P9-CLW-997

The **Killing** **Tide**

ALSO BY JEAN-LUC BANNALEC

Death in Brittany
Murder on Brittany Shores
The Fleur de Sel Murders
The Missing Corpse

The **Killing Tide**

—∗ A BRITTANY MYSTERY ∗—

Jean-Luc Bannalec

Translated by Peter Millar

Minotaur Books
New York

This is a work of fiction. All of the characters, organizations, and events portrayed in this novel are either products of the author's imagination or are used fictitiously.

First published in the United States by Minotaur Books, an imprint of St. Martin's Publishing Group

THE KILLING TIDE. Copyright © 2016 by Verlag Kiepenheuer & Witsch. Translation copyright © 2020 by Peter Millar. All rights reserved. Printed in the United States of America. For information, address St. Martin's Publishing Group, 120 Broadway, New York, NY 10271.

www.minotaurbooks.com

Designed by Devan Norman

Library of Congress Cataloging-in-Publication Data

Names: Bannalec, Jean-Luc, 1966–author. | Millar, Peter, translator.
Title: The killing tide / Jean-Luc Bannalec ; translated by Peter Millar.
Other titles: Bretonische Flut. English
Description: First U.S. edition. | New York : Minotaur Books, 2020. |
    Series: A Brittany mystery; 5 | First published as Bretonische Flut in
    Germany by Verlag Kiepenheuer & Witsch.
Identifiers: LCCN 2019036389 | ISBN 9781250173386 (hardcover) |
    ISBN 9781250173393 (ebook)
Subjects: GSAFD: Mystery fiction.
Classification: LCC PT2662.A565 B73413 2020 | DDC 833/.92—dc23
LC record available at https://lccn.loc.gov/2019036389

Our books may be purchased in bulk for promotional, educational, or business use. Please contact your local bookseller or the Macmillan Corporate and Premium Sales Department at 1-800-221-7945, extension 5442, or by email at MacmillanSpecialMarkets@macmillan.com.

Originally published as *Bretonische Flut* in Germany by Verlag Kiepenheuer & Witsch

First U.S. Edition: February 2020

10 9 8 7 6 5 4 3 2 1

For L.
For Zoé

Diaoul—pe verzud?
The devil—or a miracle?
—BRETON PROVERB

The Killing
Tide

Day One

"What a load of shit," Commissaire Georges Dupin muttered.

The stench was appalling. He felt sick to his gut. He had been overtaken by a fit of nausea almost to the point of fainting. He had had to lean back against the wall to support himself; he wasn't going to last much longer if he stayed here. He felt cold sweat running down his forehead. It was 5:32 A.M., but no longer night and noticeably cool. Dawn was creeping slowly across the sky. Dupin had been dragged from his bed by a phone call at 4:49 A.M., when it was still the middle of the night. He and Claire had only just left the Amiral shortly after 2:00 A.M.; they had been at one hell of a party to mark the beginning of the longest day of the year: the summer solstice. In Celtic they called it Alban Hevin. Brittany was naturally blessed with enthralling light, but at this time of year it became magical. The sun didn't set until 10:30 in the evening, and yet long afterward a brilliant light lingered in the atmosphere; the horizon was clearly visible across the Atlantic, yet at the same time the brightest stars could already be seen. This "astronomical twilight," as they called it, lasted almost until midnight before total darkness united sea and sky. There was so much light it almost made you drunk. Dupin loved these days. Really loved them.

The room, with its yellowish tiles reaching up to the ceiling, was cramped and cold in the harsh neon lights, with its tiny windows tilted open but not letting in anything like enough fresh air. Half a dozen dark gray containers as high as a man stood on rollers in two rows of three.

The young woman—in her midthirties, Dupin guessed—had lain in the container to the front on the left; a cleaner had found her. Two policemen had turned up here at the fish auction hall in Douarnenez harbor right away. Together with the crime scene team from Quimper, who had taken the body out of the container and laid it on the tiled floor before Dupin arrived.

It was a revolting spectacle even for the hardened observer. Dupin had never come across anything like it in his whole career. The body was covered in rotting fish, guts, stomachs, intestines, a mixture of all the more or less liquid waste that had been in the container. Even whole pieces of fish, tails, and bones stuck to the woman, to her hair, her hands, and—though there were only a few places where their original color could be made out—her light blue sweater, bright yellow oilskin pants, and black rubber boots. Her short, dark brown hair was tangled with sardine heads. Her face was a mess too. Fish scales glittered in the light, particularly maca-bre where one extremely large fish scale covered her left eye while her right eye was wide open. The slimy mess on her upper body had intermingled with the woman's blood. A lot of blood. There was a four-to-five-centimeter cut across her lower throat.

"Dead as a dormouse," said the wiry pathologist with red cheeks, shrugging. He didn't look in the slightest like a comedian and didn't seem in the slightest bothered by the stench. "What is there to say? The cause of death is no more a puzzle than the woman's state of health. Somebody cut her throat, probably yesterday between eight P.M. and midnight, though I'll spare you the reasoning behind that." He glanced at Dupin and the two crime scene specialists. "If you have no objections we'll take the young lady to the lab. And the barrel too. Maybe we'll find something interesting." There was a jovial tone to his voice. Dupin was overcome with another wave of nausea.

"Not a problem for us. We're done. There's nothing more to be added to the crime scene investigation for now."

The chief forensic officer from Quimper, Dupin had been pleased to note, was away on holiday, and his job was being done by two assistants, both of whom had the same unbounded self-confidence as their lord and master. The shorter of the two took over: "We were able to take a number of fingerprints from the top of the container, where it opens—twenty or so different prints altogether I'd say, although most of them weren't complete or were one on top of the other. Hard to say much more at present. Even though we will," he hesitated a moment, "need to look more closely at the interior."

Kadeg, one of Dupin's two inspectors, who seemed fully awake and composed and stood too close to the corpse, cleared his throat. "We could do with a little bit more information. On the knife for example." He had turned toward the pathologist and mimed for the experts: "I believe the blade must have been very sharp; the wound looks almost surgical."

The pathologist wasn't going to be impressed. "We'll examine the wound carefully in due course. The state of the wound depends not only on the blade but also on the skill of the perpetrator, as well as the speed with which he made the cut. Someone who knows his knives can make almost any cut with any knife, even in a fight. Mind you, I would probably rule out a machete"—he clearly thought this really funny—"but any of the hundred, maybe two hundred knives carried by the fishermen who use this hall could have done it."

"Just who might be carrying a knife with him," the smaller forensics man said ironically, "isn't a question you're going to get very far with here. Everybody who lives by the sea, whether they fish, hunt, collect mussels, own a boat, or are looking for work—in other words virtually everyone who lives here—owns at least one good knife and knows how to use it."

Kadeg looked as if he was about to make another objection, then dropped it and quickly changed the subject. "How often and when are the barrels emptied? Have you been able to find that out? There must be a regular schedule."

He aimed the question at the rookie policeman from Douarnenez, who, along with his colleagues, had been the first to turn up and seemed a down-to-earth local.

"Twice a day, we already know that. The men who gut the fish sometimes work late into the night and so the barrels are emptied very early in the morning before the first fishing boats come in. And once again around three P.M. The cleaners who empty them were totally distraught and called in one of the warehouse staff, who reported the incident to us at the police station. Then he closed off the hall."

"Without even glancing into the barrel himself to see if he might know the person?"

"There was only a leg visible."

"What about a phone?" Kadeg asked. "Did you find a cell phone on the body?"

"No."

"Okay," the pathologist said, obviously in a hurry. "Then let's pack up the corpse and—"

"Boss," Riwal, Dupin's other inspector, interrupted. He was standing in the doorway of the little room, which was already too full. There was a woman behind him who looked remarkably similar to the dead woman, except that she was probably about fifty years old.

"Gaétane Gochat, the chief of the harbor and the auction hall here, she's just turned up and—"

"Céline Kerkrom, that's Céline Kerkrom." The harbor chief had stopped in her tracks, staring at the body. It took a few moments before she got her voice back.

"She's one of our coastal fisherwomen. She lives on the Île de Sein and usually brings her catch here to sell."

Gaétane Gochat sounded completely unmoved, no trace of shock, horror, or sympathy, which, Dupin had learned, meant nothing whatsoever. Each person reacted totally differently when it came to sudden brutal or tragic events.

On his last case, in the Belon area, they had moved heaven and earth to find out who the murder victim was; here the identification of the deceased seemed remarkably simple.

"I need a *café*," Dupin muttered. It was only the second sentence he had spoken since he arrived. "We have a few things to talk about. Come along with us, Madame Gochat. You too, Riwal!" He was in no state to hide the grumpy tone in his voice.

He suddenly tore himself away from the wall, walked past all of them without waiting for their reaction or noticing the puzzled, surprised expressions on their faces, and was out of the door. He needed coffee. And now. He needed to shake off the stupor, the infernal stench, and the exhaustion that meant he was seeing everything as if through a hazy veil. To put it in a nutshell: he needed to come to himself, to plunge back into reality, and quickly. Get his mind wide awake, clear, and sharp.

The commissaire made his way through the big halls to where he had on his way in spotted a stand with a little bar, and a large coffee machine and a couple of scuffed bar tables. Riwal and Gaétane Gochat had trouble keeping up with him.

Everyday professional life in the plain tiled fish market had resumed, paying little heed to the dramatic news which had obviously already done the rounds; things were busy. Fishermen and fish sellers, restaurant owners and other customers were going about their business. Hundreds of flat plastic boxes were spread around the big hall on the damp concrete floor, in garish colors: fire red, neon green, signal blue, bright orange, just a few in black or white. Dupin recognized the boxes from Concarneau; they were a standard item in all the fish warehouses and the chief utensil in all the auction houses. They contained heaps of ice, on top of which lay everything the fishermen had caught in their nets: vast quantities of fish and sea creatures in every shape, form, color, and size; every sort of exotic sea creature you could imagine in your wildest fantasy. Huge, prehistoric-looking monkfish with their jaws ripped open wide, shining mackerel, fierce-looking lobsters, grayish black squid squeezed together, masses of langoustines, different types of sole, top-quality examples of sea bass (a fish Dupin loved, primarily served as carpaccio or tartare), delicious red mullet everywhere, gigantic spider crabs. There were also fish and shellfish Dupin didn't know the names of, as well as some he had never seen before, at least not knowingly, maybe already prepared on his plate, but not like this. He had to admit that as a good Frenchman his culinary interest went far beyond the zoological. In one box he came across a sadly confused-looking shark, in another next to it, a meter-long, almost completely round-bodied yet at the same time somewhat flat fish with a disproportionately large back fin. A sunfish, if Dupin's memory served him well. It was only recently that Riwal had shown him one in the Concarneau fish hall. Brittany was a paradise in many ways, particularly for lovers of fish and seafood; nowhere were they better or fresher. That was why the adjective "*breton*" stood alongside the name of almost every fish dish in almost every starred French restaurant: *Langoustines bretonnes, Saint-Pierre Breton*—there was no higher praise.

The busiest part of the hall was the rear, where the auctions took place. Along the sides were half-open rooms where some of the fish were already being prepared. Men in white protective suits, with hairnets, white rubber boots, and blue gloves worked with large, long knives at stainless steel workbenches.

"Two *petits cafés*." Dupin had reached the stand quickly, despite having to zigzag between the boxes. The old lady behind the counter gave him a suspicious look but placed two cardboard cups beneath the machine.

Dupin turned to the harbor chief, who was standing next to Riwal.

"Are you related to the deceased, madame?" The thought had occurred to Dupin because they looked so alike.

"Not at all," said Gaétane Gochat dismissively. It seemed she had been asked the question more than once.

"Have you any idea what happened here?"

"Not in the slightest. Was she killed here in the auction hall? At what time was the murder?"

"Apparently between eight P.M. and midnight yesterday evening. Whether or not she was killed here is something we don't know yet. How late were you here yesterday?"

"Me?"

"Yes, you, madame."

"I think up until about nine thirty. I was in my office."

"Whereabouts is your office, if you don't mind me asking?"

She replied with an impassive face. "Directly next to the auction hall. That's the administration center for the harbor."

Madame Gochat was the prosaic type, one who concentrated on doing the things that needed to be done, speedily and rationally. She was a stocky person with presence, short brown hair, brown eyes, little worry lines around her eyes and lips; businesslike rather than stubborn. Dupin thought she could be feisty if it came to it. She wore jeans, a fluffy gray fleece, and the obligatory rubber boots.

"What sort of fishermen come here? Those from the big boats too?"

"The deep-sea trawlers come in around five in the morning, the ones that have been at sea for a couple of weeks; the local boats that have been out for a couple of days come in around midday; and then at about five in the afternoon we get the coastal fishermen who've set out at around four or five in the morning, while the sardine fishers have gone out the evening before. The auctions begin as soon as the boats have come in. We were very busy yesterday. It was the beginning of the holiday season; a few of the coastal fishermen were still here by the time I left."

"Did you see Madame Kerkrom?"

"Céline? No."

The elderly lady behind the counter had set the two *cafés* down in front of Dupin. The expression on her face as she did so was hard to decipher.

"What about earlier?"

"About seven P.M., I think, I saw her briefly then. She was carrying a box into the hall."

"Did you speak to her?"

"No."

"What were you yourself doing in the hall at that time?"

There was just a hint of testiness in Madame Gochat's look.

"Every now and then I look and see if there's my sort of guy."

Dupin drank down his first *café* in one gulp. A proper *café de bonne soeur,* a "nun's coffee," as the Bretons called weak coffee. *Torre,* bull coffee, was what they called a strong one. For really bad coffee, undrinkable and disgusting, there were a multitude of names, serious Breton names: "Bardot piss," which supposedly meant something like "mule piss," or *café sac'h,* water squeezed through an old pair of stockings.

"You said Céline Kerkrom *usually* brought her catch here. What do you mean by that? How regular was she?"

"Almost every day, just as the auctions were starting. She specialized in *lieu jaune*—pollock—bass, and bream. Most of the time she fished with a line. She rarely used a net, as far as I know."

"So yesterday she brought her catch here?"

"Yes."

"But not every day."

"Maybe she missed out five or six days in the month. Every now and then she would sell direct to a couple of restaurants." To judge from her tone of voice, Madame Gochat wasn't happy with that.

"The killer could more or less reckon on her being here?"

Madame Gochat looked irritated for a brief moment, before continuing. "Absolutely."

"Did she have a crew? Fellow workers?"

"No. She always went out on her boat alone. Lots of the coastal fisherfolk are one-man or one-woman operations. It's a hard way to earn a crust."

"We need to know when she came in yesterday, who last saw her, and where and when. Everything."

"Obviously," Riwal replied.

"If I understand properly"—Dupin had turned back to face the harbormistress, pulled his red Clairefontaine notebook out of his pants pocket, and his Bic ballpoint from his jacket—"I imagine none of the fishermen who were here this morning were here last night."

"Certainly not."

"Who, apart from the fisherfolk, is here during the auctions?"

"At least one of my colleagues, the customers—fish merchants, restaurant owners—the workers who're already working on some of the fish. And two people to deal with the ice."

Madame Gochat noticed Dupin's curious look. "Everyone needs vast amounts of ice. There's a huge ice silo directly next to the auction hall. It's a service we provide."

"We need as soon as possible a complete list of everybody who was in the hall last night between six P.M. and midnight and/or who had been at the quayside beforehand."

"My colleagues will work on that," Gochat said. She seemed used to giving instructions. "We'll get together the people who were in the hall, but it will be harder to find out who was on the quayside. That part of the harbor is freely accessible. Anglers really like the quayside and there are always biggish groups of them there. Tourists like to pass by too; there's always something to see. Apart from that, three Spanish deep-sea trawlers have been moored there since midday yesterday, each of them with at least eight crew members."

The entrance was open, at least ten meters wide, and once in the hall it wasn't far to the little side room where the body had been found.

"I want to know about everybody who was here." Dupin repeated his instruction, stressing the "I." "What each and every person who was here was doing, from when and until when. And then we can tackle each and every one of them."

"It'll be done, boss," Riwal replied. "Our colleagues from Douar-nenez have in any case already spoken with the member of Madame Gochat's staff who was here last night and closed up the hall. Jean Serres. At 11:20 P.M. The last fisherfolk had left shortly before. He had seen Céline Kerkrom a few times in the course of the evening."

Like Kadeg, Riwal gave the impression of being lively and re-laxed, but then that had been the case ever since the birth of his son, Maclou-Brioc, four weeks earlier; despite the lack of sleep, his pater-nal pride had left him looking invincible. "He didn't notice anything unusual or suspicious. So far nobody's said they noticed anything."

It would have been too easy.

"At what time did this Jean Serres see the fisherwoman last?"

"None of our men said."

Dupin drank his second *café*. Yet again down in one gulp. It didn't taste any better than the first one. Never mind.

"One more, please," he said. Right now it wasn't about taste, it was the effect that mattered. The woman at the stand fulfilled the order with the slightest of glances.

"Madame Gochat"—Dupin turned to face the harbormistress— "I would like to call your colleague and ask him when he last saw Céline Kerkrom last night."

"You mean you want me to call him *now*?"

"Now."

"As you wish."

Madame Gochat took her cell phone out of her pants pocket and stepped aside.

"Jean Serres," Riwal continued, "said that at about nine P.M. there were some ten to fifteen fisherfolk in the hall. Of those, five were preparing the fish, and there were maybe five buyers, and a couple of men dealing with the ice. At about nine P.M. the first coastal sardine fishermen had come in from the nearby harbor ba-sin. It was busy on the quayside. The afternoon rain had suddenly stopped about six P.M. and the sun had broken through, which had brought the anglers and promenaders out."

In Concarneau, Dupin himself was one of the promenaders who always strolled by the fish auction hall. He liked the lively, colorful goings-on around the harbor, the way it was reliably repeated every day, perfectly choreographed. There was always something going on.

The elderly woman on the stand had set a third paper cup on the counter in front of Dupin, and was now dealing with four older fishermen who had just turned up.

"I want all the workers in the hall put stringently under the microscope, Riwal," Dupin said loudly.

"Leave it to me, boss."

Dupin threw back the third *petit café*.

The harbormistress came back over to them, her phone still in her hand. Serres said he had last seen Céline Kerkrom about 9:30 P.M. In the hall. He reckoned she had come in around 6:00.

"Did he notice anything in particular?"

"No. She'd been absolutely normal. But then he had no reason to pay her any particular attention. They didn't speak."

"I want to speak with the man myself—Riwal, tell him to come here now."

"Consider it done." Riwal left the counter and headed toward the exit from the hall, where a small group of police was standing.

"How long do the coastal fish auctions last usually, Madame Gochat?"

"It's very variable, it depends on the season and the weather. December, coming up to the holidays, is the busiest time. Even busier than in June, July, and August. At that time of year we work until after midnight. Now it's up to about eleven P.M. or eleven thirty."

"What do the fisherfolk do after the end of the auction?"

Madame Gochat shrugged. "They go back to their boats, take them to their moorings. Sometimes they hang around for a while, tinkering with their buoys, chatting on the quayside. Or maybe they go for a drink."

"Here?"

"Down at the Vieux Quai, Port de Rosmeur, right next door."

For the first time that morning Dupin's features lit up. The *quai* and the area behind it were fabulous; he could spend hours on the old pier side with its fishermen's houses painted in shades of blue, pink, or yellow, sitting in one of the cafés or bistros watching the world go by. His favorite was the Café de la Rade, painted in bright Atlantic blue and white, a former fish canning factory. Everything there was unstaged, nothing put on for show. There was a view of the harbor and the bay of Douarnenez, breathtakingly beautiful. Dupin liked Douarnenez, in particular its wonderful old market halls—the coffee there was great—and the Port de Rosmeur, the charmingly aged harbor quarter, built in the nineteenth century, the golden age of the sardine. If you needed to name a center of operations in Douarnenez, then the Café de la Rade was the perfect place. The commissaire, who had a tendency toward ritual, in every one of his cases designated either a bar, a bistro, or sometimes even a location out in the open air as "center of operations." It would be the scene for interviews and, if necessary, for official interrogations too. Dupin was famous for his dislike of offices of every kind, in particular his own. He escaped from them as often as possible. He solved his cases from the scene of the crime, not from a desk. Even when the police prefecture was close by, Dupin needed to be outside, in the open air, amongst other people. He had to see things for himself, speak to people himself, live in their world.

"Did you know any more about the deceased, Madame Gochat?"

"No. Like I said, she was a coastal fisher from Île de Sein. She'd been married. As far as I know her ex-husband was one of the technicians in the island lighthouse." The harbormistress, even now, talking about the dead woman, showed no sign of emotion.

"When did they get divorced?"

"Oh, that was years ago, ten at least. They get married young on the islands. And if it goes wrong, they're on their own again young."

"What else? What else can you say about her?"

"I don't know, she was thirty-six, one of the few women in this business. She spoke her mind and had a few hefty disagreements with some people."

"She was a rebel, a fighter," said the elderly woman at the coffee stand, who was busy with a few glasses at a little washbasin. She seemed angry.

Displeasure was written all over Madame Gochat's face. Dupin was quick to follow up. He was curious.

"What do you mean, Madame . . . ?"

"Yvette Batout, Monsieur le Commissaire." She had now positioned herself directly opposite Dupin on the other side of the counter. "Céline was the only one who stood up to the self-appointed 'king of the fishermen,' Charles Morin, a criminal with a big fleet, half a dozen deep-sea trawlers and more coastal boats. *Bolincheurs* primarily, but a couple of *chalutiers*. He has more than a few skeletons in his closet, and not just in the fishing business."

"That'll do, Yvette." The harbormistress's tone was cutting.

"Let Madame Batout say what she wants to say."

Madame Batout batted her eyelashes briefly at Dupin. "Morin is unscrupulous, even when he plays the *grand seigneur*. He uses giant dragnets and drift nets, even along the sea bottom, causes piles of unnecessary catch, ignores the quotas—Céline even caught him out a couple of times inside the Parc Iroise, right in the middle of the conservation area, even though he denies it all and threatens his critics. Céline reported him to the authorities several times, including those at the *parc*. She had the balls to do it. Just last week six dolphins who'd been crushed in one of the nets were found dead on a beach at Ouessant."

"Did he threaten Céline Kerkrom directly?"

Dupin was making thorough notes, in a rapid scribble that looked like a secret code.

"'You need to take care, you'll see,' he told her here in the hall, back in February, in front of witnesses."

"He was threatening to take her to court for slander, not to kill her, there's a bit of a difference, Yvette." Gaétane Gochat's memory was curiously mechanical; there was no way of knowing what she actually thought.

"What exactly happened back in February?"

"The two of them," the harbormistress said before Madame Batout could answer, "bumped into one another by chance here, and they quarreled. Nothing more."

"It was more than a quarrel, Gaétane, and you know it." Madame Batout's eyes were blazing.

"How old is Monsieur Morin?"

"Late fifties."

"What did you mean about 'skeletons in the closet, and not just in the fishing business,' Madame Batout?"

"He had a finger in the pie in a whole raft of criminal affairs, including smuggling cigarettes across the channel. But for some reason or other nobody ever caught him. Three years ago a customs boat was close on his tail and nearly caught him, until he sank the boat. The only piece of evidence! And there was nothing else to hold against him."

"Be careful what you say, Yvette!"

"Has Charles Morin ever been the subject of a police investigation?"

"Never," the harbormistress said firmly. "Everything against him, I'll say it outright, amounts to nothing more than extremely vague accusations. Rumors. I think that given the number of illegal actions he's accused of, the police would have been on his tail at some stage."

Dupin unfortunately knew all too many cases where that hadn't been what happened.

"Great," he mumbled.

His first conversation and already he had not only one hot topic but two: illegal fishing and cigarette smuggling.

Fishing was a huge affair in Brittany. Anyone who regularly read

Ouest-France and *Le Télégramme*—and Dupin did so with particularly strict regularity—came across news from the fishing industry every day. Almost on a par with agriculture and tourism, it was one of the most important branches of the economy, a proud Breton symbol: nearly half of France's fishing catch came from Brittany. A venerable branch of the economy that was deep in crisis. There were several factors at work causing trouble for the Breton fleet: overfishing; the destruction of the seas by industrial large-scale fishing; the rising temperature and pollution of the oceans causing serious damage to fish stocks; climate change and the associated quirks in the weather which led to ever-diminishing catch sizes; the brutal, almost lawless international competition; fishing policies that had long been failing, on regional, national, and international levels; and fierce arguments, bitter quarrels, and conflicts.

And the prefecture had—to the commissaire's chagrin—been on them for years about the tobacco smuggling. No matter how bizarre it might seem in modern times in the middle of Europe, tobacco smuggling really was a serious problem. A quarter of all the cigarettes smoked in France entered the country illegally; the loss to the public purse was a multibillion sum. And since sales over the Internet had been banned, the situation had got even worse.

"Thank you very much, Madame Batout. That was extremely helpful. I think we'll have to have a chat with Monsieur Morin straightaway. Where does he live?"

"Morgat, on the Crozon peninsula. He has a grand villa out there. But he has other houses too, one here in Douarnenez, in Tréboul. Always in the best places." Madame Batout continued to look at him dourly.

"And was he here too last night?"

"I didn't see him." Madame Batout was clearly disappointed to tell him this.

"He comes here very rarely," the harbormistress butted in, "but there would certainly have been some of his fishermen here. He—"

"Madame Gochat!" A thin young man in a thick blue fleece sweater had come over to them and tried to attract her attention. She gave him the slightest of nods.

"We need you upstairs, madame."

"Anything to do with the dead fisherwoman?" Dupin was quicker than Madame Gochat. The coffee was finally beginning to work.

The young man looked at a loss.

"Answer the commissaire, we've nothing to hide," Madame Gochat encouraged him.

It was an interesting scenario. The young man was clearly afraid of her.

"It's the mayor, on the telephone. He says it's urgent."

"He will have to wait a moment," Dupin told him.

It seemed Gaétane Gochat was about to say something to the contrary, then let it pass.

"Going back to the deceased, Madame Gochat, is there anything else you can tell me? Has she been involved with anyone else?"

The harbormistress made a sign to the young man and he took off immediately.

Gochat hesitated a while and appeared to be weighing her words. "She campaigned for sustainable, ecologically sound fishing, and got involved now and again with projects and initiatives down at Parc Iroise."

"Parc Iroise"—Madame Batout butted in again, having in the meantime dealt surprisingly quickly with two other orders—"is a remarkable maritime nature park. There's nothing quite like it. Here on the extreme west coast of Brittany between the Île de Saint, Ouessant, and the Channel. Our park boasts the greatest maritime diversity in Europe." There was unbridled pride in the dogged old lady's voice. Dupin almost thought he was listening to Riwal. "More than one hundred and twenty types of fish live here. There are also several colonies of dolphins and seals. And the largest algae field in Europe! There are more than eight hundred different varieties, the seventh largest algae field in the world. And even—"

"The *parc*," the harbormistress interrupted Madame Batout, "is a major pilot project. Apart from the scientific research it's primarily designed to be a model for a functioning balance between human use of the sea—fishing, algae harvesting, leisure, and tourism—and a functioning ecology, protection of the sea."

Nolwenn and Riwal had frequently talked about the—undoubtedly extraordinary—project, but to tell the truth, Dupin knew very little about it. And right now his interest was elsewhere.

"I mean: Has Céline Kerkrom had arguments with anyone else recently?"

"Oh yes, it wasn't just Morin," said Madame Batout.

Gochat shot her a warning glance, and took over the conversation: "Céline set up an initiative for alternative energy generation on the island, to replace oil that they use to produce electricity and water desalination. She got the whole island worked up. She wanted to set up several small tidal generators, a sort of pipe system."

"And that annoys you?"

Gochat hadn't sounded quite so neutral in her previous sentences.

"I only mean that she would definitely have made enemies."

"Who in particular?"

"Thomas Roiyou, for example. He's the owner of the ship tanker that supplies the island with its oil."

Dupin was writing it all down. "And they quarreled?"

"Yes. In March, Céline Kerkrom wrote up a 'manifesto' for her island movement and distributed it everywhere. *Ouest-France* and *Le Télégramme* reported on it. Then Roiyou gave an interview in which he talked about it."

The annoyance clearly in evidence on Gochat's face grew.

"I've got all that. We will definitely have a conversation with this gentleman too. Do you know"—Dupin made a point of addressing both women—"if Céline Kerkrom had any family? Or if she had friends among the other fisherfolk?"

"I couldn't say," Gochat said, looking genuinely clueless. "She seemed to me to be a loner. But I could be wrong. You need to speak to somebody who knew her better. Ask the people on the island. Everybody there knows everybody else."

Dupin turned to Madame Batout. "Do you have any concrete idea what might have happened here?"

"No."

A surprisingly blunt response, given that she'd been so ready to get involved previously.

There was a brief pause.

"But you need to bring the perpetrator to justice."

Dupin smiled. "We'll do that, okay, Madame Batout. Have no worries on that account."

"In that case . . . I need to fetch milk from the cellar." And with those words, Madame Batout headed off, looking very pleased with herself.

"Will you . . ." Gochat was obviously concerned about something. "Will you be closing off the hall now?"

Dupin was about to say yes; he was famous for sealing off a crime scene extensively and for quite some time.

"No. Initially at least we'll just seal off the little room with the waste barrels in it."

In this case it would be smart to let everyday life and business in the hall continue as normal.

"One last question, Madame Gochat. How is business doing in the harbor here? You must be finding it difficult, as all the other harbors are."

"We're struggling, yes. But we're fighting back. For the past few years we've been fourteenth out of all French harbors in size of catch: forty-five hundred tons of fish a year, the majority, of course, in sardines. They are our traditional strength." The subject hardly seemed to bother her.

"But the number of boats registered here must have dropped?"

In Concarneau, and throughout Brittany, that was a regular topic.

"For several years now things have been more or less steady. We have twenty-two boats registered, eighteen of them coastal."

"And the share of the catch auctioned here has also remained steady?"

Dupin had noticed a slight flash in Gochat's eyes. Riwal would have been proud of his knowledge of the subject. This was another topic that was heavily debated in the commissariat: international firms, Spanish for example, used the Breton harbors, but only to unload. Their catch was immediately loaded onto freezer trucks.

It took a moment for her to answer.

"No. But in response we've increased charges for using the harbor." For the first time there was a hint of bitterness in her voice. "Our harbor is in a very privileged location. Even in high seas, the water here is calm, the conditions are almost perfect. Do you see some link between the economic conditions in the harbor and the murder?" She looked at him demandingly. Defiantly.

Dupin ignored the question. "That's it for now, Madame Gochat. We will need to speak again." Dupin didn't mind if it sounded like a threat.

The harbormistress was back in control of herself. "I'm here all day. *Au revoir*, Monsieur le Commissaire."

She had already turned away when Dupin—who had remained standing by the counter—called after her: "After you leave your office about nine P.M. or nine thirty, where do you go?"

He didn't bother to add a phrase like "Just a routine question," or "It's something we ask everyone."

She came back a few steps. "Straight home, into the shower, and then to bed."

Even this follow-up hadn't jarred her.

"How far is it from here to your house?"

"A quarter of an hour in the car."

"So you were in bed by ten thirty P.M.?"

"Yes."

"Any witnesses?"

"My husband is on a business trip, he only gets back this evening."

"Did you make any calls from your landline?"

"No."

"That was very useful, thanks once again." With those words Dupin set off decisively in the direction of the exit, just a few steps away.

He would take a look around outside until he came across the colleague of Madame Gochat's he wanted to talk to.

The "look around," a particular way of wandering about aimlessly, was one of Dupin's favorite disciplines. It was a way he often discovered details that initially seemed irrelevant, but then suddenly became very important. He had solved more than one case on the basis of one of these inconspicuous details that he had stumbled across while wandering around.

* * *

Dupin stood on the quayside. It was light by now.

He had been looking around for a while, strolling about rather aimlessly, looking at this and that with particular attention—even though it was of no importance.

He looked at the auction hall. The building was flat, long, and simple, painted white, like the other buildings here around the harbor. Next to the entrance were two forklift trucks, diagonally across the quay as if the drivers for some reason had hastily abandoned them.

Business was going on as usual all around, people doing what they normally did. It was all as the harbormistress had said: the auction hall was right in the middle and anyone could have wandered around it without being noticed. There were narrow footpaths on the ground, part earth, part grass, behind and in between the various buildings. Dupin even saw two rectangular camper vans with deck chairs beside them.

The still noticeably fresh air did him good, sharpened the senses and the mind, and then there was the caffeine from the three *cafés* as well.

As was his habit, he had walked right to the very edge of the pier, the toes of his shoes almost over the edge. The slightest careless movement and he could have fallen over, a fall that at this ebb tide would have been three or four meters.

In front of him lay the wide bay of Douarnenez, which stretched from the long beaches at the end of the bay to Cape Sizun in the southwest and the Crozon peninsula in the north, and eventually to the open Atlantic.

A vast natural bay and an impressive panorama. Dupin understood why the whole world said it was the most beautiful bay in France. One of the most beautiful in Europe.

The still, deep blue water, the light-colored concrete jetty and closed-off harbor, and the water again beyond it, even bluer. Postcard blue. Serene. Already there were a few light sailing boats gliding along, and there would be more and more as the morning went on. People were in holiday mood. Above the broad strip of sea lay the gentle green landscape with the low, soft swell of the hills. The Crozon peninsula. And beyond that finally the endless, clear pale blue of the sky, decorated with a few perfect white clouds. It was summer and the temperature would rise by the hour. A heavenly day lay ahead. For anyone who didn't have to deal with the tragedy that had taken place here.

To the right lay the Vieux Port, also protected by a long pier. To the left of the hall, some two hundred meters away, the quay took a right turn and ran as far as the harbor pier. Thick car tires hung on ropes against the pier as bollards for the boats. A few anglers were already out trying their luck at this early hour of the morning. Three pretty fishing boats, moored with multiple ropes, were named *Vag-a-Lamm, Ar Raok,* and *Barr Au.* They looked like the fishing boats Dupin had seen in the movies as a child, the way painters in Pont-Aven had depicted them. Made of wood, one in bright turquoise, striped yellow, and lower down paprika red, the other with its upper half bright red, and the lower Atlantic blue, the third in various shades of green, from dark to pale and then blaring white below the waterline. There was nothing arbitrary about the colors. Every fisherman or company chose their own colors or combination of colors, Dupin knew: it was a deliberate signature, as conspicuous as possible so that it could be identified at sea even from afar.

Dupin studied the technical equipment on the deep-sea trawlers behind them: boats of a completely different dimension, forty or fifty meters long, tall. This part of the harbor, the halls, the machinery, had none of the charm and flair of the Vieux Port. Everything here was functional, technical, made of concrete, steel, aluminum, constantly fighting off rust, the sea, time itself. It was obvious everywhere that this was hard work, a world where only extreme professionalism counted. Any mistake could prove fatal. Knowledge, experience, ability, those were the currency if you had to deal with the sea. Bravery, endurance. Dupin was in awe of it. Even as a little boy he had loved the harbors, the sea in general and its stories. It was as if he was obsessed; he had read every story that came into his hands. More than anything else, the sea had become a subject of romantic imagination, even if he was becoming increasingly unwilling to take boat trips of any sort. It might even have been his fantasy at work: the vast number of creatures, horrible monsters that he had imagined, and, like those of Jules Verne, lurked in the dark depths: giant squid, sea snakes, shapeless twisting beasts. The world below was as black and featureless as the world above; the universe. The fearful unknown; the fearful wonderful.

Dupin headed over to the anglers. Only one road led into the harbor area. Dupin had left his car farther up, not far from Chanterelle-Connétable, the world's first ever fish factory. It had been set up in 1853, Riwal recited like a prayer. It had been Napoleon himself who had set up the French industry as a way of preserving fresh food for his campaigns. The tin can had been invented and Douarnenez and other Breton regions had become very rich, although to be more precise it was the sardine that had made them all rich. Dupin was crazy about the red cans with sardines, mackerel, and other fish, above all the incredibly tender tuna fish. In the heyday of the sardine, toward the end of the nineteenth century, more than a thousand boats had been based in and around the Port de Rosmeur, and there had been all of fifty "*fritures*," canneries. Nolwenn had given Dupin a book with early photographs of Brittany. The pictures showed the hectic lifestyle, the colorful crowds and—though you could only imagine it—the penetrating smell of fried fish which must have been everywhere in the air. Penn Sardin, sardine heads, was what the local people had called themselves.

"Boss! Boss!" Riwal was running toward the commissaire. "I've been looking for you. I . . ." He stopped and stood in front of Dupin. "Jean Serres, the harbormistress's colleague, should be here in a few minutes. It's taken a while, he had to use his bicycle because his car wouldn't start and he lives quite a way out." He held an arm out but it was unclear which direction he was supposed to be pointing. "Our men have already spoken to three of the fishermen who were here last night. One of them remembered seeing Céline Kerkrom shortly before ten P.M. He says she was on her own and standing near the entrance. The three of them gave us the names of a lot of others who were here last night. And a few customers. I don't think we'll have a problem putting our list together. But so far nobody has had anything unusual to report."

"Find out from as many of them as possible what they know about"—Dupin pulled out his notebook and glanced at the first page—"the so-called fisherman king. Charles Morin. I want to know primarily what the police think of him. Whether or not they think he's a criminal. One they haven't been able to lay hands on so far."

"Consider it done, boss. Meanwhile the press have turned up, the pair from *Ouest-France* and *Le Télégramme*, they're over at the coffee stand next to Madame Batout."

"Tell them we're completely in the dark. It's the truth, after all."

"Will do."

Dupin was standing right at the edge of the pier again, looking out across the wide bay.

Riwal did the same. Passersby would have assumed they were two laid-back day-trippers.

"You know, don't you"—it was a rhetorical form of speaking used by his inspector when he began telling a story—"that it was here on the Bay of Douarnenez that the mythical city of Ys is supposed to have been, an unimaginably rich city with red walls in which even the roofs were made of pure gold, and one day it just sank beneath the sea. It was where the famous King Gradlon ruled, whose wife gave him a wonderfully pretty daughter called Dahut. There are many stories and tales, 'ancient Breton things.'" Riwal obviously stressed that element. "The story is undoubtedly the most well-known of all French sea sagas."

Of course. Dupin knew the story only too well. In fact every child in France knew it.

"Next year a long-planned thorough scientific expedition is due to search the bottom of the bay. Researchers had found that it was covered in several meters of sand and mud, dragged into the bay by big storm floods. Back in 1923. During one of those once-in-a-century ebb tides after a total eclipse of the sun, several fishermen reported seeing ruins in the middle of the bay."

Dupin felt like saying there had also been a number of expeditions looking for Atlantis.

"And just there," Riwal made a vague nod, "just before you get to the western end of Douarnenez, is the Île de Tristan with its unusually large variety of wildlife and its mysterious ruins. According to the legends, they are supposed to be the last remaining bit of Ys. And not only that," he was speaking reverently now, "the island itself is linked to many mythical wild, ghoulish, bloody but also wonderful stories and legends. Including the greatest and most tragic love story known to humanity: that of Tristan and Isolde. Both of them doomed to die. A *Breton* story," once again Riwal stressed the word, "a story of Cornouaille, the famous medieval kingdom that stretched from the Pointe du Raz as far as Brest and Quimperlé, and," his tone became ever more celebratory, "a story that became one of the most important elements in Western literature. It dates back to as early as 1170 when already it states that Tristan came from around Douarnenez, then capital of Cornouaille. Quimper," he gave a dismissive look, "only became the capital much later. Before that it was Ys.

"Isolde is a Breton. In one of the innumerable versions of the story, Tristan was about to throw himself off high crags into the sea in despair at the death of his beloved, when he was taken by the wind and set down gently on the island. But even there he soon died of his incessant grief. And there they lie for all time, the two lovers, beneath two trees with their branches intertwined," Riwal sighed emotionally, "somewhere in the northwest of the island. Nobody knew where they lay save the king who buried them. The remnants of his castle stand near Plomarc'h by Plage du Ris . . ."

"Riwal." However much he loved sea sagas, Dupin was getting impatient. "We need to know who had the closest personal contact with Céline Kerkrom, search her house, talk to her friends and neighbors on the Île de Sein. Above all, the islanders. Go to the island as soon as possible."

"No problem, boss." Riwal loved boats.

"Find out who knows most about her and then bring that person back to the mainland."

Dupin wanted, as far as it was possible, to avoid having to go to the island himself.

"Consider it done," Riwal said. "By the way, I have a cousin here in Douarnenez."

Dupin refrained from asking the follow-up question, not that it made any difference. "He's president of the Association du véritable Kouign Amann, the *kouign amann* association."

The Breton butter cake. Dupin involuntarily found his mouth watering. Breton butter—an elixir—lots of it, a bit of flour and even less water but more sugar, the simplest of ingredients, but the great art was to caramelize them into an ambrosian delicacy.

"In the middle of the fourteenth century," Riwal said quickly, glancing briefly aside at Dupin, "a baker here in Douarnenez had to make cakes for a big celebration, but during the night most of his ingredients were stolen and he was left with just butter, flour, and sugar. My cousin has made it his mission to preserve the original recipe. It can't be improved on."

"I need urgently to make a phone call, Riwal. And you need to get going. Kadeg can take over here."

"I'll get a boat sent over. On the subject, Kadeg and a few colleagues are inspecting the fisherwoman's boat," Riwal said.

That was important.

"And?"

"We'll report the minute they're finished, boss. See you later." Riwal ran back into the hall.

Dupin stayed standing on the pier.

He pulled his cell phone out of his jacket pocket. He was missing an important part of his ritual: the first phone call in a new case with Nolwenn, his personal assistant. He would have to ring Claire too, given that he had just vanished, leaving only a short note on the table. They had agreed to sleep off the night before, have a convivial breakfast together at the Amiral, and lunch together too. Dupin had intended not to turn up at the commissariat until the afternoon. They had spent all too little time together in the last few months, Claire and he. Not at all what he had planned—and wanted—when he had dragged Claire to Brittany the previous year and she had taken over the post of head of the cardiology department in Quimper. The sad thing about it was that Claire had the morning off—precious hours they might have spent together—before she had to go to Rennes for a medical meeting and would have to stay the night too. Back in Paris, during their early relationship, it had been exclusively Dupin's fault that they saw each other so seldom; now it was the other way around. Dupin frequently had to drive to Quimper late at night to collect her from the clinic. Then they would sit on Claire's little balcony and drink red wine and eat cheese that Dupin had bought at the Concarneau market. Often Claire was so tired that they simply sat in silence next to one another looking at the lit-up ancient alleyways. Nowadays they rarely went on excursions as they had earlier when Claire had come to Brittany from Paris on her days off. Dupin missed that.

He had already tried Nolwenn from the car but the line had been busy. As always she would already be in the picture, well informed. Dupin had long ago given up trying to figure out how she knew what and from whom, and simply assumed she had telepathic abilities. Druidic abilities, it would seem. Nolwenn picked up the phone.

"The woman is a rebel, Monsieur le Commissaire, I know her through my husband's aunt who's a friend of hers." Dupin might have guessed, even if this familial link didn't exactly open up the case. Nolwenn was, in principle, on the side of the opposition—a genetically anchored, wonderfully anarchic reflex. She knew everybody who had fought back against injustice, arbitrary judgments, and bad management.

"Did you know her personally?"

"As good as. I'll try to find out what I can."

"Absolutely."

It couldn't be better. Nolwenn took charge of the business.

"It's more than just about the tragic death of this wonderful woman." Nolwenn was livid. "That shouldn't put more pressure on you but it's something you need to know. And you know what immense courage it takes to go out amid tossing seas, waves several meters high, and whipping storms, in total darkness, to put yourself at the mercy of the sea, alone? Daily? That's how a fisherman or fisherwoman earns their daily bread."

Dupin considered it a nightmare.

"They're heroes! It's a magnificent job! A mythical calling indeed," Nolwenn said.

Dupin had no intention of contradicting her.

"Jean-Pierre Abraham"—Nolwenn's favorite author, who had for years been a lighthouse keeper and later lived on the Glénan islands—"once wrote, 'Going out to sea means something new every time, to leave the land of the living with no guarantee of returning to it.' In comparison the work of a police commissaire was just thumb-twiddling!"

Dupin didn't take it personally.

Nolwenn left a dramatic pause.

"You have to come down hard on this mafioso Morin, he's responsible for everything."

"We'll do that, Nolwenn, we'll do that."

"Céline is bound to have made many enemies."

"Riwal is going out to the island."

"Excellent. He knows how to speak to the people there. But really you should go with him." Advice seriously meant. "And by the way, in case you're wondering, I will be working from Lannion today. But I'm contactable at any time."

Dupin hadn't the faintest idea what her work from Lannion was about.

"And—"

"Boss, boss!" It was Riwal again, but this time he came charging right up to him. There was a look of horror on his face.

"I'll call you back, Nolwenn."

"We've got—" Riwal stopped in front of Dupin, gasping for breath. "We've got another corpse, boss!"

"What?"

"I'm not joking, boss. Another corpse. A new one."

"Another dead body? Who?"

"It's a woman again—and guess how she was killed."

"Her throat was cut."

Riwal stared at him in confusion. "How did you know?"

Dupin brushed his hand through his hair. "It can't be true."

"A dolphin researcher from Parc Iroise. Her throat cut. And guess where?"

Before Dupin could say anything, Riwal answered his own question: "On the Île de Sein!"

The island had now assumed an indisputable role in events.

"A dolphin researcher?"

"Yes."

"The woman at the coffee stand said something about dead dolphins."

"There are two groups of great porpoises in the Parc Iroise. About fifty around the Île de Ouessant, and another twenty around the Île de Sein. The Parc Iroise also has various different types of dolphins, little porpoises, blue dolphins, and roundhead dolphins. The dolphins are very important to the scientists in the *parc*: we still know very little about their highly evolved social relationships, their remarkable intelligence. In addition, the condition of the dolphins is an important indicator of the ecological conditions in the *parc*, the quality of the water . . ."

"Did the two women know each other?"

"I can't tell you that."

"When was the dolphin researcher killed?"

"We don't know that yet either."

"That's completely crazy."

Dupin had only just begun to deal with one murder. "This means we need to go out to the island together. Me too."

"I'm afraid so, boss."

There was no way for Dupin to avoid it.

"The sea is still going to be a bit rough," Riwal said. Dupin knew that all too well, but was aware that there were more important things at the moment. Even so. For the past few days, up until midday yesterday, there had been a storm. But today was summer. High summer. The water in the bay was beautifully calm, but—he was no longer a newbie in Armorica, "the land by the sea"—it would still be seriously choppy farther out.

"Unfortunately we can't use the helicopter. The prefect is using it, on the four-day simulation exercise for a—"

"That's enough, Riwal."

Dupin knew he would only get worked up. It was always the

same. Whenever they needed the helicopter, the prefect was using it. This time the prefect had announced weeks ago that there was going to be a practical simulation of something that for Dupin personally was a particularly dubious issue.

"We can go out from here in a police boat, or . . ." Riwal checked the time, "or take the regular ferry from Audierne, we could make that, we're twenty minutes from the stop."

Dupin gave him an inquisitive look.

"The ferry would be much more comfortable. It sits deeper in the water and is more stable. But we need to leave right now."

Dupin liked the word "regular" when he needed to go out on the water.

"Are there any of our colleagues there already? Is there a gendarmerie on the island?"

"No. But the deputy mayor takes care of everything. He's also the island doctor and president of the national lifeboat organization."

"Sounds promising."

"There's a police boat already on its way. From Audierne."

"It's a shorter distance from Audierne than from Douarnenez?"

"Yes."

"We'll take the ferry. The regular one. We can set off right now. In your car. Call the ferry company and tell them to wait for us. Kadeg can take over here. Tell him our priorities. He'll call for reinforcements."

With that Dupin set off, Riwal following him.

The whole thing was absurd. Two slit throats within a few hours—that was no coincidence. Both victims were women and both came from the Île de Sein, had to do with the sea. Obviously it was one and the same case. Dupin was in no doubt.

* * *

The swells were three meters high at the dock, up to five meters a bit farther out—long, forceful, rolling waves with astonishing troughs—and now that they were past the last piece of land, the Pointe du Raz, the waves reached as high as seven or eight meters. And they had nine kilometers more of open sea until they reached the island.

The classic blue-and-white *Enez Sun III*—the island's name in Breton—was neither as long or as big or as solid as Dupin had imagined it from Riwal's description. The promised "much more comfortable" and "more stable" were unnoticeable. The regular ferry flew upward toward the sky in challenging leaps and turns only to fall deep into the waves the next moment.

It was complete chaos. Up and down like the scariest roller coaster. But not just the *one* up-and-down movement, but lots of other movements too, all completely different, and what made it worst of all, they were all simultaneous: backward and forward, a sudden drop, a slithering and sliding. Neither body, soul, nor senses could find a rhythm. And on top of this horrible sensation the whole body was subject to the unbearable vibration of the entire boat, produced by the motor, situated right beneath the commissaire. And the deafening noise.

Dupin tried to fix his gaze on the horizon. Everyone said that helped. It was just unfortunate that Riwal and he hadn't found seats on the upper deck—the ship had waited twelve minutes for them, and they had to stand on the open deck at the rear, two meters above the theoretical water level, from where the horizon wasn't visible because it was regularly obscured by mountains of water. The ship was absolutely booked up with day-trippers and island dwellers who had been on the mainland overnight.

They would have to remain standing for the whole journey, and not even in the middle of the deck where it might have been just a little bit better, in that the sideways slipping and sliding wasn't quite so bad. But a fat couple with a tiny dog and masses of luggage had made themselves comfortable there.

Dupin wondered if the police boat might have been the lesser evil. But it was too late now.

He was reminded of a story that Nolwenn had told him about how the Romans had referred to Brittany as the end of the world and all life. *Finis terrae,* they had called it, meaning the Atlantic. The Atlantic had literally been the end for them, the end beyond the end, the ultimate landfall, the *mer extérieure,* that had nothing to do with the harmless civilized Mediterranean, the *mer intérieure.* "It's completely different," Caesar had noted in his last decisive sea battle against the Gauls, "traveling across an enclosed sea to going out into an immeasurable ocean, a sea without end that is an end in itself."

Dupin had the feeling that his whole body was a swaying movement. He needed to distract himself. Riwal was standing on the other side of the deck with a provocatively jovial expression on his face, looking out delightedly at the gigantic waves.

It might be best if they talked over a few things.

Carefully, feeling his way for a handhold, Dupin worked his way over to the other side of the deck, some five meters in all.

"Ah, boss"—Riwal's tone of voice had changed—"a wonderful trip. You know what the fishermen say: 'whoever sees Sein, sees his end,' or 'God help me survive the crossing from Raz, the boat is small and the sea is big.' We're making one of the wildest, most dangerous crossings there is. Strong currents, swirling seas and swells, the sea on the 'Bay of the Dead.' Majestic soaring crags for kilometers all along the route."

It wasn't exactly the distraction Dupin was hoping for. Riwal went on unperturbed. "From 1859 to now there have been one hundred and seventy shipwrecks officially recorded here. In reality it was more like three times as many! You need precise high-tech navigation technology here, and even that doesn't always help. Take a look: jagged rocks everywhere. It's as if some lazy giant had sat on the Cap du Van and tossed rocks into the sea for fun, like kids do with pebbles."

It was a pretty image, but it only made things worse.

"Even the devil had a problem reaching the island, boss. The story of his failed attempt explains why the sea is so wild here. Just the introduction makes it clear that it was inevitable.

"The devil demanded the souls of the islanders. So he had to deal with Saint Guénolé, who had promised the islanders he would build a bridge to the mainland. To reach the island the devil first disguised himself as a man. But the boat caught fire because of his hellfire hooves. Then the devil thought up a fiendish ruse: he would persuade Guénolé to build a bridge for him. That put Guénolé on the spot: if he didn't build the bridge he would be breaking his sacred oath, which was a serious sin, and the devil would take his soul. And those of all the islanders too, because Guénolé wouldn't be able to carry out his missionary work amongst them. In desperation Guénolé asked God for help, and God used his mighty breath to blow on the sea and create a bridge of ice. The devil thought he had won and quickly ran onto the bridge. But it melted beneath his feet and he fell into the tossing waves. Failed again."

As far as Riwal was concerned the punch line had fallen surprisingly flat.

"The heated water between the mainland and the island—here, in other words," the inspector waved an arm over the railing, "turned into a giant maelstrom that prevented the devil from getting any farther and saved the island from him. Even today the fishermen cross themselves in thanks when they pass the Pointe du Raz. The spot where the devil fell into the sea is called the 'hell of Plogoff' and is marked on all maritime maps."

A crazy story, Dupin had to admit. But even that wasn't distraction enough.

"Call the prefecture in Quimper, Riwal. Ask if there have been any other murder cases in Brittany recently where the victim has had their throat cut."

"Have you got an idea, boss?" Riwal was suddenly disturbed. "Are you thinking . . ." he hesitated, ". . . we might have a serial killer?"

"I'm just checking, only checking."

The expression on Riwal's face indicated he regarded Dupin's answer as disconcerting.

"On our right here we have the two mythical lighthouses Tévenneg and Ar Groac'h." Now it was Riwal who seemed to be looking for distraction. "You might glimpse one of them amidst a dip in the waves. Just two bare, rough rocks in the middle of the sea. They built towers on them. Great architectural achievements. Unfortunately, Tevenneg is cursed. The last lighthouse keeper fled in panic in 1910. Today it's run by remote from the Île de Sein. Do you know what lighthouse keepers call solitary towers in the sea? Hell. Those on the islands they call Purgatory. And those on the mainland, Paradise."

They were on their way to further an investigation into a capital crime, a brutal murder, the second within a few hours; "Hell" seemed the right word for their excursion to Dupin.

"Above all, we have to find out what link there was between the two women, Riwal. That's what we need to work out."

"I imagine we'll find out something on that when we get to the island."

Dupin was concentrating on something Riwal had said at Douarnenez harbor. Going back over things in his head, reworking them, was one of the commissaire's oblique but effective skills.

"You mentioned that the state of the dolphins' health was an indicator of the quality of the water, and other factors about the sea."

"Indeed."

Obviously Riwal was waiting for a conclusion that would let him understand why the question had been asked. Instead Dupin simply changed the topic.

"Do the ferries only go from Audierne?"

"*One* ferry. The *Enez Sun III*. Which is what we're on now. In July and August there are others, one of them from Douarnenez even. For the rest of the year there's just this one. Forty-three meters long, eight meters across, fifteen knots top speed, double 1750 horsepower. She belongs to Penn Ar Bed—the Celtic name, in other words the real name, for Finistère—a private company that deals with the three islands, Sein, Molène, and Ouessant, on behalf of the state. The *Enez Sun III* goes once a day."

"Only once?"

"It leaves Audierne in the morning and leaves the island in the afternoon. That's it."

"There must be other ways to get from the island to the mainland and back?"

"If there's a medical emergency the helicopter comes from the clinic in Douarnenez. Apart from that, no. At least no public means of transport."

That meant the island was very isolated from the rest of the world. A factor of some significance in their investigation.

"Depending on when the murder occurred," Dupin mused aloud, "the murderer could still be on the island. Either way is possible: someone who came from the island and had to go to the mainland to commit the crime, or someone from the mainland who had to go to the island."

Spoken out loud, it sounded stupid. Riwal took things a bit further.

"The people who live on the island call themselves 'islanders,' and those on the mainland 'French,' which to them more or less means 'tourist.' Just to avoid any confusion in our investigations. Sometimes they even refer to themselves as 'Americans.'"

Dupin gave him a confused look.

"Beyond Brittany, there's only America," Riwal replied.

Dupin knew this wasn't just trivia or quirkiness; things like that were important in Brittany if you didn't want to sound like a fool.

"In general they're stubborn. Like the island itself. It doesn't belong to this world, boss. It's wonderful. France is far away, a lot farther than just the actual nine kilometers. You'll see. A tiny dot of rocky land in the wide oceans, shaped like some long-tailed mythical creature in the face of the elemental forces of the Atlantic. Two and a half kilometers long and in some places just twenty-five meters wide, mostly flat, barely two meters above water level. During real storms gigantic waves sweep over the island, putting it totally underwater. All in all just less than a single square kilometer in area. Rough, barren, wild, lonely. I love Sein and its people."

Riwal sounded as if he was talking about another species. Another planet. "An island of magical forces, with an extreme aura.

You'll feel that too. Sometimes it can make you scared." Riwal was speaking with serious respect. "In prehistoric times cults were based here, even today you find menhirs and dolmens, standing stones. One important burial mound was destroyed by greedy gold robbers. Later, according to Celtic belief, the island was the closest place to the realm of the dead and the immortals. A place of fairies, nymphs, and druids, lots of the latter buried here. You absolutely have to be prepared for a trip to Sein, boss, inwardly prepared," Riwal said, a deep seriousness on his face.

Dupin hadn't the strength to tell Riwal to calm down. In any case, most of it had gone straight over his head. For one thing the boat had taken another leap, and then plunged way down again. Dupin had clung so tightly to a steel brace behind him that his wrists were aching. For another thing, he was trying as hard as he could to concentrate on the vital questions in the case.

"How big is the crew on the police boat that's coming from Audierne?"

"Four men, plus the crime scene team."

"How many people live on the island?"

"All year round, two hundred and sixteen, in summer some six hundred. Most tourists only stay until the ferry leaves in late afternoon. Just a few spend the night."

"Four police plus the two of us isn't enough for all the people we need to talk to." Dupin rubbed his temples. "Does the ferry have a passenger list? Do people use their names when they buy tickets?"

"Yes, they have to, for security reasons. But if it's the same killer in both cases, he can't have used the ferry. If he had been on the mainland between eight P.M. and midnight yesterday, this is the first ferry he could have taken since, and the dolphin researcher was murdered either last night or early this morning."

Dupin's brain wasn't exactly working at full speed yet, he realized. He needed more caffeine.

"But obviously there are lots of private boats as well as boats owned by companies and institutions that run to and from the island, some of them regularly. There are also specialist boats, such as the waste disposal and oil delivery boats. The ones Céline Kerkrom protested about. Then there are the tourist boats that come out dolphin-spotting, even though there aren't that many. Or the boats used by scientists and researchers, and the Parc Iroise guards. The deceased would have had her own boat too, as one of the *parc*'s scientific team."

That meant that, despite how out of the way it was, there were lots of possible ways to get to and from the island without problems.

"No matter, Riwal, we have to check the arrival and departure of every single boat between yesterday morning and this morning."

"That won't be easy. I've only listed some of the boats, and like I said, anyone here can be out in their own private boat at any time."

"We . . ." Dupin didn't finish the sentence. The *Enez Sun III* had merrily ridden a particularly big wave. *Piquer dans la plume,* the Breton seagoing folk called it: "riding the feather." The white horse of the breaking wave.

Dupin breathed deeply in and out.

He had forgotten what he wanted to say.

Riwal took advantage of the moment.

"The story about the Île de Sein that has most resonance is by a Roman writer who visited the island about the year 20 AD. He writes about a Celtic goddess's oracle served by nine virgin priestesses who carried out ritual ceremonies. They were called the Gallicènes, and are the earliest witches ever reported. They could make the sea and the winds rise with magic spells and could transform themselves into any animal they wanted, heal the sick and the dying. Or tell the future. Truth seekers from all over the world came to them, just like us." Riwal wasn't joking, that much was clear. "One of them was Morgan le Fay." The inspector said the name as if she was a friend. "The one you know from the King Arthur saga. It was on Sein that the nine priestesses were supposed to have healed Arthur from a wound suffered in battle: Avalon!"

Dupin didn't react. He was deep in thought.

"Riwal, call the Parc Iroise and find out about the incident with the dolphins."

"Are you thinking of something in particular?"

"No. Ask them about irregularities in the quality of the water. Pollution, if there is or has been any."

"Straightaway, boss. Nolwenn is dealing with Charles Morin. I've spoken to her. She'll do her research thoroughly and she's organized a meeting with him. She's also spoken to the prefect, and told me to tell you she's put him in the picture."

"Very good. Do you happen to know what Nolwenn is doing in Lannion?"

"An aunt."

"She has an aunt in Lannion?"

Dupin had already heard about a lot of aunts, but not one in Lannion.

"Jacqueline Thymeur. I think she's the third sister of her mother. Early seventies."

Fine. Nolwenn could work anywhere. It didn't matter.

"Is it something special?"

During their last big case Nolwenn had had to go to a funeral. Of another aunt.

"She's fine. If you mean the aunt."

"Riwal." Dupin had just had an idea, a good idea. "Call Goulch! He should get ready and come and collect us from the Île de Sein later."

Dupin was pleased at his inspiration. Kireg Goulch of the water protection police might steer one of those dreadful speedboats, but for one thing the ferry wasn't the slightest bit better and for another Dupin trusted the tall, lanky Goulch, whom he had worked with on a complicated case on Glénan. Not that Goulch's handling of the boat back then had exactly been a pleasure, but Dupin's fear of traveling by sea—a lot worse than just seasickness—hadn't been as bad in Goulch's company as it was normally. On top of that: Goulch was an excellent policeman. And an expert on the sea.

"Gladly." Riwal beamed.

Goulch and he had become good friends over the years.

Once again the boat shot sharply into the air, seemed to sway there for an endlessly long moment, then crashed mercilessly down with a fearful fury. As if the Atlantic were playing with it. Not cruelly or angrily—that would be something different—but playfully, coquettishly. Just to pass the time, maybe. All of a sudden, for no obvious reason—the island was still at least a kilometer away and the boat hadn't changed its speed—the sea calmed, as if they had passed through some magic border that blocked the forces of nature. If Dupin hadn't been so preoccupied with himself, his queasiness, his now cramplike tension—following the chat with Riwal he had crept into a corner of the deck and tried hard to get at least an occasional view of the horizon—this mysterious change would have been yet another reason for worry, but he just accepted it.

To the right, bizarre-shaped rocks stuck out of the sea. Dangerously sharp and dark, several meters high, rising up against the marvelously blue sky. Some of them with bright green trails of seaweed. Wary seagulls stared at the boat.

The ferry passed unnecessarily close to the rocks. It was only very late that it took a sharp curve around a stony islet in front of the harbor, and then all of a sudden there it was: the Île de Sein. Very real and breathtakingly beautiful.

The harbor, a few jetties in front of a black-and-white picturebook lighthouse, Men-Brial, a solemn, surprisingly large church just sitting there, a curved quayside with a small sandy beach in front of it. Behind lay small houses painted yellow, bright blue, and bright pink, though most were simply white or just stone with window shades painted Atlantic blue. All a bit faded, battered, whipped by the perpetual wind, the spray, the sun. The sea reflected the light from all sides, multiplied it until it seemed like a psychedelic vision.

The harbor was a natural bay with a sturdy pier built around it, and enclosed a group of rocks opposite—also with a bright white sandy beach. The concrete and the defensive rocks had over the years turned yellowish. Behind the quay and the village and tow-ering over everything was the elegant, gracious, extremely tall is-land lighthouse. Dupin knew it from picture books: Goulenez—le Grand Phare. A famous landmark, as were all the lighthouses in Brittany, all of which had their own names and were listed in an un-official rating depending on how inaccessible and difficult to main-tain their position was.

The boat headed for the outermost pier; their course left no doubt, that was where they would disembark.

"At ebb tide the boat stops at the first pier, the water at the others isn't deep enough," Dupin heard one of the tourists say, who were beginning to come down the steel steps from above.

Within seconds there was a line. Dupin was glad to join it. He would soon have his feet on dry land again, even if there wasn't much of it.

A hefty thump. The boat had docked.

"Here, here!" A vigorous, high-pitched woman's voice from the pier. Dupin started to gingerly make his way down the narrow, steep ladder. "Monsieur le Commissaire!"

A stocky, elderly lady with crinkly gray-blond hair was waving frantically. The passengers were staring curiously at the lady and even more so at the commissaire, as she called out more loudly. "The corpse!"

The day-trippers looked suddenly concerned and distraught at this dramatic opening to their stay on the island.

Dupin, his legs wobbling, had finally reached the pier. Immedi-ately the little woman was standing in front of him. The expressions on her face were as vigorous as her voice: tough, stubborn, ruthless. Dupin knew the type: hard-nosed to the bitter end. She must have recognized him from a photo in the newspaper.

"I'm Joséphine Coquil, director of the island museums." She turned her gaze casually to Riwal. "And you must be the inspector. Right, I'll take you to the corpse," she raised her eyebrows, "to our second corpse! This is quite a drama for the island." She sounded more exhilarated than dismayed.

"First the murder of our Céline, and then the dolphin woman. The poor girls! Such a shame! Do you know anything yet? Have you an initial clue?"

"Céline Kerkrom has only just been found, madame." Dupin moved his weight from one foot to the other, trying to get an even stance again.

"You know what they say, 'See Sein and you've seen your end.' Ha!"

"I've heard say it's the 'island's motto,' madame." And he reckoned it wasn't going to be the last time.

"Is it true that Céline had her throat cut? The same thing happened to the dolphin researcher. There's no doubt about that, I can tell you."

"There was no doubt in the fisherwoman either."

"There's a monster at large here!" Madame Coquil exclaimed, without sounding in the slightest shocked by her own statement.

"Céline was brave, she changed things. And Laetitia Darot was a strong woman too," she hesitated, "even if she didn't really know anybody well. She was usually out on her own on the sea. She only talked to Céline, and occasionally to the deputy mayor. What a mess, she only arrived on the island in January." She shook her head grimly. "She was only interested in our dolphins. She came into my museum four times. Even if she didn't talk to anybody much, she had our interests at heart, our island's. Its history, its flora and fauna. When you come here again, Monsieur le Commissaire, not for some terrible murder, then you must come and see my museums, three of them altogether, one about the island and life on the island, another on the Second World War resistance, and one on the lifeboats, I—"

"Where is the dead woman's body, madame? Do we have a car?" Dupin was impatient.

He was met with a glare that suggested he should know better.

"There are *no* cars here. Just four motor vehicles—two fire engines, a gas truck that carries the oil for the lighthouse and the electricity and drinking water facilities, and one emergency vehicle. That is used only for the most urgent cases," she concluded firmly.

Dupin was about to say that this might be considered one of the most urgent cases, but Madame Coquil was ahead of him.

"And the woman is already dead, so why would we need an emergency vehicle. We will go on foot. You don't have any luggage. Come along, no need to dally."

She set off at a pace down the long, wet pier. Despite her age and her small size, she set such a bracing tempo that Dupin had to work to keep up with her. The same went for Riwal, who had a grin on his face.

"This is your first time on the island, I'm right in thinking?"

It wasn't exactly a question.

"Yes, madame."

"How long have you been working in Brittany?" Dupin didn't miss the implied criticism. "Whatever, you're here now. In July and August we get a lot of your Paris friends come to visit, most of them only for a few hours."

It sounded as if Dupin was supposed to know them all. "But do you know when things were busiest here? Back in the Roman days! Sein and Ouessant were the most important resting points between Britain and Germany, the most important shipping route for trade and military. The Romans here also met the nine witches who—"

"I've heard the story, madame."

"Or in the Hundred Years' War! In 1360, eighty ships landed here, carrying fourteen thousand men! All on this island. In order to plunder it."

That sounded like a lot of men to the commissaire, just for this little island. Even practically it was hard to imagine. Fourteen thousand men!

On the quay to their right, four men in yellow oilcloth pants were standing against the low wall, which had a few handsome crabs lying on it, the fruit of some successful *pêche-à-pied*. They had big knives in their hands.

"After that things were very quiet on the island for a long time." There was a tone of deep disappointment in Madame Coquil's voice. "So quiet that the Sun King decreed that all the inhabitants be exempt from tax in order to make the island more attractive. The decree is still good today. He said, and I quote, 'To tax Sein, already depressed by nature, would be to tax the sea, the storms, and the rocks.'" It was clearly something she could repeat even in her sleep at night. "How right he was! Nor did it help when the missionaries introduced agriculture, which obviously did no good, producing no more than a few measly potatoes in some years, and some miserable grain, so little that the women still had to use roots to make bread. Most of the fish caught goes to Audierne. The dried biscuits and the low-quality salted fish that get brought to the island every couple of weeks aren't much help either. The islanders had to gather seaweed to eat and to make fire. There was nothing left for them but to become pirates, beach robbers, and plunderers. What else were the poor people to do?" Her expression was one of deep, if dubious, understanding.

Madame Coquil took a deep breath.

"Do you know what they call us in France? Wild men, barbarians, sea devils, and the island they call the rocks of hell. Just because we have nothing to eat and no priest, which is obviously because not one of those milksops dared come here. Wagging tongues have suggested that some of the islanders even opposed the building of the first lighthouse, on the grounds that it would reduce the number of shipwrecks. We only got wine if some unlucky ship had any on board."

They walked past the pretty black-and-white lighthouse on the quay. A forklift truck was heading down the pier to the ferry to pick up the containers with baggage and shopping in them. Dupin realized all he had to do was listen. They would find the islanders ready to engage. And it would clearly be no disadvantage to their investigation if they were to learn more about the islanders and their "realm."

"Today there are about five or six times as many rabbits on the island as there are people. The mayor before last let loose three pairs, and that had, as we put it, consequences. He thought it would be a good idea to have some meat to eat for a change. Everyone can go hunt for their own roast. Previously it was nowhere near as comfortable as it is today. People are getting softer. The more pleasant life has become over the past decades, the greater the numbers leaving. In 1793 we were three hundred and twenty-seven and we gnawed on dried fish and died of hunger. By the end of the nineteenth century we were nearly a thousand. By 1926 we were even one thousand nine hundred and twenty-eight! But in the second half of the twentieth century there were fewer and fewer. And by then we had electricity, water, a mail office, a supermarket, cafés, restaurants, television, a school with six students, even sport facilities on the beach at low tide, a grand church, handsome menhirs, a mayor and a deputy mayor who's also the island doctor, three fisherfolk—" She corrected herself: "Two fishers and an LTE mast for perfect cell phone reception. Nobody here needs a landline anymore! And"—the LTE mast obviously wasn't the high point— "we're one of just five places in France to be awarded the Ordre de la Libération. After General de Gaulle, on June 18, 1940, made his appeal from London for the establishment of an army of liberation, all one hundred and forty men on the island, without exception, set off in six boats, on the same day. One of those proud boats, *Le Corbeau des Mers*, still exists."

Everyone in France knew that deeply impressive story. It somehow represented the soul of the island.

"Only the women, old men, children, the priest, and the lighthouse keeper remained. Twenty-five percent of the men who turned up in London in response to de Gaulle's appeal were ours. In a celebratory speech later, the president declared to the nation *'L'Île de Sein est donc le quart de la France'*—The Île de Sein is a quarter of France! Us. Nobody was as heroic as us. The president came in person to award us the Ordre de la Libération. 'You were the ones who saved France,' he told us. *That*"—she took a deep breath— "Monsieur le Commissaire, *that* is the Île de Sein, that is its spirit! The 'wild men' were the ones who saved France."

"How far is it to where the body is, madame?" But Joséphine Coquil wasn't finished yet.

"And now, now Sein is on its last legs."

She turned to Dupin and shot him a withering look. Dupin had no idea what he was supposed to have done.

"It was in the papers yesterday. An important professor from Brest, Paul Tréguer, said that Sein will be one of the first islands to disappear under the water if the sea level keeps rising. A study has shown that the increasing *extreme weather conditions*"—she spoke the phrase as if it were some deep-sea monster—"are going to hit the islands particularly badly. As always, people will only learn when it's too late, and by then Sein will have long been history. That's the tragedy. And if the Gulf Stream collapses, all Brittany will be in the Arctic . . . We're considering going to the International Court of Justice and accusing the world like other islands have done, in the South Seas and such . . ."

"I . . ." Dupin pulled himself together. "You're absolutely right, madame," he replied seriously.

"It's quicker if we go through the village," Madame Coquil said, and took a sharp turn between two houses, down an alleyway so narrow that Dupin would almost have missed it, barely a meter wide, but still with a proud street sign: Rue du Coq Hardi. They went one after the other, with Riwal last.

"Just so you know"—the museum chief's anger seemed to have abated somewhat, apparently thanks to Dupin's ready agreement— "we have fifty-four streets, the most important obviously the two quays on either side of the harbor, Quai des Paimpolais and Quai des Français Libres; we just call them Quai Nord and Quai Sud, north and south. And the great east–west axis that links the village with the other end of the island. Last week we had a great event: all the streetlights were fitted with LED bulbs. They give out stronger light, use much less energy, and are indestructible. Only Monaco in Europe has LED streetlights, and cities like Los Angeles in America."

The old lady had turned left, then right and then left again down other streets that were little wider. The house fronts all looked the same, plastered white, occasionally pale yellow or pink. All close together as if they had been pushed. A proper labyrinth. Quite unique. Dupin had lost all sense of direction, something that normally never happened.

"The houses are all squeezed together to keep the wind out; they all protect one another."

Yet again Madame Coquil had turned one way and then the other. Dupin had the impression they were walking in a circle. He wouldn't have been surprised if they came out back at the quay. Yet again they took a sharp left and came out on a broad concrete path.

"*Voilà,* the east–west axis, la Route du Phare."

A car would have found it difficult here. There were little gardens and courtyards to the right and left, but not a soul to be seen.

"If the weather stays fine, everybody will sit outside here and eat." She cast a wary glance at the sky.

"Madame Coquil, how might we find out which boats came and went from the island yesterday?"

Before Madame Coquil could answer him, Dupin turned to his inspector: "Riwal, see to it that no boat leaves the island before we have registered it, and spoken to the passengers. No exceptions."

"That's a thing you're asking, Monsieur le Commissaire. Two tasks fit for Sisyphus at once," Madame Coquil said. "Obviously there's no central list of which boats come and go. How could you imagine there would be? Particularly now in the summer: all the leisure boats, sailors, divers, anglers, Bretons, French, and other foreigners. And then the boats from Parc Iroise . . . You mustn't forget them! And then there are the official boats. The oil boat that comes every Thursday, as well as the food boat for the minimarket. And normally the hairdresser is here at this time on a Thursday."

"The hairdresser?"

There really were a lot of boats. And a hairdresser.

"He comes in his own boat to the islands. Mondays and Tuesdays he's in his salon in Camaret, on the Crozon peninsula. He used to be a fisherman, who occasionally cut his friends' hair. Then he turned it into a full-time job. He's very good at it. We have a lot of older people on the island who're pleased they don't have to go to France to get their hair cut. Oh yes, not to forget the priest. He also uses his own boat to get around the islands. But you can write him off the list of potential murderers straightaway: he's been in Zanzibar for two weeks!"

It was all too strange, and at the same time very plausible: people living out here, cut off and with a minimum of infrastructure and social life, had to organize things differently. Even so it was a mad idea to have a priest and a hairdresser commuting between the islands. And committing murders. Like something from an Agatha Christie mystery.

* * *

They had come to the last houses in the village, where the island narrowed disconcertingly, with the ocean lapping on either side. Inevitably—this was the only street on the island beyond the village—they headed toward the big lighthouse, even though it was still a ways away. Riwal had dropped behind a bit, with his phone to his ear.

Uneven coarse grass everywhere, kept short by the sea, salt, wind, and almost certainly also the rabbits. It was a low, undulating landscape, bright shining green, that petered out into stony beaches along the coastline. It was a remarkably empty landscape, without trees or bushes. But here and there were pretty pink flowers in full blossom, which lent a certain appeal to the rough, barren landscape.

"Where does the oil boat come from, Madame Coquil?"

"From Audierne harbor. It comes to us first, then goes on to Molène and Ouessant."

Those were the other two large islands that formed the unique archipelago that made up the extreme west coast of Brittany. The rest was comprised of countless tiny islands, islets, and some that were little more than chunks of rock. The most imposing by far was Ouessant, but Molène too—only slightly larger than Sein—had its reputation.

"I assume we're talking about the boat Céline protested against."

"Not the boat, but the wrong state of affairs that everything is done with oil here. There are alternatives."

"When does the boat usually get in?"

"Between seven and eight in the morning. And leaves again between ten and eleven."

"And the provisions boat?"

"Around eight. It isn't always punctual."

"Also from Audierne?"

"From Camaret. On the Crozon peninsula."

Dupin knew the peninsula well. Particularly Crozon, as well as Morgat, a summer spa with a little harbor. He had very good friends in Goulien, next to one of the peninsula's breathtaking beaches.

"Did it get in before eight today?"

"Just after."

"And when did it leave again?"

"It's still in the harbor. The two captains are sitting in one of the bars we passed."

Naturally Dupin had seen the bars on both quays. They looked wonderful, perfect even.

"Riwal." The inspector had finished his phone call. "Where is the police boat at the moment?" Dupin hadn't seen it in the harbor.

"It's anchored in the bay over there, look." Madame Coquil was pointing in the direction of the lighthouse. "Apart from the harbor, that's the only other jetty on the island usable by a ship no matter what the state of the water. But actually nobody uses it anymore. We'll be there in a moment."

"By the way"—Riwal had caught up with the commissaire—"there hasn't been any murder in which someone's throat was cut in Brittany in recent years, definitely not. And as for the matter of the dolphins, Parc Iroise can't say anything at present, but it happens all the time. One of the problems with the nets. It's appalling. They said we need to speak to the *parc*'s scientific director. About water pollution too. And the boats: I've organized everything."

Dupin turned back to the museum boss. "Is there one of the Parc Iroise boats nearby at the moment? Have you—"

Dupin's phone rang.

A Parisian number he didn't recognize.

He stopped reluctantly and took it.

"Yes?"

"There is also a train at six twenty-seven A.M.," said a rapidly rattling voice in full flow, "then you would get there at eleven seventeen A.M. The one at eight thirty-three A.M. only gets to Paris at one twenty-three A.M. That would be a shame because by then it would be packed, my dear Georges. I'm sitting here with your aunt Yvonne, going through everything. Down to the last detail."

Dupin was too puzzled to say a word.

His mother.

The "big event."

Obviously he hadn't given it a thought in the last few hours. Nor had he thought of the likely, almost certain explosion that he was unquestionably about to create. But not telling his mother the situation or inventing excuses would only make things worse in the end.

"I . . . we . . . we have a murder, two murders, in fact. Brutal murders. Just, just a few hours ago." He sounded more pathetic than he intended, but perhaps that was the right thing. "I'm in the midst of a case." He took a deep, deliberate sigh.

There was a silence—two rabbits pattered down the east–west axis—then: "It is my seventy-fifth birthday, my dear Georges." Her voice was a cold, suppressed hiss. "You will be in Paris the day after tomorrow, come what may. You and your fiancée." Which was how she referred to Claire even though there had been no talk of an engagement to date. "At seven P.M. precisely. You will sit at my right side at the table of honor with your sister on the left." A lengthy silence; perhaps she was calming down, a little at least. Then she cleared her throat theatrically. "Very well then. In that case, the eight thirty-three train. I'll agree to that. You already have those tickets."

A second later she hung up.

The seventy-fifth birthday of Anna Dupin.

The preparations had been under way for a year now. She went in for big celebrations, obviously, or in her words, "appropriate." It would be what a Parisian from a *gros bourgeois* family would consider a highly elegant, highly ceremonial affair.

There would be exactly one hundred guests and she had rented one of the restaurants at the Hotel George V, no less. Dupin had had at least a hundred telephone calls since the planning had begun, three yesterday alone, in which he had for the umpteenth time discussed the most minute of details.

Obviously he had no idea how long he would be busy with this case, but he had never solved a major case in just two days. It was out of the question.

Dupin ran his fingers roughly round the back of his head. He had to get a grip on himself.

He joined Madame Coquil and Riwal again. The little group continued on their way.

"The Parc Iroise boats—that was my question, Madame Coquil—whether there are any here right now, on the island?"

"I don't know. But watch out for Captain Vaillant, the pirate smuggler, he turns up anywhere he likes. Including here."

"Captain Vaillant?"

"Some folks consider him a knave, others a hero who thumbs his nose at the state." It wasn't clear which Madame Coquil considered him to be. "A fisherman with a crock of a boat, a chancer. He basically makes a living from smuggling, alcohol smuggling. Eau-de-vie. He buys the stuff from various illegal distillers and sells it in England. But so far nobody's caught him at it."

Smuggling as a topic yet again. And alcohol and cigarettes every time. And another shady character whom nobody had any proof of anything against.

Dupin had got his notebook out again and taken a few notes while walking—in his hieroglyphic script. "Vaillant, you say?"

"Captain Vaillant, nobody knows his first name. We're almost there."

Some fifty or sixty meters to their right was a large group of people: police, people in plain clothes—probably the crime scene investigators—and among them a woman and a boy.

"You should know," Riwal turned to Dupin and said, "that smuggling has a long tradition on the British Isles, just as smuggling has had a long history of links with piracy in Brittany. Smuggling began in the early seventeenth century. The next three hundred years were the heyday of smuggling in the Channel, with the main route leading directly from Ouessant—"

"Riwal!" Dupin stopped him. He was getting out of hand again. Dupin knew the history and also that smuggling had made no minor contribution to the economic prosperity of Brittany, and that places such as Roscoff or Morlaix had become famous and wealthy nationwide on that account. There were whole strips of land, including the magnificent coastal route that Dupin so loved, that were basically just smuggling routes, to the extent that the concept even today had a remarkably romantic sound to Breton ears. Something that had nothing, absolutely nothing, in common with the modern smuggling that took place on the seas of the world and had a very different face, a particularly brutal face.

"This Captain Vaillant." Dupin turned toward Madame Coquil; he didn't want to get any further involved in the digression. "Was he on the island yesterday or today?"

"You'll need to ask around in the bars along the quays. They head directly there after they've concluded their business. They don't see much more of the island."

All of a sudden celestial Celtic notes rang out—Riwal's cell phone. The inspector took a few discreet steps to one side.

"What about Charles Morin, the big-time fisherman? Has he been seen on the island recently?"

"Now there's a *real* criminal!" This time Madame Coquil was leaving no doubt about what she thought. "Not that I knew it. No. He has a large Bénéteau, you see it straightaway. Every now and then you find him sitting in Le Tatoon. You get the best *lieu jaune* in the world there. Caught by our fishermen."

Dupin made another note.

"Well, here we are: the cholera cemetery."

"The cholera cemetery?"

A man came toward them with a deliberate pace.

"Antoine Manet. Our deputy mayor. And the island doctor!" Madame Coquil had assumed a businesslike voice. "The mayor is on holiday. Jokkmokk. Lapland. Elk watching. Did you know they make elk salami there?"

The deputy major—in his late fifties, maybe early sixties—was lean and sporty with thick, short, light gray hair and an open, serious tanned face with intelligent eyes. Young man's eyes. Jeans, black leather shoes, a polo shirt, a gray all-weather jacket, and a dark green shoulder bag.

He held out a hand to Dupin and smiled.

"What a load of shit!" he said, and gave him a forceful handshake.

Dupin stood there as if struck by lightning. He found himself incomprehensibly irritated. It was the deputy mayor, not him, who had sworn, and used Dupin's most common swear word expression.

"That was all we needed on the island!"

Dupin had no reply to that.

"Come along, Monsieur le Commissaire. The dead woman is over here." He spoke casually but formally. "You know the phrase, 'See Sein and see your end.'"

Without waiting for any reaction from Dupin, the doctor had turned around sharply.

There was no sign of Madame Coquil retreating, quite the opposite:

"We were struck by a serious cholera epidemic in 1849," she

said, as if she was talking about something that had occurred only a month ago. "In the seventeenth century we were also hit by plague, which almost wiped us out. The surviving islanders had to repopulate the island in the following years and sought partners from the mainland." It was easy to tell the last sentence was important to her. "But going back to the cholera, it was stupidly accompanied by a sweating fever that had come from the mainland! The doctor had cautiously isolated the bodies of the first to die and brought them here to be buried in a separate cemetery, rapidly laid out. The island's black traditional dress dates back to the epidemic. Even today people still wear the black bonnet."

It all sounded particularly tragic and morbid, particularly given that Breton traditional dress was usually marked by its richness in bright colors.

Dupin followed the deputy mayor. The cholera cemetery lay on one of the scrubby fields, grazed down to the ground by rabbits, that here ran right up to the rocky beach. It was a perfect square with one entrance on the east–west axis. Little clumps of the pink flowers clustered in the shelter of the walls. On the other side, opposite the entrance, a modest, weathered stone cross, no more than a meter high. On both sides of the square were huge granite slabs lying parallel to one another. With no inscriptions. Totally blank.

That was it. The whole cemetery.

It was a crazy place. A flat, naked nothing below an endless beautifully blue sky. Thirty meters farther and the endless ocean began, a few strangely shaped chunks of granite on the waterline, and a few more jagging out of the sea beyond them, like obscure sculptures, cryptic signs.

"They have to share the cross." Madame Coquil had seen Dupin's look. "In the end there were no more than six cholera victims; the cemetery could have taken far more." She obviously regretted the waste of space.

The policemen, the men in plain clothes, the mother and boy were standing next to the stone cross, looking over at Dupin. The deputy mayor was waiting by the entrance for the commissaire, Riwal, and Madame Coquil.

"Seven, I think? Seven surely," Dupin remarked in passing.

He had counted five stone slabs on the left and two on the right.

But it was unnecessary.

"Pardon?" The museum chief had stopped on the spot, hearing Dupin. Her face bore a look of horror. Something awful must have happened, even if Dupin had no idea what it was.

Even Antoine Manet had noticed. "Joséphine, don't scare the commissaire! We have important work to do here. And he's supposed to be the best."

Madame Coquil tried to regain her composure, but it clearly wasn't easy.

"You—you said you counted seven graves? Five on the left—*five* graves? Five? Is that right?"

"I must have miscounted," Dupin said after he had taken another look and only seen four.

He had made a mistake.

"They say that anyone who sees a fifth grave in the western row"—she was trying hard not to appear too dramatic, but in vain—"has seen his own grave. And in the next few days will be struck by something dreadful. The last time it happened was four years ago, a man from Le Conquet, a butcher, he—"

"Joséphine! Stop it!" Manet said sharply. He was serious. Which hardly made things better, Dupin thought. Why was he taking it so seriously? It was only a silly superstition.

Dupin shot a glance at Riwal, who was still holding his phone, but said nothing. Riwal just stood there rooted to the ground, glancing back and forth between Madame Coquil and Dupin.

He wasn't going to be any help.

"What's up, Riwal." Dupin walked over to him.

"Kadeg." Riwal was trying in vain to keep his voice calm. "He just called: the pathologist put the time of death at approximately ten P.M., give or take an hour."

Dupin had expected nothing different.

"Apart from that, he confirmed all his initial assumptions. Nothing new. And they found nothing unusual on Kerkrom's boat either. So far it all seems unremarkable. But Kadeg wants to let a fisherman whom the Douarnenez police trust have a look. It's possible he might notice something we missed."

A good idea.

"A cell phone," Riwal said. He still didn't seem very calm. It was as if he was trying to calm himself down as he spoke. "They didn't find one on the boat, but Kerkrom had one. The murderer must have taken it."

"Find out the network and connection."

"We're already doing that, but you know that will take time. Kadeg talked to Jean Serres, Madame Gochat's colleague. But to tell the truth nothing came of it. He only repeated what we already knew. The list of customers who were at the auction is ready. That means the agreed list of lists is ready as far as we know: a list of everybody who was in the auction hall that evening. Interviews are still going on but we will be notified if there is anything important."

"Good."

Kadeg was in charge of the whole systematic procedure.

"But boss, you . . . you shouldn't dismiss the seventh grave thing lightly." Riwal looked deeply worried.

Louder than he intended, Dupin replied, "Everything's fine, Riwal, everything's fine!"

Riwal was about to contradict him, but caught himself.

"I'll deal with the boats and their crews, boss. You can get me on the cell phone." He paused. "Call me if something happens. Anything."

The inspector gave himself a shove and went over to the uniformed policemen. "We've got a few urgent tasks to deal with, messieurs. Follow me."

With an inquisitive look on their faces they tagged after him like puppies, back to the east–west axis.

Dupin turned to Manet. "The body? Where is the body?"

He hadn't seen it anywhere.

"Behind the last grave," Antoine Manet said, and walked up to the cemetery wall. "Over there," he waved a hand vaguely, "right at the back. The grave was dug but never used. Over time it's fallen in on itself. The body isn't visible from the road. Anthony found it this morning while playing."

That had to be the boy, maybe nine or ten years old, standing next to his mother. Dupin introduced himself to everyone.

"Why would she have been left in the cholera cemetery, of all places?"

Manet, who had stayed next to the wall, shrugged slowly. "We have no idea."

Dupin had reached the last stone slab. Then he saw the body.

The corpse of Laetitia Darot, an extraordinarily pretty woman, there was no other way to say it, aged somewhere around thirty, lay on its back as if peacefully in bed. She had long, slightly wavy brown hair with a copper-red glow. Fine features, but in no way weak, a curved mouth. It almost looked as if she was asleep. Dark jeans, low blue rubber boots, a blue wool jacket, and a gray, roughly knitted woolen sweater beneath it.

"I imagine it happened this morning. Probably between six and seven o'clock. A straight cut, through the windpipe and the vocal cords." Manet's brow was furrowed; he seemed to be concentrating. "She wouldn't have been able to make any noise after that. The brain would have got no more oxygen and blood would have poured down her windpipe and suffocated her." Manet took a step back and let his eyes run down the victim's body, Dupin's following his. "Her right wrist is a bit swollen, presumably where the killer held her. There are no real signs of a struggle though. No other visible wounds."

"Would it take a specialist to make a cut like that, do you think?"

The question had already come up that morning.

"Not particularly. By the sea there are so many people who use a knife and are masters at doing so. Proper masters."

One of the crime scene team took a step forward, a younger

version of Kadeg. "The pathologist should be here any moment," he said, a jaunty, enthusiastic tone to his voice. "I think we should wait for the expert."

"I have all the information I need about the body," Dupin mumbled.

The island doctor smiled gently. Dupin's taking sides hadn't been necessary. Manet wouldn't be so easily unsettled. He gave the impression it wasn't the first time he had seen something like this.

"The murder was probably carried out here, or nearby," said the other of the two men, older with thick white hair, making a confident gesture. "There is a lot of blood soaked into the ground next to the body, and she can't have lost that much in two different places. She can't have moved after she was placed in the ditch; the blood all flowed the same way."

Manet nodded in agreement. "Laetitia Darot would already have lost consciousness by then—it normally happens in about ten seconds."

"Just to be sure, we've searched the entire cemetery for any other signs of blood. And found none. Not on the grassland around the cemetery. Absolutely nothing of note. And on ground like this," the older of the two glanced down pointedly, "there's no point even starting to look for footprints. We haven't found anything suspicious on the clothing or the body. We'll inspect everything once again after the body's been removed."

The competent impression they gave seemed confirmed.

Dupin had walked around the ditch.

"She must have met up with the murderer here, very early." Dupin's gaze wandered toward the shore. "If he had come here with a largish boat he would have anchored by the jetty, exactly where the police boat is now."

"Or . . ." Madame Coquil spoke up for the first time since the "incident" with the graves. Dupin had the impression she was still giving him a strange look. "He could have anchored farther out and come in on a tender, or," her face darkened, "he lives on the island."

"Exactly when did your son find the body, madame?"

The two crime scene men had set off toward the jetty with their two heavy silver cases. Dupin had remained behind with the boy, his mother, Antoine Manet, and Madame Coquil.

"At seven twenty-four A.M."

The boy had chosen to answer the question himself.

His eyes were sparkling. It was quite clear he was in no way cowed.

"How do you know that so exactly?"

The boy proudly showed the commissaire a shiny black digital watch. "Precise timing is important in criminal cases. School starts at eight thirty, but I can play outside until eight fifteen and then I have to go."

His mother felt obliged to add: "We live in one of the first houses, at the front. Normally Anthony isn't allowed to come this far. But then nothing can happen here." She noted the irony. "Normally, that is."

"Was the body lying exactly like this when you found it?"

"Yes, exactly like that."

"Did you notice anything else unusual, Anthony?"

He was a very bright boy. An adventurer. Stubbly dark blond hair, a roguish smile. Filthy jeans, sneakers, a faded blue T-shirt. All the pockets of his jeans, front and back, were bulging: it seemed he had all sorts of stuff in them.

"Rabbits. Six rabbits, who were having a look at the body. They were sitting all round it. And Jumeau was out there."

"One of the island fishermen, with his boat," Manet said, looking admiringly at the boy.

Suddenly Dupin was wide awake.

"How far out?"

"Halfway," Anthony said, and pointed into the distance, at the open sea. It wasn't a very useful answer.

"Perch, line fishing. For a few days now, he's been out there at the same spot every morning. You have to add that fact, or else the commissaire might think it suspicious. But you only have to say what's most important." Anthony's mother wrinkled her brow.

The boy wasn't going to let himself be browbeaten: "Do you know that the president visited with us in our house? And over there," he pointed in the direction of a stone monument a little way away: a soldier next to a curious double cross standing on a large stone plinth, "he made a speech last year. Because we were so brave and it was the anniversary of that bravery. We were all there, the whole school. After the speech I went up to him and invited him to lunch. It was midday."

Anthony's mother laughed in embarrassment. "It's true. He really came back to our house. For half an hour."

"We had turbot with fried potatoes."

Dupin had other interests. "What was the name of this fisherman you mentioned?"

"Jumeau."

"Does he have a first name?"

"Luc."

Dupin made a note. He already had quite a few names on his list: *Gochat, the harbormistress; Batout, the woman at the coffee stand; Morin the fisherman king* . . . Struggling to remember names was the hardest thing in all his cases. It had been like that in Paris, but it was harder still with Breton names. To be honest, Dupin reflected occasionally, it was a weakness that should have made him unsuited to his job, and a few others too.

"Ten years ago," the museum chief added, "there were still twelve fishermen."

"What else did you notice, Anthony?"

"Nothing that would be relevant to an investigation, Monsieur le Commissaire." Even so, he seemed to be thinking hard. "But I'll let you know if anything occurs to me—that's the way to put it, isn't it?"

"It's time for you to get to school now," his mother said in a tone that brooked no argument. "You've missed enough already."

The boy's eyes lit up again.

"School's not quite the same," his mother explained apologetically.

Dupin understood the boy well. "Many thanks. You've been a lot of help."

Dupin reckoned that were it not for Anthony, the body would not have been discovered so quickly. The distance from the east–west axis was at least fifty meters. And the body in the ditch could really only be seen from next to it. It could have taken a lot longer, days perhaps.

The next minute, the boy was up and away with his mother following him.

Dupin walked over to Antoine Manet and Madame Coquil. "Who comes regularly to this part of the island?"

"Me, for a start," Manet replied. "When I come to see the four technicians at the lighthouse, and the equipment itself." He laughed. "But there are others too. People just going for a walk. The path out to the lighthouse is very popular, not just with island folk, but day-trippers too. There aren't that many paths here."

Dupin let his gaze drift over to the lighthouse.

It was no more than a kilometer away. And there was nothing in between.

"The three houses between the village and the cholera cemetery," Manet nodded toward the village, "are only occupied in July and August. Maybe for a week at Easter."

Dupin rubbed his brow, one of those gestures that along with several others became a tic when he was on a case.

"Have you any idea what might have been going on here? Two women from the Île de Sein killed. You knew both of them."

Madame Coquil wasn't going to get worked up. "We've had worse. They won't beat us that easily. But there's something nasty going on. Something very nasty. I can't tell you any more. But you need to look out for yourself too, Monsieur le Commissaire. The seven graves!"

With those few words she turned on her heel. "I need to go back. My museums. I'm supposed to open at nine. I'll look forward to you getting the chance to visit, Monsieur le Commissaire—I know a lot."

With that she rushed off.

"You have no idea either what might have happened here, Monsieur Manet?"

"To be honest, no. I haven't the slightest idea."

"Tell me about the two women. What they did, who they were connected to."

"One moment. I must get in touch with the pathologist and the helicopter. We shouldn't leave the body here too long."

Manet took a few steps to the side. It came into Dupin's head that he might be able to fly with them, and avoid the trip back on the boat, even though it was obviously too early. He still had lots of people to talk to.

The commissaire pulled out his cell phone and dialed his inspector's number.

"Riwal, one of the uniformed police officers should come to the cemetery here and keep an eye on things until the body is removed. I want to close the cemetery off."

"Very good, boss. I have placed one of our men down at the harbor to make sure that no boats leave the island before we're told about it. The oil boat is still there. And the hairdresser too. I've told them we want to talk to them. They're waiting for us in one of the bars. The food supplies boat had already gone though. People get hungry. It will be more difficult with the list of all the boats that arrived or left between yesterday and today. There's no harbor office. But we can try. We'll talk to everyone, and the bar landlords will help us."

"Very good."

"Even so we won't be able to catch up with every boat. In summer there are always some that arrive late in the evening and leave again very early the next morning. They don't have to report anywhere, just come and go as they please. Even during the day, boats come for just a few hours, the people go for a walk through the village, get something to eat, and head off again."

There was no chance of them putting together a systematic record. They would have to rely on pure luck. Dupin sighed.

Antoine Manet had finished his phone call, but remained a few meters away out of discretion.

"As I said"—Riwal made it sound as if it were encouraging—"it is always possible the killer lives on the island."

If the killer were an islander, he would have had to have taken a boat trip to Douarnenez before eight or nine the previous evening—on some boat or another—and another back after the murder there. Either during the night or very early that morning, to have time to carry out the second killing. Or, there was another scenario: the killer lived on the mainland, in which case he would have had to have taken a boat to the island yesterday between eleven o'clock in the evening and six o'clock this morning. But if there was an accomplice involved then there were any number of alternatives. Dupin didn't even want to start working them out.

"I want us to go by every house and make inquiries—maybe somebody saw something that might help us. Somebody going for a walk very early this morning, for example."

They were going to have to trust on luck, or at least to give it a chance, no matter how improbable it might seem.

"I've already requested additional reinforcements that should be here soon. Another two boats. Eight police in all." Riwal knew his boss. It would be a minor invasion. "Between the south quay and the north there is a row of sheds and huts used by the fishermen, among others. They store their nets and buoys and so forth in them. Both Céline Kerkrom and Laetitia Darot rented one. A colleague of the mayor will show them to us. I already have two of our men in Kerkrom's and Darot's houses, taking a first look around. Laetitia Darot's boat is actually in the harbor here. Obviously we'll take a look at it."

Riwal was concentrating seriously on the business, which pleased Dupin, because it meant he could concentrate on his own ideas.

"See you soon, Riwal."

Manet came over to Dupin. "Come along. If you accompany me to my patient's house, we can talk along the way. She has a badly inflamed knee, just a minor accident in a wooden boat, as it happens, but a nasty splinter."

The island doctor had already set off while he was talking. Dupin followed him. Two particularly nosy rabbits that had been sitting by the cemetery gate shot off.

"I used to have a drink now and then with Céline. Usually at Chez Bruno. We talked about everything under the sun: life, the island, fishing. Serious conversations but we also had a lot of laughs. She was a serious woman, sincere. Very quirky. Very involved. I'm sure you've already been told that. A loner, but not antisocial. Not grief-ridden, or constantly moaning about the world. By and large I think she was at ease with her life, including her failed marriage. She loved her job, despite how hard things are for the fisherfolk." It was a balanced résumé. "When the dolphin researcher arrived on the island in January, they immediately became friends. It was remarkable. Particularly in recent times, over the past two or three months, I frequently saw them together. Sometimes they would come in their boats at the same time of an evening, or occasionally one of them on the other's boat."

Manet rubbed the back of his head. "The unfortunate thing is that the pair of them knew more about each other than anybody else on the island."

"What can you tell me about Laetitia Darot?"

"Not much. Laetitia was shy, but not unfriendly. Not introverted or arrogant. She just didn't go out of her way to make contact. Here on the island we let people get on with their lives the way they want. It's a unique blend of community and solidarity on one hand and an exceptional individuality on the other. Obviously this closeness, the fact that we're all crowded together, can lead to conflicts too. But as I said, Laetitia wasn't really part of the village, which is why I don't know what she might have got involved in. Some people thought she was a bit secretive, but nobody had a bad word to say against her. People respected the fact she was a scientist. And worked with the dolphins."

They were already walking on.

"She was out at sea most of the time," Manet continued.

"Do you know what she did in Brest before coming here?"

"All I know is that she was working for the *parc* there too."

"Who on the island could tell me more?"

"Nobody, I'm afraid. But I'll keep my ears open. If there's anything to report, if anybody saw or heard anything noteworthy, I'll soon hear about it, and not just concerning the two of them." Antoine Manet smiled.

Dupin believed him. It was obvious. Anything newsworthy would do the rounds like the sails of a windmill on the island. And a doctor was a person of trust; he would hear everything.

"Fine. Did Céline Kerkrom have contacts with the other island fisherfolk?"

"Yes, both of them did, but I never heard of any problems. She was closer to Jumeau. But if they were really friends, I couldn't say. Fishing is a hard life."

An elderly couple came toward them on the way to the village.

"Pauline, Yanik, *bonjour*."

"What a tragedy! Will you be able to make it, Antoine? Are we still on for this evening?"

"Of course."

Obviously everybody on the island knew Manet. Deputy mayor, doctor, and president of the lifeboat association. But he gave no impression of being authoritarian, no superiority complex, no put-on airs. On the contrary he gave the impression of being wise. A friend to everybody, it seemed.

"See you later then, Antoine."

"A meeting to prepare for the big festival to celebrate the one hundred and fiftieth anniversary of the lifeboat association," Manet explained after the couple had passed them. "Yanik has been a member for fifty years and was an active lifeboat man for a long time. We'll drink a toast to Céline and Laetitia. In situations like this it's better for people to stick together. Murder is something we've never had on the island."

"I believe Céline Kerkrom had arguments with a lot of people?"

"Not that many. With a certain few, for sure. Every now and then she caused a fuss on the mainland, but not so much here. Life here goes along at its own unshakable pace."

"What about the row over the oil? Her action for alternative energy supplies on the island? I heard something about that." Dupin leafed through his notebook. "Tidal generators, a piping system."

"Most people think the same as she did. Just a few worry that it wouldn't give us a stable supply, but we'll convince them. There's a feasibility survey going on at present. It's not just small tidal generators, but a combination of other alternative energy sources. That's why the real row was with the oil boat boss. One morning he hung around her boat swearing at her."

That was more concrete than anything Dupin had heard so far.

"Did he lay hands on her?"

"He pushed her about a bit."

"Did he come late in the morning . . . I mean wouldn't she have long been out at sea?"

"Normally, yes. But sometimes she went out late. It depended on the weather."

"What's the man's name?"

"Thomas Roiyou."

Dupin looked in his notebook. "I'd like to talk to him right away. My inspector has already made contact with him."

Manet nodded.

"Has there been any trouble or incidents related to fishing recently?"

"Not that I know. I've heard nothing from anybody. Fishing is a hard life. But it hasn't been any harder this year than in the last few. Céline got by, at least she never complained about financial difficulties. But you should probably speak with the people in charge of the harbor in Douarnenez. Céline took most of her catch to the auction there."

"We're . . . ," Dupin said as neutrally as possible, ". . . already in contact."

They had reached the first village houses and were about to enter the labyrinth. Manet stopped at the first left turn.

"And I've heard about Charles Morin. And the incident between him and Céline Kerkrom," Dupin said.

"You need to think of him as a sort of Breton godfather. He never gets his fingers dirty in his dodgy enterprises. He pulls the strings in the background."

"I want to meet him."

"You should."

"Do you share the belief that Céline Kerkrom was right that he practices illegal fishing—or facilitates illegal fishing?"

"That's not the question. The question is whether anyone can find any proof."

"What sort of illegal practices would these be?"

"Morin doesn't pay any attention to anything, whether it be with his trawlers outside the *parc* or with his *bolincheurs* inside it. He ignores the catch quotas, the catch limits, the regulations on nets. And not just sometimes, I'm certain, but systematically. His dragnets cause a huge amount of accidental catch. And some of the fisherfolk have seen his boats leaking seriously polluted wastewater into the sea. All serious stuff."

"And the fisherfolk have reported this? And the other transgressions?"

"As far as I know there have been a few reports, but there's never been a prosecution. The worst of it is that nobody knows the most of it. Nobody sees what happens on the boats."

Hopefully Nolwenn would have something a bit more exact to relate.

"Smuggling? Have you ever heard anything about cigarette smuggling?"

"I've heard about it. There are rumors. But I've no idea if there's anything to it. Sometimes people fantasize."

"Has he allies?"

"A few, yes. Including some of the most powerful people in the region. Primarily because of his polemics against the Parc Iroise. Most of the fisherfolk support the *parc*. The coastal fishers at least, but others claim the whole idea is to throttle them, the big industrial fishers mainly. For them the *parc* is a brain-baby of bureaucrats and ecologists out of touch with reality, a Parisian gimmick to take over their control of the sea. They say overfishing and the poor quality of seawater are just invented. Obviously it's all humbug even if there is excessive bureaucracy. That is a huge problem, we can't deny. The Breton and French fishermen are obliged to keep their catch to ecologically acceptable measures, enforced more stringently in the *parc* than elsewhere. Other countries do whatever they like; it's complete anarchy on the global seas, barbarism if you like. Even within the European Union the fishing regulations are different. The result is that the local fisherfolk here are at a disadvantage to the competition. Stricter standards are important, but they need to be global. Or at least Europe-wide."

Without noticing it they had made their way through the maze of alleyways and were standing in front of the church Dupin had seen from the boat, on a small square with a well-kept lawn.

"Those are the pregnant woman and the warrior, two of our standing stones. They're talking to one another, night and day. Sometimes you can hear them." Unlike Riwal or Madame Coquil, Manet didn't go in for colorful storytelling; he related even the fantastical without elaboration.

As it was, the standing stones really were unusually shaped; without using too much imagination, it was easy enough to recognize the pregnant woman and the warrior.

"Are there frequent breaches of the fishing regulations in the *parc*?"

"Every now and then. There was a serious one just last week. A *bolincheur* fisherman was caught in Douarnenez Bay." He noticed Dupin's questioning look—there had been a reference to that back in the auction hall. "It's a fishing method that uses a net fixed to two buoys and a ball in the water, a circular net, primarily to catch sardines, anchovies, mackerel, and scad. He caught two tons of sea bream, which is illegal." And very delicious, it struck Dupin.

"And this *bolincheur* belongs to Morin's fleet?"

"I don't know. They haven't released the name. The trial is ongoing."

They would get the name straightaway. A job for Nolwenn. Madame Gochat hadn't mentioned the case that morning.

"All through the winter there was trouble in the *parc* between the *bolincheurs* and the coastal fishermen with their small boats. The *bolincheurs* make life hard for the small fishermen. When a couple of their boats with their big round nets have dredged an area, there isn't much left for the little guys. But then the *bolincheurs* themselves are just 'small fish' compared to the trawlers. And even the trawlers come in different dimensions, right up to the huge floating fish factories." It was easy to tell from Manet that the subject was a hot topic, frequently discussed. "It's not easy. There's a *bolincheur* union led by one of Morin's fishermen. Céline had a few confrontations with him too. Frédéric Carrière. His mother lived here on the island. She died a couple of years ago, but he still owns the house."

Yet another name to add to the list in Dupin's notebook.

"Was Céline Kerkrom somehow involved in this argument about the *parc*?"

"On the fringes of it."

"And what sort of rows did she have with this Carrière? Putting it plainly?"

"Verbal attacks. From both sides. During the auctions primarily."

The harbormistress hadn't mentioned anything about that either. "Recently?"

"I only know about their quarrels last winter."

By now they had left the square in front of the church and were back in the labyrinth of houses.

"All this fishing stuff," Dupin said, and ran his hands through his hair, "it's a very complicated business."

Complicated enough to cause a few crimes in the area. Including murder.

"You can say that, all right." Manet laughed.

"Have you heard anything about incidents of pollution in the *parc*? In the last few weeks or months?" Dupin was obsessed by the topic, without knowing why.

Manet raised his eyebrows. "I know of two instances. A blanket of oil on the water, not large, but even so. North of Ouessant. It's a hugely busy area with all the traffic in the Channel. The second instance was an extreme case of chemical pollution caused by the dock workers in the harbor area at Camaret. They used horrible stuff to treat the stern of the boats against erosion and rotting. Morin's deep-sea trawlers are based there."

"Were the works being carried out on his boats?"

"No idea. You need to talk to the science chief at the *parc*. Pierre Leblanc. He knows everything. About all the things that have happened at the Parc Iroise. He has an eagle eye on it all."

The science chief had already been mentioned. Dupin made a note of his name.

"He would have been Laetitia Darot's boss."

"Indeed. He works on Île Tristan, which is where the *parc*'s scientific center is located."

Dupin needed to talk to him first and foremost, as soon as he was back. In France.

It was the same as always. Dupin would have liked to talk to everyone at once. He didn't like having to talk to people one after the other in a specific order. If he had his way—it was dreadful for himself and everyone else too—everything would happen at once, and he was not just frustrated but angry every time it turned out not to be possible.

"The *parc* has several water-quality control stations, including one here on the island. Leblanc comes once a week to take the readings."

"Which day?"

"Fridays. In the morning."

"And what about the dead dolphins last week?"

"By-catch. A result of drag-and-dredge fishing. It's infamous, and so far the European fishing commission hasn't managed to pass a total ban on these nets."

A dreadful topic. Even Nolwenn talked about it often.

"The collateral catch also includes the seal colonies in the north of the archipelago. Also the various whales and the sea turtles. In general it includes many types of fish that are forbidden to catch."

"Have there been incidents recently?"

"Talk to Leblanc. He can tell you precisely what it was Laetitia was working on. I can't. Nor can anybody else on the island, I imagine."

"I'll do that."

Manet had stopped next to a pretty old house with a steep gable, surrounded by hollyhocks. It appeared this was where the patient with the knee infection lived.

"There's something else I ought to tell you," he furrowed his brow, "even if it is just a rumor and normally I don't heed rumors. I have no idea if there's any truth to it. But who knows whether or not it might be important: Laetitia Darot is said to be Morin's illegitimate daughter."

Dupin stood stiff. "Darot, Morin's daughter."

That was one for the books. Would be one for the books.

"He's supposed to have had an affair with Darot's mother. Given that people knew so little about Laetitia, that led to speculation. You know what I mean."

"Did Darot herself say anything about it?"

"Not that I know."

It would be a script worthy of a classic drama: father and daughter, one an irresponsible, destructive fishing boss, the other an ecologist and researcher who had dedicated her life to the dolphins.

"Do you know anything about Darot's family?"

"Not a thing. And I doubt anyone else does either."

"And Céline Kerkrom? What about her family?"

"An only child. Her parents died a few years ago. Shortly after one another. Islanders. Going back generations. Céline's father worked on a deep-sea trawler. Tuna fishing. Her mother collected edible seaweed, like many people here do."

It sounded tragic, the pair of them lonely women, but then maybe Dupin was getting it wrong.

"I need to go in here now," Manet said in a low voice, "and then afterward I'll have a few forms to fill in. I've no idea what sort of a report I'm supposed to file on a murder. And we need to think about the funerals."

"And I need to go in search of my inspector." The juxtaposition sounded comic, though Dupin hadn't intended it to. "And carry out a few more interviews."

"If you need me, it's not hard to find anybody on the island."

With that, Manet disappeared into the house with the hollyhocks, without ringing a bell or knocking on the door, as if he lived there.

* * *

The Quai Sud was a magnificent place. As if somebody had sought out all the ingredients that constituted Dupin's idea of an ideal place and brought them together to a real one. The bay was a gentle semicircle, with pretty little fishermen's huts: white, pale green, bright blue. Dupin had emerged from the confusion of streets and houses at the end of the quay—having got lost twice—and now had the whole quay in front of him.

A magical light illuminated everything here, a clear light that reinforced all the contours sharply but without being glaring or unpleasant.

The quay was surrounded by a defensive stone wall in good condition, which was visible everywhere on the island, and was intended as protection against the lashing storms and raging floods that came to mind the minute you set foot on this tiny piece of land, even if with today's calmly lapping sea in the well-protected harbor basin the idea seemed remote. Wonderfully pretty little wooden boats painted in Atlantic colors bobbed up and down in front of him. Directly opposite lay the glitteringly white sand bank Dupin had seen from the ferry, which formed part of the harbor's protection.

Something strange happened to the world on the island. Dupin had tried to grasp it the minute he arrived. The quay, the houses, the whole village, indeed the entire island seemed squeezed together, as if the vast sky above was literally crushing them beneath it. At sea the sky seemed far away, enormously far away, but here on the island it seemed to be farther still: it seemed inflated, spread, stretched, yawned in every direction, even the mighty Atlantic seemed no more than a thin shining line beneath it. It was just like using an extreme wide-angle lens while lying down, that was exactly what it was like, Dupin thought. And this impression, it was quite clear, was part of what gave the island its peculiar atmosphere, a feeling of endless distance, that made one feel tiny—and free. Perhaps dangerously free. Obviously only in the amazing summer weather. In stormy weather, beneath furious towering black clouds in the midst of an angry sea, left at the mercy of the primitive powers of nature, there would be none of that.

One of the other defining qualities of the island was a curious silence. All the usual background noise of civilization was missing: no cars, no waste trucks, no trams or trains, no machinery. The few noises that existed seemed to be gently swallowed up by the Atlantic, with the result that when they ceased, the silence seemed even more absolute. Lots of things were different here. You noticed it the moment you stepped onto the island, but it took a long time to work out what it was that made this world particular.

"Boss." Riwal appeared next to him as if out of nowhere, causing Dupin to flinch. "Our colleagues have taken a quick first look around the houses of Céline Kerkrom and Laetitia Darot. It doesn't look as if anyone else has been there. Everything seems normal, nobody has gone through the drawers or anything. But then it's hard to say, because neither of them locked their doors. Nobody on the island does. The killer could just have walked straight in. And obviously could have simply taken something without us finding out now. The crime scene team are going to go over them again shortly."

"Whereabouts are the houses?"

"Not far from each other, behind the Quai Nord. If you're coming from the cholera cemetery along the outer path next to the sea, you don't even need to go through the village. But as I said, at present there are no indications that anybody was in either of the two houses. On the other hand, however, there is still no sign of Darot's cell phone."

"I want to take a look at the houses myself. And you check out Darot's phone calls."

The list of things that had to be gone through immediately was still growing.

"And the sheds the pair had. Have our men already taken a look at them?"

"At first glance, both of them are crammed full of all sorts of stuff, mainly things they needed for work. Kerkrom's was full of nets and buoys, totally chaotic. Darot's is relatively tidy: old diving suits, bottles, buoys, a small rubber boat. Nothing suspicious so far. Obviously somebody could have gone through them, Kerkrom's in particular. We have no idea what was in there, and what might be missing."

"The crime scene team needs to check them out as soon as possible too."

"They're on it. Otherwise they've found nothing suspicious on the pier. And Kadeg has reported in: they found a large quantity of human blood in the barrel. They believe Céline Kerkrom was thrown in there very shortly after her throat was cut, probably immediately. That means she was probably killed in that room."

It wasn't hard to imagine.

"Whom can I talk to next, Riwal?"

"The hairdresser has already left the island. He has appointments in Molène, and we couldn't force him to stay."

"Did you try?"

"We threatened him with everything we could. Even telling him he would have to come to the prefecture in Quimper. He said there were four elderly people waiting for him on Molène." It was easy to tell from Riwal that that was what had weakened his resolve.

"Two of our colleagues," the inspector was quick to add, "checked the boat over first and found nothing unusual. Apart from dozens of sharp blades."

Dupin assumed it was meant as a joke; everyone who figured in the case so far had a knife: the fishermen, the harbor workers, the staff at the *parc*, the doctor, and even the hairdresser, anyone who had a boat, who went to sea, all of them.

"It's a relatively small boat, seven meters eighty, but with a powerful engine. And, do you know what?" Riwal made it sound exciting: "Both women were customers of his! Kerkrom and Darot. He last cut their hair, both of them, three weeks ago. One after the other. The fisherwoman had been a customer of his for years. Like nearly everybody else on the island."

Obviously the hairdresser was an interesting figure. Lots of people chatted with him in the unusually intimate and yet business-like situation of having their hair cut.

"Did he say anything? Had either of them told him anything that could be meaningful in the light of the circumstances?"

"He seemed clearly disturbed, I have to say, but nothing automatically occurred to him. He said Darot had been friendly, but she had only exchanged a few words with him. He and Céline Kerkrom had talked about the sighting of orcas."

"Orcas?"

Dupin had recently seen a documentary in which powerful orcas had mercilessly played Ping-Pong with a poor seal for a few minutes, flicking it to and fro with their powerful tail fins, before eating it.

"The big orcas that come from the same family as dolphins. A large one can grow as big as ten meters long. In summer they sometimes come up to the coast in groups. Recently a pair were spotted in Audierne Bay."

That was where they had docked on the ferry that morning.

Dupin shuddered.

"Occasionally you also find large porpoises or razorback whales in the Parc Iroise. Sperm whales too."

Dupin wasn't going into it any further; he was rather going back to the case. "Did the hairdresser make home visits to the two women?"

"Yes. After that he would go on to Ouessant, and then back to the mainland. He lives in Camaret."

"And where was he yesterday evening?"

"At home, with a friend. He gave us the name."

"Hmmm."

One of those special alibis.

"And this morning?"

"He arrived here just before eight o'clock, he says."

"We need to check everything thoroughly."

"Clearly. In the meantime, Goulch has arrived. He's checking Laetitia Darot's boat. And he's ready to go anytime." Riwal gave an unnecessary grin.

Dupin's cell phone rang. Given that he was on a case, it had been silent for an unusually long time. Even Nolwenn hadn't called again.

It was Kadeg's number on the screen. Dupin grabbed it testily. "Riwal has already told me what you reported."

"A fisherman called anonymously. One of the coastal fishermen who was at the auction yesterday."

All of a sudden Dupin was wide awake. Kadeg paused theatrically.

"He claims Madame Gochat had asked him a few times over the past weeks if he had seen Céline Kerkrom in the *parc*, and where."

"What is that supposed to mean?"

"I think she meant where she was fishing."

"Why would Gochat want to know that?"

"I'll talk to her straightaway. I—"

"Leave it, Kadeg. I'll do it myself. I have a few questions for her in any case."

Dupin was too eager to find out what the harbormistress would say. In any case he needed to go back to the mainland when he had finished his interviews here. To meet the *parc*'s scientific chief. And to speak to Morin.

"Talk to you later, Kadeg."

His phone rang again. They were still standing in the middle of the quay.

It was Nolwenn. She sounded clearly unhappy and—unusually for his assistant—tense, stressed.

"It's goddamn useless, Monsieur le Commissaire. I can't find out anything interesting about Céline Kerkrom. Only stuff we already know. I spoke to the friend of my aunt's"—in Brittany it wasn't just families that built fully fledged clans across the generations, they included close friends too—"but she knew next to nothing. Céline Kerkrom was very intelligent and remarkably stubborn, she said, even more hard-necked than your average Breton. A 'good girl.' She was totally in shock but couldn't help."

"And that's it?"

"That's it."

It really wasn't much.

"There is no other family."

Dupin could hear voices in the background. Nolwenn was on her way somewhere.

"And what about this Morin guy?"

"As a matter of fact there are two accusations against him. Both relating to fishing regulations in the *parc*. And there's been a whole series of them over recent years. That said, not one from Céline Kerkrom. It would seem that was just a rumor. But so far there have been no charges. Morin has a pretty wily lawyer. I've spoken with people in several positions. Including the chief of police in Douarnenez. He says he's given up; nobody is likely to prove anything against Morin. They would need photographs or video, not just circumstantial evidence or witnesses who'd seen something from a hundred meters away. That is usually the problem with things at sea."

"What sort of accusations, and when were they made?"

"One of them was about throwing back fish from one of his trawlers."

"Oh yes?"

"It's all to do with the so-called 'upgrading,' which is strictly illegal. The fishermen make a grand show of throwing back fish they've already caught and are already dead, to make space for better fish or cheat on the quotas. For fish that they can sell at a better price than those they caught earlier. We're talking about huge quantities here. It's disgraceful."

This was news to Dupin.

"It's another one of those things," Nolwenn said. "How do you prove it? Even if you board a boat—and there's no legal justification for doing so—and could prove that purely by chance every catch was the best it could be, which is hardly possible, even then you'd only have indirect evidence, not actual proof. And that would never work. The public prosecutor has said upgrading can only legally be proven if they are caught in the act. We urgently need a law that specifies boats must install cameras!"

"Just recently," Nolwenn hissed between her teeth, "a deep-sea trawler on a three-week fishing trip in the North Sea was found to have thrown overboard one thousand and five hundred tons of dead herring. A ship that over the last fifteen years had received twenty million euros in subsidies. A heroic commissaire uncovered the case. A magnificent woman!"

"Who made accusations against Morin?"

"A young fisherman from Le Conquet. A brave man. I've just

been speaking to him." Nolwenn was just brilliant. "He didn't know Céline Kerkrom personally though. There's no evidence of any ties between them."

"And the other accusation?"

"One of Morin's fishermen has regularly been caught with too large a catch of *ormeaux*. He was given a small disciplinary fine. The *ormeaux* were sold on to Japan at a horrific price."

Ormeaux were a form of abalone, Dupin's favorite shellfish, with mother-of-pearl shells and firm, white flesh to be quickly seared like an entrecôte steak, with salted butter, *fleur de sel* salt, and *piment d'espelette* pepper. Delicious.

The commissaire tried to concentrate again.

The opportunities for indulging in illegal practices in relation to the fishing industry seemed to be impressively wide.

"Has Morin said anything about all this?"

"Not as far as I know. No."

"The water around the Camaret harbor area was polluted with chemicals recently. Because of the stuff they use to prevent rot around the stern of the boats. Have you heard if they were Morin's boats?"

"Not all of them, but primarily. There's a big installation at the end of the Quai du Styvel. In Le Conquet and Douarnenez too. The foul business with the water pollution has been going on for years, but I haven't heard anything about it getting worse."

"Have you heard anything about cigarette smuggling? What does the customs office say?"

"They were on the heels of a smuggling ring three years ago, tobacco smuggling, by sea. In fishing boats. Two of the investigators came across two of Morin's boats involved, apparently spotted a few times on the English side of the Channel, just where they suspected there was a smugglers' meeting point. They managed to nab the boats, but they openly found proof of smuggling through the Channel Tunnel in big trucks." As ever, Nolwenn's investigations had been fastidious. "Therefore they closed the investigation into

Morin. Also because there were no other indications against him. As far as the customs people go, Morin has a spotless character."

"Well and good, but we have one more rumor to go on, Nolwenn. The murdered dolphin researcher is said to be Morin's illegitimate daughter."

"Well, she certainly would have deserved a better father," Nolwenn said, completely unperturbed. Then she took a deep sigh. "I certainly haven't heard anything about that, Monsieur le Commissaire. But I'll look into it. Morin is married and has no children, legitimately at least."

"What else do you know about him?"

"His private wealth is estimated at around ten million. That makes him greedy; we Bretons say *hemañ zo azezet war e c'hodelloù*: he sits on his pockets." Nolwenn treated personal characteristics like facts. "He has a spectacular property empire, most of which he inhabits himself. His main home is near Morgat, and the other houses—by which I mean those I could find out about—are in Tréboul, Saint-Mathieu, Cap Sizun, and Molène."

The most attractive places, spread all along the west.

"His four deep-sea trawlers are registered in Douarnenez." Nolwenn had switched her voice to a staccato reporting style, as if she was in a rush again. "His other boats are seven *bolincheurs* of the twenty licenses for the *parc*, and three *chalutiers* spread between Le Conquet, Douarnenez, and Audierne."

Dupin had noted it all down.

"You're meeting him today at four." She hesitated slightly, which was unlike her, then added, "If that suits you. Otherwise I can rearrange it."

"I'll see how long I need here. First of all I need to see the head of the *parc*, then I need to talk to the harbormistress again."

Nolwenn was silent. That was unusual too.

"The harbormistress," Dupin said, "wanted to know where Céline Kerkrom had been fishing over the past few weeks."

"Have you any idea why?"

"Not the slightest."

"I'll send you, Riwal, and Kadeg all the telephone numbers you need right now. Those of all the people involved."

Dupin was only half listening.

"One more thing, Nolwenn." He was glad to have remembered the fact, he had almost forgotten. "There's a court case currently under way against a *bolincheur* charged with illegally catching two tons of pink gilthead bream. I want to know who it was and whether or not he belongs to Morin's fleet."

"Fine. I'll come back to you—until then, Monsieur le Commissaire."

Dupin jumped in. "Nolwenn?"

"Monsieur le Commissaire?"

"Is everything okay?" The rumble of voices in the background had got louder. "Where are you actually?"

"We need a few more signatures, we're working on it now."

"Signatures?"

"You know the economics minister in Paris has signed off on the demolition of the sandbank in the bay. A scandal! My aunt Jacqueline is the local head of the Peuple des Dunes, one of the local opposition groups. We need to get mobilized again and I'm helping them out."

Dupin let it go.

Nolwenn had explained everything as if it were all a matter of course. She had made it clear that further questions would not be welcome.

Lannion had been a big issue throughout Brittany for weeks now. The anger was simmering, and with good reason: since the beginning of the year there had been big demonstrations and other acts, but none of it had done any good. Dupin had read a long interview in *Ouest-France* with a professor of biology. A company had got an agreement with the French central government to extract vast quantities of valuable sand, and shell-containing sand used as a construction material, from the bay of Lannion. Or to put it another way, which was the truth, to destroy an underwater landscape which was both geologically and biologically unique: a gigantic underwater sand dune, four cubic kilometers in size, Trezen ar Gorjegou. Both the smallest and the biggest fish, sea mammals and birds, all of them depended on the plankton produced en masse in the area; all the sea life relied on it. The entire biological equilibrium of the marine region would be seriously damaged, with severe consequences also for the smallest coastal fisherfolk, who were already struggling to keep going. The most cynical part of it was it had been decided to halt the process between May and August, so as not to disturb the tourists. In his last case Dupin had had to deal with the sand-stealing phenomenon in which a criminal firm had been stealing sand illegally; to have it done here—by a company sanctioned by the state—would be more monstrous still.

Nolwenn was in full flow: "We're inviting the whole world to the biggest-ever climate and environment conference, presenting ourselves as the barbarians."

Dupin heard frenetic hand-clapping in the background, loud cries of support.

"Just like the ban on deep-sea fishing that France blocked in the European Union!" More loud applause in the background. "And why do people let this happen? Because people don't see the damage underwater. People only realize the catastrophic consequences later when it's long been too late."

Enthusiastic cheers broke out. It seemed Nolwenn was part of a large crowd.

If Dupin understood correctly, Nolwenn would be working on this case from behind the barricades. But that wouldn't hinder her amazing work, and the commissaire would be busy with other aspects of the situation.

"You're absolutely right, Nolwenn."

He had to say something, and in any case, it was true.

"You need to get involved too, Monsieur le Commissaire, if you think like that. But back to the case, we have no time to lose. I'll call back, like I said."

A second later she had put down the phone.

Dupin had to get his head together. It was all getting very complex.

Riwal had used the time during Dupin's phone call to make his own.

"I'll be there straightaway, see you soon," he now said. Then he turned to the commissaire. "We have an initial sketch of which boats left the island last night and which arrived this morning. Obviously only the boats that were seen. I'm going through it with colleagues."

"Get in touch with all of them, Riwal. Check them out." Dupin was still thinking about Nolwenn and the barricades. He pulled himself together. "Check out all of their alibis, all of them, without exception."

"I'm on it, boss. Thomas Roiyou is waiting for you. The man from the oil boat. He's sitting up front at Chez Bruno. With his two crewmen. He's been waiting quite a while."

And with that Riwal disappeared.

* * *

The bar owner had chosen a warm, summery yellow for the façade and a bright lemon yellow for the gable of his narrow house. A neat little white wall with a green wooden door and a bright pink strip high up on the wall, a green awning out over the terrace. *Chez Bruno* was painted in big letters on the awning. The terrace in front of the entrance to the bar was made of faded wooden planks. There were a few round bistro tables and comfortable wicker chairs. Hard to find anywhere better to sit, with a view of the harbor, the pier, the sandbank, the sea behind them, and the wonderfully blue sky above.

Dupin glanced at his notebook to refresh his memory and mounted the terrace steps.

"Thomas Roiyou?" They were sitting at the corner table.

All three of them were in worn, dirty blue overalls. The whole terrace smelled of oil. In front of each of the men were two *petits cafés,* an empty Fischer beer glass, and a heap of crumpled Gitane cigarette ends in a red Ricard ashtray. On the next table lay three pairs of oil-smeared gloves.

"She wants to put me out of business on account of a couple of liters of oil." The tall, chisel-jawed man in the middle of the threesome, with reddish-blond hair and high cheekbones, opened the conversation on an aggressive note. "It's madness. She should busy herself with something else. I'd like to see it. I mean, they can do what they want, it's not my island. But she can lick my—"

"*She* has been murdered."

The man sneered at Dupin. "Oh, and you think . . ."

"Where were you yesterday afternoon, last night, and early this morning, Monsieur Roiyou? And what witnesses do you have?"

Dupin had taken an empty chair from the next table and sat himself down casually. Opposite the threesome, with their boss directly in his sights.

"I don't have to tell you anything."

"I'll be happy to ask you the same question after inviting you down to the police station." Dupin had lowered his voice, and he pronounced his words coolly and emphatically, leaning the weight of his body into every syllable. It was a routine that rarely failed him. And didn't here either.

"So what?" Roiyou said, trying to calling his bluff.

"It'll take a whole day of your time. Possibly two, depending on the circumstances. Obviously we'll arrange a time for you in Concarneau, maybe tomorrow morning, but you can imagine how much urgent police work there is to do in a case like this. You will have to come in and wait. And then I might have to push the schedule back and you'll have to wait again. I'll be very apologetic."

Primitive as the tactic was, it seemed to have gotten Roiyou to think about it. Which didn't help.

"You're not scaring me."

"Have the police checked out your boat yet? If not, we'll do it now."

"You can't do that without—"

Always the same old tune. Dupin was losing his patience. "Yes, we can. Without any search warrant. Two brutal murders have been committed just a few hours ago. You and one of the victims had a serious altercation. And apart from that, you're behaving oddly. That's grounds enough for reasonable suspicion."

Dupin was bluffing. But by now he was ready to go to extremes.

"Last night, where were you? Between nine and midnight?"

The man seemed to be thinking again. If you could say that. But not for long. "At that time I'm asleep."

In principle it might be true: his day clearly had a very different rhythm. As did the whole fishing world, and the sea.

Even so.

"Who can confirm that? That you were asleep at that time?"

"My old lady?"

"And this morning?"

"We left Audierne at six in the morning and got to the island at five past seven."

The dolphin researcher had probably been murdered between six and seven, according to the island doctor. But it might also have been a little later.

"The oil transporter was already waiting for us. Everything here takes its time. We refilled the tanks twice. When transport headed out to the lighthouse the first time, we hung around the boat."

"Were you and your men together the whole time?"

"I think so." It was one of the men with a sunbeaten face who replied. Both of them were grinning stupidly.

"Was there anyone else with you?"

"Just the driver. Or do you mean somebody else?"

More grinning.

"How long was he away, taking the first load to the lighthouse?"

"I'd say half an hour."

Dupin made a note. "We'll check that," he mumbled. "How long did it take for the tanker truck to fill up and set off?"

"Ten minutes, I'd say. Tops," Roiyou said.

"So that would have been about seven fifteen. And he drove off immediately?"

"Yes, what would he be hanging around for?"

"And you had your boss in sight all the time from when you docked?" Dupin had turned his attention back to the two crewmen.

"Yes," they answered simultaneously, if not quite so obviously as the nodding of their heads. But it meant nothing.

Dupin was thinking things through.

"You could comfortably have made it to the cholera cemetery and back again in the time from when they docked." Roiyou's alibi was anything but convincing. "Did the truck driver see you before he set off?"

"No idea. I was busy on the boat. Right, that's enough."

Roiyou stood up abruptly. His voice was harsh and his facial expression hard. His force of movement knocked over the chair he had been sitting on, with a clatter so loud the whole island must have heard it.

For a moment Dupin didn't rule out the possibility that Roiyou was going to tackle him physically. The conversation had turned into more than just a verbal skirmish. Apart from anything else, the man made Dupin furious.

"We'll see each other very soon then." Dupin had remained seated, not showing the slightest reaction.

The other two men had got to their feet too. They followed Roiyou onto the quay toward the harbor.

Dupin grabbed his phone. "Riwal, listen up. Send a few men right now onto Thomas Roiyou's boat. They need to search it thoroughly. If Roiyou complains, tell him to call me. Ask around in the harbor and the boats of the Quai Nord if anyone saw him this morning, either on his boat or near it. And what time exactly the boat arrived. Oh, and one more thing: get the man who drives the oil truck to confirm what time he left after filling up the first time, and when he got back. And whether or not he had seen Roiyou when he set off."

"Got it, boss, but watch out. Roiyou is directly descended from the Vikings, one of our policemen knows the family—"

"Nolwenn will find out if he's had problems with the police before." Dupin sighed and put down his phone.

Already during his conversation with the oil boat captain he had heard unusual dull sounds that had sounded far away but were quickly getting closer.

The helicopter.

Dupin searched the sky in the direction of the mainland, clearly visible in the distance: France. And found it: a spot on the horizon, like an insect.

The noise got louder and louder.

The helicopter was heading directly toward the island. They were coming to collect the body.

The young woman had woken up on the island on this beautiful morning with nothing before her but a day with her dolphins—now she was lying dead in a bag, ready to be flown to her autopsy in the forensic laboratory in Brest. It was strange; sometimes one little thing in the wake of a murder made it more real than the news of the murder itself. That was how it was for Dupin now. All morning long the whole thing had had a strange element of the abstract to it. Even the sight of the body—strangely, that was almost the most abstract moment of all.

Dupin followed the helicopter with his eyes. It had now reached the island and was thundering low above the harbor, the noise deafening. The pilot was going to land on the stubble grass directly next to the cemetery.

For a while Dupin stood there lost in his thoughts. Then his cell phone rang. Kadeg.

"Yes?"

"Is that you, Commissaire?"

Who else could it be? This habit of Kadeg's was maddening.

"The fisherman has taken a look at Céline Kerkrom's boat."

"And?"

"It's called *Morweg*—Mermaid. Nine meters thirty long. She fished with lines and gillnets. Loach, red mullet, turbot, brill, whiting, hake. Her lines are no more than seventy meters long. He saw nothing unusual about it. He said the boat was old, but still in remarkably good condition. One of the good old wooden boats. She had recently had a new lifting arm installed. For the nets. That lifting arm can really handle stuff, the fisherman said."

"Anything else?"

"I spoke on the phone with Kerkrom's ex-husband. He has four children, lives on Guadeloupe, and seems a happy guy. He's had no contact with her for over ten years."

Céline Kerkrom's past appeared to give them nothing to work on.

"Have you interviewed Madame Gochat, Commissaire?"

"I want to have her in front of me when I speak to her."

"Don't you think we need to pursue a clue of such importance right away?"

Kadeg was particularly insufferable when he talked like this.

"See you later, Kadeg."

Dupin hung up and leaned back.

He really ought to talk to the harbormistress soon. Riwal could take over on the island and conduct the interviews that had to be carried out, including the one with the fisherman Kerkrom apparently had a connection to.

Dupin still had his phone in his hand. He dialed the number of his inspector.

"Riwal! We need to chat." Dupin had spotted a restaurant at the far end of the quay, where they could meet up soonest. "Let's meet up in . . ." He tried to read the name at a distance. "Le Tatoon." Somebody had already mentioned it. "At the end of Quai Sud. And tell Goulch we'll be needing his boat shortly. I want to go to Île

Tristan, to speak to the *parc*'s scientific boss." He thought for a second, then added, "Tell you what, bring Goulch along too."

The young policeman had his complete trust.

"Goulch has inspected the dolphin researcher's boat. And was extremely impressed. It has very expensive, very high-spec sonar equipment." Riwal seemed no less impressed. "As well as a whole row of other high-tech equipment. A tracker system for fish and marine mammals with a program that allowed her to keep them under continuous surveillance. That means—"

"Anything suspicious?"

"No. But—"

"We'll talk in Le Tatoon, Riwal."

"One more thing. The pathologist verified Antoine Manet's suggested time of death for Darot."

"I thought she might."

Dupin left the terrace of Chez Bruno and walked past another bar that also looked wonderful. There were several of them along the quay, each of them a coffee shop, bistro, restaurant, and bar all in one. Everything seemed tranquil and relaxed.

All of that also contributed to the impression the island gave of being "another world"; the tempo, the rhythm, all slowed down. Everything seemed to happen—for outsiders at least—in a contemplative calm. It was as if it were a state of mind. Things moved differently. Dupin could get on remarkably well with it. Normally calm made him nervous. There were rumors that at one stage when it had been suggested from the prefecture that he should be sent on a relaxation seminar he had almost drawn his weapon. Rumors that weren't totally false.

* * *

Le Tatoon was splendid.

An old white stone house with a Breton pointed roof and window shutters painted a bright green. A pretty terrace, large ceramic pots with olive trees in front of it, tables and chairs made of untreated wood that had developed their typical patina. A few more tables than Chez Bruno, but still the same inconspicuous narrow slates on either side of the entrance with the menu on them—which was primarily what the island fishermen had pulled out of the sea a few hours earlier.

Dupin had chosen the table outside in the first row of the terrace. He had taken his jacket off and draped it over a chair. By now, just before midday, the temperature had risen to at least twenty-eight degrees Celsius. There was a gentle wind. As expected, the cool morning had turned into a perfect midsummer's day.

Before sitting down he had popped inside to order a *café*.

Riwal and the gangly young policeman were walking along the quay.

"Goulch!"

Dupin was happy to see him.

They only saw one another once or twice a year. Either at a police party or the Festival des Filets Bleus, a Fest Noz, a traditional Breton music affair.

"Commissaire!"

A particularly hefty handshake, but a friendly one.

"Nasty business."

"Really dreadful."

"I would love to have the kind of equipment on my police boat the dolphin researcher has on hers," Goulch said with a smile. "Riwal has already told you. It doesn't look as if anybody else has been on the boat. The killer would have been taking quite a risk: the boat is at the end of the quay, just before the storage huts. It's busy there from early in the morning."

Riwal and Goulch sat down.

"Do you know the history of this restaurant?" Riwal asked. Of course Le Tatoon had to have a history, just like everything in Brittany had a history. And of course Riwal knew it.

"The chef ran a two-star restaurant in Monaco, but one day he was visiting his friend in Brest and they came on a trip to the Île de

Sein. The chef fell in love with the Quai Sud, saw this house was for sale, sold everything in Monaco within a month, and opened Le Tatoon. Now he conjures up delicious menus here. He works together with the . . ." Riwal faltered a second, "the two fishermen on the island, and until yesterday with Céline Kerkrom too."

"S'il vous plaît, messieurs." The waitress, a smiling blonde with a complicated hairdo, brought the coffee and set it down on the table in front of Dupin. "I suspect my colleagues will want one too." He glanced at Riwal and Goulch, who both nodded.

He downed his—wonderful—*café* in two swallows.

"Netra ne blij din-me,' vel urbanne kafe!"

Dupin had been planning for weeks to try this sentence out on Riwal. He had hoped to stun him, and it seemed he had succeeded: the inspector was staring at him open-mouthed. Paul Girard, boss of the Amiral, had given Dupin a book about Brittany and coffee, in which Dupin had found a few magic lyrics from an old song. He had made a note of this one: "Nothing makes me as happy as a slug of coffee."

Goulch grinned. Riwal needed a moment to master his confusion—quotations and wandering digressions were supposed to be his business. As if changing the subject without mentioning it, the inspector set his notebook down on the table and opened it, still without saying a word, to reveal an impeccably neat double page. He began to read out his report mechanically.

"That is all we could find. All the boats that docked either yesterday or this morning. As I said, it's also possible to dock at the jetty at the other end of the village. And with a tender, of course, you can pull up to the land anywhere on the island."

It wasn't much help.

"Oh yes, our colleagues did a full examination of Roiyou's boat. Nothing to be found, even though they took a fine-tooth comb to it."

"Pity," Dupin grumbled.

"We've also talked to the technicians at the lighthouse and the supply sheds: they didn't see any suspicious boats, nothing out of the ordinary."

The waitress came with the *cafés* for Riwal and Goulch and a little slate with the specialties of the day: *fricassé de praires au piment d'espelette, filet de lieu jaune et purée de pommes de terre maison*—that was the dish the museum keeper had raved about, the sensational fish with potato purée—and for dessert *soupe de fraises à la menthe.*

Dupin hadn't been thinking about eating when he had suggested Le Tatoon, even though he had already been on his feet for seven hours.

"I'll have another *café*."

Dupin leaned down over the list of boats, which was longer than he had imagined.

Riwal spoke up: "The majority are private individuals. Nine of them islanders. We're already checking them out. We've had widely differing reports as to who arrived in the harbor overnight and left again first thing in the morning. Between three and eight boats. For the sailors, the summer season has already begun. That makes it all the harder—nobody knows where they came from and where they are going."

"We have to try."

"We spoke to the captain of the food delivery boat," Riwal said. "He has a crew of three."

Dupin had forgotten all about it.

"During the day yesterday they loaded up all the orders for the islands, particularly for the Metro. They worked until late, until around eleven thirty, with the help of a few packers, from whom the two of us have witness statements. The boat then left Camaret this morning—the harbormaster there verified that—and couldn't have been on the island before eight."

That ruled out the food delivery boat too.

"They were bringing half a Charolais bull for Le Tatoon here."

Dupin wasn't to be distracted. He was still taken up with one name on the list.

"Vaillant? Madame Coquil mentioned him. Captain Vaillant? Isn't he the pirate?"

Goulch grinned. "He's even more famous than I thought. An anarchist swashbuckler. A *bon viveur*. He was here in Le Tatoon last night, with his crew."

Dupin couldn't help it; everything about Vaillant smacked of adventure stories and classic sailors' yarns. He imagined him to look like a relative of Captain Haddock from the Tintin books.

"When did they come in?

"Late. After eleven o'clock."

"Where from?"

"Douarnenez."

"How long does it take to get here in their boat?"

"Seventy minutes, maybe eighty."

That would have made it tight for the murder of Céline Kerkrom. But there would have been just time enough.

"With his whole crew?"

"One of them wasn't there. We've already set someone on his tail."

The friendly waitress brought Dupin's second *café*.

"Good. Where does this Vaillant live?"

Dupin downed his second coffee in a couple of swallows.

"On the Île de Ouessant, that's where they all live. They have three houses in Le Stiff, a hamlet on the east end of the lighthouse, close to the lighthouse and the main pier."

The piracy business seemed to be going well.

As soon as the waitress was out of hearing range, Riwal commented, "For twenty euros you can have a complete three-course meal here. And it's said to be excellent."

As it happened, the restaurant was just the kind Dupin loved: down-to-earth, cozy, and not in the slightest way chic.

"And what about the smuggling? Is there anything to that, do you think?" Dupin had ignored Riwal's comment and turned to Goulch.

"I've had a bit to do with Vaillant myself. He pops up everywhere along the coast. A couple of years ago we searched his boat along with the customs guards when he came into French waters.

We couldn't find any cigarettes, but we did find alcohol. Various expensive eaux-de-vie in canisters. In quantities that went above the legal limit, but not excessively. But we also found a load of canisters we suspect he had poured out before we boarded. I think he's a smuggler all right, but in small quantities."

"Who does the patrols in the *parc* here? Whose authority does it fall under?"

"Boats from the Affaires Maritimes, the sea authorities, as well as customs and excise, the Gendarmerie Maritime, and the boats from the *parc* itself."

"Has Vaillant ever been prosecuted?"

"Only small fines."

"But he fishes too? I mean, gets involved in actual fishing?"

"Yes. But not every day. He uses long lines. For the more expensive fish. Sea bass. *Lieus jaunes,* as many people now do in the *parc.*"

"Did they still go back to Ouessant after eating here last night?"

"They moored here overnight. One of the landlords on the Quai Nord saw them leave, about seven in the morning."

That would have been just about right for the timing. Goulch understood straightaway.

"They claim not to have left the ship after that this morning. And we have no witnesses to the contrary. Not that that means anything."

That was the way it was.

"A lucky chance," Dupin said, primarily talking to himself. "They hardly come to the Île de Sein for dinner that often."

"The harbor landlords say they come to the island about once a month. So it's not that seldom," Goulch added drily.

"Okay, onward." Dupin would have to meet the man. His list was growing ever longer. He bent down over Riwal's notes. The inspector resumed.

"Two boats came from the *parc* yesterday, one in the morning, one in the evening, about seven o'clock. Both routine."

"What were they doing precisely?"

"They patrol regularly, primarily to keep tabs on the fishing and environmental rules. They take samples to see if anything suspicious comes up. They check a few boats, their nets, their catch."

"We've already spoken to the captains of both boats," Goulch added. "They didn't come across anything unusual yesterday, and they'd asked their colleagues too, with the same response. The same goes for the boats belonging to the other authorities. Nobody reported anything anywhere that could have to do with the murders."

"Have you chosen?" The blond waitress was standing in front of them again.

"Lunch today, sadly not." Dupin wanted to be off. He was feeling impatient.

"You're making a big mistake," she said, and turned away smiling, Riwal looking glumly after her.

"Had anyone from the patrol boats had anything to do with Laetitia Darot?"

"No. The *parc* scientific department operates completely independently and isn't involved in the patrols. Their boss is Pierre Leblanc."

The man whom Manet, the island doctor, considered extraordinarily competent and who was on the list of people Dupin hoped to talk to soon. Maybe he had been too quick to say no to the friendly waitress. If he left here right now he would undoubtedly get nothing to eat over the next few hours.

"How about Darot's relations with her colleagues?"

"There are six scientists in all. Leblanc will be able to tell you more."

Dupin leaned back.

His fellow officers had done good work. The factual investigations were going ahead well, even if to date they had brought nothing concrete to light. But then who knew, maybe somewhere in the sieve, covered in sand and mud, was a lump of gold they would only discover later.

"Goulch, have you heard anything from the Gendarmerie Maritime about water pollution in the *parc* that has happened recently?"

"No."

"Riwal, have you had the opportunity to talk to the island's two fishermen?"

Their names too were on the list.

"I've spoken to both of them, albeit not for long. They're out at sea. Neither noticed anything unusual either last night or this morning."

"And where were they themselves last night and this morning?"

"Marteau, that's what the older fisherman is called, was out at a little birthday party here on the island—until midnight. There are witnesses. And this morning he was up at six for a meeting on the wharf in Douarnenez. That's confirmed too."

That eliminated him.

"Jumeau says he was back in the harbor at five thirty yesterday. He brought six large bass to Le Tatoon, drank a beer, and sat around for a while. There are witnesses to that. By nine he was home and went straight to bed, because he goes out earlier than normal at the moment: four thirty today. He lives on his own. He's a bachelor."

"So last night he could have done anything," Dupin murmured, "and the same goes for this morning. The boy who found the dolphin researcher saw him to the north of the island, in visible range. He could have come ashore for half an hour at any time."

"Correct," the inspector confirmed.

"The pirate and the fisherman." Dupin folded his hands behind his head. "Both were here in the restaurant yesterday."

He was really talking to himself. There was no volume in his voice.

"Maybe," Dupin began hesitantly, "maybe we should have something to eat after all," quickly adding, "just a little."

Relief spread across Riwal's face. It was as if he had hoped things might go this way. Goulch too nodded keen approval.

"Very sensible," Riwal said, and nodded heavily. "It will be our only chance before this evening. And in any case you have to try the oysters, boss. Just for your stomach's sake." His eyes turned misty. "Docteur Garreg will be very proud of you."

It was a clever move. On their last case, Dupin had had a lot to do with oysters, which up until then he had shunned. Certain circumstances, accompanied by medical advice, had led him to start eating them. And despite his initial skepticism, they had turned out to be an efficacious therapy for his sensitive stomach. And a new delicacy in his life. Ever since, for medical reasons, he had eaten three every evening. From then on, his stomach had been much better and he had shaken off the wretched "Gastritis C," which meant he could once again drink as much coffee as he liked. He could be himself again.

"Oysters from the island! A young couple has recently opened up an oyster farm, L'huitre de Sein. An absolute treasure. The phytoplankton around the island gives off extraordinary aromas: powerful, raw, wild aromas, absolutely wonderful, and above all not dominated by iodine."

Dupin had discovered that it was true. Eat an oyster and one was eating the sea itself, the seawater from which they had come.

He waved at the waitress. Yes, they would have something to eat. And support the young couple. Riwal beamed, Goulch no less so.

"Do you know who else dropped in here last night? And drank a bottle of red wine on his own?" Riwal seemed to want to illustrate that you could continue to work while eating. "This Frédéric Carrière. The *bolincheur,* the one who fishes for Morin."

Dupin pricked up his ears. "Here in Le Tatoon?"

"Here in Le Tatoon. Late on, about midnight."

Yet another coincidence. And his mother's house was here. He obviously knew people round about. This was a very close-knit community.

"Was there anyone with him?"

"No."

"Hmmm."

The waitress was standing in front of them. "You've changed your mind?" She couldn't restrain her satisfaction.

"The *menu du jour*, please. And a few oysters first. Eighteen."

Riwal and Goulch nodded in agreement.

"Menu of the day three times. Oysters beforehand," the waitress confirmed. "Maybe a bottle of muscadet to go with it, monsieur?"

The temptation was unconscionably great, here in the sun, along with the endlessly delicious white meat of the *lieu jaune*.

"No thank you," Dupin grumbled. "Just water."

He pulled himself together and turned back to Goulch and Riwal. "Do we have an alibi for this Carrière? What was he up to on the island?"

"We haven't spoken to him yet."

"Do so. Where is his boat moored? I mean which is his harbor?"

"Douarnenez. He lives there too. We'll deal with him."

"Good."

"That's all we can tell from the list for now, boss."

The stupid thing was, it could take a lot of hard work over a long time to find out who arrived at or left the island, and all the while it might be a waste of time. They had to get a grip of some sort on the story, at least something to start from.

* * *

The oysters, the mussels in allspice, and the *lieu jaune* were all on the table in the twinkling of an eye. None of the effusive praise for the restaurant had been exaggerated; everything was sensational. The place was perfect.

In the meantime the colors had acquired a surreal intensity: the opal blue of the sky, the deep blue of the sea, the bright green of the seaweed and the algae at the edge of the harbor bay in front of them, the blinding white of the sandbank opposite, the orange and red of the gently bobbing wooden boats, each and every color magnified to the max, no faded, diluted tones, no shades.

They had exchanged a few more thoughts before the meal, Riwal,

Goulch, and the commissaire, but none of them had in any way changed the world or the case as each of them had increasingly frequently turned their eyes to the door of the restaurant. Dupin's stomach was really grumbling.

But the first oyster was followed by a deep, ecstatic sigh.

It had gotten warmer while they had been sitting there, in that the last bit of wind had ceased. The sun was now incredibly strong. Sweat was running down Dupin's brow. He'd never been able to bear hats and as a result never wore one.

His eyes flitted lazily over the pretty quay and the bay, a number of things simultaneously going through his mind.

"Really good decision, this! I reckon you've never eaten as splendid a fish as this in your life. Am I right?"

Antoine Manet had appeared on the terrace, along with Madame Coquil. They must have come along the path by the seaside, not along the quay.

"Have you found out any more yet? Was it one of us?" The museum chief couldn't restrain herself, and yet again she sounded more as if she were curious, rather than worried.

Dupin found himself involuntarily grinning. He put in his mouth the last morsel of the baguette with which he had cleaned his plate of the remains of the heavenly creamy potato puree.

"As of now it might still be anybody . . ." He hesitated, then added, "Almost anybody. Almost anybody from the island, or anybody from anywhere else."

Antoine Manet pulled up two chairs from the next table, and he and Madame Coquil sat down.

"We have a little news." Manet's expression was serious. "People are saying the dolphin researcher met up with Luc Jumeau, the young fisherman. They were seen walking together two weeks ago, out by the dolmens, about nine o'clock in the evening. And it wasn't the first time."

Obviously the islanders had been talking amongst themselves about the two murders. And this and that had cropped up. The phrase "people are saying" was clearly a distillation of everything the island doctor had picked up from all his meetings and visits during the morning.

"You mean they were in a *relationship*?"

"Possibly."

"That landscape gardener certainly thinks so," Madame Coquil said definitely.

"The landscape gardener?"

Manet explained: "The local regional authority has recently assigned a landscape gardener to each of the islands. Ours has been here two years, an amazing guy. Since he's been here the *arméries maritimes*—a particular type of sea carnation—have been growing again. You must have seen them: little pink flowers. And he has a wonderful wife."

"When will this Jumeau guy get back in from the sea?"

"About five o'clock."

"That's too late. Call him now. We need to talk to him."

They should have done it ages ago. It was all the more important now. Of course it could be a tragic love story. The region was apparently known for them. Worldwide. Riwal gave the commissaire a look to see just exactly how urgent it was. Within a second he was on his feet with his phone in his hand.

"Natalie's husband," Madame Coquil said, "the pair of them own the restaurant on the Quai Nord, directly opposite the main pier—he saw Laetitia Darot hanging out a strange fishing net in the little garden next to her house."

"What was strange about it?"

"It had little bits of apparatus around the edges," she said. "More than a few of them."

"What's that supposed to mean?"

"He didn't rightly know himself." She gave Dupin a challenging look.

"What could that be about?" Dupin had turned the question to Goulch, but he just shrugged.

"We'll need to discuss it with an expert. I'll ask the *parc* chief when I see him shortly. Did the crime scene team mention a net like that?"

"No, they found no equipment at all in Laetitia Darot's house. It seems she kept everything in her shed. I have no idea why she might have needed a net. There certainly wasn't one in her boat."

Riwal came back to the table. "I couldn't get through to Jumeau, but asked one of his colleagues to get hold of him on the radio."

"Good, so what else is there?" Dupin looked expectantly at the two islanders.

Madame Coquil's face looked fierce. "There was a sighting of Dahut, just three days ago. That's always a bad sign. Our eldest girl, Annie, spotted her. Where she's always seen. Not far from the ruined burial mound."

Manet realized an explanation was in order. "She's talking about the daughter of King Gradlon. She became a sea siren." He thought nothing more of the sighting than if Madame Coquil had been talking about the sighting of a dolphin or orca.

"She's spotted every couple of years. And every time something bad happens afterward." Madame Coquil gave Dupin an inscrutable glance. "There are witnesses for many of these things, just in case you think we're rambling here. In 1892 a priest who'd come to say mass spotted her. He saw a spectacularly beautiful woman with long hair and a fish's tail in the midst of the waves. Dahut swims around here endlessly, wanting to bring everything back: the glittering balls and parties, the expensive clothes, the excess."

Much as he tried, Dupin hadn't a clue how to respond to this.

"And as if that weren't enough," Madame Coquil drew her eyebrows together in yet more consternation, "the Bag Noz has been sighted too! The Boat of the Night. Down at the western end of the island. Not far from the chapel."

Once again Manet came to their assistance. "The maritime equivalent of the Garrig an Ankou, the Chariot of Death."

Dupin knew the stories of the Grim Reaper who came to collect the corpses of the dead in his coach.

"The Boat of the Night turns up," Madame Coquil continued, "when dark things are happening. Your eyes can't ever see it clearly, it's always blurred, and when you get closer, it gets farther away. Every now and then you can hear heartbreaking wailing from the boat. The first drowning victim of the year is always doomed to become the boat's ghostly helmsman."

A lengthy silence followed that statement. Riwal was fidgeting uncomfortably back and forward on his seat.

"Is there anything else—of news?"

"Just a little." Manet glanced meaningfully at Dupin. "But perhaps the most important. The ladies and gentlemen of the press. I've put them into one of the bars on the Quai Nord, as far as possible from what's going on. I've told them you're bound to drop in."

"Then I'm headed straight back to the mainland."

Dupin's phone rang. An unidentified number.

"Yes?" He had pushed his chair back and dropped his voice.

"Charles Morin here. Am I speaking with Commissaire Georges Dupin?"

A remarkably polite tone of voice. Dupin himself didn't know why, but he wasn't very surprised by the call.

"That's me."

"Your assistant called me. It seems you want to speak with me?"

"Indeed."

"Four p.m. would be good. I'm, let's say . . ." A slight pause followed. ". . . extremely curious to know how your investigation is going."

Despite the excessively accommodating choice of words, there was no suggestion of sarcasm or obsequiousness in Morin's voice. Dupin had expected a very different tone from Morin. He had imagined him to be a totally different character, more like Roiyou, except hiked up a grade.

"Because Laetitia Darot was your daughter," Dupin retorted out of the blue.

Morin's response contained no trace of aggression. On the contrary, it sounded in control of itself, self-confident, worldly, without the slightest intent of provoking the commissaire.

"We don't need to go into all that, Monsieur le Commissaire. I feel responsible. I live and work here and have done for decades. The sea, the *parc*, the people—this is my home."

"Your empire, you mean." Dupin too had adopted a convivial tone.

"Up to a point you could say, yes. You will understand that I am interested"—he spoke more slowly—"when two young women become victims of a crime that doesn't appear to have been committed by an outsider. That worries me. In a big way."

"I'll see you at four o'clock, Monsieur Morin."

"Your assistant said you would come to see me here, in Douarnenez."

"Gladly."

Nolwenn had forgotten to mention that. But that was no bad thing.

"I look forward to our first meeting," Dupin said, but Morin had already hung up. He got to his feet. Charles Morin made any particular interpretation difficult. Quite a skill.

"Time for us to go."

"Good luck," Manet said to encourage them, simultaneously signaling he understood why they had to go so suddenly.

"We're here when you need us, Monsieur le Commissaire. And you will," Madame Coquil said with a smile. She wasn't so much making an offer as making a point.

"Indeed, Madame Coquil. We need you. No doubt about that."

"And don't forget the inscription on the monument by the cholera cemetery: 'The soldier who never surrenders is always in the right.'"

Goulch and Riwal had also gotten to their feet.

Dupin disappeared inside Le Tatoon to pay the check.

A short while later he came back out onto the terrace and said good-bye to Monsieur Manet and Madame Coquil. Riwal and Goulch were already waiting for him on the quay.

"Riwal, you take charge here on the island. Kadeg will continue to do the same in Douarnenez. Keep in touch regularly, and if you come across anything new." Riwal gave a routine nod. "And give Nolwenn a ring. I want to know what's up with Morin's paternity. She should do whatever she can to find out about it."

"I'm on it, boss."

Riwal set off, turning left into the labyrinth of alleyways, acting as if he knew the place like the palm of his hand.

"One more thing, Riwal, just briefly." Dupin took a few paces after the inspector.

"The butcher from Le Conquet"—Dupin was unintention-ally speaking softly—"the one who saw seven graves, of which five rather than four were in one row"—he tried to speak in a louder voice—"whatever happened to him?"

Riwal looked at him worriedly for a moment, so that Dupin was already regretting having asked the question.

"He fell out of the boat he'd gone fishing in. In a calm sea and good weather. Dead. His heart. Despite there being no previous history or warning signs. Just like that."

Dupin's eyes widened, even though he had tried to restrain any reaction. He shook himself. It was ridiculous. Now he was paying attention to ghost stories. Fantastic fables come from crazy supersti-tion.

"You . . ." Riwal hemmed and hawed. ". . . you need to watch out, boss. I mean, watch out particularly carefully, twice or three times as much as normal, if you're going to Île Tristan."

Dupin stared at him.

"You've just heard: Dahut, the daughter of King Gradlon, is now a ghostly siren in the bay of Douarnenez. If you think you see something odd in the waves, some strange form in the spray, under no circumstances take another look. Her gaze drags you into the sea after her."

But before Dupin could say anything, Riwal had vanished amidst the houses.

* * *

"The boat was right at the end of the Quai Nord."

Goulch was striding out decisively as they headed toward the harbor area between the two quays, where the huts belonging to Céline Kerkrom and Laetitia Darot stood.

"Are you aware—" Dupin's cell phone rang again. A Rennes number.

"Yes?"

"Xavier Controc. Affaires Maritimes. Head of fisheries department. Commissaire Dupin?"

"What's this about?"

"I'd like to tell you about something in complete confidence. I think it might be of importance, even if it's not related to this case."

Dupin had automatically stopped in his tracks.

"But first I need you to swear not to utter a single word to anyone about this. Can you do that?"

"Go ahead."

"This afternoon we are going to carry out a major 'joint services action' in the Parc Iroise, controls at sea. We will be taking part alongside a unit from the Gendarmerie Maritime, and Ifremer, the Institut Français de Recherche pour l'Exploitation de la Mer. We're investigating apparent breaches of the catch regulations for red lobsters. Are you familiar with the matter?"

Dupin was already familiar with almost every possible subject connected to the fishing industry; not that one, however.

"It's a local type of lobster, found primarily in the Chaussée de Sein, which was nearly driven to extinction through overfishing in 2006. On that occasion they introduced a total ban on fishing for the species, which led to something of a recovery. But the ban is still in effect, and there are some who think they no longer need to heed it."

"Is your operation aimed at anybody in particular?"

"In theory, no, but there are one or two who we believe are ignoring the ban. Over the past few weeks, some boats refused to let inspectors carrying out spot checks come on board."

"Charles Morin's boats?"

He hesitated. "There are several boats involved, but yes."

They seemed to be taking it seriously. Even the chief of police in Douarnenez, with whom Nolwenn had spoken, apparently didn't know about this, or at least hadn't mentioned it.

Dupin had remained standing on the spot. "So who knows about this operation?"

"Only a few staff of each organization involved. From yesterday, of course, the control boats and their crew."

"And what happens if infringement of the ban is proved to be happening? I mean, what are the stakes here?"

"A few of them were caught at it last year. This time around, for a repeat infraction, there could be fines of up to fifteen thousand euros, or in an extreme case a jail sentence. Up to six months. That's when it gets serious."

"And the boats undertaking the operation are authorized to take control against the will of the captains?"

"Absolutely. We have permission from the courts."

If Dupin understood properly, an operation like this could be a real slap in the face for Morin.

"Could Laetitia Darot have known about this operation?"

"The dead dolphin researcher?"

"The murdered dolphin researcher."

"In theory it's impossible. This has nothing to do with the *parc*'s scientific department."

"Darot's boss, Pierre Leblanc, does he know about it?"

"He's in on the secret."

Dupin had no firm idea, no clear plan to follow, but the whole business was of great interest.

"However, seeing as you are investigating within the *parc*, I thought it proper to inform you."

"I am very grateful to you, Monsieur . . ." He had of course already forgotten the man's name.

"Controc. Do you see—" Controc paused for a moment. "In the circumstances of your investigation at present, do you see any possible connection between this operation and the murders?"

"I can't say for now," Dupin replied honestly.

"Everybody here is very worked up about it."

"Here too, Monsieur Controc. I suggest we keep in touch with one another in case there are any new developments."

"Agreed."

Dupin hung up. Goulch was waiting for him a few meters farther on. Dupin caught up with him and put him in the picture.

"They must have real grounds for suspicion. I can't remember anything on this scale in recent years," Goulch said. He had started walking on, and Dupin with him.

They were walking along the last stretch of the quay, mountains of colorful fishermen's nets in big wooden boxes along the way. To their right a concrete slipway led down to the sea. Straight on led to the harbor area, with a handful of long, low, flat-roofed buildings, the storage sheds.

"You didn't find any net on Darot's boat," began Dupin, returning to a point he had been mulling over. "With little bits of equipment attached?"

"Certainly not."

The sheds were worn by the wind and the sea. There were just a few painted white, while most were bare concrete that over the years had taken on yellow or green tones. Bright orange patches of lichen. Narrow doors with tiny windows next to them. The frames of the doors and windows were painted in bright colors: turquoise, bright blue, petroleum green, sunlight yellow. Between the barracks lay buoys, anchor chains, all sorts of rusted bits and pieces.

Outside one of the barracks stood two policemen, the Gendarmerie Maritime.

These had to be the sheds belonging to Darot and Kerkrom.

Dupin slowed his pace.

"I just want to take a quick look to see if we can find this net." For some reason the strange net was nagging at him.

Without waiting for any reaction from Goulch, Dupin went up to the policemen.

"Which is Laetitia Darot's shed?"

"This one here, Monsieur le Commissaire."

An extremely carefully painted door—reddish ocher. The frames of the narrow windows were deep blue. There was a small wooden bench in front, with two empty plastic boxes on top. Two old window boxes with a few wind-blown flowers still managing to be in bloom.

"The one next to it"—the policeman pointed to the door a few meters away—"belongs to Céline Kerkrom. The crime scene team have already documented everything."

"Is it just by chance that they're next to one another, Darot's and Kerkrom's?"

"Apparently."

What else was the poor uniform to say?

Goulch had followed Dupin. "I'll follow up again with the colleague who checked out the houses. About the net. Just to be sure."

"Good."

Dupin headed toward the reddish-ocher door, which was half open. He opened it wide. And walked in.

The dusty window didn't let much light in, and the light bulb fixed to the ceiling didn't help much. It took Dupin's eyes a moment to adjust. There was a rather musty smell, but not unpleasant. In the right-hand corner—the room was some five meters by two and a half—lay a few buoys.

They were different shapes, most of them oblong and orange, which to Dupin looked like those used by divers. There were at least a dozen of them.

Then there was divers' equipment on metal shelves half a meter high, which took up most of the room: bottles in different shapes, breathing apparatus, diving masks, neoprene suits. A handful of knives.

The rear part of the room was occupied by a large table with an unusual hodgepodge of objects on it: sticks of driftwood, rusty bits of metal, a largish ship screw, things that Laetitia Darot had brought up from the sea bottom, pretty shells in various shapes, dried seaweed, unusual stones.

No nets.

Not even one.

Dupin walked out again.

Goulch seemed still to be on the phone.

He would take a quick look at the other shed.

Perhaps it had been Kerkrom's net. And for some reason or other she had kept it in Darot's shed.

The room was the same size. But it created a completely different impression. It was impossible to say if it was random chaos or the result of what had actually been a systematic collection of things that over the years had been picked up and put down, which in the end would give an outsider the same impression.

There was a rusty old fridge directly to the right of the door, and next to it, piled up against the wall, lobster cages, fish boxes in various shapes and sizes, paddles. Then buoys, much larger than Darot's, mostly in fire engine red, and reaching into the far corner, mountains of nets. Dupin pushed his way through them. With meshes in different sizes and colors. Dupin rooted around a bit. They looked as if they were no longer used. Amidst them were lines, lots of long lines, wrapped around logs. A bucket full of fishing hooks, a bucket of lead weights.

But nothing with little gadgets attached.

Everything seemed to belong here, nothing out of the ordinary.

Dupin turned around and left the shed. The light was so blinding, he had to hold his hand in front of his eyes.

"We have already made progress," said Goulch, who was standing directly in front of him. "The crime scene team have been through the dolphin researcher's house in detail, and are now on the fisherwoman's. They definitely found no net at Darot's. There were a couple at Kerkrom's, but none with some sort of gadgets attached. Nor did they find a cell phone on Darot's boat. Nor a computer or laptop. Just a battery charger. No laptop at Kerkrom's either, and it was a big fifteen-inch notebook, from what we know by now."

In which case the killer had been into the houses. Maybe he knew there were clues on the machines, or at least was afraid there might be. In which case maybe he had also taken other things.

"We need somebody to go through their email accounts straightaway."

"That's complicated, as you know. But we're working on it."

"Good. Okay, let's go."

Dupin had already set off; his voice had sounded grumpy.

He was unsatisfied. And nervous.

It wasn't long before the shakedown on the sea was due to start, the so-called "joint services action." That would stir things up. Maybe even throw up things to do with their case, speed things up, bring them to a head.

* * *

This boat trip was torture too. Neither the calm sea, the beautiful weather, nor Dupin's trust in Goulch and his team changed anything. Nonetheless, there was one good thing to say: it was definitely not as bad as that morning.

They had just gone around Cape Quillien in Douarnenez Bay, and straightaway, there it was, with the sun framing it: the Île Tristan. An apparition. A secret island of adventure, a pirate island like in picture books. A legend.

Half a kilometer long, half as wide, stretched out evenly in almost an oval shape. To the west soared high, rugged rocks, dark at the bottom, turning to dark gray and then light gray. Bright sprouting vegetation that made the island look like it might be too small and be overwhelmed by it. Tall spreading trees in every shade of green—some nobleman in the last century had imported unusual and also exotic trees and plants, and laid out a botanical garden, which had gone wild. Different types of bamboo, myrtle, araucaria. Fruit trees too: miniature red apples, plums, apples, pears, medlars.

Ancient stone walls enclosed meadows and heathland, defiant remains of a fortress, an atmospheric ruin. A fallen-down house next to an equally dilapidated pier, a small weather-worn lighthouse. There were endless unbelievable stories about the island—Nolwenn was keen to tell the story of a fearsome devil pirate—and even for Brittany the legends and historical poems were extraordinary.

"We're steering round to the other side of the island and will dock right by the old fish cannery, which is now where the scientific department of the Parc Iroise is located. We'll be there in two minutes. Leblanc has been informed. He's waiting for us in his office."

Goulch's precise information brought Dupin back to reality.

The commissaire had made several calls on board the boat: to Riwal, Kadeg, and Nolwenn.

They had got hold of Jumeau, the young fisherman, who had grumbled but then without too much resistance given up on fishing for the day and come back to the Île de Sein. Dupin just listened to the barest details, as was his habit.

In fact, he would have been prepared to have seen him himself. He would still do that. A young lad, not unfriendly but sparse with his words; Riwal hadn't managed to get much out of him. He had drunk a beer occasionally with Céline Kerkrom—"once a month maybe" was as precise as he could be—and chatted about this and that. "Nothing in particular." Obviously they had bumped into one another regularly down at the harbor, and exchanged a few words, though their boats were moored far apart. He had also occasionally run across Laetitia Darot, mostly down at the harbor too, and then, Riwal had obviously asked him about their "walk" together; they would take a few steps together in the direction of her house. On those occasions they would talk about anything and everything. He had no idea what had happened, what could have led to the murder of the pair, and there was nobody who seemed suspicious to him. Dupin was convinced Riwal had done all he could to drag anything more out of him. But he knew the type.

The inspector had also spoken with Frédéric Carrière. These days the *bolincheur* spent the night more frequently on the island, as he was fishing in the far west of the *parc*. He claimed that he had been on Sein around nine o'clock, but so far no witnesses had been found. He had been in his mother's house and he had only been seen by anyone else when he arrived at Le Tatoon. This morning, by his own account, he had been out at sea by five. Around ten he had had to go to Douarnenez for a brief appointment. Right now he was on his own boat west of the Pierres Noires lighthouse. Riwal had asked him about his row with Céline Kerkrom. Carrière had spoken about his anger openly, without seeming in any way reluctant to admit it. Their major falling-out had occurred in the auction hall in January. Kerkrom had accused him and the other *bolincheurs* of using catch methods that were wiping out the coastal fishers' living. That was the conflict Manet had mentioned.

At the end of their conversation, Riwal had asked Dupin how he was, if the journey had gone "smoothly." In reply Dupin had simply grumbled testily: "Everything's in order."

He had gone over the agenda for this afternoon's interviews again with Nolwenn. She had pulled all the levers to find out what she could about Morin's much-rumored paternity issues, setting a whole information machine in motion: amidst relatives, girlfriends, and her husband, who all wanted to hear everything, all of whom would put out their listening ears too. Concentrated particularly on Douarnenez Bay and western Finistère beyond. That was the maximum; there was nothing more anyone could do. It had always been successful in the past.

Nolwenn had of course also come up with the name of the *bolincheur* who had been caught with two tons of pink bream: it had indeed been one of Morin's boats, but not Frédéric Carrière. A heavy fine had been levied, but nothing more. Dupin hadn't asked about the protest demonstration in Lannion; it was better to leave that alone.

Obviously, the commissaire told all three about the maritime raid about to take place. They needed to be aware of it.

Riwal had handed the hairdresser and oil boat man over to Kadeg. He had spoken to the hairdresser's "friend," with whom the hairdresser had spent yesterday night. It had turned out, all too comically, that "the friend" was the mayor of Camaret, which raised the question why the hairdresser hadn't said so in the first place. It would have greatly increased the credibility of his statement. Kadeg had made a few discoveries: the mayor was highly regarded on the peninsula, and in Quimper, which seemed to put the hairdresser out of the picture. On the other hand the reputation of the oil boat man, Thomas Roiyou, was pretty poor. Kadeg had heard a few unpleasant stories. Over the past few years, Roiyou had been involved in several serious scuffles, one of which had resulted in charges, curiously withdrawn a few days later with no explanation. It was a fact that nobody on the island had seen his boat before 7:05 A.M., not that that mattered much given that the boat could have lain unnoticed on the northern side of the island, by the jetty not far from the cholera cemetery, for example. He also had a tender. But two of the islanders had confirmed they had seen the whole crew—including the captain—on their boat between the oil tanker's two trips. In which case the only time that could have mattered—according to Manet's estimate and the forensic pathologist's—was before they moored in the harbor. What was likely to be impossible to be sure of was his assertation that he had gone to bed early last night.

The Douarnenez side of the island came into view. They had been going along the long side of the island at the same tempo and the boat had only now begun to slow down.

They could see the long, whitewashed building of the former fish canning plant, with its sharply pointed high roof, white chimney, and bay windows, and behind it, at an angle, another long building made of stone. A little farther on, partly concealed by flowers and shrubs, was a rather dilapidated but still noble manor house, a building of substance. All the buildings lay only a stone's throw from the water. There was a concrete quay running along the western side of the island with a pier at either end pointing toward the mainland, no more than two or three hundred meters away. A clutch of weary seagulls were dozing in front of it. Between the houses, pathways led into thick woodland, with inviting shady patches under the tall pine trees. It was a little paradise.

In this weather the island had a delightful light and contemplative aura, radiating a bright strength, not in the least reflecting the sinister world of the stories told about it; on a day like today there was no trace of a dark aura—quite the opposite. Dupin was relieved.

The boat headed for the first pier.

"Goulch, I'd like you to keep a close eye on the action taking place in the *parc*. Get in contact with the operational boss, confidentially of course. He needs to keep you constantly informed."

"Consider it done. We'll be waiting for you here. It's too late today to get to Douarnenez by foot. The tide will be coming in."

Dupin hadn't thought of that.

One of Goulch's young team leaders—none of his men were older than thirty—had climbed into the bow and was using a hook to skillfully bring the boat parallel to the pier.

A few moments later Dupin was on dry land. He had to admit he had been particularly careful getting out of the boat; he had reluctantly found himself thinking about the stupid story with the butcher.

He walked across the unkempt lawn and found himself in front of an apparently recently built entrance to one side of the building with a white placard declaring *PI-Antenne Sud du Parc Naturel Marin d'Iroise.*

Dupin opened the door.

"You must be the commissaire," announced a cheerful young voice wafting toward him. It belonged to a particularly beautiful woman with fine features and chestnut brown hair. She was wearing casual jeans and a dark blue T-shirt. She seemed to be expecting him. "I'm Pierre Leblanc's assistant. We saw you dock. Come in."

The original internal factory architecture of the building had been forced to accommodate a wholly functional layout, to fit in as many offices as possible.

The young woman was already standing on a spiral staircase leading from the entrance to the upper stories, and practically flew up it.

When they got to the third floor they found themselves in a workroom with a row of desks and large screens on one side and on the other a professional maritime map of the Parc Iroise.

"Come in!" called a deep, dynamic voice. "We need to talk urgently." The tone was almost friendly.

A suntanned man—in his early forties, Dupin reckoned—came toward him with his hand stretched out. Short frizzy hair, almost black, a modest V-necked T-shirt, faded jeans—a surfer type. The most striking thing about him—so striking that they seemed to define his personality—were beaming pale blue eyes.

He shook Dupin's hand, strongly, engagingly.

"She was our best scientist. Already a distinguished expert at such a young age. Nobody else was as close to the dolphins. Some people said she was one of them." There was real tragedy but also sincere warmth in his voice.

"One thing is sure: she belonged to us, human beings, a lot less than she belonged to the dolphins." Leblanc paused. "None of us can come to terms with what has happened. It's terrible."

They went into the room next door, a signally untidy room: stuffy, small gray carpet, white walls with charts, diagrams, and photos hanging all over them. In one corner was a desk with a computer and an outsized screen. On the wall opposite the door was a little table with four chairs. That tabletop too was covered with papers. The remarkable thing about the room was the extraordinarily superb view from the bay window.

"What was Laetitia Darot working on, Monsieur Leblanc?"

"Various things. As opposed to what most people think, we are still in the early days of research into dolphins. Laetitia had been primarily involved in studying dolphins' exceptional cognitive and social facilities. Chiefly among the great porpoises that live in the *parc*, the *Tursiops truncatus*, but not just them. For example, they are capable of learning simple sign language; Laetitia properly established a friendship with certain individuals of the two populations in the *parc*. The dolphins had even given her a name of her own. They know one another by whistle names, you should know; even after twenty or thirty years, their memory functions excellently."

Dupin was envious—his own memory for names lasted barely two minutes.

"Laetitia had put all that together in one coordinated project."

"And this project is all stored on your computers and servers?"

"Obviously." Leblanc gave Dupin an inquisitive look.

"I assume she had her own notebook, her own computer?"

"Of course. We give all our researchers laptops."

"And they have their own hard drives?"

"Yes. Running special software, programs that automatically sync their data with our cloud. And all their notes too."

Dupin had begun taking notes of his own, in his Clairefontaine paper notebook.

"But she could have had data on her laptop that only she had access to? In a word processing program, for example?"

"Absolutely. Most of the researchers also use their laptops for private matters. It's explicitly allowed."

"What about email?"

"The email runs on our client server. But it is strictly limited to professional use. Private communications have to run on private accounts."

"Do you know if she had a private account?"

"Unfortunately I don't know."

"We didn't find a laptop either in her house or on her boat—could it be somewhere here?"

"Definitely not. It was her everyday work tool."

"Did she have an office here?"

"She didn't want one. And didn't need one."

So the killer had to have taken her laptop. Or got rid of it.

"Tell me more about Darot's research work."

Even if it was specialized, Dupin wanted to know more. You never knew what might turn up. He had come across deciding factors before in the most improbable subjects.

"She was chiefly concerned with showing that with each dolphin we were dealing with a specific personality, with specific individuals with different mental and emotional attributes. More developed and closer to humans than in the case of chimpanzees. Dolphins are, after humans, the most intelligent creatures on our planet. That also applies to their neuroanatomy. Seen purely anatomically and physiognomically, the brain of a dolphin is closer to that of a human than that of any other animal." He was getting carried away now. "Despite the fact that it evolved along an entirely different route. Laetitia had not only come closer neurologically, but over meticulous behavioral studies of individual dolphins, demonstrated wholly consistent, complex personality depictions: a distinct sense of self and awareness, including awareness of the future that permitted making plans for the future. Most important of all, they also exhibit highly nuanced emotions that lead them to behave in groups the same way humans do.

"That was her second focus, after the question of individuality: the social life of dolphins. She studied the highly complex structured manners in which dolphins live together. They are capable of learning, and she studied how they passed on their learning, actually teaching one another. Animals released into the oceans, for example, can teach their wild fellows the artistic tricks they've learned in those dreadful dolphinariums: in a distant part of the Caribbean all of a sudden whole populations began swimming on their tails. Other dolphins use sponges as tools to extract little sea creatures from rocky ground—a learned trick passed on from dolphin mothers to their children."

Dupin was deeply impressed. But it was the dolphin researcher he was interested in, not the actual dolphins.

"What was a standard working day like for Darot? How should I imagine it?"

Leblanc had gone over to the bay window. Dupin followed him.

"She spent it either on her boat or in the water. With the dolphins, one way or the other. That was her working day. Like I said, she wasn't really interested in people. Every two weeks she came to see me and we talked over her latest discoveries."

"Was she the only dolphin researcher in the Parc Iroise?"

"Yes."

"What about you? What is your area of research, Monsieur Leblanc?"

"Marine ecology. I'm mainly involved in long-term studies in two areas: overfertilization and excessive acidation. Parc Iroise, like all seas, suffers from eutrophication, from phosphates leaked into the sea by industrial farming methods, which lead to the production of poisonous phytoplankton and excessive green algae. Only"—his face darkened—"to give an example of the consequences: last year in Douarnenez Bay certain types of shellfish couldn't be fished for a hundred and fifty days because of an exaggerated concentration of toxic plankton. I'm sure you know about the consequences of the green algae."

The commissaire nodded.

"Humanity's excessive production of CO_2 is acidifying the oceans, which has already had fatal consequences: one-third of all life in the sea is now threatened, countless species are already extinct. This is no alarmist futuristic scenario, but has already long been reality. Just like the tangible warming of the Atlantic, take cod for just one example: the temperature has risen so far that the fish are laying their eggs even farther north, because they need cooler water. But there isn't enough of the nourishment they need there, so they die after hatching."

Leblanc rested his case on that topic.

"Sorry." He was speaking calmly in a deep voice once again. "We had a meeting with politicians yesterday and I'm still angry. The current reform of EU fisheries policy doesn't go far enough, and even now we're getting fatal decisions about quotas. The reality is that we need significant reductions in the allowed catches, and support for small fishermen along the coasts, which lies at the heart of our ideas here at the *parc*. But the quotas are being shared out in the same old way: the fishing barons, and their fleets with their destructive drag fishing, get the lion's share, which leaves the small-scale fishing businesses and the independent fishers hugely disadvantaged and driven further into ruin. Just look at the quotas for trawler fishing of sole in the Channel, beginning north of Ouessant and taking in all of northern Brittany. Along with the devastating overfishing it ends up with huge waste catch."

"Was Laetitia Darot at this meeting?"

"No. She hated all that."

"Do you think—" The monotone chirping of Dupin's cell phone interrupted him.

Paris.

His mother. Unbelievable. There was absolutely no point in answering; what was he to say at this junction, except that it was getting less and less likely that he could come.

"Do you think"—Dupin took up where he had left off, letting the phone ring—"Darot's murder might have something to do with her work? Directly or indirectly?"

"How do you mean?"

"In recent weeks numerous dolphins have washed up dead."

"Happily none from our populations, but all the same, Laetitia was apoplectic, with anger and despair. They were probably caught up in the collateral catch of the sole fishers north of the *parc*. The dolphins hadn't been dead longer than a day, the inquest said. So they must have died locally."

"Had Darot anything to do with the inquest?"

"No. It was a veterinarian from the Gendarmerie Maritime."

"So what happens now?"

"Nothing."

"Is it possible"—it was pure speculation, but still—"she could have caught out the culprit?"

"Unlikely—and even if she had, nothing would have happened; the culprit had nothing to fear. In this year alone three thousand killed dolphins have been washed up on French shores. In the north Atlantic, on our side of the Atlantic, dolphins are at risk of going extinct."

"What type of nets are banned in the *parc*?"

"There are six different kinds of fishing practiced in the *parc*. Drift nets are forbidden, dragnets and gillnets only allowed up to certain sizes. On top of that, the catch quotas for the different types of fish are strictly enforced. Those of us here at the *parc* are only involved in the recommendations made; the legal binding regulations are then decided on by politicians, and then put into law by the prefecture. We've been trying for years to implement a special program to make major reductions in the by-catch. We're just beginning to have some success."

"If there are no legal consequences, proof that the dead dolphins in the last weeks were by-catch victims of one of the local big fishing businesses would seriously damage the owner's reputation, and maybe also his business?"

"You mean Morin, the so-called fisherman king?" Leblanc didn't wait for an answer. "I should think so. But Laetitia didn't go out to sea that often. And in any case she would have filmed it or taken photos; she would have gotten close up."

"Maybe it wasn't Laetitia Darot who witnessed it. Maybe it was one of the fisherfolk? Who told her about it later. Céline Kerkrom maybe? The pair of them were friends."

"Even that's extremely unlikely."

But possible. Obviously that too was pure speculation.

"Or"—Dupin was thinking again—"somebody had laid down the banned dragnets inside the *parc,* north of Ouessant. More than once. Or ignored the quotas, caught banned species of fish . . . And perhaps the women had systematically checked it out, documented it, over weeks, months?"

"You think the two women might have been spying on Morin?"

Dupin didn't reply. Something had just occurred to him that he hadn't mentioned yet.

"What could be the connection of the strange net that was seen at Laetitia Darot's—a net with little bits of apparatus attached to it?"

The answer was prompt. "That was one of her current projects. Those little bits of apparatus were sonar devices that send out ultrasound signals to warn dolphins and other mammals. They ought to keep them from getting trapped in the nets in the first place. The *parc* is in charge of doing scientific tests of their effectiveness. In some parts of the world where conditions in the sea are even worse, there have already been positive results collected."

That was the mystery of "bits of apparatus" solved. But not the fact that the net was there and what else it could be used for.

"And this test net is currently here with you in the *parc*?"

"I think so. I can ask. Is it important?"

"I'd like to know."

"The *parc* worked together with several fishermen." Leblanc paused for a moment's thought. "I don't know whether or not Kerkrom was one of them." It sounded as if he was kicking himself for not having thought of that already. "I'll find out right away." He walked over to the telephone—the same ancient old office sort that they also had in the commissariat, the same ghastly green—and pressed the key for a preprogrammed number. "Mathieu, just a quick question: Laetitia's program with the sonar devices, was the young fisherwoman from the Île de Sein, Céline Kerkrom, involved?"

He listened for a moment, then nodded and said: "Yes, dreadful."

He listened again.

"Ah, right. Thanks, Mathieu. Do you know anything about how they got on? Did Laetitia say anything to you about it?"

A brief answer.

"Thanks, do you still have the net? . . . Good. And send me a list of who else was involved."

He hung up.

"That was the technical assistant in the scientific department. So, yes, she was there. Along with three other fisherfolk. From the north of the *parc*, where the major population of dolphins lives. Near Molène and Ouessant. You'll have the list soon."

"Thank you."

Well, that was something. An actual factual connection between the two women apart from their friendship.

"Also the test nets are for now still with us. All four. My colleague didn't know anything more about it, he's not been here long."

"Do you think the ordinary fishermen would take to nets like that?"

"There'd be very different reactions. The large part of the fisherfolk cooperate well with us—apart from the odd skirmish here and there—because they know that it's in their own interest for the sea to be kept in good order. But not all of them, of course."

"Have there been rows over the nets?"

"No."

Dupin looked out of the window.

The view was superb. The silver shining sea; to the right Douarnenez, which looked particularly picturesque in this light. The air was so clear he could even see the broad beach of Quillien at the far end of the bay; it looked as if it were close enough to swim to it. He could see the pier, Goulch's boat, the seagulls still snoozing. He turned round to face Leblanc.

"If I understand rightly, you were the only one of all the staff who had regular contact with Laetitia Darot?"

"I think so. Not that Laetitia was particularly unfriendly to the others, not at all. Quite the opposite: she was a very warmhearted, likable creature. It was just that she didn't seek out contacts, human company just wasn't her thing. But I know next to nothing about her private life. We had a purely professional relationship, she never told me anything about herself."

Leblanc pulled a sheet of paper from the printer and handed it to Dupin. "The list of the fishers involved."

Dupin put it in his pocket. "About the rumors that she was a love child of Charles Morin, do you know anything?"

"Somebody mentioned it to me once. But I don't listen to rumors; I couldn't care less. They only say something about the people who spread them."

Dupin was of the same opinion.

"She never referred to it herself?"

"She never would have."

"So you don't know anything about her family situation?"

"No. I've had somebody look through her personnel files to see what information we had about her. There's no more than date of birth, place of birth, school career. We have extensive documents only about her studies and her scientific positions. She studied maritime biology at the University of British Columbia in Vancouver, passed everything summa cum laude, has excellent scientific references. She went on to work there for two years, and following that, three years in Halifax at the famed Bedford Institute of Oceanography. She's been here now with us for three years, even when she was still living in Brest. She can hardly have had much time for a private life; she was already spending most of the time with her dolphins. I can't tell you much about her time in Canada. But I can send you a copy of all the documents we have."

"That would be good. Do you know why she moved from Brest to the Île de Sein?"

"To be closer to her dolphins. There's a large population of great porpoises living around Sein, and if she was lucky she could see them just by looking out of her window in the morning. And then—I think this was also a reason—there were fewer people on the Île de Sein."

"And why did she suddenly come back to Brittany?"

"Her contract in Halifax ran out, and here she had all the scientific freedom she wanted. Maybe there was a bit of homesickness too? To be honest, I just don't know."

There was a pause for the first time in the conversation.

"There's a big collective action taking place in the *parc* today, as you know."

Dupin had just dropped the sentence into the room.

Leblanc nodded. "We're counting on catching one or another of the culprits red-handed. The regular controls and checks aren't enough. It's easy to see that more reaches the market than can legally be caught."

"Do you have a suspicion who it is that's not keeping to the catch quotas?"

"It's no secret—we talk about Morin's boats. But not only his. There are another two big-time fishers who are suspect."

"This could be a big thing then?"

"I hope so."

Dupin glanced at the clock.

"That was all very worthwhile information, Monsieur Leblanc."

"Let me know if I can do anything to help. I hope . . ." He hesitated, then continued in a firm voice, ". . . that Laetitia's murder had nothing to do with her work. I mean this collaboration between the two women in the net project." He broke off.

"What would a possible story in that respect look like—how would you imagine it?"

The question was, how could the thing have evoked such a force that could have led to murder; two murders.

"I'm a scientist." He smiled with a sad expression on his face. "I need facts, empirical facts. My imagination isn't that well developed."

"Call if anything occurs to you."

"I'll do that. You can count on me."

"Thanks."

Dupin turned away, left Leblanc's office, and strutted rapidly across the anteroom; the assistant's workplace was empty.

He found his way on his own.

A minute later Dupin was out of the building, grateful to be in the open air.

He walked toward the pier. Goulch waved at him. Suddenly Dupin stopped dead and turned around. He let his gaze drift over the fabled island. He had the strange impression that, however bright and pretty it might appear, it simultaneously belonged elsewhere. In other, darker realms.

A vague, indescribable feeling of unease crept over the commissaire, though he himself had no idea why.

* * *

It had been a brief trip. Harmless. A speedy crossing. Dupin had sat in the bow to watch Douarnenez harbor coming toward him.

It reminded Dupin of the little town ferry in Concarneau that one took to get from the Ville Close, the medieval old town in the mouth of the Moros, to the eastern part of the town, just a stone's throw, maybe a hundred meters. An enjoyable tour in a little green boat; it went through the sheltered harbor and had nothing whatsoever to do with a trip on the sea. Sometimes, when he needed to think, the commissaire would take a walk along the fortified walls of the old town as far as the wild garden on the hill and the church, then take the little boat and cross over. Not to get out on the other bank; he stayed in the boat and took it back again. He had the picturesque view of the fortifications, the harbor, the town, a bit like a bus trip in the old days on the open buses. It was one of the commissaire's many enjoyable rituals; his whole life and work were filled, if the truth be told, with an extremely rich and well-stocked storehouse of such rituals. Including those that might be categorized by others as tics, quirks, or foibles.

Dupin had told Goulch about his conversation with Leblanc. Despite the minimal information, a picture of Laetitia Darot as a person was slowly emerging. Dupin was getting an idea who this wonderful dolphin researcher had been.

Goulch's speedboat, the *Bir*, had moored at the quay right in front of the auction hall, between two larger boats flying Spanish flags. Dupin and Goulch, who had emerged from the captain's cabin, were already standing to the rear, from where Dupin was going to take to the land.

"Here is the list of the other fisherfolk involved in the net project," he said. "Talk to them. I'm interested in everything. Particularities of the project, incidents of any sort. Ask them also what they know about Darot and Kerkrom. What they spoke about with them."

Goulch took the list and glanced at it. "Do you think this might have something to do with the case?"

Dupin didn't know, but he did know it was bothering him. First and foremost: at this stage of a case they had to put their feelers out in all directions.

"We have to check everything, Goulch. And we mustn't neglect Céline Kerkrom." The sentence was primarily directed at himself.

"We've just gotten the information on the radio. Operation Red Lobster is going according to plan. Every boat currently fishing in the *parc* has been ordered to halt where it is. I've just spoken with the head of the operation."

"Good. We'll see how it goes. Any news from Kadeg, Riwal, or Nolwenn? Anything new from the island?"

"Not so far."

"See you later, then. I'm going to remain on the mainland for now."

Dupin sprang enthusiastically ashore.

Goulch went back to the bridge.

Dupin looked around. He was standing almost exactly in front of the entrance to the auction house, just where he had been standing early that morning. It was busy now too. He saw the big ice silo and next to it a functional office building, which had to contain Gochat's office. The sun shone as bright as ever, there wasn't a breath of air, just a strong smell of fish, seaweed, salt, oil, and rust—the smell of a harbor.

Dupin was intending to head for the office building when out of the corner of his eye he spotted a figure coming out of the auction house and heading toward him with resolute steps. Madame Gochat.

He stopped in his tracks.

She was looking down at the ground.

He waited.

She walked straight past him.

"Madame Gochat!"

The harbor chief started in shock.

"Ah, Monsieur le Commissaire."

They crossed glances.

"I was on my way to see you, madame."

"I'm afraid it's not convenient right now, we're—"

"You asked a fisherman to follow Céline Kerkrom. To watch where she stopped at sea, where she fished. Something that you can imagine makes you look suspicious in our eyes. More so than anyone else up to now. That might be the reason why you were so taciturn during our conversation this morning."

She replied to him promptly, without showing the least sign of annoyance. "I had no motives."

"I'd like to check that out, Madame Gochat."

Just a second of hesitation, then she said: "I like to see things are done properly. That's what I do. It's my job."

"You'll need to explain a bit more to me."

She seemed to be thinking.

"You know Céline Kerkrom fished with small gillnets, but for sea bass and *lieus jaunes,* she mainly used a line. That means she was primarily in three areas: around Ouessant-Grabens, the Pierres Noires to the west of the Molène archipelago, and in the Chaussée de Sein. Never in Douarnenez Bay; in that area you'll find completely different fisherfolk with different boats and different nets. Yet it was right there that I'd seen her with her boat recently, four weeks ago and again three weeks ago." She sounded almost sarcastic.

"And I wanted to know why. That's why I asked one of the fishermen from the bay if he would just keep an eye on her now and then. A harmless request."

"Had you any particular suspicion?"

"No, nothing in particular."

Madame Gochat was saying no more.

"What could possibly have been her reason?"

"I couldn't tell you."

Or wouldn't.

"And how did you happen to see Céline Kerkrom there?"

"My husband has a boat, and every now and then we take it out for an excursion. Usually in the afternoon, when I don't work."

"How big is your husband's boat?"

"Eight meters ninety."

"That'll take you wherever you want."

Anywhere in the *parc.* Or out to the Île de Sein.

The harbormistress gave Dupin a piercing look.

"Do you know about this experiment the *parc* is carrying out with these nets that send out signals to warn dolphins and other creatures?"

"I've heard of it. But only peripherally. It's *parc* business," she said, once again in the deliberately neutral tone of voice Dupin recognized from the morning. "I supported anything that tried to unify professional fishing with ecological and animal welfare."

"Of course"—Dupin affected a ponderous tone—"the *parc* might be seen as your enemy, Madame Gochat? At a time of economic stress, ever more requirements, regulations, restrictions all make things harder."

"You've got it all wrong, Monsieur le Commissaire," she said. "The direction the *parc* is taking is the only one that over the long term is viable for economic survival."

Dupin couldn't be certain whether or not she was having him on. It had sounded as if she was talking from deepest conviction. But it also might all have been a show.

"So you also support controls by other official bodies?"

"We support all official bodies."

Nor did she show any emotion at the use of the word "controls." But that meant nothing. Maybe she knew about the big operation after all. Dupin accepted she could have that much self-control.

She hadn't moved a centimeter. It was an extremely tense conversation.

"I need to get back to my office, Monsieur le Commissaire. They're waiting for me."

"Is there something in particular going on?"

She shook her head.

"Can the auction hall"—Dupin spoke in a way that made it clear he had paid no attention at all to her last sentence—"be held responsible if it sells fish caught by illegal practices? Or if the catch quotas have been disregarded?"

"No, and nor should it be. We have no way of checking where the fish come from. The fishermen just tag them. They are the only ones responsible for their declarations. In any case, there are different regulations outside the *parc* and they may have come from there. Anyway, we've already discussed the fact that the majority of the catch doesn't get sold at the auction. Or the boats go to other harbors outside the *parc*. If you want to put a stop to illegality the fishermen need to be caught in flagrante. The harbors can't do that."

"What were you doing down here in the hall, Madame Gochat?"

"I wanted to see if after the excitement of this morning all had returned to normal."

"I—"

A phone rang.

Dupin took his cell phone from his pants pocket. "Just a minute, please." He took a few steps to one side, toward the water. There was serious irritation written on Madame Gochat's face.

It was Goulch.

"You're not going to believe this," the normally calm Goulch said excitedly. "The first boats they checked were Morin's. They found nothing, not a thing. Not a single red lobster, not even as accidental by-catch. Completely clean, every one of his ships; it's not possible. In comparison they found loads on the ships of two other fishermen, so that means—"

"Morin was forewarned. Somebody tipped him off."

Dupin was finding it hard to keep his voice calm.

"The project leader thinks it's not possible."

"Humbug."

Dupin realized he wasn't exactly keeping calm.

"Should we talk to the other two fishermen?"

"Take their names. That'll do for the moment. Have a chat with the man from the Affaires Maritimes, the one who called me. Tell him there's a leak somewhere."

If only half of what Dupin had heard about Morin's godfather status was true then it was no wonder. Quite the opposite, in fact.

"He'll deny it."

"Anything else, Goulch?"

"Not right now, the operation is still going on. But Morin's boats have got through."

Dupin hung up and went back over to Madame Gochat, who had remained standing exactly on the same spot.

He had lost the thread, but it didn't matter.

"I'm afraid now I have to—" the harbor chief began, but Dupin interrupted.

"There were a few other things you left unmentioned this morning, Madame Gochat."

She looked as if she hadn't a clue what Dupin was talking about.

"Let's take those charges against Morin that actually were successful: criminal jettisoning of caught fish, high-grading the catch so only the most expensive were sold, exceeding the permitted numbers of *ormeaux* mollusks."

"I repeat what I said this morning: so far Monsieur Morin has never been convicted. And I haven't the time to deal with the countless allegations."

"One of his *bolincheurs* is about to get a heavy fine. He's been found with pink gilthead bream."

"I'm afraid that happens now and then. The authorities have to react as swiftly as possible, there's no space for error. The question is whether Morin gave the orders."

There was no way of getting around her.

"And the serious row between Frédéric Carrière and Kerkrom—did that not seem worth mentioning?"

"Have you any idea how long it would take if we talked over every quarrel Céline Kerkrom had with somebody or other? I assumed your question about unusual occurrences was aimed at things of importance?"

She could hardly have been more callous. Everything rolled right off her.

"That'll do for the moment, Madame Gochat." There was no point in carrying on the conversation. Dupin had lost patience. "We'll see each other again. Soon." Even this gruff end to their conversation didn't disconcert Madame Gochat. She feigned a smile and immediately set off, at the same time as Dupin. She headed straight to the entrance of the office block.

Dupin went in the opposite direction. He had to go along the harbor road a bit to where his old Citroën stood.

He was early. He would head to Tréboul, then drive around a

bit, to reflect, pull his thoughts together. The events of the morning had hurtled past.

He pulled out his cell phone and called Nolwenn's number.

"Nolwenn, I'm going to—"

"I just had my phone in my hand to call you. It's like a curse. I simply can't find out anything about Morin's possible paternity." He could hear that she felt as if her honor were at stake. "I'm still sitting here with a scanned copy of Laetitia Darot's birth certificate, issued at the clinic in Douarnenez. It lists the parents, I mean the mother and father, the birth parents, as Francine and Lucas Darot."

"That sounds good."

"It would hardly be the first time that a birth certificate has been forged. It's not all that long ago, but those were different times. Obviously Morin could have had an affair with Francine Darot which had consequences. According to the certificate, Darot's father was forty-two and her mother thirty-seven when their daughter came into the world. They lived just outside of Douarnenez. The mother died two years ago, the father twelve years ago. Also in Douarnenez. I'm trying to find out more about the pair of them. Laetitia Darot had no siblings at the time of her birth, and nothing changed."

Nolwenn was in the best of form despite her apparent despondency at the beginning of the call. It would have taken Dupin longer to find out all that information thirdhand.

By now the commissaire had arrived at his car not far from the famous Connétable sardine factory.

He had wanted to hear something in particular from Nolwenn, which was why he had picked up the phone, but he could no longer remember what it was. It was something that happened to him more often recently, and he would have mentioned it to Docteur Garreg, if he hadn't been too afraid of the treatment he would prescribe.

"What about you, are you still in Lannion?"

It sometimes helped him to remember what it was if he talked about something else until it hit him all of its own.

"We're at my aunt's. Her living room is a fully equipped communications center. An astounding broadband width, superfast network, two computers, high-resolution scanner and printer. Just what is needed for things like this."

"I understand. I'm . . ." Dupin left off asking another question, instead saying, "I'm on my way to see Charles Morin."

"Have you already spoken with Madame Gochat?"

"Just now."

"She seems to lead a tough regime. A typical Douarneniste! The Douarnenez women have a reputation for being strong, busy, and efficient. Breton women in general, but in particular those from Douarnenez. It's a matriarchy," Nolwenn said, a dry statement of fact. "It goes back to the fisherwomen in the nineteenth century who worked in the fish factories. The 'whitebait daughters.' Their men would spend weeks and months at sea and most of the time couldn't support their families, so the women earned the money, did the housework, brought up the children, organized the commune and the town. Everything. '*Rien*' got done without her, she did '*tout.*' Nothing happened without her, and everything that did get done got done thanks to her, that was the Douarnenistes' proud boast. Actually the proud boast of all women!"

Certainly Nolwenn didn't come second to them, and seen like that, there was also a matriarchy in the commissariat.

"You've got to Tréboul a bit too early. I would recommend that you go to the Ty Mad for a coffee, just a stone's throw from Morin's house. It's a remarkably fine hotel and restaurant, with a fabulous terrace. You'll be completely undisturbed there. Max Jacob, Picasso, Dior were all there in the thirties, a place with an extraordinary soul. The Ty Mad is run by a woman too."

A quick *café* absolutely belonged to Dupin's idea of a reflective sit and think, but of course he was aware Nolwenn knew him very well, so he felt a bit caught out.

"See you later then, Nolwenn."

* * *

With the help of his car GPS—a ridiculously minute display that did more to cause confusion than provide orientation—Dupin made it as far as Chapelle Saint-Jean, and left the car there.

A narrow path led from the chapel to the bay with its pristine white sand and bright blue shimmering sea, hemmed in on both sides with spiky rocks. The chapel, the narrow little path, and the old houses seemed as if they had come from ancient times, with prolific vegetation of elegant trees, extravagant shrubbery that cast welcome shade, palm trees with tousled tops. A rare alluring charm. A tiny seaside resort from the end of the nineteenth century, pretty but not overexaggeratedly prettified. The fishermen from here once sailed as far south as Andalusia, Morocco, and Mauretania to catch lobsters, and had called their quarter "*petit* Maroc."

According to the map, Morin's house had to be on the other side of the chapel. A wonderful footpath led by the sea, above the little beach, meandering along the cliffs and by a big cemetery in the direction of Douarnenez's town center. From here too you could see the Île Tristan, barely half a kilometer away. It must have reached high tide because there was no sign of the dark lower part of the cliffs.

Dupin decided to drink his *café* first before walking on. He turned around and walked back to the Ty Mad.

There was rough white gravel on the hidden inner courtyard, which had the atmosphere of a beautiful little garden. On the left was the old stone house, overgrown with vines gone wild, dark shutters; a tall building under the circumstances here, with three floors and an extended roof space.

The terrace was filled with a sea of flowers in different colors, beguiling scents mixed with one another, little rows of tender green bamboo, lacy tall grasses, profligate rhododendron in blinding white, dark green pots with olive trees, tables, chairs, and cozy sun beds all over the garden in the midst of the green.

A magic place.

An oasis.

Pairs of lovers sat at two half-hidden tables, with eyes only for each other.

Dupin chose a table by a high bamboo tree.

He had scarcely sat down when an elegant woman came out of the house, down the stone steps, and directly over to him. Maybe early fifties, of a particular, unique beauty; wild dark locks of hair gathered into a bun from which a few loose strands had strayed; wise, dark, velvety eyes; a singular complexion. Bright pink linen blouse, a deep red skirt, a long string of glass beads of differing sizes.

A smile that came from deep within beamed at him. "Nolwenn said you would be coming."

Nolwenn hadn't mentioned she knew the owner. Only now did Dupin notice she had an espresso cup in her hand, which she set down on the table with a casual gesture.

"Thank you." Dupin was a bit embarrassed. But mostly he was delighted.

"I knew Céline Kerkrom. A little." Her voice was gentle but strong. "Every now and then she would bring us sea bass. Caught by line. Incredible fish. My chef said they were the best. She was an extraordinary woman."

"When was she last here?"

"She brought us some just two weeks ago. We were having a big party. A birthday party. With a special menu."

"Do you know Monsieur Morin, madame? I mean personally." They were, after all, virtually neighbors.

The owner of the Ty Mad took a chair and sat back, all quite casually.

"There are people who unbalance the world. People who damage it, poison it." She was thinking it aloud to herself, calmly. "I've never consciously had anything to do with him. I've always avoided him."

Dupin downed his *café* in a few small sips. It was strong and gave off an irresistible aroma.

"The Morin family has tyrannized the bay for generations. The whole region. They're domineering types, always have been. Morin's father was a judge, renowned for his toughness. The Île Tristan belonged to them once upon a time. The mid-twentieth century. Before it was taken by a poet, and then bought by the state. Do you know the island?"

"Just the bit in front of the pier, the building belonging to the Parc Iroise."

"The island has two faces. If you see it in beautiful sunshine like today, you're looking at the bright side. That's the aura projected by the lovers in their graves," the Ty Mad's owner told him without the slightest hint of the dramatic. "But there is another side too. In the sixteenth century the island was a bastion of a gory pirate and warlord." That had to be the bogeyman Nolwenn told him about now and again. "Guy Éder de La Fontenelle, 'the Wolf.'" She held a long pause but it didn't seem to be for effect. "The Wolf turned a small band of thieves and thugs into a garrison of nearly a thousand warlike men, with whom he terrorized the region under the guise of religious war. They massacred thousands of people, peaceful farmers, fishermen, everyday town and country dwellers, and laid waste to whole strips of land. They raged like storms of destruction; in Douarnenez the Wolf forced the citizens to tear down their own houses to give him the stone to build his fortress on the island, then he had them executed." She pushed strands of hair from her face. "He built a huge fortune from his robberies, primarily gold. He was obsessed with gold and piled it up in hidden caves across the island, where it still lies today. Somewhere out in the western cliffs, near the half-collapsed pier where the grottos are, that's the entrance. Before long there was so much gold that he had to hide it in other caves the length of the bay." She gave Dupin an inscrutable look. "People here remember everything. They make no distinction between yesterday and today."

Dupin was aware of that. It was a basic trait of Brittany and its people. That was the way things were, and you had to know that.

He wiped a few beads of sweat from his forehead. The heat had become unbearable.

"There's a tiny place beyond Tréboul where the locals still talk about the landing of Viking ships as if it were just something that happened last week. They claim they can tell you the exact site of the Viking Thingstead, their parliament. A few years ago a team of archaeologists searched the area and indeed found the Thingstead. There were lots of remains, and exactly on the site they had indi-cated. People pass these things on from one generation to the next; a thousand years is nothing, just a chain of twenty or thirty human lives. It's the same with the Wolf. There are locals who can tell you everything about him, what routes he used to get to the island, who his lovers were. Everything."

Dupin believed every word.

"And these treasures"—the question had fallen off his tongue, and now she seemed somewhat unfriendly toward him—"do people look for the treasure?"

"People are always looking for it," she said, sounding disdainful. "People will do anything to get rich. They would commit any murder."

It was tragic but true.

"From time to time this darkness visits the island. But believe me, it doesn't turn off the island's light."

The sentence had barely faded away when Dupin's cell phone rang.

"I'm sorry, madame, I have to take this."

"Please, go ahead."

Dupin pulled the phone out of his jacket pocket.

An unfamiliar number.

"Dupin. Who is this?"

"Antoine Manet here. Jumeau was just here. He admitted to me that he had a relationship, a relationship with both women. Al-though loosely. One after another, sort of. Maybe not quite after one another. I can't be certain."

Dupin's attention had already been grabbed by the first sentence. He had to pull himself together not to speak too loudly.

"With both? A relationship with both women? For how long?"

"If I understand correctly, that with Céline had already ended, but in March they . . . 'saw' each other again. By then he had already started up with Laetitia Darot. But it was very relaxed. He only met up with her three times, so he said."

The impact of this information was immense.

"That makes Jumeau our most prominent suspect."

"I know." There was clear resignation in Manet's words. "I told him I would inform you. And that you yourself would want to speak to him. He accepted that with a shrug of his shoulder. On both counts."

"Why had he not already told my inspector?"

"He needed time to think if he ought to tell anybody at all."

"Did he mention any quarrels, or allegations? Jealousy?"

"He and Céline split up amiably, and remained friends as they had been before. And Darot knew all about it. Even the subsequent time. There hadn't been any problems. For any of them, so he said."

Sort of a ménage à trois. It was the first time there had been anything that complicated.

"Was he nervous when he spoke to you?"

"Jumeau's never nervous."

"Tell him a police boat will come to collect him."

"I will."

"He's to stay at home. I'll let my inspector know."

"Fine."

Antoine Manet hung up faster than Dupin.

The hotel owner had sat there fascinated throughout the phone call, without letting him know she had been listening to the whole conversation.

She put her head to one side and looked Dupin straight in the eye. "I'm holding you up, you need to get on. I do too. I have to pick up my two daughters from the airport, they're staying all summer, two months." She beamed warmly; the dark stories she had just been relating now seemed unimaginably distant. "The season is starting, my daughters will help me, along with my best friend. Come for dinner next time. You'll enjoy it."

Dupin had already spotted the dining room, a cast-iron annex in Art Deco style. It would be magnificent sitting in there, staring out at the blue of the Atlantic through the greenery of the garden. Claire would love it.

"I'll do that."

The Ty Mad's owner stood up, turned around, and a moment later was gone. Dupin hadn't heard her light feet on the gravel.

He sat there a while longer.

Then he called Riwal's number.

"Boss?"

"Fetch Jumeau in one of the speedboats." Dupin told him about Manet's call. "I want to see him. Make it . . ." Dupin thought for a minute, ". . . at the Ty Mad in Tréboul." Why not? A quieter place would be hard to find. "I've spotted a little jetty, not far from the Chapelle Saint-Jean. You can dock there."

Apart from that, it would save wasting time driving.

"Are you in the Ty Mad now, boss?"

"I'm on the way to see Morin."

"Aha. Apart from that . . ." Riwal dithered a bit and then added, "Apart from that, all's well with you?"

It took a minute for Dupin to understand. "I'm fine. In the best of form. And I think it was actually just four graves I saw that first time. I was just a bit tired. There's not the slightest reason to worry."

He was going to have to ditch this idea once and for all.

"Okay, boss." Riwal sounded far from convinced.

* * *

On the way to Morin's, Dupin still worried over the spectacular news of Jumeau's multiple affairs. That, and the growing barrage of events, and his interviews. Dupin wasn't making any assumptions.

He was in the midst of the confusing whirl of events, and confused by them himself. His thoughts were bouncing endlessly from one thing to another. What he needed more than anything else was some distance. But obviously this stroll was much too short even to get a bit of distance. He was outside Morin's house in the wink of an eye.

A belle époque villa, visible from afar. A relic of the glittering era of the aristocracy. Nothing swanky. Rather discreet nobility. An elegant narrow house built of interlaced L-shaped red stone, the obligatory steep roof in natural slate, unostentatiously laid. Ornamental dark brown brickwork around the numerous windows, on the first floor a balcony full of ornaments from which there had to be a superb view of the bay. The most notable thing was a weathered rosebush in a winter garden built of elaborate woodwork. In front of the balcony was a single tall palm tree, and apart from that a few ancient, overgrown pines on a deep green lawn. Everything looked well cared for, none of it overly extravagant.

Dupin had to walk around the extensive grounds enclosed by a wall and with a cast-metal gate on the side away from the sea. A black Volvo SUV stood in the entrance. There was no name on the bell, one of those old-fashioned black buttons on a convex gleaming steel plate.

Dupin pushed the button. Once. Then once again, quickly one after the other.

It didn't take long for the gate to open. Almost immediately a man appeared through the heavy wooden door of the house.

Dupin waited for him to speak first.

"How are your investigations going, Commissaire? Have you brought anything new to light?"

That same tone of voice that Dupin already knew from the phone: paternal, considerate, but pressing at the same time. Once again Morin didn't waste time with pleasantries but cut straight to the chase.

"Tell me what I can do to help you. You know it's a matter of deep concern to me."

"You could help me by telling the truth."

Morin had come a few paces toward Dupin, but now that Dupin had reached him, he nodded briefly, turned about-face, and headed back toward the door of his villa.

He cut a robust, stocky, burly figure, a singularly strong neck sticking out of a white shirt with vertical beige stripes, dark cloth pants, and black suspenders. Black hair, two bushy eyebrows, and pushed up onto his hair a pair of dark sunglasses which, like everything else he was wearing, looked as if they had cost no more than a few euros. The fine features of his face were a complete contrast to his otherwise coarse appearance.

"You must know that I have more than a few contacts, not unimportant ones. I know what levers need to be pulled and where in order to get information or anything else. I know the ways and means. We should be working together, Commissaire."

The way Morin pronounced those sentences was supposed to appear not so much a threat as an offer of cooperation.

"Somebody warned you about the control operation today, monsieur. Your boats had been informed." Dupin had spoken without any hint of implication; calmly, almost deliberately.

Morin showed not the slightest reaction. Rather he held the door open for Dupin and led him down a long hallway into a bright, spacious living room, decorated—or so it seemed—in the style of the same era as the building. Exquisite furniture, a glossily polished dark brown table with curved legs, modest but ornately decorated high-backed chairs. There was the smell of beeswax, dust, and mothballs, an idiosyncratic scent that Dupin recognized from long ago, from the grandiose house of his Parisian grandparents, who ended up only using the lowest floors. Morin was unlikely to spend much time here. Even now it seemed they were alone in the house.

Morin steered them to two deep armchairs directly in front of a window with a superb view: the deep blue of the sea with a bright sparkling surface. He sat down and waited for Dupin to do likewise.

"It's a joke, the effort, the expense—childishness."

There was no malice in what he said. He had made the statements simply facts. That it was taken for granted he had known about the operation. It meant nothing to him.

"I want to know who killed Laetitia Darot."

For the first time there was a hardness evident in Morin's expression.

"She could have been a witness to your numerous illegal activities in the *parc*. You wanted to get rid of her. Perhaps she had also got together with Céline Kerkrom to systematically monitor you and your boats."

"I'm not going to answer that, Commissaire."

"Eventually, Monsieur Morin, eventually, we'll find out everything. Nothing will be left in the dark. I can assure you of that."

Dupin had made a point of leaning back in his armchair as he said that, not letting his eyes leave Morin for a second. His face showed nothing more than a calm aplomb.

"We *know* . . ." Dupin let a few seconds pass; he obviously had to try it once more: "We know that she was your daughter."

This time too, Morin showed not the slightest trace of reaction.

"I've heard that the two women were friends. And that they were working on a research project together. Other fisherfolk were involved too. I know them."

Morin had his contacts, obviously. That was no surprise. Dupin would be damned if he'd engage him on the topic.

"Your trawlers' dragnets and drift nets kill hundreds, thousands of the animals your daughter dedicated her life to. The animals she fought to protect."

Morin's eyes had drifted over to the window. He was silent.

"We know about the bream you let your men catch despite the strong regulations, the large numbers you throw back, the *ormeaux*. We also know your boats fish for red lobster, even though they weren't caught with any today. That you use forbidden nets and fishing methods on a large scale. We know about all of it."

There was no point in going through it all in detail, and in any case it was probably only a small part of what went on, but Dupin felt the need to do it.

"As I said, laughable. But that's not the issue, Commissaire. I've been listening. You're a reasonable man, a clever man. At least I hope so. I hope so very much."

He was still staring into the distance.

"Where were you yesterday evening, Monsieur Morin? Early yesterday evening."

"Is this really necessary?"

"It is."

Morin groaned. "Around seven thirty P.M. I was at home. In Morgat. My wife and I had eaten, we chatted, watched television, and about ten thirty P.M. we went to bed. I had a meeting with my fishermen this morning at ten."

Calmly Dupin fumbled his red Clairefontaine out of his pocket and opened it to the page with his list of persons.

"With Frédéric Carrière, I believe. Where did you meet?"

Morin remained unimpressed. "Here, in Douarnenez, by the harbor."

It would have been no problem for Morin to have been in the auction halls yesterday evening and on the Île de Sein this morning. It was a trivial thing, but that was how it was. And the more complicated and tricky a case was, the more important it was to know the simple things. The banal facts.

"In other words, you have no alibi of any kind, Monsieur Morin?"

"Perhaps we shouldn't talk about me, but about what the two dead women had to do with one another, hmm?" Morin's forehead had developed deep creases. "They were both seen together at the entrance to Douarnenez Bay, on Laetitia Darot's boat. And also on Céline Kerkrom's."

"We know that." Dupin had immediately reacted. It wasn't true. They hadn't known that. It was an interesting piece of news, but it could probably be explained by the project with the specially equipped nets.

"Why were they together on one boat? What were they doing?" Morin was speaking quietly and not necessarily directed at the commissaire.

"Perhaps testing the special nets which give off a signal; a real thorn in your side, I imagine. It must cause you a lot of expense."

"I've already checked out all the fisherfolk involved in the project. There's nothing in that. You can save your time, Commissaire."

Morin kept going. And it wasn't Dupin's idea. He was doing it of his own will.

"Madame Gochat," he continued calmly, "was having Céline Kerkrom watched. Here again we have to ask 'why?' And the boat of that hippie-pirate Vaillant has been seen a few times not far from Laetitia Darot's boat. The devil knows what he had to do in the entrance to Douarnenez Bay."

It was uncanny. And depressing. Yet again Dupin would have loved to have known how Morin knew all this—and above all, if he knew more. He didn't ask.

"And he was on Sein last night, of all places." Morin gave a grim look.

Dupin didn't react, even though he found it difficult.

"So far you've always gotten away with things. But nobody has that much luck forever."

A curiously calm smile played around Morin's lips. He tried to catch Dupin's eye. Then he leaned back in his armchair. Relaxed. Master of the situation.

"Young people don't understand the big world yet. They are necessarily naïve. I was too at that age. The world is complicated. Life is complicated. They think it is simple."

He wasn't impressing Dupin at all.

"Complexity is one of the most frequent excuses, especially for oneself," the commissaire replied.

"You should accept my help, Commissaire. We should exchange information and work together."

"You're one of the suspects, Monsieur Morin. And high up the list." Dupin's voice was surly.

It wasn't a problem for Morin to put the gentle smile back on his face. "Commissaire, our world has rules of its own. Apparently not everybody adheres to them." Morin got up slowly. "But I'll deal with that, I promise you. And if not with you, then on my own."

He was on his feet. The conversation was at an end.

Dupin stood up too. Unhurriedly.

"*Au revoir,* Monsieur Morin."

Dupin set off and it was not long before he found himself on the coastal path. The silvery glitter of the bay through the villa window was no more than a cheap shadow of the unending sparkle out here.

* * *

"Jumeau insisted on coming in his own boat. Two officers are with him."

It was unorthodox, but why not? Dupin was, after all, the embodiment of unorthodox procedure. He wouldn't criticize Riwal's decision.

"He should be here any minute, our colleagues have just called in."

"Okay." Dupin would be there in a few minutes; he could see the chapel, but he hesitated. "Let's do this differently, Riwal. I'll meet Jumeau on his boat, not in the Ty Mad. I'll head to the quay."

"I . . . okay, that works too, I'll tell them . . . By the way, we can scrub Thomas Roiyou, the oil boat captain, from our list. Two fishing boats saw him coming out of the long harbor neck at Audierne a few minutes after six P.M. He still had to go by the auction hall; his little oil depot lies beyond it."

"I understand."

It was almost a shame. They might at least have let him stew a bit longer, Dupin thought.

"One more thing, Riwal. Ask Nolwenn to organize a meeting

with this Vaillant. This evening." Just to be safe, he quickly added, "Somewhere here on the mainland."

"Consider it done."

Dupin had reached the chapel, on his left the little beach that suggested the Mediterranean.

Something had occurred to him. Something important.

He looked for the numbers Nolwenn had sent him, and found what he was looking for.

"Hello? Monsieur Leblanc? Commissaire Dupin here."

Maybe the scientist could make sense of it.

"One second."

He could hear dull thuds.

"I was just in the technical area. I'm yours now. All ears."

"Laetitia Darot and Céline Kerkrom stayed a while in Darot's boat at the entrance to Douarnenez Bay. Was that one of Darot's areas? What could they have been up to there?"

It was clear to Dupin that there were two questions: Why were the two women on one boat? And: Why had they stopped there, there in particular? What were they doing in that area? If he wasn't mistaken, it wasn't one of their usual sites.

"Really, in the bay?"

"In the mouth of the bay, yes. You said Darot's dolphins lived near Sein, Molène, and Ouessant, right?"

"Recently? That was recently?"

"In the last few weeks, yes."

"What obviously occurs to me is the round-headed dolphins. They follow the cephalopods and mollusks: squid, octopuses, their preferred food. In summer these retreat into the rocky coastal areas of the bay, and the dolphins follow them. I know Darot watched them last summer. This year she didn't mention it, but that means nothing."

Dupin thought he remembered Riwal mentioning round-headed dolphins that morning, but so far nobody else had.

"Are they rare?"

"They're only around our area in the summer. The round-headed dolphins grow to about four meters. A few examples can weigh up to six hundred and fifty kilos. They have a bulky forehead that falls away vertically, a broad, short snout, a sickle-shaped fin, and—"

"Could there be something politically charged about these dolphins?" Dupin interrupted him.

"I don't know. All I know is Laetitia watched them for several weeks last summer. Their arrival is always something special."

"Thank you, Monsieur Leblanc." The curved path down to the sea was fringed with several tall pines. To the right was the cemetery behind an old wall. To the left the Île Tristan. It looked as if you could be there in just one long jump.

Dupin could already see the pier. And at the end of the pier a boat was just docking.

Snow white, a bright blue stern, rounded off at the front, a paprika red edging all around. The bridge was glazed from waist height and had orange-and-yellow-painted sides, on its roof the usual antennas and transmitters. Dupin reckoned the boat was about eight or nine meters long. In the bow there was a big red box, two pink buoys, and a tower of plastic boxes.

Dupin reached the pier. Even though the tide was still high, there were at least two meters between the pier and the waterline.

He could now make out two policemen on board and a slim young man with collar-length hair. A black sweatshirt and bright yellow oilskin bib overalls. That had to be Jumeau.

Dupin headed for the rusty narrow ladder at the end of the pier, the same as there were everywhere along the coast. The two policemen noticed the commissaire and waved to him; Jumeau just gave him a fleeting glance.

Clambering down the ladder was a dicey business, and Dupin sighed when he reached the bottom.

"Everything go normally?" Dupin asked, and pushed himself past his two colleagues standing between the buoys and boxes. Jumeau hadn't thought it necessary to come to the bow.

"All okay."

When Dupin had made his way around the bridge, Jumeau was busy emptying two boxes by the side, as if he'd come here to work. Then he stood with his back to the railing, leaning on his elbows. A casual pose.

"One of the two women will have been jealous. Probably both," Dupin said without skipping a beat.

"It was just small stuff. Nothing more." He had almost shrugged his shoulders, or at least it looked like that. But it was clear Jumeau didn't mean it disparagingly.

"Occasionally we spent the night together. Mostly not even the whole night, just a few hours."

Dupin eyed him.

"I liked them a lot. Both." His eyes moistened.

He was undoubtedly a good-looking guy. A handsome face, if a bit lean; harmonious features, gentle, mild, boyish, with melancholy dark green eyes. Wiry, slender fingers and hands.

"Was there an argument? Between you and the women? Between Kerkrom and Darot?"

"Never."

Hard to believe.

"It all just sort of happened of its own accord, en passant."

"Did you tell them? That you were also having—a relationship— with the other?"

"They both knew, yes. The thing with Céline was over sooner, back in March, actually."

"Did you prefer one? Laetitia?"

It took him a while to answer.

"Maybe, yes." He suddenly seemed terribly sad.

"You know that this 'small stuff' has made you a prime suspect?"

His eyebrows rose slightly.

"Your . . . meetings with Laetitia Darot, when did they start?"

Jumeau blinked and for the first time looked directly at the commissaire. "In March. Then we saw one another a few weeks later. And last night."

Dupin pricked up his ears. Unbelievable. Manet had said nothing about that.

"Last night? You were together with Laetitia Darot last night?"

"Yes."

"The night before she was murdered?"

A barely noticeable nod.

"From when until when?"

"From eleven until twelve, more or less."

"That was just a few hours before her death."

He said nothing.

"Where did you meet? At your place?"

"Hers."

"And then—where did you go afterward?"

"Home. To sleep."

"And did anyone see you by chance, on your way home?"

"I don't think so."

"Did you mention to anyone the next morning you had met? Give a hint?"

"Not a word."

"Did she seem different to you last night? In any way? Did anything strike you?"

"She was the same as always."

It was exhausting. He had to drag every word out of the fisherman. Dupin stood next to Jumeau. Stared at the water. Across the bay. Followed with his eyes a boat sailing leisurely toward the Île Tristan.

"Last night, prior to eleven o'clock, what were you doing?"

"I was at home, alone."

"Before that you were in Le Tatoon."

"Yes."

Seen objectively, Jumeau hadn't a trace of an alibi. He could easily also have gone to Douarnenez.

"I went out again." It was the first time that Jumeau had begun to speak of his own accord. "I couldn't sleep. I bumped into Laetitia by chance. At her shed. We hadn't arranged anything."

Dupin paid keen attention. "What was she doing at her shed?"

"I've no idea. She was standing by the door."

"Did she have anything with her?"

"No."

"When you were in her house, did you see her laptop?"

"No."

"But you have seen one at her place?"

Jumeau looked as if he was thinking hard. "On the table in the living room."

"Not last night?"

"We weren't in the living room."

Dupin sighed audibly. "Did she tell you anything about her work? About her project?"

"She told me a lot about the dolphins."

"Including the dead dolphins over the past few weeks?"

"She was so furious."

That was almost certainly the right word.

"But she didn't talk about it much. She didn't want to."

"Did she have a theory, about how they were killed? And by whom?"

"She hated the whole industrial fishing industry."

"Did she say that?"

"Yes."

"Did she link Charles Morin to the dead dolphins?"

"No, she never mentioned Morin. But of course he has countless dolphins on his conscience."

Dupin walked over to the railing opposite. Jumeau appeared to take no notice. The view from there was the yacht harbor.

"What do you think? Is Morin her father?"

"A father isn't a father, just because he's a child's biological parent." For a moment it was clear Jumeau was internally agitated.

"Was he her father?"

"I don't know."

There was no point to this.

"Was she preoccupied by anything? Did she seem worked up? Was there anything unusual?"

"No." He was looking at Dupin, but at the same time seemed to be looking through him. "She was the same as always."

"What did she talk to you about yesterday?"

"She told me about some dolphins getting high."

"High!"

"How a group of young dolphins were getting high on the poison from a blowfish. They were inhaling it like a joint. One after another would take the fish in their mouth and squeeze it gently so that the fish exhaled its poison in tiny doses. They were all completely high, doing the craziest tricks, backflips and so on."

The anecdote was too weird.

"Did she tell you about the project with the signal emitters on the nets?"

"I saw the net once down at the harbor. She had mentioned it when we met up three weeks ago. Saying that all the fishing boats in the world should be immediately equipped with them, that the small-scale fisherfolk can't afford them and that the big ones don't give a shit about them."

"Anything else?"

"No."

"Not even—"

The penetrating ring of Dupin's cell phone interrupted the sentence.

"Riwal, I'll call you right back, I'm—"

"Boss, we've—" The inspector was hard to understand, his voice weak. "We've—" He stumbled again. "We've got another murder. Yet another throat cut."

Dupin froze.

"On the Crozon peninsula. Lostmarc'h Beach. The craggy tail

that hangs into Douarnenez Bay." Riwal gradually pulled himself together. "On the other side of Morgat, a totally isolated—"

"Who is it?"

Dupin pushed his way past the bridge and ran into the foremost part of the bow.

Anxiety showed in the eyes of the two policemen who had come with Jumeau. Dupin had almost shouted at them.

"A professor emeritus, seventy-five, living alone, he—"

"An old professor?"

"A Parisian like you. Similarly been here in Brittany about five years. Has a house across the beach. A neighbor found him, when she was out with her dog. On one of the dunes. She knew him. An extraordinarily well-read man, she said, he—"

"His throat cut?"

"That's how the police there described it."

"Who's there?"

"Four police from Crozon. I know two of them. Good men."

It was hair-raising. Insane.

"I'm heading there right away. We can meet at the scene. Kadeg needs to come, you too . . ." Dupin thought for a moment. "Then again, no. You stay on the Île de Sein, Riwal. Kadeg needs to drop everything. I'll call Nolwenn."

The case had taken on serious proportions. Completely unaffected by their investigation. Now there were three. Three murders within less than twenty-four hours. That was going to cause giant waves.

"Boss, do you think now we're dealing with a serial killer?"

"No, that's not what I think."

"I know we're only a tiny blip in the statistics. But they exist even so. Think back to the serial killer we had last year in Normandy. Nobody had thought that possible either."

"It remains distinctly unlikely, Riwal."

His conviction was less than convincing, he realized.

"We have spent the whole day tracking down the corpses the killer left for us to find."

The conversation was crazy.

"What was the professor's subject?'

"Virology. Professor Philippe Lapointe."

"A physician?"

"Virology falls into the divide between medicine and biology."

"We need to find out the time of death as quickly as possible."

Obviously what Riwal had said was true. The killer was doing a proper tour. Douarnenez yesterday evening. The Île de Sein this morning and—maybe, probably—the Crozon peninsula afterward. And there was another thing: mixing the two earlier victims with this murder was curious, at least at first glance. A young fisherwoman, a dolphin researcher—between whom there were however several things in common and certain overlaps—and now a retired Parisian professor of virology. What could link them?

"The pathologist is on the way. The same as on Sein this morning."

"Do we know anything about the professor's contacts?"

"So far all we've had is the agitated call from his neighbor to the gendarmerie. And the few bits of information I've just given you."

"See you later, Riwal."

Dupin put his cell phone in his pants pocket.

The two other policemen had stared at him continuously.

"Tell Jumeau I'll contact him again."

Dupin was already at the rusty ladder.

On the almost one-hour trip around the wide bay, and despite the car's breakneck speed, the commissaire had managed to speak three times on the phone to Nolwenn.

She had never heard the dead man's name but she was already researching it as they spoke, and very shortly had gathered a pile of information. Professor Philippe Lapointe was a virologist and immunologist, and clearly had a substantial national and international reputation, had recently studied at the Paris Université Descartes's Institute for Molecular Virology. For years, however, there had been no new publications. It seemed he really was in retirement;

the list of previous publications took up several pages. There was nothing about him personally except for the fact that he had turned seventy-five in March; the other data only related to his scientific work. By her third call—it seemed she was still sitting in her aunt's "head office"—she had turned up an assistant from the former Paris faculty who was going to try to find other information for her.

Between Dupin's first and second calls, Nolwenn had spoken on the phone to the prefect, who had let "his" commissaire know that they had "both been assigned to very important business." That of course he was involved in the investigation, even from afar, and that he had full confidence in their "so thoroughly successful investigative work so far."

Meanwhile Nolwenn was on the tail of Laetitia Darot's mother's neighbors, friends, and acquaintances. So far in vain. But it was still of importance.

Goulch had tried to get through to Dupin but ended up talking to Nolwenn. He had checked out the fisherfolk who were involved in the net project. They had all only tried out the net a few times. The people they dealt with were the technical department at the *parc,* not Laetitia Darot. There was no indication of any communication between them, not anything that would make any of them in any way suspicious: Goulch had come to the same conclusion as Morin.

Dupin had made it—strictly following his GPS—down bumpy roads as far as the lonely high cape. The last part of the route had been an unpaved, dusty track. Potholes, large stones, and deep sand tracks alternated. The rocking back and forth of the car reminded Dupin of the ferry that morning. The path came to an abrupt end before meter-high brambles. Not so much a parking place as a dead end, with just a glimpse of the bay here and there. It couldn't be far to the beach. Dupin hadn't seen a car anywhere, so there had to be another way here, probably from the north, from the village.

He left his car where it was.

He battled his way down a steep path through a jungle of thorny blackberry bushes. Suddenly, completely unexpectedly, they opened up to reveal a breathtaking view.

Only moments ago, in Tréboul, he had found himself in a gentle Mediterranean dream of a bay with babbling turquoise water and a couple of decorative rocks. Now he was on top of a great cliff hemmed in on all sides by wild beaches stretching for kilometers, reminiscent of northwest Scotland or Ireland. On both sides the craggy landscape stretched endlessly, deep bright green on the hills. Overwhelming. There before his eyes, his ears, he could feel it, smell it: the wide-open Atlantic, crashing tumultuously against the beach. The tossing, whipping winds, the torrents of water coming together crossing thousands of kilometers to crash onto the land. The old continent. The Atlantic with all its power, its forces, its size. The ancient feel of Brittany—it was in places like this that you really felt it. Dupin always thought it had to be at a place like this that a Roman had once stood and determined: this is where it ends, here it is, the end of the world.

Back in Douarnenez, there hadn't been even the slightest breeze. But here there was a strong wind blowing incessantly, as always bringing the sea surf with it. Nowhere, Dupin thought, did the Atlantic smell as good, as wide, and as free as in this wind from the sea. No sooner did the spray hit your face than you could taste it.

Here even on the calmest, most beautiful days there were still waves: real waves. Long, calm, stately waves. A meter high.

Even the sun and the sky were different, more ancient, like at the beginning of the world. You had the impression of having been traveling for days, so distant did this landscape seem in comparison to Tréboul.

He could see a group of people at the end of the beach, looking tiny and lost, down there where the beach turned into long, extenuated dunes, thickening as they moved inland.

Dupin headed down at a swift pace toward the beach, which

looked even bigger when you were down there, and trod through the heavy sand.

Kadeg, who must have parked in a better place than he had—he couldn't have driven any faster—spotted him and headed toward him.

"Brutal. Same stab wound. An ice-cold killer." Kadeg loved pithy utterances that could have come from a dramatic movie script.

"Is the pathologist there yet?" Dupin had made out eight people.

"Yes."

"Did she mention anything about the time of death?"

"She only arrived just before me. She would have done better to have parked here at the northern end of the bar, as—"

"And the woman who found him?

"She's gone back home."

"His neighbor?"

"Exactly."

Dupin thought for a moment whether he ought to have her fetched. But he wanted to go to the village anyway shortly. To take a look at the professor's house.

"How big is the place?"

"Ten, fifteen houses, no more. We've already been through everything down here." Kadeg gave the impression he'd done it all himself, even if it had to have been their colleagues from Crozon or Morgat. "We found nothing. Nor did the crime scene team. Nothing around the body on the dune and nothing on the path leading down here. It must have happened in the shifting dune sand. There are only vague footprints to be seen, barely imprints, two people most probably."

They had almost reached the group. Dupin greeted them all round.

"Kadeg, take the officers here and knock on all the doors up there. I want to know everything anybody has to say about the professor. Whom he had contact with, how he passed his days. Everything."

"Shouldn't I wait here until—"

"Immediately, I want you to start asking questions straightaway. I'm coming up too, shortly." That way he could prevent the unnecessary gathering of people here at the scene.

Kadeg turned away with a childishly sulky face and made a snappy gesture to the police. They hurried toward him. Together they plodded up the dune. Only one of them stayed behind.

"We'll go into the professor's house together," Dupin called out loud enough for Kadeg and his people definitely to hear him. "Nobody's to set a foot inside before I get there."

Dupin walked the last few meters to the corpse.

It was a gruesome sight.

Philippe Lapointe lay on his back. Unlike in the case of Laetitia Darot, a large quantity of blood had spread all over the body. Into his bright blue sweater, which was saturated with it, and beneath his clothing as far as his jeans. A lot of blood. His head was brutally bent backward, down into the soft sand. Probably the professor in his agony had used his last ounce of strength to try to snatch a gasp of air. It was easy to see the intense agony that this death had involved. The eyes were wide open, staring emptily at the sky. The arms were curiously fixed by his side, almost straight; his legs, on the contrary, were at crazy angles.

The virologist was of average height, neither fat nor thin. A distinguished face, even when so ferociously distorted; narrow lips; thick white hair, cut short; a notable high forehead.

Dupin was standing directly in front of the corpse, just a few centimeters from the black sneakers the deceased was wearing.

"Body temperature twenty-eight degrees." A pleasant voice. Dupin turned around to find a young woman in her late thirties standing next to him, her light blond hair in a ponytail, no makeup. He had only caught sight of her out of the corner of his eye; she'd been standing with her back to him, busying herself with a silver case. "Given the pleasant temperature today, the body will have lost about one degree per hour. That suggests ten hours. Plus or minus an hour." She said it as a matter of routine, but in a tone that reflected the seriousness of the situation. "The pupil test confirms that. His pupils hardly reacted to eyedrops, but still just noticeably, which also suggests about eight hours. And my gut feeling says the same." The pathologist sounded detached, as if looking back over innumerable corpses she had seen in her professional life.

"Good." Dupin was satisfied. "That's a great help. It fits exactly with our scenario." It sounded accidentally comic. It already appeared that the killer had come here from the Île de Sein more or less directly, without much of a detour. Either he had come from the Île de Sein to the mainland directly with his boat, and then here in a car, or come here directly in the boat.

"We're dealing with a hardworking killer here." She gave a grim smile.

"You think it can be one and the same person?"

"Just looking at the cut here I would say at first glance it's perfectly possible. But I'll have to check that out in the lab. Compare the wounds. By the way, we've found nothing else unusual in the case of the dolphin researcher."

"Do you see anything out of the usual here?"

"There's a hematoma on the right wrist. Maybe the killer overcame him and held him tight. He certainly couldn't have put up much resistance."

"Do you think it happened right here?"

"He would have collapsed straightaway. Yes."

That too seemed to be part of the killer's modus operandi. He met his victims in lonely places, murdered them there on the spot, and left the bodies where they were, without moving them. Everything was thought out thoroughly. According to a precise plan. As far as Darot and the professor were concerned, the killer must have made an arrangement to meet them. He couldn't have lain in wait for them, that would have been far too unreliable. That was also true for Céline Kerkrom, actually: she needed to have had a reason to come to the out-of-the-way room with the waste barrels. The perp had known the places he had chosen. And known them well. The whole area.

"Did the professor have anything in his pants pocket? A cell phone?"

"Nothing. We're taking the body with us now. I'm calling the van, so it'll take a while. It can only get here from the other end of the bay."

"Thanks." Dupin smiled. The pathologist returned his smile with a friendly, professional glance. "And let me know if anything occurs to you."

"I'll do that." She took a phone from her bag and stood to one side.

Dupin made a gesture to the uniformed policeman who had stayed behind, an impressively portly man with a head round as a ball, who had been following everything attentively. "You stay here and mark the spot where the body lay. Clearly."

"Consider it done."

Dupin took a look around.

Although the land rose only gently toward the interior of the peninsula, at the edge of the beach, high cliffs rose with dangerous overhangs. Dupin found himself staring at them, and the policeman noticed.

"There's a Celtic defensive structure up there, where the Gauls fled to from the Romans."

Dupin sighed gently.

There was nowhere without stories and history. No single place where something important hadn't happened. That was Brittany for you.

He moved toward a narrow footpath he had noticed amidst the dunes.

The policeman had noticed that too.

"The path is the best way to the village, Monsieur le Commissaire."

This man wouldn't miss anything down here at the crime scene; he was undoubtedly the right man to keep watch.

Dupin set off.

* * *

"Madame Lapointe, yes, I've already spoken on the phone to her. She lives in Paris. In the Marais district. They separated fifteen years ago, been divorced for twelve."

Nolwenn had been working hard. Her idea about the assistant at the institute had been spot-on, and she had come across Philippe Lapointe's ex-wife.

"They parted on good terms. No intrigue. They even saw one another occasionally. They went out for dinner. But not for the last year. She was taken aback by the news."

"Had he still been doing any work? Had anything to do with the faculty? In any way at all?"

The path up to the village was longer than Dupin had imagined. It was only now that he saw the first houses. From here on, the road was paved. There were four police cars by the side of the road and he recognized Kadeg's.

The rough harshness of the Atlantic reached up here, limiting the vegetation to bare bushes, shrubs, grasses, moss, heathland. Nothing soft and pretty up here. In stormy weather the spray would swirl through Lostmarc'h, as if the hamlet were only a few meters from the sea.

"She couldn't say. She didn't know what he'd being doing in his 'exile,' as she called it, indeed if he still had anything at all to do with his research, as he had no laboratory anymore. He spent a lot more time reading, she reckoned, having taken his entire library with him to Brittany: the great literary and philosophic classics. That was his great hobby."

That was only of peripheral interest to Dupin. They needed to find out how Lapointe spent his time. Dupin had already been thinking about that in the car. Had the great virologist, biologist, physician, come across something unusual in the *parc* somewhere along the coast? Had he got wind of something he realized was a disaster? Something that only he would have noticed. These were all hazy thoughts. But all the same, there had to be some connection to the two women, a decisive—even fatal—link. What could be the story in which these three people could have played a role? Each on their own or the three of them together, knowingly or unknowingly? Up until now they had no more than a few loose threads, or not even that, a few themes that could link them: the fishing industry, possible offenses, illegal practice, the dead dolphins, water pollution, smuggling, intertwined topics, a suspicious family relationship, including a possible highly complicated paternity. But none of those themes were really urgent. They might also even be totally irrelevant, all of them leading in the wrong direction. And the one thing that hadn't even stirred so far was Dupin's nose, his scent of a trail. The one thing he had always relied on in messy situations. Like this.

"Was he in a new relationship?"

"She didn't know that either. She herself had got remarried." It sounded like *and just right, too.*

"Does she know if he had friends here in Brittany?"

"His best friend died two years ago. They had talked about that the last time they met up. He hadn't mentioned any new friends. She did mention what good shape he had been in, kept very fit and did a lot of walking. Not that it helped him."

Dupin had walked farther along the street but not met anyone.

"And just so you know, the press have already got wind of the professor's death. I'll spare you the first headlines." According to her tone, they left Nolwenn cold. "Obviously the ghost of the serial killer is doing the rounds. They're having a feast day."

Obviously, Riwal wasn't the only one with a contagious imagination.

"That's it for the moment, Monsieur le Commissaire. We're getting ready for an all-out day tomorrow. I'll come back to you when I get anything new. See you later."

Nolwenn hung up.

The "all-out day." Things like that always disquieted him. He quickly turned his thoughts back to the case, and the professor.

"Commissaire!"

Kadeg's voice.

Dupin looked around, but didn't see him.

"Over here."

He was standing in the doorway of an old, flat-fronted stone house with a reed thatch, the sort you saw often in the little hamlets. It was quite a ways away; he had shouted loudly.

Dupin walked quickly toward him.

"This is the house of Madame Corsaire. The neighbor. Back here," Kadeg waved vaguely, "is where Lapointe's house is."

But before Dupin reached the old stone house, a head with impressive gray curls popped up next to Kadeg in the doorway. It belonged to a dainty lady in a pink apron dress. She blinked curiously at Dupin, who was standing almost next to her on a narrow piece of land between the road and the house, with the same stubby, bushy grass as on the cliffs.

"This is Madame Corsaire, she—"

"He's been away a lot recently. In Brest and Rennes. In libraries. He loved old books, old maps, old documents. All that. His whole house is full of it. An eccentric if you ask me. Have you any idea how much dust it creates?"

She passed Kadeg by and took a step toward the commissaire.

Dupin was glad there was no great prologue. "When you found him down on the beach, did you see anyone else? Or at any time on your walk?"

"Is he still lying down there, the poor man? The wind down there is even worse than up here." She shook her head. "Nobody, not a living soul."

"Did anything else unusual strike you, Madame Corsaire?"

"More unusual than a corpse?"

"So you didn't notice anything in particular on the beach today, or among the dunes?"

"No. And all of this today, just when my husband is away in Roscoff! And I'm here all on my own!"

"Was there maybe a car in the parking lot you didn't recognize, for example?"

"No. Nobody comes here."

The murderer had been there.

"Do you know if Monsieur Lapointe had been particularly busy recently, with something special that had happened? Here in the Parc Iroise? In the water, or along the coast?"

The old lady's face looked extremely skeptical. "What on earth might that be?"

"Something he might have mentioned that was worrying him? Pollution? Animals, wounded or dead? Dolphins? Anything at all."

"He went for a walk every day. Always along the shore. He loved it, that's why he moved here, he said. Either along the beach or along the cliff tops. Sometimes he went on 'walking excursions,' that's what he called them. Along the coast of the Pointe du Raz or in Douarnenez Bay. On those occasions he took his car."

"Did you see him often?"

"Not every day, but two or three times a week. We always stopped for a chat."

Dupin would have another go. "But Professor Lapointe never mentioned anything he'd been busy with of late?"

"He gave the impression of being very upbeat in the past few weeks. He was in a good mood."

"So there was nothing."

"I don't think so—"

The penetrating tone of Dupin's phone interrupted them. Dupin snatched it into his hand.

His mother.

To be honest he had been wondering—her last attempt had been hours ago. Normally she was a lot more persistent.

The elderly lady looked at him queryingly.

"You were saying"—Dupin put the phone back in his pants pocket—"you don't think . . ."

She was immediately back on topic. "I just wanted to say I didn't think there was anything on his mind." She shook her head energetically. "That he had any worries. Or worse."

"Do you know if he still had anything to do with virology?"

"Not that he mentioned to me."

"Did he have friends, acquaintances? Did he get visitors sometimes?"

"Not many. An elderly man came by from time to time, not someone I know."

Dupin took out his notebook.

"He came in a tiny car, but the professor never told me who it was. Maybe once a month. Then they went for a walk together, and came back and sat in the professor's house. But I don't know what they did there."

"You have no idea who it might have been?"

"No. It was a white Citroën C2. From Finistère."

Dupin made a note.

He turned to Kadeg. "Have the colleagues in the village ask around, maybe somebody knows something more about this man." Then, turning back to Madame Corsaire: "Any other visitors, madame?"

"Marie from the citizens' movement, she was there a couple of times last week."

"Yes?"

"The citizens' movement against chemicals."

Dupin waited. In vain.

"Can you tell me any more about those chemicals, madame?"

"They use them in Camaret harbor, to clean boats and treat them against rot. They belong to Charles Morin, the Fisher King."

"We know about this."

Only about protests, a citizens' movement, nothing else, but even so: this was the first potential link. And to Morin.

"It all ends up in the sea. It's a disgrace. The politicians don't dare do anything. So a few people have got together."

Morin, again and again, Morin.

"You just said Professor Lapointe wasn't involved in anything, but it would appear he was, in this water pollution."

"There was nothing recent; this business with the chemicals has been going on for years."

"But it would appear things have suddenly got worse. You said a woman from the citizens' movement was there a couple of times last week."

"You'd need to ask Marie Andou yourself, she's a kindergarten teacher."

Yet another note. And another instruction for Kadeg.

"Go round to see the teacher and talk to her. She must be able to explain. Any other visitors?" Dupin asked.

"The island doctor from Sein came to see him twice . . ."

"Antoine Manet?" That was unexpected.

"You know him?" It came across more like *I wouldn't have thought you up to it.*

"What did he want from Professor Lapointe?"

"How should I know?" Madame Corsaire said indignantly.

Dupin was still dumbfounded. "When was this?"

"Once in April, then again in May, I think. I'm not absolutely sure."

"I'll deal with him," Kadeg interjected. His eyes sparkled.

"I'll talk with Manet myself, Kadeg."

"That . . ." Kadeg forced himself to swallow it.

"How long was Antoine Manet there?"

"Maybe an hour, not longer."

"Do you know how the two of them got to know one another?"

"How should I know that?"

He needed to talk to the island doctor straightaway.

"Do you have keys to the professor's house?"

Triumphantly she held up a small key that must have been in her hand all along.

"Did the professor always lock his door?"

"Yes, obviously an old habit from the capital." She sounded sympathetic.

The funny thing was that no key had been found on the professor.

"Good, that's it for now, Madame Corsaire. Thank you very much." And with those words, Dupin was off again.

"Bring the key straight back to me," Madame Corsaire said.

"I think the police will hold on to it for a bit."

Dupin headed for the narrow unpaved track that led from the house. He had his phone already in his hand. There it was, Antoine Manet's number. It took a few moments before the call was answered:

"Hello?"

"Dupin here."

"Oh, Commissaire, I've just heard. I knew Monsieur Lapointe. This thing is getting crazier still." Manet sounded deeply upset.

"You visited him twice in the last few months."

Dupin let the sentence hang in the air. Manet didn't seem at all irritated.

"Yes, we both belong to the Patrimoine et Héritage Culturelle de la Cornouaille organization, for looking after and maintaining the cultural and historical roots of the region."

There were countless organizations like that in Brittany, in every region, every village. The most disparate types of people got passionately involved in them.

"These two visits, was there a reason for them?"

"I wanted him to become the new chairman. He had lots of knowledge and a lot of spare time."

"And?"

Dupin had reached the end of the path. On his right was a simple house with a raised ground floor in the mundane "*nouveau bretonisme*" style from the seventies and eighties, narrow with a very steep roof. It appeared to have been painted recently; the white shone pristinely.

"He wanted to mull it over. I think he would have said yes. He was as crazy as I am. And lots of others here. He was interested in everything local and regional. He knew every path on the Crozon peninsula, every tree, every stone, every building, and above all: every story about every tree, every stone, and every building, Which dwarf, which fairy lived where and what they got up to. We got along well. He passed on some material to me."

"Material?"

"I collect anything to do with our island here. It's going to be a big library."

Dupin was silent for a bit. As corny as it seemed, it sounded plausible, very plausible for Brittany.

"How long have you known one another?"

"About five years, as long as he's lived on the peninsula."

"And every now and then you met him alone, I imagine, not just at meetings?"

"Apart from the two meetings over recent months, maybe three times. No more."

"Did he seem in any way different when you last met?"

"Not at all. No."

"Nothing that seems somehow relevant, now, in hindsight? Something that could have been keeping him busy?"

"No."

"Do you know if he was still doing research? Privately, on the quiet?"

"I don't think so. At least he never mentioned anything. Last year I asked him for advice about a chronic viral illness one of the islanders had; he was a real genius in his field."

"So I believe."

"My feeling is he wanted to draw a line under his past when he came to Brittany. He didn't even have a computer. Just a cell phone."

"You know for certain that he had a cell phone?" He had forgotten to ask the neighbor that.

"I can send you his number if you want."

"Please."

"Do you think the professor could have had anything to do with the two women?"

"I had been hoping you were going to tell me something about that, at least if they had known one another?"

"Very unlikely, I imagine. But I don't know. I'll ask around on the island. We have a lot of money in the organization, to be shared out; we got a large sum from the region. The chairman has some influence on how the money is spent."

It took a moment for Dupin to react.

"You think this could be about some cultural or historic project? About handouts? Money?"

"I have no idea in particular."

"Was there an argument about something in the organization? Allegations?"

"No, as it happens. But of course you can't see into people. In Brittany least of all."

Dupin was baffled. But it was an interesting point. But how could that have any connection to Kerkrom and Darot?

"I'm sure I'll come back to that. Thank you, Monsieur Manet."

"And I'll get back to you if I come across any possible connection between the three."

"Good."

Dupin hung up.

He got a move on. Kadeg and the crime scene men would be here shortly. He clambered up the steep steps to the house doorway. The key stuck and the door hadn't been locked. That obviously explained why the key hadn't been found on the professor. The perp had been here, therefore. In Lapointe's home. As he almost certainly had been in the cases of Darot and Kerkrom. They would test the key thoroughly for fingerprints or any other clues, but Dupin didn't expect the killer to have left them a gift.

Dupin went all through the house for a first sweep, and found nothing unusual. Apart from the kitchen and bathroom, the house was filled with shelves from floor to ceiling, all of them filled with books, books, books, books; there had to be thousands of them. The shelving was fitted to the rooms, every centimeter properly used. Literally everywhere, in the dining room, the adjacent living rooms, as well as in the three rooms upstairs: a bedroom, a tiny room with a cot, and an office.

Dupin had already finished his tour by the time the two men from the crime scene team arrived. Kadeg was on the phone outside.

He indicated the key to his colleagues.

"We'll sort that out straightaway." The elder of the two men set down the case with their work tools. A pragmatic attitude, the solution right at the scene. Dupin liked that. "I'm upstairs if you need me."

Dupin took the stairs. He wanted to take another, more thorough look around Lapointe's office in peace and quiet. An outsize desk in front of the window, a magnificent view of the beach, the cliffs, the bay. Even the desk had to serve primarily as a storage space for books. A simple wooden chair, and in front of it, on the desktop, a small area of free space. No notebooks, no paper, nothing. Not even a telephone. A little patch of empty space, which looked strange, because it was the only one in the entire room.

The books on the desk covered a variety of topics and genres: novels, lots of history books, biographies (Charlemagne at the top), but not one factual book on medicine or biology, nor any scientific magazines.

Two piles of magazines, on history, philosophy, or cultural topics. Particularly high up, and clearly read, were several books on Breton and regional topics. One pile lay at a slanting angle, while all the others were in solid upright piles. Dupin came closer to look at them, without touching anything. He put his head on one side and read several of the titles on the spines. *Celtic Myths and Legends of Finistère, Ancient Armorica, The Revolution in Brittany, The Christianization of Finistère, The Iroise Sea as a Cultural Space.*

Dupin's glance flitted over to the shelves. Mallarmé, Flaubert, Apollinaire, Maupassant, Baudelaire, the French nineteenth century.

It was only just now that he noticed that between the two piles on the table there was one book lying at an angle, *The Life of Sea Mammals in Brittany*.

That was interesting. Dupin pulled it out carefully and flicked through it. First came the whales, many types, then orcas, and dolphins. He flicked more slowly. He was looking for something: marks, underlining, notes in the margin. Whatever. There were impressive photos of dolphins. He put the book back. It was quite clearly no book for experts, but for the layman.

He hadn't the faintest idea whether or not one of these books or magazines could give something away under the right circumstances. Their investigations were now relying on a coincidence—in combination with a stroke of inspiration. They needed luck. But obviously the killer would have removed anything that would have given him away. Anything obvious, including notes. But perhaps on a second glance, there might be something. The killer hadn't had time to do a complete search. He might have missed something.

"Commissaire? Where are you?"

Kadeg plodded up the stairs. "Madame Corsaire wants to see you again," he said. "And I've already spoken to the woman from the citizens' movement, the kindergarten teacher. The professor was effectively the citizens' movement's scientific advisor. Amongst other things he helped them send water samples from the Camaret harbor area to a laboratory and evaluate the results."

"And?"

"They regularly found noticeable concentrations of certain toxic materials. Always at approximately the same level. The use of the noxious substances was not reduced as a consequence."

"And?"

"The citizens' movement is submitting more documentation to the authorities. The Parc Iroise is supporting them. Some of their staff have taken their own samples, with the same results."

"Has there been any escalation?"

"How do you mean?"

"Arguments with people from the facility where the boats are dealt with? With the boat owners? With Charles Morin?"

"The kindergarten teacher didn't mention anything like that. Just that there had been reports in the local press."

"Was it widely known that Professor Lapointe was helping the movement?"

"Yes, there was even a quote from him in the last article. How devastating these materials were, stuff like that." Kadeg pointedly cleared his throat. "I also, as ever, asked about any connections of any kind between the movement and Kerkrom and Darot—to no avail. The kindergarten teacher had only heard of Kerkrom by name. She'd never heard at all of Darot."

"And did she say anything about Morin?"

"Only that some of the boats belonged to him."

"Anything more precise?"

"No. Her anger was primarily directed at the people who run the facility."

"And what does the neighbor want with me?"

"I don't know."

They needed to move forward with something, finally get their hands on something concrete. "Kadeg, I want to find out from a few people where they were this morning. Think of all of them as potential witnesses and check everything they say meticulously. Get Riwal to help you. As many people as you need."

"Who are we talking about?" Kadeg asked.

"The harbormistress, Madame Gochat, claims to have been in her office the whole morning, apart from nipping into the fish hall from time to time—somebody must have noticed that; Jumeau, the fisherman from the Île de Sein, says he was at sea from four thirty A.M.—for the man with the multiple affairs it would have been easy to make a detour to the peninsula." Dupin flicked through his Clairefontaine. "The boy who found the dolphin researcher saw Jumeau at seven twenty-four, not far from Sein. That is the only thing we're sure of so far."

"He could have killed Darot beforehand, and Professor Lapointe afterward."

It was true.

"And let's also talk with Pierre Leblanc, the scientific chief at the *parc*." Dupin had seen him around two o'clock. There would have been enough time before that.

"I'll speak myself to the pirate, who was also on Sein last night, Captain Vaillant."

Put so generally the operation seemed a bit casual, the commissaire knew, but as far as he was concerned it didn't matter.

He already had Morin's statement. He had allegedly met up with his *chef bolincheur* at Douarnenez harbor at ten, but there was no confirmation.

"And, most important, ask this Carrière if he has witnesses. Anyone who saw him and Morin this morning at the harbor. Otherwise, their alibi is no good. And also, find out how long they claim they stayed there."

"Noted," Kadeg said. "We'll let him feel our teeth."

"Find this man who came to see the professor once a month. And have the crime scene team make a list of all the titles and topics of all the books here on the desk and in the office."

"Are you looking for something in particular, Commissaire?"

Dupin didn't go into it. "Professor Lapointe had a cell phone. We need to get our hands on his itemized bill as soon as possible. And find out if he used the phone for email, if he had an account."

"Noted too." This time it didn't sound quite so euphoric.

"And work on getting the call logs of Darot and Kerkrom."

"Yessir!"

"Is Madame Corsaire waiting for me in her house?"

"She's outside, in front of the door."

Dupin left the office without another word.

In an instant he was standing in front of Madame Corsaire. She sought out Dupin's eyes with an inscrutable look on her face. The old lady hesitated for a second, then seemed to give herself a shove.

"I've just spoken to my husband on the phone." She sounded seriously worked up. "He thinks there's something I absolutely have to tell you. Something private. About the professor."

"You should tell me everything, Madame Corsaire."

"Over the past few months he would receive occasional visits from a young lady. A very young lady."

There was no allegation, no condemnation, no shock in her voice. Quite the opposite. What seemed to be troubling her was the fear of being indiscreet.

"Did you know the woman? Do you know who it was?"

"We'd never seen her before."

"Can you describe her?"

"Long hair, nothing more. And young . . . What do you think? We weren't spying on him, you know. Our houses aren't quite that close together. My husband just thought she ought to be part of the picture. Maybe the young woman might know something."

"You would help us with a few general details of her appearance, madame."

"Probably dark hair, not very tall. Pretty, I think. I only ever saw her briefly. She wore longish jackets, usually with a hood."

That wasn't much help.

"Do you think she didn't want to be seen? That was why she wore the hood?"

"That was the impression it gave."

"When did she start calling on the professor?"

"My husband and I asked ourselves that too. I think since the end of April. My husband thinks it wasn't until May."

"And how often was she there?"

"We think five times. More or less. For how long each time, we can't say. But they weren't short visits."

"Did you see her car?"

"No."

Dupin pricked up his ears. "What does that mean?"

"There wasn't a car. Once I saw her walk past our house on her own. Once with the professor."

"How did she get here?"

"Maybe somebody dropped her off. Or she took the bus to Saint-Hernot and then walked the rest of the way. We do that ourselves sometimes. Even though my husband still drives."

"Or . . ." Dupin broke off. Or she came by boat.

Something had suddenly occurred to him.

"I'm going to have to check on something. I'll be right back," he said.

Madame Corsaire stared at him, perplexed.

Dupin took a few steps along the grassy path with its innumerable rabbit holes, and called Nolwenn. She would have it figured out within a minute. And so she did. An email almost immediately arrived on his phone, with the attachment Dupin had been hoping for: a photo.

"Is that her?" Dupin held his phone up to Madame Corsaire's face. "The young woman with long hair who visited the professor?"

The forensic lad in Brest had taken it. Laetitia Darot's facial features hadn't been harmed, she was easy to recognize from the photo.

Madame Corsaire's eyes widened. "Oh my God, that's her."

"Are you sure?"

"Yes."

Laetitia Darot had known Philippe Lapointe. She had come to visit him several times at home in Lostmarc'h.

That was it, just what they needed; now they had a direct connection between the women and the professor, even if they didn't yet know what sort of a relationship they'd had.

The problem was: Who could or would know that? Who knew anything at all about these meetings? And would they reveal the background? The most likely person, Céline Kerkrom, was dead. But nonetheless they had to do everything they could to find out.

After his conversation with the neighbor, Dupin exchanged a few more words with Kadeg. In their investigations of the professor's call list they now needed to look for possible conversations with Darot. Had he and Darot been in contact long? Had they spoken often on the phone? These could be further points to fill out the character of their relationship.

From Lapointe's house Dupin did not turn left onto the little street, but right onto the path he had walked down to make his phone call. Toward the bay and the beach. Then he would have to take a left at some point to get to his car.

He could only spontaneously think of a few people he could try. He would just have to give it a go. He had already dialed the first number.

"Monsieur Jumeau? Commissaire Dupin here."

It took a while for him to get an answer.

"Yes," Jumeau responded sluggishly.

"I have another important question. Did you know," Dupin said, trying to keep it neutral sounding, not suggesting anything, "that Laetitia Darot used to go to see a certain Professor Lapointe?"

A long silence.

"We didn't have a firm relationship. She could do whatever she wanted."

"I'm only interested in whether you knew. Did she ever mention it to you? Maybe she was consulting the professor about something in particular?"

"Consulting?"

"You knew nothing about this contact?"

"No."

"Did you . . ." Dupin gave up. It was hard work. "Thanks. My colleague will be in touch with you again soon. "

The path came to an abrupt end by shoulder-high thorny bushes; he would have to walk along the side of it. He would keep trying. Maybe he'd get lucky.

Dupin had his phone to his ear again. The scientist picked up immediately. "Pierre Leblanc here."

"Commissaire Dupin." There was no need for formalities with Leblanc. The commissaire came straight to the subject. "Did you know about any contact between Laetitia Darot and a certain Professor Lapointe? Philippe Lapointe. He lives on the Crozon peninsula. A distinguished virologist from a Paris university."

"The name means nothing to me . . . is he the third murder victim? I just heard on the news."

"I'm afraid so."

"That's dreadful." His reaction was automatic, and there was a deep horror in his voice. "Terrible—I'll ask my colleagues here at the institute if anyone knew about such a contact, which is in any case highly unlikely."

"That would be good, Monsieur Leblanc."

"I'll be in touch if I hear anything. This case is achieving monstrous proportions."

"Indeed it is." Dupin thought for a moment. "Did Laetitia Darot ever mention an illness, an infection going around among the dolphins? Were there animals who'd been affected?"

"No. And she certainly would have. For sure."

It was a plausible possibility.

"One more question, Monsieur Leblanc. Where were you this morning, let's say between six o'clock and eleven?"

The answer was clear and calm.

"In the office, here, from nine o'clock. Then at half past nine I was at Pointe Saint-Mathieu, where we're building a new measuring station, which we want to start using by the end of the year. Something that was very important to Laetitia, as the dolphins often stopped around there. I was back by half past eleven."

"And prior to nine o'clock?"

"At home. I live in Tréboul, on my own, as it happens. I realize that is very hard for you to check." Leblanc had said the words with almost scientific concern. "I'm trying to think if anyone might have seen me. Possibly on the way."

"Were you on the boat?"

"Yes, just me."

"How long does it take to get there?"

"From here, an hour and a half."

"And nobody saw you there either?"

"Probably not. The station is a jagged headland, hard to reach from the mainland."

"What about when you came back? Around midday?"

"My assistant. She was waiting for me for a meeting."

"So did your assistant also see you at nine?"

"She wasn't there yet. But some of the technicians must have done. Certainly somebody here. I was up here briefly before I went down to the boat."

"How about last night, between nine and eleven o'clock?"

"I was here at the institute for a long time, maybe up to midnight."

"And did you bump into somebody who could bear witness to that?"

"I know it's unfortunate, but I don't think so. I'm usually the last to leave."

A very factual briefing. But Leblanc's alibi was as weak as those of the others.

"Thank you, Monsieur Leblanc. One of my inspectors will be in touch again. He will want to talk to your assistant too."

Dupin had reached the end of the thorny hedgerow. A little footpath led straight down toward the beach. Another led parallel to the beach; theoretically he ought to come to the path that led to his car.

It had been through this pair—as far as Dupin could say for now—that he had felt that he might have had a chance of finding out something about the meetings between Darot and the professor.

Then he thought of Manet. He got his phone out again.

"Hello?" Manet answered.

"Commissaire Dupin here." He didn't need to go into formalities with the island doctor either. "Laetitia Darot was in contact with Professor Lapointe—she went to visit him in his house in Lostmarc'h a few times over the past few months." Dupin refrained from asking a question.

"That's interesting. Why?"

"That's what I'd like to find out. You didn't know?"

"No, I would have mentioned it." He didn't seem irritated.

"Have you any idea what these meetings might have been about? Or what sort of a relationship at all they might have had?"

"Not in the slightest. No."

"Does anyone else occur to you who might have known about it?"

"Céline, that's all."

That was the problem.

"Two other things, Monsieur Dupin. The tide will be particularly high tomorrow. Coefficient 116. That can cause the weather to turn rough. We will have to bring the boats into the innermost part of the harbor, for safety's sake. Including Darot's. Only so you know.

"Also: there's registered mail for Céline Kerkrom. The woman from the post office was just here to ask me what she should do with it. It has to be collected by hand."

"Inspector Riwal will pick it up. I'll talk to him."

"Thank you. Thanks."

"See you later, then."

Manet hung up. That was it, then, the people who could have helped him. Dupin swore aloud.

His sense of orientation hadn't let him down. He had stumbled onto the path that led to his car. It went remarkably steeply uphill; he hadn't noticed before.

He glanced at the time. Quarter past eight. He lost all sense of time when he was on a case. He needed to call Claire straightaway. He had been intending to do it all day long. And, there was no alternative, his mother too.

He realized how worn out and exhausted he was. His night had been over by five in the morning, and the day since had been a solid turbulent marathon. And it was by no means over yet. He needed a *café*. Urgently.

* * *

Dupin already had his phone to his ear, about to call Claire, when it rang. He was almost at his car at last.

"Extraordinary news, boss!" Riwal burst out. "Guess who cut the professor's hair?" Riwal left a rhetorical pause, before continuing excitedly. "Yan Lapal."

Yet another pause.

"The hairdresser with the boat, who also cut the hair of Darot and Kerkrom. His salon is in Camaret. Professor Lapointe went there. Lapal cut the hair of all three."

"Really?"

The hairdresser had a rock-solid alibi, Kadeg had told him, at least for last night.

"That's just a stone's throw from the new murder scene. And it would only take him five minutes from his house to get to his boat in Camaret harbor, I've checked on the map. From there he could get anywhere within an hour. Including the islands."

It was all true. And it was a funny coincidence that all three had used him. But there was no chance of it being him—and there was no reason to think differently—if you continued to assume there was just one killer, which the pathologist also considered probable.

"Think it over. A hairdresser who could get in his boat to the most isolated areas, and commit murder undisturbed. Nobody would suspect him."

That applied not just to the hairdresser but also to their serial killer. Dupin should have known that.

"Anything else, Riwal?"

"I've spoken to a few men from the island who enjoy spending time on the quays. Sitting in the bars, watching the world go by, the boats coming and going," Riwal said.

"And?"

"They say that recently Kerkrom spent more time out at sea than normal. That she used to take one day off a week but hadn't done so for a while."

"We need to ask around in Douarnenez harbor. Maybe they could—"

"Already done that. One of Madame Gochat's staff has been told to send us a list of which days Céline Kerkrom brought her catch to auction, from March on. That's all that's on record, not whether or not she docked in Douarnenez harbor. But even so."

"Excellent, Riwal."

Dupin should have thought of that himself, first thing that morning.

"She also fished to order for certain restaurants, sea bass and *lieus jaunes*. On those days, obviously, she wasn't registered at the auction. Their best watcher, in any case, was the little boy you spoke to this morning at the cholera cemetery, boss, and he often hangs about the harbor. He knows the fisherfolk well. And even he said that recently Kerkrom was at sea most of the time. Darot too. And occasionally both of them in the same boat."

"Which?"

"Either. Darot's and Kerkrom's."

"How often?"

"Sometimes, was what he said. I couldn't get him to be any more exact."

"And why did they go out together? Did he say anything about that?"

"He thought they were rod fishing together. But he didn't know."

"Did the two of them tell him that—that they were line fishing?"

"No, it was just what he thought."

"And did he add where exactly they went to?"

Another one of the crucial questions.

"No." Dupin turned a narrow corner. He didn't remember the path from his car to the beach being this long.

"Anything else?"

"Once or twice Kerkrom would give him a fish or a crab when she came back. So would the other fishers. He used to help them sorting out their nets, at their sheds. And if the fishers had found anything on the seafloor, he would take it to the museum. There's a room there where they collect things that have been found. Madame Coquil showed me it, they keep everything, even really old stuff." Riwal sounded impressed. "Cannonballs, two huge anchors, bits of boats, even a few Roman coins and ceramics. Amazing things, remnants of shipwrecks and settlements over six thousand years. They ought to—"

"Is that all, Riwal?"

Dupin needed to stop his inspector's habit of meandering away from the topic. Current matters were too important.

"Yes."

The commissaire would have very much liked to have spoken to the boy himself.

"Good, Riwal, we'll speak again soon."

"I need to pass on to you something from Goulch. The authorities have produced their decisive conclusion to the 'joint services action.' Things remain the same: nothing to be proved on any of Morin's boats. Red lobsters were found on two other fishing boats, whose captains, as you know, had nothing to do with Morin. In one case it was almost certainly the result of by-catch, in the other it really was a breach of the regulations, which will now be punished. Everybody assumes Morin had been tipped off about the operation. There's a lot of talk going on. Xavier Controc of the Affaires Maritimes is beside himself."

Speculative talk to be sure.

Two more points occurred to Dupin, both ones he had almost forgotten. "You need to go by the mail office and pick up a registered letter for Céline Kerkrom. And I want one of our people there when they move Darot's boat into the inner harbor. Antoine Manet said . . ."

"The weather's going to change tomorrow."

"Like I said, we need somebody watching."

"Consider it done, boss. By the way"—Riwal's tone of voice had changed oddly—"are you well, physically I mean?"

This time the commissaire understood immediately. "I'm fine, Riwal. Now, enough of this."

He would not speak another word about it.

Dupin shoved his phone into his pocket.

A seagull flew crazily close over his head. It had done that a couple of times ever since he walked along the blackberry hedge, almost as if it was aiming at him. Squawking. Maybe she had chicks and had a nest nearby.

At last Dupin caught sight of his car.

And not just his.

A few meters behind the Citroën was a second car. Big, black, and shiny.

Charles Morin was leaning on the door of the Citroën and looking at Dupin. As if it was the most obvious thing in the world that he should be standing there.

He waited until Dupin was only a few paces away.

"The pirate clown had been diligently on the tracks of both of them, we've found out. Vaillant spent days at sea near them. When they were out together on Kerkrom's boat. Apparently without them noticing. By the entrance to Douarnenez Bay," Morin said with the same self-confident, relaxed tone of voice and gestures as in their last conversation.

"How did you know where to find me, Monsieur Morin?"

"I think you need to deal with Vaillant. I certainly would."

"How did you come to be here, Monsieur Morin?" Dupin really wanted to know.

"I was on the way home. My wife's waiting with dinner."

The uncanny thing was not that Morin was near the scene of the crime—the media had already reported that—but that he was here, by Dupin's car, in the middle of nowhere. It was a demonstration of power.

"The murderer," Morin said thoughtfully, "was obviously in a hurry. He wanted to stop his intended victims warning one another."

That was one aspect, undoubtedly. But Dupin wanted to go his own way without any middle-man input from Morin.

"Professor Lapointe was involved in the citizens' movement against the use of poisonous chemicals on your ships. You had a reason to undertake something against him. Who knows what he knew."

"You think I'm going to kill somebody because of their ridiculous allegations against me? About cleaning material?" Suddenly Morin sounded downcast. "And why Madame Gochat had the pair of them followed remains also completely in the dark. We absolutely need to concentrate on these questions, Commissaire. Believe me."

With those words he let go of the car door and went over to his own vehicle. Without even looking back.

Dupin opened the door of the Citroën, climbed in, and fired up the engine. Even before Morin had started his motor, Dupin drove off.

* * *

The commissaire had intended to see Vaillant anyhow. But obviously what Morin said had made his intention more pressing, even if it went against the grain to follow a "tip" from Morin. He might not have wanted to give it to the "tipster," but Vaillant was nonetheless still high on his list of suspects. There was no doubt Morin had a cunning intelligence.

But it posed an urgent question, if true. What was the reason behind Vaillant following the two women in his boat? What was he after? Captain Vaillant was the second to be tailing them. And it always revolved around Douarnenez Bay.

Dupin was to meet Vaillant in Le Conquet in the fishing harbor. Nolwenn had arranged everything.

Kadeg had got hold of Frédéric Carrière, whose meeting with Morin had taken place by his high-seas trawlers, in the harbor area that wasn't open to the public. Because they allegedly had to take a look at a problem with one of the boats. Of course the only person to see them was another of Morin's employees; nobody else confirmed what he said. Carrière claimed he had come out again at eleven o'clock. Kadeg made no secret of the fact he found the whole meeting suspect. As indeed it was.

All the other alibis also seemed extremely vague; it could hardly be otherwise. Gochat had definitely been seen at twelve, but the last time in the morning at half past nine. In between she had "retreated" into her office. Jumeau claimed that apart from his conversation with Dupin, he had been at sea the whole time until six o'clock, but there was no way to confirm that.

Dupin subsequently spoke with Riwal. The post office was obviously long closed. Dupin had been around the Bay of Brest before; it was a good hour's drive. Vaillant would also need an hour. Dupin could be there in a few minutes.

He had discovered Le Conquet and this part of the extreme west coast for himself last year for the first time. He and the whole commissariat had gone on a "work outing," organized by Nolwenn, to the most westerly part of Brittany and France, the Pointe de Corsen, an excursion that despite Dupin's deep skepticism about such outings had been very nice. They weren't back until midnight and in an extremely good mood. It was not just the most westerly part of France, but apart from a tiny piece of Portuguese and Spanish land was the most westerly part of the European continent, and more: the entire European continental plate which rose some seven thousand kilometers away, including Siberia and China, from the Pacific. It was a reasonable Breton superlative and every upstanding Breton made the pilgrimage to the Pointe de Corsen. Naturally that was part of Nolwenn's deeper reason in choosing the destination, yet another symbolic act in Dupin's Bretonization.

They had begun the excursion in bright sunshine at Saint-Mathieu—a magic place with innumerable legends, with high cliffs buffeted by wind and sea, with a picture-pretty lighthouse and next to it the atmospheric ruins of an old abbey from the sixth century—then ate lunch sumptuously in Le Conquet and from there drove to the Pointe de Corsen and the pretty little town of Porspoder and on to the almost unearthly beauty of the beaches of Lampaul-Ploudalmézeau. It was perhaps the stretch of Breton coast that had impressed Dupin most. He knew it was a stupid thing to say but he had done so many times. In any event it was the most remote, isolated, roughest, and wildest stretch. In "the south," in "his" region, the land—fields, forests, meadows—mostly ran straight to the coast, and then suddenly there was the sea. Up until then it was clearly land. Here it was different. Here the monstrous forces of the tossing Atlantic and the whipping winds, the endlessly fine salty spray that was carried for kilometers, shaped nature far inland. Above all, that meant that everything, apart from the few oaks or pine forests, was barren, with little plant life. The typical stubby grass, ferns, bushes, brush, sandstone, rocks, cliffs. Yet with that the excess of green tones seemed to act as competition to the absence of any other beauty, from the darkest black-green to the brightest yellow-green. These were grand, powerful, superlative landscapes, most impressive perhaps to be seen on the road that ran directly by the water from Penfoul to Trémazan, but even better on the endless smugglers' paths along the coast.

Even the houses seemed more solid, more massive than those on the south coast, the granite darker, a little stronghold that wanted to say: I resist, over centuries. They were pushed close together, just like those on the Île de Sein.

Dupin had reached Le Conquet, steered through the narrow streets toward the town center, and then on to the modern fishing harbor, where the ferries to Ouessant and Molène also docked.

All at once he could see the almost tubular bay, the beginning of the narrow sea arm that was one of the best protected natural harbors, opposite a rocky peninsula with a green top. From the harbor quay it was hardly two hundred meters to the peninsula, which gave enough space to maneuver, even for bigger boats. A long pier stuck out at the entrance to the basin. At the end of the arm of sea lay the Vieux Port, directly next to the picturesque center.

Dupin parked his car on the big square behind the quay, where the day-trippers going out to the islands parked. He walked along next to the water. There wasn't a soul in sight, not anywhere on the pier. Two ferries had tied up on the long pier; proud letters on one spelled out *Penn Ar Bed*, the same company as that to which the *Enez Sun III*, which he had seen this morning, belonged. A few fishing boats lay tied up to brightly colored buoys in the harbor basin.

Vaillant—Captain Vaillant—would only be able to tie up here at the pier. He wasn't there yet. Nor was there any boat to be seen on the bit of sea visible at the exit from the harbor. Toward the northwest and Ouessant the peninsula blocked the view. On the other hand, even though it was just before ten, the sun still hung high enough to peek over and shine its mild, milky light into Dupin's face. It was still remarkably warm. Definitely over twenty degrees.

A magnificent summer's evening. It had gone through Dupin's head while parking the car that it couldn't be far to the restaurant where the whole gang from the commissariat had eaten. They had taken a walk down here to the harbor after dinner. He would be back in a quarter of an hour, a lot more lively and attentive. Dupin didn't think long about it. Vaillant would have to wait if needs be.

Five minutes later he was standing outside the Relais du Port, down at the old port. It was an old stone house with a lot of flair, but a simple restaurant, an everyday one, the sort Dupin loved. You could look out at the Vieux Port while eating. It didn't get any better than that. Right now that meant looking at the seabed and the boats laid up on the sand. Even on such a fine summer evening very many of them still had something melancholy about them. There were lots of patches of seaweed on the beach, glittering yellowy green in the light. Directly in front was a bright blue wooden boat, beyond that an orange one, a turquoise one, then a red—a crazy field of colors.

Dupin chose a table in the first tow of a cozily roofed terrace.

Perfect. He had downed his coffee in seconds. It was then that his glance—unintentionally—landed on the menu: *Steak tartare, frites, salade.* One of Dupin's favorite dishes, just behind entrecôte steak. There was a lot the commissaire would do for a good tartare.

He reached for his phone.

"Nolwenn?"

"Monsieur le Commissaire?" Nolwenn said cheerfully.

"I've been held up. Tell Vaillant I'll be there in—let's say, twenty minutes."

It didn't take long to serve up a tartare, and he needed to eat something. The last bite he'd had was ages ago. Apart from that, the Amiral would probably be closed by the time he got back to Concarneau. That did it.

"I imagine you're sitting in the Relais du Port. Just right, Monsieur le Commissaire!" Nolwenn said it as if it was common sense. "The pirate will just have to wait."

Dupin had too often been a witness to Nolwenn's uncanny ability to guess his whereabouts to be surprised.

"I assume you are aware"—Nolwenn's tone of voice had changed and her choice of words also signified that she was not amused—"that your mother has several times tried to get ahold of you. And every time she's been put through to me."

As far as Madame Dupin was concerned, everybody outside the metropolis was a provincial, particularly people from such remote regions as Brittany, which was the epitome of provincialism. And she let them know that. Nolwenn had her own way to counter that. She avoided clashing with her and instead calmly and without sympathy let his mother dangle starving on the end of an outstretched arm.

"You need to talk to her."

What that really meant was that she wasn't going to do so anymore.

"I will talk to her, Nolwenn. First thing tomorrow morning."

"Good." Already she sounded happy again. "Apropos, as you happen to be in the region of Ys: Do you know when Ys will rise from the waves again? When Paris sinks into them. That's the way the Bretons have talked for centuries about Par-Is: meaning 'on a par with Ys.'"

Dupin chuckled.

"We're turning the lights out here now, Monsieur le Commissaire. We've made our preparations for tomorrow and are trying to get some sleep, so we're back at full strength tomorrow. But you know I always have my phone with me. Riwal, by the way, is going to spend the night on the island. We found him a room in the only hotel. Simple but clean. It'll probably be the first night he's slept through since Maclou-Brioc came into the world. Kadeg decided to come back. How are things with you? It's a good hour and a half's drive. I have—"

"I'm still coming back." It was a reflex answer.

"One and a half hours."

"It's not a problem, Nolwenn."

"As you wish."

"Another thing," Dupin said, massaging his temples. He had already involuntarily come back a couple of times to one of the stories the woman at the coffee stand in the auction hall had told him this morning. "This boat of Morin's, the one suspected of smuggling, people say the customs men really did tail it into a corner, and, on Morin's instruction, they sank it in order to get rid of any proof."

"I haven't heard anything of a story like that. The chief customs officer, whom I spoke to this morning about Morin, didn't mention anything like that. But I'll keep on it."

"That would be good, Nolwenn. And ask where the incident is supposed to have taken place.'

"I'll do that. *Bonne nuit*, Monsieur le Commissaire."

"*Bonne nuit*, Nolwenn."

Dupin leaned back and made a gesture to the friendly waitress who was just bringing something to the next table.

"I'd like the tartare, please. And a glass of Cornas. The 2009 Empreintes."

For most things, Dupin had a lousy—recently damn lousy—memory. But for wines, their names and where they came from, he had no problem. They had drunk the Cornas on their work outing.

"Of course, sir."

Dupin had to admit that Nolwenn's "day of action" still made him nervous; he would like to have known exactly what was going to happen. Why it was important to be "at full strength." But he should probably just stick to his instinct, which told him it would be best for everybody to say as little as possible about it. But there was another thing going through his head. And even though it required effort, he ought to do it.

He reached for his phone again.

"Riwal?"

"Boss, I was about to—"

"I want to talk to the boy again, myself." Dupin had lowered his voice. "The one from the island, who hangs around the harbor all day. I want—"

"I've got the registered letter," Riwal said. "I bumped into An-toine Manet in Le Tatoon. He knew that the mail woman had been invited to dinner this evening. He knew where and asked her to get me the registered mail quickly. Manet is—"

"Riwal, what is the piece of mail?"

"It's a cautionary note, from a laboratory in Paris, for an unpaid check."

Riwal paused unnecessarily.

"And?"

"A specialist laboratory, one that does chemical, physical, and biological analyses of materials of all sort, fabrics and liquids."

"What?" He hadn't been expecting that.

"The firm is called Sci-Analyses."

"And what exactly was the issue?"

"Like I said, it was a cautionary note, with a copy of the check. All it says is 'RfS-Analysis.'"

"Nothing else?"

"Nothing else. I checked on the Internet, but all I found was FRS-analysis."

"And what does that mean? I mean the thing you found."

"Distance X-Ray. It's a form of analysis used in orthodontics."

"Orthodontics?"

The waitress placed the glass of wine and a basket of bread and butter in front of Dupin.

"Exactly."

"When does the check date from?"

"April 27."

"And how much is it for?"

"1,479.57 euros."

An expensive operation.

"Have you already tried to call the firm?"

"They're only taking recorded messages at this hour."

Obviously. Riwal went on: "I looked down the page to find the directors, to try to call them direct. Neither are in the phone book. We'll have to wait until tomorrow morning. I'll keep at it."

Riwal had done a lot already. He knew that in situations like this Dupin would go to great lengths, no matter how crazy and complicated it was. But if they were to get in touch with somebody from the firm tonight it would mean getting the big guns out. Without knowing if the matter had anything to do with their case.

"Okay, and like I said, I want to talk to the boy again."

"You'll need to come early then, Monsieur le Commissaire; he'll be in school from eight thirty."

Dupin sat back. He had instinctively, without thinking about it, assumed they would meet on the mainland. But that would obviously be hard to arrange. To take the boy out of school for the morning and bring him to Douarnenez on a police boat. For an interview based on nothing concrete.

That meant he would have to make the boat ride himself.

"Goulch will take you, boss. You just need to let him know."

"I'll see. Maybe it was a crazy idea, to see the boy."

"The pathologist from Brest has submitted her report. She compared both wounds, and had the photos of the examination of Kerkrom sent to her. It could certainly be the same knife. No doubt about it. But there was nothing specific, for example she didn't find anything that would have caused particular damage to the blade."

"Hm." A pause. "Anything else, Riwal?"

"Not for the moment. The news media are already reporting on the 'big day of action' tomorrow. It's going to make the headlines," the inspector said, obviously delighted. "That's the way to go."

"Meaning . . . ?" Dupin didn't finish the sentence. "See you later, Riwal."

The commissaire put his phone back on the table. And lifted his wineglass instead.

What had Kerkrom been looking for with this scientific analysis? By a specialist laboratory in Paris?

The wine was rich and velvety, the way Dupin liked it. He took a chunk of the baguette, and spread salted butter on it. It was good.

It had been a hard day, harder than any Dupin had yet experienced in his career. Three murders. Clinically calculated. Each one carried out quickly after the other. In three different places, each one roughly an hour distant from the other. It wasn't possible to investigate them jointly. Each time they had to start again, from the beginning; could never deepen the investigation, never dig down.

The waitress brought his meal, poured him more wine.

The tartare looked fantastic. And tasted as good as it looked. The French fries were excellent too. They were something Dupin had loved since he was a child. His godfather had at some stage moved to Brussels, and every time he visited him they had eaten fries in big paper bags full to the brim, conjured up instantly as if by magic from a few sheets of paper. Served with delicious sauces. They were superb: crispy outside, soft as butter inside. Eaten standing up, at a nondescript stall on some shabby square; his bourgeois mother was dismayed every time, but his father loved them, as did he.

* * *

Dupin hadn't exactly hurried. It was a quarter to eleven when he got back to the quay. There was now a third boat on the long dock behind the two ferries. A conspicuous boat, in a light faded blue with a narrow white stripe that ran all around it below the railing. It was totally made of wood, to the front unusually high and sweeping like a sperm whale. A bow shape that Dupin had never seen before. It was at least fifteen meters long, pretty wide overall, and it sat low and heavy in the water. A captain's cabin and the usual electronics. A curious boat, like something from a Jules Verne movie. A sign on the bow read *Pebezh Abadenn*. It had to be Vaillant's.

Even on the longest day of the year it happened: Brittany had turned away from the sun—or as people said, the sun had gone down. It had turned the sea, out there where it sank, bright orange and seemed even to have set the sky alight. It seemed the entire horizon was on fire, a crazy orange-red. Only at its far fringes did it turn blue-black. The one thing that a Breton knew was that it was an occasion to relax, to remain calm, and not to fear the world was about to end.

On the deck of the *Pebezh Abadenn* stood a group of men. One of them was busy tying up the boat, an indication that it hadn't been there for long.

Dupin stopped by the pier, then walked along it to the last of the three concrete ramps that led down into the sea, so that, as on the Île de Sein and everywhere along the coast, you could get on or off a tied-up boat at whatever the height of the tide.

"Here comes the cop."

Dupin heard it as clearly and plainly as everybody else. But it didn't sound antagonistic.

He had reached the height of the railing.

One of the men began walking toward him silently. A somber-looking guy with a deeply tanned face, notable rings under his eyes, slightly swollen eyelids, a great wild mop of black hair that dominated his whole appearance and reminded Dupin of seventies rock bands. The reflection of the bright orange just increased that impression. He wore a dark green linen shirt with the top buttons open, jeans, black rubber boots. Dupin put him in his midforties.

"We couldn't resist, there was a huge swarm of mackerel beneath us, we just had to throw a few lines down."

Vaillant nodded toward a few plastic buckets full of flipping, flapping fish. It was intended to be an explanation for turning up late—which at the same time meant that if Dupin hadn't been in the Relais du Port, he would have been waiting here on the quay for three quarters of an hour.

"I'll pack up a couple for you. They're really delicious." He meant it seriously. Only now was it obvious that there was a little door set into the thick wooden railing. Captain Vaillant opened it and was about to take a large stride onto the ramp.

"I'll come to you," Dupin said.

"Of course." Vaillant retreated. He seemed completely calm.

"Inspect as much as you will." There was no sarcasm or aggression in the tone of his voice. "Take a look round everything. We've nothing to hide."

Dupin took a long stride, almost a little jump, and was on board the *Pebezh Abadenn*. "Monsieur Vaillant, you followed and watched Céline Kerkrom's boat, which Laetitia Darot was also on board, for several days. At the entry to Douarnenez Bay. Two women who were murdered between yesterday evening and this morning. Why?"

The other men on board had all got out of the way, disappeared up to the bow or beneath the deck.

"Didn't you find them extraordinarily good-looking? For myself I'm happy to be around good-looking women," Vaillant said, neither unpleasantly nor condescendingly. He laughed; a rough, deep laugh.

"Why did you follow Céline Kerkrom? What did you want from her?" Dupin said gruffly.

"They were being followed by Gochat's fisherman. He had been on their heels for several days, just keeping his boat far enough away so as not to be conspicuous."

"That's no answer." But Vaillant had admitted it frankly. Dupin continued: "What was the reason for *you* following them?"

"Maybe I was just concerned and was following the fisherman who was following them." Vaillant's eyes gleamed. "Or I was simply, let's say, 'curious.' Curious what the two of them were up to." He made a mischievous face.

"No, seriously, in summer, we like to be toward the front of the bay, reeling in the fat squid. They also attract the dolphins. We weren't following anybody. Even though the attractiveness of those women alone would have been grounds enough."

Vaillant wasn't giving anything away. He was lying, of course. He had been following them. That wasn't by chance.

"How well did you know Céline Kerkrom and Laetitia Darot?"

"Nobody knew the mermaid. Not even me. She was as mysterious as the depths of the Atlantic itself. And as for Céline, we'd chatted pleasantly a few times. I have to say I personally wouldn't have minded chatting with her more often." For the first time he seemed serious. "But she wasn't interested. I wasn't her type. I think she'd already given her heart to that fisherman from the island."

"Jumeau?"

"Indeed, Jumeau's the kid's name."

Dupin was wide awake. "Did somebody tell you about Kerkrom and Jumeau?"

"I didn't need anybody to tell me. I could feel it."

"What was it that you . . . felt?"

"That she was after him."

"When did you last speak with Céline Kerkrom?"

"Monday, this week. In Douarnenez harbor. At the auction. We don't often bring a catch in there. But we had a large number of red mullet."

"And what did you talk about?"

"About the large number of red mullet."

Dupin took a hard look at him. "Did she say anything specific?"

"She told me about Laetitia's project. With the transmitters."

"Did she mention Morin?"

He hesitated a brief moment. "No."

"Did she—" Dupin cut himself short. He'd felt faint for a moment. He'd already felt it on the way to the Relais du Port. It was familiar to him, this tiredness. More than that: deep exhaustion. Neither the meal nor the two cups of coffee had helped.

"Monsieur Vaillant," he began again, "did you know Professor Philippe Lapointe?"

He blinked at Dupin bemusedly.

"The third victim, the one found on the beach at Lostmarc'h?"

"Ah, of course, it's been on the news already."

"And?"

"I didn't even know this professor existed."

Dupin walked around the fish boxes, the buoys, and the nets. This boat was a total mess.

"Along with fishing, I've been told you also enjoy acting as old-fashioned smugglers." Dupin made a point of looking around him.

"We get by. But obviously we stay within the limits of our respected laws." Vaillant was flirting shamelessly.

"So strictly that you've had a series of fines, I've heard. Primarily for illegal quantities of alcohol."

"Trivia. We like drinking. We like smoking too. Nowadays they count as much less serious matters than capital crimes. Like I said, look around all you will. We've got time, and you won't find anything."

"What about Morin, does he smuggle too? Cigarettes. Big time?"

"I don't smuggle," Vaillant said with exaggerated annoyance. "And I haven't the faintest whether Morin is involved in this lucrative business. I wouldn't be surprised."

Dupin was now standing directly in front of Vaillant. "Céline Kerkrom or Laetitia Darot saw something, maybe even documented something so that they had proof," he said, wrinkling his brow. "Or maybe they found something. Whatever it was, it had to do with illegal action by Morin."

He looked Vaillant directly in the eyes. "Something so concrete and provable that he couldn't wiggle out of it as easily as he used to. And you in turn knew about it. You got wind somehow. And now you're in danger too."

Dupin had to give it a go. Make suppositions. Try his luck. Cut swathes through the thorns. If that was really what had happened. If they really had found proof of something, and others knew it, or even just guessed or speculated that they had, then it would be an explosive shock not just for Morin but for the whole region. In that scenario, Morin wouldn't just be looking for the murderer, but for others who might know about it. The unknown factor remained what role the professor played.

"If I really knew something I would have seen to it that Morin was in jail long ago."

"I don't believe a word of it."

"Go ask Gochat, the iron lady, why she sent her fisherman spy out after Céline." He sounded bitter.

"You'll know that we consider you a chief suspect, Monsieur Vaillant. You followed two of the victims. You were on the Île de Sein last night. You could have murdered Céline Kerkrom before that in Douarnenez, then Laetitia Darot this morning on the island."

"We're regularly on the island and usually sit in Le Tatoon. I wasn't aware that this was a cause for police suspicion."

"And this morning? You left the island at seven, where did you go? Where were you between seven and eleven?"

"We were fishing for sea bass. Up until midday. Over by the Pierres Noires to the west of Molène." This was one of the places Kerkrom also fished for sea bass, Madame Gochat had said. "We sold the bass at noon to two restaurants in Ouessant. And ate a couple of them ourselves. Go and ask at the restaurants if you want."

"I assume you have no witnesses for those four or five hours of fishing."

"No."

Vaillant put on his ironically contrite face. Dupin let it go. He was tired. He didn't want to keep at it. And he couldn't. In any case it was clear Vaillant didn't have a shred of an alibi. Dupin had intended to take a closer look around the boat. But he didn't bother with that either.

"That'll do for today, Monsieur Vaillant." He turned abruptly away and made for the little door in the railing. "But I think we'll be seeing one another again soon."

"And you really don't want to take a couple of mackerel with you? You won't find them anywhere as good as they are in the Mer d'Iroise," Vaillant called after him.

Dupin took another determined stride.

He walked up the ramp and then he was back on land. He didn't react, even to the last sentence.

"I hope you have a pleasant evening, Monsieur le Commissaire."

Two minutes later Dupin was standing next to his car. The conversation with the crazy pirate had sapped the last of his strength. He was angry, felt he hadn't been good enough. Not crafty enough. But even in top form he probably wouldn't have got more out of the guy.

He leaned for a moment on the car door and took a deep breath.

Nolwenn had been right. It was hardly a stone's throw back to Concarneau. He forced himself reluctantly to think of the one-and-a-half-hour drive. And if he really wanted to go out to the island to talk to the boy tomorrow morning, then he would have to be on Goulch's boat by seven at the latest. That meant getting up before six if he wanted to have a *café*. That meant very little sleep once again. And he wasn't going to see Claire today anyway: she was in Rennes and it was probably too late to organize something now.

He got his phone out.

"Nolwenn?"

"Monsieur le Commissaire." She sounded wide awake.

"Maybe I should stay here, overnight—spend the night here."

Nolwenn knew every guesthouse, every hotel, every room for rent.

"Château de Sable. Porspoder. Twenty minutes from you. They're expecting you. The owners are friends of Alain Trifin, the owner of the Ar Men Du. There were no more rooms free in the nice La Vinotière in Le Conquet. They'll bring a toothbrush and so forth up to your room."

It was unbelievable. Nolwenn was unbelievable.

"Thanks."

"I'd thought as much."

"Tomorrow morning I'm going out to the island first thing.

Riwal might need your help. Something to do with a laboratory in Paris. We need information urgently." It wasn't that he didn't trust Riwal with the job, but Nolwenn could work wonders.

"We've already spoken on the phone."

"I . . ." He was too worn out, too exhausted.

"You need sleep, Monsieur le Commissaire. We all do."

"Yes."

A rare confession.

"Till tomorrow morning."

Nolwenn had already hung up.

* * *

It was magnificent, the place, the hotel, the room. Even if Dupin was looking at it all through a veil of exhaustion.

The Château de Sable lay in a landscape of rough dunes, the sand grown up around the omnipresent stubble of greenery and high cliff formations. It was as if the earth had just exploded. A big wooden terrace facing the Atlantic, and two outcrops of land, one to the left, the other to the right, had closed the spreading sea into a gentle bay. They had also come to Porspoder on their work outing, but only briefly, primarily so they could go down the "Route Mandarine" to see Nolwenn's friend who made luxurious natural soaps from aromas of the earth, the plants, seaweed, and the sea itself. Dupin enjoyed going over the top in situations like that and had bought the whole selection for Claire. They had poetic names like "Ciel d'Orage sur Ouessant," "Avis de Tempête," "Envie d'Ailleurs." One even bore the name of his favorite song by Serge Gainsbourg, "Sous le Soleil Exactement."

Dupin opened the terrace door and went out. To breathe in the wonderful air once again, but also maybe to get a moment of relaxation after such a day.

Then he would lie down and be asleep immediately. The bed looked extremely promising.

The sky to the west still held the slightest trace of light. The last light of the day, a dark glimmer, blue verging on black but not quite there yet. The sea was brighter than the sky, even if that was theoretically impossible. Dupin had noticed the phenomenon a few times in recent years, although not as noticeably as here. The water of the bay glowed, shone, the light clearly coming from below. As if the sea itself were a source of light. As if it had somehow stored the light, in a bright shimmering and shining. Silvery ocher, metallic, an unearthly color. A flat, magical expanse, no waves, not even a wrinkle.

It seemed to be getting even brighter, turning on its end the natural order of things, Dupin thought. It wasn't the sky illuminating the sea, but the sea illuminating the sky—not just the sky but the whole world. Along with these strange sensations came strange thoughts and images, going back to his first boat trip of the day, as if they'd been strangely distorted, seen from a distance. Pictures of the dark shadows on the Île Tristan, thoughts of the seven graves. Dupin had to stop himself getting lost. He held tightly to the terrace railing.

Suddenly he heard a noise.

Dupin pulled himself together. He was almost relieved: the noise had shattered his bizarre impressions.

The noise was coming from above. Far above, somewhere to the front of him. A sort of thunder, rolling, then getting increasingly loud.

Dupin stretched his neck, scanning the sky with his eyes.

All at once, Dupin was practically thrown around, the sound now clearly coming from behind him. For a few seconds it became weaker. It wasn't his imagination. It had become clearly weaker, then stronger again. And sounded as if it came from all around. Even the nature of the sound had become strange: technical, artificial, and yet completely natural at the same time. It reminded him of a storm cloud or a volcano coming from deep in the earth.

Dupin stood stock-still for a moment.

He shook himself hard, ran a hand through his hair.

What had it been? Had it been his state of exhaustion that caused him to feel this? Were his senses playing tricks on him?

He turned around, went back inside, and fell on the bed. He found it difficult even to take his shoes off. He couldn't call a single clear thought to mind.

Day Two

Once again Dupin was jarred from sleep early. A particularly restless, troubled sleep. He had indeed immediately passed out but then quickly woken up again, then waltzed into a half-sleep of confused thoughts, before finally drifting off again. He had only really fallen into a deep sleep—for half an hour at most—shortly before Kadeg's call at seven minutes past five.

"You say we can't, I mean we've no way," Dupin said, stumbling on his words, "of getting to the email, to know who sent it."

"For now that's the way it's seems; we've forwarded the email to experts in Rennes."

"Gochat's garden house? We need to search the harbormistress's garden house?"

Dupin was sitting in bed, his back against the headrest. It had been hard enough for him to get into this position. He was not even up to being in a bad mood.

"Exactly," Kadeg said. "There's that one sentence: 'Search Gaétane Gochat's garden house,' but no address, no subject, nothing."

"And no hint as to what we might find there?"

"Just that one sentence."

"We need to start the action straightaway." There was an insuffer-able enthusiasm in the inspector's voice. "I can be there in an hour. Where are you, by the way?"

"Porspoder."

"What are you doing in Porspoder?"

Dupin ignored the question. "It could be a joke. Some idiot, who finds it funny. Or it could be the killer himself. Trying to di-vert our attention or confuse us. Leaving false tracks."

"It could solve the case."

"Maybe."

"And prevent any more murders."

Kadeg loved the drama in the tone of his voice. But that was true as well. It wasn't impossible, that it could have important con-sequences.

"Good, we'll search the garden house, Kadeg."

"You will need to get the search warrant, Monsieur le Commis-saire."

"A *dangerous delay*," Dupin growled.

Even when it was tricky, and Dupin had had problems more than once, his motto was: better problems afterward than acting too late. If necessary a public prosecutor or a commissaire himself could, in an emergency, order a search, if they could prove they had consulted a judge. Nolwenn would deal with that.

"I'm on my way immediately." Kadeg was in dynamo mode. "We'll see each other there. I'll deal with getting support in Douarnenez, we'll need a few colleagues."

It didn't take Dupin long to think about it. "You do this on your own, Kadeg." He quickly added, "I mean I'm appointing you as leader of this important operation, Inspector."

There was a brief silence. Dupin could almost genuinely feel the effect that was having on Kadeg, how he was torn between the impulse to protest because the commissaire wasn't going to be there and that meant the importance of the measure wasn't that far-reaching, and on the other hand pride that he was going to lead something that might be decisive.

"Fine." Pride had won out. "I'll keep you fully informed."

"You do that, Kadeg," Dupin said, and hung up.

It wasn't as if he thought the anonymous email was meaningless. Not in the slightest. But his original plans for this morning still seemed the best to him.

Dupin was still sitting in bed. Only now did he realize he had a headache, behind his forehead, his eyes. He hated that. He felt totally wrecked. A brilliant start to what would be another stressful day.

The email, though. What did it mean? Who sent it? Obviously it was tempting to think of Morin, and his own investigation.

He looked at the clock: 5:15 A.M.

The most important thing was: Where at this time of day, with people still asleep, was he going to get a *café*?

He pushed himself to get up. Dupin had had one hope and it had come to pass, even if not totally. The little fishing harbor where he had met Captain Vaillant the previous evening. And where Goulch was going to pick him up to take him out to the island. The fishermen would be up and about early here to set about their work, Dupin had reckoned. There would be people here needing coffee. And they had it. Only not from a coffee stall, but a machine. Still, better than nothing.

* * *

There had been nobody to be seen so early at the hotel. Dupin had taken a quick shower and simply set off. He had given them his details when he checked in last night. From the room he had called Nolwenn, who—obviously—was full of life and already in the picture about the anonymous email. She had made an agreement with Goulch and was now going to talk to the judge.

Dupin had found a bench near the fish hall, right by the water, and now had two brown plastic cups in his hands with a double espresso in each. The coffee tasted of plastic but it was hot and gave him the caffeine he was after.

It had been getting lighter for a long time now, and before long the sun would be up. The tide was dangerously high; ten to fifteen centimeters more and the water would be slopping over the quay. Coefficient 116, that was what Antoine Manet had said yesterday. That was enormous—the maximum was 120. And only a total eclipse of the sun would cause that, a miracle that would only happen three times in this century.

In the little fish warehouse, the one that was open to the quay, it was already busy. Fishermen in yellow oilskins, blue plastic boxes scattered around on the ground, a great water basin to the rear, for crabs, spider crabs, and lobsters, Dupin assumed. Three brightly colored fishing boats—coastal fishers—looked as if they were ready to set out, their heavy diesel engines already growling.

It had remained unusually mild overnight; the air was damp and smelled particularly strongly of salt and iodine. Dupin tried hard to muster his first clear thoughts, to come to his senses. It wasn't easy.

By the time Goulch's boat came into the harbor, twenty minutes late, he had almost fallen asleep on the bench. It took the third double espresso he fetched to have any effect.

Dupin took mechanical steps along the pier to the very end. There was no need of the concrete ramps with a tide like this. Goulch gave the commissaire a brief greeting. He looked tired too. Dupin was pleased to meet another person looking tired at this hour of the morning.

In next to no time he had steered out of the harbor, and it didn't take long before they had got beyond the last defenses of the peninsula. Goulch put his foot on the gas.

The only good thing was the strong tailwind, which astonishingly had more effect on waking Dupin up than the *cafés*—six of them when he counted them individually. As always, Dupin had positioned himself in the stern. The young policemen on Goulch's team understood and left him in peace.

To the north and northwest extended a whole row of islands, as far as the eye could see. With white sand and broad lagoons. It was easy to pick out Molène, the second-biggest island, and then beyond Ouessant, with the island's high cliffs at the eastern end and the great lighthouse, near which Vaillant and his team lived. Amidst the bigger islands, some of which were just a few hundred meters apart, innumerable smaller islands and rocks stood out, despite the high tide. This had to be where the seal colonies were that Nolwenn and Riwal had been so keen to tell him about, the ones on lots of postcards.

It was a breathtaking sight, as Dupin slowly came to. You could see and feel just how much the Mer d'Iroise was almost completely surrounded by the land, embraced and protected. Everything seemed peaceful, as mild as the air. The water was calm as a mirror, shining silvery blue in the first light of the sun. The boat glided gently and in a straight line across it, undisturbed by waves or wind. Almost sliding. Dupin had no fear at all of the calm, peaceful sea here.

He stood there almost without moving when the penetrating tone of his cell phone tore him away from his thoughts. He had obviously assumed there would be no reception here. But he saw five bars. And Riwal's number.

"Boss. I tried to get through to you last night, but you didn't reply."

Dupin had seen no indication of a missed call on his mobile, but then he had been half asleep. The inspector left an inscrutable pause.

"Go on, Riwal."

"The experts in Rennes looked through the bank accounts and transfers between each of the three deceased. There was a transfer of ten thousand euros between Laetitia Darot and Luc Jumeau on June 6 this year. Both had accounts with the Crédit Agricole in Douarnenez."

It wasn't easy to make out what Riwal was saying, what with the noise of the vehicle and the wind.

"With some particular business in mind?"

"No. At least there is no reference to what the sum was for."

Jumeau had said nothing. Which wasn't very clever, even if it was harmless. He should have known something like that would come out sooner or later.

"I'm on my way to Sein."

"I know."

"I'll talk to Jumeau myself."

Already the second piece of unexpected news for that morning.

"He's already out at sea."

"Get in touch with him. He must return to Sein."

"Okay, boss."

"Do we already have details of the victims' itemized phone calls? And what about their email accounts?"

"The experts are working on it. It's complicated."

"They need to let us know as soon as they manage it."

"They'll do that."

Dupin glanced at his watch. "We'll be there around a quarter past seven. Tell the boy's mother."

"Will do, boss. Did you . . ." Riwal was doing his level best to sound unconcerned, without succeeding. ". . . sleep well, then? And do you feel all right this morning?"

Dupin just hung up.

He wondered how long the—what should he call it? "Plague incubation time"?—might take in Riwal's mind. As long as it took, as long as possible.

Then his mind switched to the latest piece of news. Ten thousand euros, that was quite a sum. He couldn't wait to hear Jumeau's explanation.

They were due to start the search at Gochat's any minute, and Kadeg would arrive in Douarnenez soon. Dupin realized that the operation was making him a little nervous. He called his inspector's number.

"Where are you, Kadeg?"

He could hear the noise of an engine. "I'll be there in ten minutes. Four colleagues from Douarnenez are already in the street where Gochat lives, waiting for me." His voice shook.

It would make a splash, that was for certain. Dupin imagined Gochat opening the door, the harbor chief seeing a troop of policemen, and making a fuss before letting them in.

"Let me know everything that happens, do you hear me? And try not to make too big a scene."

"I'll behave fittingly."

Dupin stuck his phone in the pocket of his jeans.

His eyes wandered across the wild, glistening sea.

* * *

"Hi, boss," Riwal said. He was standing on the pier, where the museum chief had held her little reception committee yesterday. It felt as if it had been days ago.

"How was the trip?"

At least it seemed as if Riwal meant the question earnestly. Nonetheless Dupin ignored it.

"When do I see the boy?"

"At half past seven. At Darot's and Kerkrom's sheds."

In twenty minutes' time, that meant.

"Very good," Dupin muttered.

That gave him a bit of time.

"You got here quickly," Riwal said with an impressed nod.

Indeed, they had come at top speed the whole way. The sea had remained calm not just out on the open water, but even on the last stretch, just lain there flat and lethargic. "Like oil," was what the Bretons said, and it painted a precise picture. On days like this you could have sworn it wasn't really water.

Even out here on the island the air was still, already warm and damp. The smell of the sea was strong here too. Dupin had learned that the sea smelled differently every day, not just some days stronger than others but also differently in aroma. What they called in Brittany "the scents of the sea." From heavy and intense—like today—to light and airy, from salty and bitter to sweet and mild, the whole spectrum. Bretons described the smells of the sea as if they were talking about perfume, with differing notes. Today it was seaweed that dominated.

"Jumeau should be here soon. He didn't react much."

Dupin could imagine.

"Great."

He headed straight past him and was already a few meters away, then he turned around again. "Come along, Riwal."

Five minutes later they were sitting on the terrace of Le Tatoon, and for the first time that morning the commissaire was in a good mood. He felt nearly at home now on the Quai Sud, a feeling that Dupin didn't get from being there often but from one thing alone: his relationship with the place.

A series of islanders were already up and about as the island prepared itself for a new day, an atmosphere that Dupin very much enjoyed, as he did on mornings in the Amiral, in Concarneau, where, almost without exception, he began his days. An old lady with shining white hair, wooden clogs and a blue apron, and two baguettes in her hands strolled along the quay; an elderly man with a faded cap and broad-legged pants was pulling behind him a hand-cart laden high with wood. A laid-back young kid in jeans and T-shirt cycled past, legs splayed wide on a rusty bicycle that was far too small for him, whistling as he went. Somewhere on the island there was a lonely dull thudding going on. Like every sound on this island it vanished immediately again into nothing, ebbed away as if suddenly there was no longer any atmosphere to carry the sound.

It was a great Atlantic day, one of those days of pure flaming colors that always made Dupin a little drunk. Every tone was intense, penetrating, dizzying. Glowing and luxurious. A real high on colors.

Dupin had already chosen the sunniest place on the terrace, right at the front by the quay. Riwal had sat down next to him, rather than opposite, so he could enjoy the sun as well.

"Have you heard anything more about the relationship between Darot and the professor?" Dupin asked.

"No. Nobody knew about it. Manet's made it into the talk of the island."

Dupin understood immediately what the inspector meant.

"But nothing came of it."

That would have been too much to ask for.

"So we've tried to get people to find out about the elderly man in the Citroën C2 who came to see Professor Lapointe once a month. A renowned literary professor. They got to know one another three years ago in the Tabac-Presse, Crozon's cigarettes and newspaper shop. Both of them were classic literature fans, Maupassant above all. We've had people check it all out. He's not remotely suspicious."

"Anything new from the crime scene team? What about the list of books?"

"There was nothing out of the ordinary in the house, and the book list is ready."

"And?"

"Lots of Maupassant. Mostly classic books. Lots about the local region: history, culture, flora and fauna, everything the heart could want for. But not one single book about virology or other natural sciences, not one scientific book. And no science magazines either—I have the list here."

He handed Dupin his smartphone. Dupin looked down the list. Right at this moment he could see nothing revealing.

It was the same pleasant waitress as the day before. Dupin had ordered two *cafés* and two *pains au chocolat*, Riwal one *café* and two croissants, and she put them on the table in front of them with a charming smile.

It did them good. And was delicious at the same time. The strong coffee, a real *torre*, washed away the taste of the plastic.

There was a good view of "France," the mainland, today—the Pointe du Raz, the high-and-mighty forbidding granite cliff, was superb despite the still air. Yet it seemed unimaginably far away. It was a basic feeling that immediately overtook anyone on the island; that of being far away from everything. Much farther than the nine kilometers it was in reality.

Despite there obviously being lots to talk about, they had automatically both stopped talking with their first sip. They had lost themselves in the taste of the coffee and the picturesque scenery.

Brusquely the pleasant quiet was broken by Dupin's phone.

Kadeg.

"Yes?"

"Madame Gochat wants to talk to you in person," Kadeg barked. "We formally requested that she let us take a look at her garden house." Gochat must have been standing close by Kadeg. She was clearly whom he was addressing. "She has dismissively declined the police request. We are asking now for your intervention to secure access."

Dupin hesitated.

"Pass her over."

It had to be. There was no other way.

"If you were to be so good," said the harbor's boss in a tone that was cutting and sarcastic, "to explain to me what you mean by all this. I have informed my lawyer, who is making a formal complaint. That's what you are causing with this serious breach of the peace."

Dupin had known this was going to cause trouble. "We are in possession of substantial indications that you are hiding something relevant in your garden house. I have no choice, Madame Gochat." Dupin's cool tone of voice was not apologetic.

"Are you trying to get a search warrant?"

"The judge has been informed"—or soon will be—"which means I have the authority to order the search. Which I am hereby officially doing. Have no fears, Madame Gochat, everything will be done by the book. Your lawyer will confirm that. And as we're speaking, do you have an explanation to give? Think well: if you do have anything to say it would be better for you to say it now rather than later."

"I have nothing to say to you, either now or later."

With that, she hung up.

He had actually imagined her reaction being more drastic.

Dupin leaned back and ate the last piece of *pain au chocolat*. "Madame Gochat is less than thrilled." He got to his feet, still chewing. "I'd better go and see the boy. Let me know as soon as you hear anything from the company."

He dropped a bill on the table, left the terrace, and walked down the Quai Sud toward the sheds.

A few minutes later he lifted his phone again. Maybe he would do well just to check.

"Nolwenn!" he said quickly. "Do we have the okay for the search at Madame Gochat's place?"

"It should come through any moment. I imagine Judge Erevan won't cause us any problems. I've had an extensive talk with his assistant, who knows him well. She suggested it would be a pure formality."

"Good, that's all for now."

"Did you call your mother?"

"I'm just about to."

"I'm not taking any more of her calls."

"I understand."

"More important, I've just been speaking to the customs people. Several people. The story about the sunken boat is complicated. They—"

"So, it wasn't just a rumor?" Dupin interrupted her. Maybe he wasn't losing his flair after all.

"It all goes back to a captain who's since retired. A report by him. From May 23, 2012. The customs at the time suspected that the sea route was being used for cigarette smuggling. At which point they increased their patrols. The captain said that they spotted a fishing boat in the mist during heavy seas at dusk. A *bolincheur*. Just outside the entry to Douarnenez Bay. No fishing boats were going out at that time. He claimed to have recognized the typical colors of Morin's fleet: bright blue, orange, and yellow. Another crew said the same, two others couldn't confirm it. It looked suspicious to the

captain and he tried to get closer to the *bolincheur*. At which point
the fishing boat doused all its lights and set off at full speed. They
followed it for twenty minutes, radar equipped with True-Track
function. Until it vanished. They—"

"Where did they lose it? Where was its last known position?"

"Beyond the entrance to the bay, on the north side, where the
panhandle from the Crozon peninsula comes down, Cap Rostudel."

Dupin stopped in his tracks. "That's more or less where Kerkrom was seen in her boat. Both the women."

"Slightly farther south, as I understood it."

Dupin didn't respond to that, but asked, "And after searching in
vain, the captain assumed the boat had sunk?"

"That's what happened. And that the crew had reached land in
the tender. In the meantime the weather had got even worse, which
of course could be the reason they lost the boat. That was what it
said in one commentary on the report. Of course, it could also have
been that the *bolincheur* hid away in another bay. Given the weather
conditions the captain obviously couldn't have searched the area
systematically."

"Did they search for the boat in the following days?"

"Two days. But with no luck. They hadn't had any exact position,
so they gave up on the search. Then the news came that the smuggling routes over the water were no longer of importance. They had
found heaps of cigarettes in refrigerated trucks driving through the
Channel Tunnel. They had hidden the packs in deep-frozen animal
carcasses."

"Was there any indication that the fishing boat had been scup-
pered? Apart from the captain's supposition? Anything concrete?"

"No. And apart from the conspicuous behavior of the boat there
was no reason for suspicion."

Dupin thought about it.

"The captain was totally convinced they'd played him for a fool.
That they'd had vast quantities of smuggled cigarettes on board."

"What's the captain's name?"

"Marcel Deschamps. I'll text you his number. He's a pensioner nowadays, but still alive."

"Good."

"See you later then, Monsieur le Commissaire."

Dupin set off again.

* * *

The commissaire reached the shed still deep in thought.

He had expected to see the boy's mother too, but Anthony was standing on his own in front of Darot's storage hut, which had in the meantime been cordoned off by police tape. The boy looked as if he had been waiting a while. He was once again wearing the dirty jeans with the baggy pockets, but a clean green T-shirt.

"I saw you come in on the police boat," Anthony said with a proud smile. "I was watching you." He spoke casually, not making a fuss.

"The whole time? Since I came ashore?"

"You went with your inspector straight into Le Tatoon. You drank two *cafés* and ate two *pains au chocolat*. And talked with the inspector. You kept running your fingers through your hair. That looked funny."

Impressive. Dupin hadn't noticed Anthony. Despite the fact he must have been somewhere roughly nearby to have noticed all that so precisely.

"You'd make a first-class spy. Did you come on your own?"

"My mother told me to tell you she couldn't come. I have little brothers and sisters." He rolled his eyes.

"My inspector tells me you also watch the fishermen when they're out spearing fish at sea, and when they come back. And when they're working here at the harbor."

"I help them too."

"With their catch?"

"With everything: bringing the catch on shore, fixing up the nets, sorting through the fish."

"Was Céline Kerkrom's catch good of late?"

"Not bad. But she only brings fish here now and again. She sells her fish most of the time in Douarnenez." He looked Dupin directly in the eye. "Why?"

"No reason. You said she was spending more time at sea than usual."

"These are proper police questions, aren't they?"

"Absolutely proper police questions."

"Yes, more often."

"Anybody else? Any other of the fisherfolk more often out than normal? Jumeau maybe?"

"No. Everything was as normal with him."

"When was the last time you helped Céline Kerkrom?"

"Last week. I couldn't say which day."

"Did you chat with her when you were helping her?"

"Oh, yes. She told me stuff about the sea, about her trips. She knew great stories."

"What sort of stories?"

"About secret places?"

Dupin pricked up his ears. "Secret places?"

"Where you catch the best fish."

"She told you that?"

There was a bench made of wooden planks on concrete supports just a few meters away, right by the water. Dupin walked over to it, the boy following.

"Yes. But I'm not saying where."

Anthony sat down next to Dupin.

"Just tell me approximately. The general area."

"Maybe," he hemmed and hawed, "maybe near the Witch."

"You mean the lighthouse?"

The boy looked at him uncomprehendingly. "What else? Ar Groac'h."

They had seen it on the crossing yesterday. If Dupin had gotten it right, the lighthouse with the memorable name wasn't in the

Chaussée de Sein but a little farther north. Which also meant: almost in the entrance to Douarnenez Bay.

"That's a secret place?"

"There are underwater caves there and particularly strong currents. With huge shoals of small fish. And for that reason it's a hunting ground for the biggest bass and *lieus jaunes*. Over a meter long. There's a lot of seaweed just below the surface of the sea; that's why no anglers go there. But if you come across a heavy bream there"—the boy's eyes twinkled—"you go down and catch it. You just have to know." Anthony looked at the commissaire triumphantly.

"Do you know how long she'd been going there?"

"Just since this year, I think. But she had been there a long time before, she said."

"Are there other secret places inside Douarnenez Bay? Where she had also been often recently?"

"No secret fishing places."

A clear statement.

"Apart from the best fishing places—maybe she was in the bay somewhere recently for another reason?"

"I don't think so. She would have told me."

"Are you certain?"

The boy looked inquisitively at Dupin. "This is important, isn't it?"

"Very."

"I don't know of any other reason," Anthony said at last. He couldn't manage to hide his disappointment, how much he would have loved to have something decisive to report.

"And Laetitia, did you watch her too?"

"Sometimes, not so often. I never knew when she would go out. Or come back. It was always different. But she was very nice. She would tell me dolphin stories sometimes."

"What sort of stories?"

"About her favorite dolphin, a female. Darius. She had two male children last year. She told me everything Darius taught her boys.

She showed them the best hunting places. She had secret places, just like Céline."

"Other stories?"

"How dolphins helped people. Last year an extreme swimmer was attacked by a white shark. Then twelve dolphins came and formed a circle around him. They swam with him for twenty kilometers. Or the story about the little boy who fell overboard in a storm and was brought to land by a dolphin. The dolphin was called Filippo. But they also come to us for help, if they know exactly who we are. Recently a dolphin got caught up in an angler's line, the hook caught in his fin. He swam up to two divers and drew their attention to the hook. When the divers had freed him, he gave them a pat with his fin to say thank you." Anthony suddenly looked at him seriously. "There's film of it. I can show you if you don't believe me."

"I believe every word."

He seemed satisfied with Dupin's answer.

"Did she talk about the dead dolphins?"

"Yes, that was really bad." There was an expression of serious distress on the boy's face.

"Did she say anything about it? About who was guilty?"

"The big ships and fleets. Everybody knows that."

"Did she speak about that big fishing chief, Charles Morin?"

"No."

A clear no.

Dupin sighed. The boy was great but there was nothing new in what he said.

"Once upon a time Jumeau found a cannonball on the seabed. Antoine said it's from the seventeenth or eighteenth century. Maybe from a real pirate ship. There were lots of pirates around here." The boy watched the commissaire carefully. "It's now in the museum treasure room. There are also real coins there, some silver, according to Madame Coquil, even if some of them are covered in chalk. Have you been to the museum?"

"Not so far."

"You have to go and see the treasure chamber! Madame Coquil has made me the treasure chamber's special envoy. I always take everything the fishermen find there. Recently—"

The phone.

Kadeg again.

Dupin feared the worst.

"Yes?"

"Commissaire, we have the murder weapon."

It sounded more comic than dramatic, even though Kadeg had tried for a dramatic effect. And then said nothing more. Dupin had sprung to his feet.

"Say that again, Kadeg!"

"A fisherman's knife, standard black model, the one you find everywhere in Breton harbors. Eight-centimeter blade, the whole thing nineteen point four centimeters long. Stainless steel, hard plastic handle."

"What makes you think it's the murder weapon?"

"There's bloodstains visible, both on the blade and the shaft."

"Where did you find it?"

A whole range of different questions were flooding through Dupin's head. He had walked on a few meters.

"The knife was hidden behind a loose wooden plank. I found it. It wasn't actually visible. It was only when—"

"I want . . ." Dupin stopped. He looked at the boy, who had stayed sitting on the bench and was staring at him with eyes wide open.

"I'm afraid I have to go, Anthony."

The boy nodded. He didn't seem troubled; on the contrary he seemed fascinated by the sudden burst of excitement.

"Commissaire, you still there?" Kadeg sounded insulted.

Dupin headed toward the quay. "The forensic people need to look at the knife as soon as possible. I want to know with absolute certainty if it really is the blood of one of the victims. And if there are any other clues on the knife. They have to drop everything else."

"Got it."

"Have you confronted Madame Gochat with your discovery?"

"She claims never to have seen the knife, that it's not hers. That she's only been living in this house two years, and has never taken a close look inside the garden house." Kadeg added derisively: "The shelves were already built in. The garden house was also never locked and is covered by two big trees."

"We're going to have to arrest her for now," Dupin mumbled, lost in his thoughts. "You'll bring her to Quimper, Kadeg."

"Like I said, the knife was quite impossible to see, it was perfectly hidden. I documented it with photos."

Dupin hung up.

Intuitively he headed south, to look for Riwal, though he couldn't see him either on the Tatoon terrace or anywhere else on the quay.

The find could be all-important. Which didn't exclude the possibility that it was a farce. Wasn't it all very strange? Too easy, above all. Even if the knife really was the murder weapon, if there were traces of blood from Kerkrom, Darot, or Lapointe, there were still several possibilities. Somebody could have planted it on Gochat. To blame her for the murders. It wasn't hard to hide a knife in a garden house—the killer would have carried out a lot of riskier operations. One thing was certain: even without Gochat's fingerprints it would have been a very effective chess move that, when taken in conjunction with the fact she had had the pair spied on, would put serious pressure on her. A primitive move, but an effective one. Without watertight alibis it would make things difficult for her. And it was just this type of cold-bloodedness that could be expected from the killer.

Or, and was equally possible: Gochat actually was the killer. Even if she didn't have the slightest glimmer of a motive. Dupin didn't know what he should think. His "gut instinct" was telling him nothing right now. Nothing at all, not even a hint. No intuition, no inner voice, no inkling. However things might go, he had to remain calm, concentrate, follow the threads, and not turn away from any twist or turn.

"Boss!"

Dupin turned around.

"Here!" Riwal called as he burst out of one of the storybook small alleys.

"It's unbelievable, boss. Nolwenn got in touch with the firm. She spoke to the chemist in the laboratory. The one who carried out the analysis." He came to a brusque halt in front of Dupin. "It's a fluorescent X-ray analysis, it's used, amongst other things, to identify precious metals, it's based on a complicated—"

"Riwal! Spit it out!"

"Gold!"

"What do you mean, 'gold'?"

"The material analysis that Céline Kerkrom asked for says that the sample she sent in contains gold. Very pure gold, nearly twenty-four karat."

"Gold?"

"It's incredible! One side of the sample, two and a half centimeters long, very thin, was very dirty, the lab man said. As if weathered, in layers, not at all recognizable as gold. Either Kerkrom didn't know what the material was, or she knew it was gold and wanted to see how good quality it was."

"And what's so unbelievable about it?"

The process didn't seem so unusual now.

"Maybe Céline Kerkrom," Riwal said, stressing every syllable, taking his time, "had seen or found something made of gold. Or Darot." He took a deep breath. "Everything would suddenly make sense. Everything!"

Dupin understood. This was right up Riwal's street: treasure.

Dupin wasn't in the mood for Riwal's fantasies. "Or she had an old gold medallion, an armband, a chain. Something she'd inherited and wanted to know the worth of. Maybe she was considering getting rid of it."

Riwal's face fell with deep disappointment. And incomprehension.

"On the Internet form that Kerkrom filled in it said 'sample.' It can't be something small. Two and a half centimeters is significant. Nobody mistreats an inherited artwork like that. Nobody has such a thorough analysis carried out for some chain."

"There are other things made of gold. Plates. Cups. You can inherit things like that too." Dupin thought of his mother's house in Paris and remembered that he really had to ring her. "And she didn't make any written reference to the origin of the sample?"

"No, we know nothing about it."

"I have to go, Riwal."

Dupin was suddenly feeling restless. He was unhappy with the abrupt way in which his chat with the boy had ended. They had now come across a topic he would have liked to go into more detail about.

He glanced at his watch. It ought to work, even if it would be close. He would make the call as he walked and then catch up with the boy at school. He headed toward the Quai Nord. "Monsieur Deschamps?"

"Who wants to know?" A testy grunt.

"Georges Dupin, commissaire de police, Concarneau."

Dupin made a point of sounding friendly; after all he was the one who wanted to know something from this man.

"And?"

"It's about Charles Morin. I'm investigating the triple murder case."

"Yes?"

"I'm interested in the story of what happened on May 22, when you tailed a suspicious boat that you took to be a *bolincheur* from—"

"Forget it."

"How do you mean?"

"That story only caused me problems. Like everything only ever causes me problems. I don't want to talk about it."

"Have you changed your mind? Did you make a mistake back then?"

"What's that supposed to mean?"

"Are you no longer of the opinion that it was one of Morin's boats that you were following? That it had smuggled cigarettes on board and it was the crew itself that sank the boat, after you'd cornered it?"

Dupin had just passed the bench where he had been sitting with the boy. He was nearly at the Quai Nord.

"Of course that's how it was. Exactly so. But nobody was interested. Quite the opposite. Once again I was the troublemaker. I'm not going to say another word about it. I'm running a small distillery with my brother-in-law. I'm happy. I don't need those old stories anymore."

Dupin found the man not in the slightest unpleasant. But he wouldn't let himself get led astray.

"Did you have proof? Concrete proof?"

Deschamps said nothing. Then it seemed as if he gave himself a jolt.

"Their boat was faster than ours—what sort of *bolincheur* has an engine like that? Normal fishing boats are barely half as fast as ours. I'm telling you, boats like that are specially equipped for smuggling."

"That's why you lost it on the radar."

"Like I said, I don't want to talk any more about this subject."

"Did anyone check on Morin's fleet numbers afterward? I mean, every boat in every fleet has to have a registration, and when all of a sudden one goes missing somebody must notice."

"I have nothing against the Parisian commissaire." Deschamps spoke smugly if not unkindly. "The best of luck in his further investigations. Excuse me, please."

Before Dupin could say a word, Deschamps had already hung up.

Dupin rubbed his temples.

He had turned off the Quai Nord. He had already noticed the gleaming white painted stone building with the big sign, *École Primaire,* the previous day.

Two children—a tall, lean kid in shorts and a disheveled little girl in a multicolored dress—were sitting on the steps. Dupin guessed

Anthony was the sort of kid who would turn up last, as a straggler. He stood at a certain distance, just close enough to see everything.

He dialed Riwal's number. The inspector was the expert on things to do with boats, and fishing.

"Boss?"

It was probably going to be a tough bit of work, but it had to be done. "The supposed smugglers' boat, that the crew themselves are alleged to have sunk, I've just been talking to the retired customs authority captain, and I—"

"I'm in the picture. Nolwenn told me about her research."

In that case he could get straight to the point.

"If they really did sink the boat, it must have been counted as missing eventually. It must be possible to find out if a boat suddenly vanished."

"As a rule, boats are officially registered at several places. But they don't keep a continuous record if the boats still exist, not even if they're still in use."

"You mean it might officially still exist all over the place even though it's actually lying at the bottom of the sea?"

"Once every four years a fishing boat has to go through a technical check, a bit like a vehicle technical inspection."

"And that might be this year." Dupin had simply come out with the sentence, without really knowing what he meant by it. "You mean otherwise it would already have been noticed?" That was probably what he had meant.

"Not necessarily," Riwal said. "Morin might simply have deregistered it. As 'put out to rest,' 'inactive.' You don't need any official documentation for that."

"We need to find out if Morin deregistered a *bolincheur* in the last three years."

That was the crux of the matter.

"Or he used a few tricks to replace it."

"How do you mean?"

"Every boat is identified by two numbers, which they also need for its registration. One is an official plate, set into the ship's stern, while the other is the engine number."

Dupin pricked up his ears. "You mean because of these two numbers a boat that was found on the seafloor could be positively identified."

"Straightaway and with no doubt."

There was a long silence. Dupin's imagination was going wild.

"You think Kerkrom and Darot might have found the boat?"

"It's possible," Dupin replied absently.

"And the professor? Philippe Lapointe—how does he come into it all?"

"I don't know."

That was an issue for Dupin. But then he had only just begun to think through the scenario.

"How could Morin have passed off a new boat as an old one to the examiners, Riwal?"

"By manipulating the two identification numbers."

"But how, precisely?"

"It's difficult, but possible. In every run of boat production there are several that are identical. They then have to be made identifiable through the two numbers, the one on the stern and the one on the engine. In the end, you can manipulate everything if you're . . . sufficiently motivated."

Riwal was right of course; it was an assumption that lay at the heart of their profession.

Dupin was keeping a close eye on the entrance to the school. The two kids got listlessly to their feet and walked into the building. Lessons were about to begin.

"Riwal, I want you to check everything out. Get some help." The number of personnel required for something like this was huge, but Dupin didn't care. "Somebody needs to make a list of all Morin's boats, all the *bolincheurs* registered over the past four years. And compare it with the list of all boats registered today. And then check out each one painstakingly. To go and see it in person, including the two identification numbers, checking for possible manipulation. We also need to find out if Morin bought a *bolincheur*—new or used—over the past three years." Dupin just rattled off the chores. "Then we need to know which boats were in for technical inspection over the past few years, and which have still to undergo it. All the permutations."

"I'll get on it straightaway, boss."

Riwal was on the job.

"Good."

"And the story," Riwal said, "will go like this. Morin will hold us for fools, will refuse to cooperate and get the investigation moving, but instead he'll have unscrupulously got rid of anyone who had found proof of his smuggling—the boat with its smuggled goods on board that was sunk by its own crew, the part of the stern with the identification number. Or the engine."

Dupin didn't reply. But yes, that's how it might have been. It had gone vaguely through his head the previous evening, although only vaguely, a story that only hung together with the assumption of a lot of bold "if"s. But it was often like that at the beginning. Almost always.

"We'll talk later, Riwal."

He hung up hurriedly. Dupin had spotted the boy.

Anthony was coming across the grass, from the sea. He had spotted Dupin too.

He was smiling cheekily. Dupin went up to him.

"More police questions?"

Dupin smiled back.

"Will I have to miss my lesson?" the boy asked hopefully.

"Just for a few minutes, but you can tell your teacher, Monsieur . . ."

"Madame, Madame Chatoux."

"Tell Madame Chatoux the commissaire needed your help."

A sly expression slipped across his face; that seemed good enough for him.

Dupin came straight to the point. "You were just saying that the fisherfolk sometimes brought things they had found on the seabed: cannonballs, coins, my inspector referred to old anchors and parts of shipwrecks . . ."

"You can see it all in the museum. Shall I show you?"

Actually, it was a good idea.

"Agreed, but in that case I had better have a word in person with your teacher."

The boy's face beamed.

"Wait here." Dupin went up the stone steps into the building.

"The room on your right. There are only two downstairs."

"I'll find it," Dupin called over his shoulder.

A few minutes later he was standing back outside.

"Done. You've got half an hour off to help with police investigation work."

"Then we should lose no time." The boy hurried to the Quai Nord, at the end of which the museums lay. Dupin had to work to keep up with him.

"Do you know if Céline Kerkrom or Laetitia Darot," he said casually, "might have made a discovery of some sort on the seabed recently? Come across something special? Might even have brought it here?"

"Céline found something."

Dupin stopped automatically.

"Mama wouldn't believe me. Nor would Papa. They say people made jokes about holy symbols. They thought I had just made it up."

"What do you mean?"

The boy had gone on ahead and made no sign of being about to stop. Dupin set off after him.

"I couldn't see it properly. It was wrapped up in a cloth."

"Céline Kerkrom brought something here?"

"Yes, on her boat."

"What?"

"A big cross. A really big cross."

"You saw a big cross?" Dupin stopped again. It sounded completely implausible.

"Yes." The boy hesitated for the first time. "At least it looked like a cross."

"What makes you think it was a cross?"

"The shape. From underneath the cloth it looked like a cross, the thing underneath it, I mean."

"It was wrapped in a cloth?"

"Yes."

"But you didn't see the actual thing itself."

"No, but I think it was a cross."

"That would be appalling."

Had they actually dug up a piece of Morin's *bolincheur*? The piece with the identification number, the engine? It wasn't impossible that provisionally covered or wrapped up it might have had a cross-like shape. Or the bit from the stern?

"When was this, Anthony?"

"Oh . . . about the beginning of the month. I know because I had gone swimming that day, for the first time this year. It was nice and warm, the water too."

Dupin recalled the little heat wave at the beginning of June.

"Mama always says my imagination runs away with me. But it's not true, monsieur."

"Did her boat already have a new lifting arm?"

"Yes."

It had to have been installed in the weeks before. Maybe even for this purpose. There was no way it could be coincidence.

"And Laetitia was there too," Anthony said.

Dupin looked questioningly at the boy. "She was also on the boat?"

"Yes. They had gone out a couple of times together on Céline's boat. And before that a couple of times on Laetitia's. But most recently only on Céline's."

Dupin had to pull himself together. "Did they bring the object ashore?"

"I didn't see. I had to go home. The following day I had a look in the treasure chamber. Before school. And I asked Madame Coquil if anything new had been brought in. And Antoine. Céline was already out fishing again."

"And?"

"They said no. That evening I asked Céline herself."

"And what did she say?"

"That it was a wooden beam she needed for her house. That she had brought it from France. But I think she was fibbing."

"A wooden beam, she said?"

"Yes."

"Where had you been hiding? Where were you watching them from?"

"Near the sheds. Between the two quays. If you're small you can hide unnoticed behind the lobster cages," Anthony said with another sly smile.

Dupin himself had been a witness to Anthony's impressive proficiency in hiding and espionage.

"I want you to show me that briefly, before we go to the museum."

"In that case half an hour won't be enough. I'll miss more lessons." The boy grinned and turned around on the spot.

They were at the huts in seconds.

"Just here, this is exactly where I hid."

He was pointing at a dozen piled-up lobster cages no more than three, maybe four, meters from the slope of the quay wall.

"Behind them. There weren't as many that day, but even so they didn't see me. And here," Anthony ran over to the water, "this is where they laid it down. The cross was in the stern of the boat among several fish boxes. You could almost not see it. It was wedged in. I don't think they wanted anybody to see it."

"What makes you think that?"

"Because it was so well hidden. And they only came into port when it was already dark."

"But you could still see them nonetheless."

"Yes."

If he had been hunkered down behind the lobster cages he would only have been a few meters away.

"And you reckoned it was a cross because of the shape?"

They'd already been over that, but it was an important point.

"It really looked like a cross, it had exactly that shape. And it was really big."

"But you didn't manage actually to see what it was underneath the cloth?"

"No."

There was nothing more to be got out of him. And Dupin had seen what he wanted to see.

"Let's go."

Dupin stopped again on the Quai Nord. The boy was still close beside him.

"And was there anybody else on the quay that evening? Did you see anybody?"

"No."

"What about earlier, did you see anybody nearby?"

"The two other fishermen had already come in."

"Jumeau first?"

"No, he was the second."

"And did he stay about longer on the quay, I mean after he had docked?"

"He was gone by the time Céline's boat came in. He had tied up his boat and left."

"Long before?"

"No, not long."

Dupin had taken his notebook out and scribbled something as they walked.

"Are you writing this down?" The boy tried to get a sideways look. "Is what I said important?"

"That depends. And did you see anybody else before the pair docked in Céline Kerkrom's boat?"

"Antoine Manet came by, just as Jumeau came in."

"What did he want?"

Dupin knew he was asking impossible questions. But children didn't know what impossible questions were.

"They talked for a bit. He stood up close to the boat. I couldn't hear them. Then he left again."

"And that was it?"

"Yes, nobody else."

"And in the days that followed, did you watch Céline again?"

"Yes."

"But you didn't see any other . . . object?"

"No, the cross was already gone the next day. They must have taken it to a hiding place." He sounded devastated. "But I'm afraid I don't know where."

There was a brief pause. There were almost back at the museum.

"Earlier you said the object was really big. Just how big exactly?"

"About as big as me, maybe."

"You're sure?"

Dupin put Anthony at about one meter forty. Could be believe the boy? Should he? Dupin thought there was no way Anthony had invented the whole story, just made it up. To get hold of him, grab his attention. But there was another question. Had he maybe just seen something quite ordinary and *then* his imagination had run away with him?

"Yes, I'm positive. Maybe the cross was made of silver or gold and Céline had to die because she had found real treasure. Do you think that's what it is?" The boy's voice sounded sad and fascinated at the same time.

Dupin gave him an urgent stare. "What makes you think of gold?"

"Just because. Gold is the most expensive, isn't it?"

Dupin sighed. "Let's take a look in the treasure chamber."

They had already turned into the museum's inner courtyard.

Dupin didn't imagine Kerkrom and Darot—whatever they'd

brought back—would have used this as a "hiding place," but nonetheless . . . he wanted to see this treasure chamber. Maybe it would give him other ideas.

"Over here, the room is in the lifeboat service museum."

They were magnificent horseshoe-shaped buildings, in the middle of a picturesque courtyard. Dupin was impressed that the lifeboat service had a museum of their own.

The boy headed straight through the entrance doors, then turned left, past an imposing glass display case in the middle of the corridor with an old lifeboat inside.

"Ah, here you are, after all. And about time too. A visit to the island without a visit to the museum is unacceptable."

The ironclad—wonderful—Madame Coquil had appeared from nowhere.

"Jacques de Thézac in person, the founder of the Abris du Marin, the shelters for stranded seafarers, built these houses. The very first shelters of all. Because conditions here were worse for people than elsewhere. And because back then lots of ships interrupted their journey here."

Her eyes beamed nostalgically.

"Anyway, this July we're having a big festival on Sein to mark the one hundred and fiftieth anniversary of the founding of the lifeboat service. You must come, Monsieur le Commissaire. No question about it. Seven thousand volunteers, and only seventy staff. The service was founded in Audierne in *1865*," she said, stressing the year as if she could hardly believe it herself. "That's where the main festival will be held, but obviously we couldn't let it go by without having one of our own. And in any case the station here on Sein was one of the very first, founded just two years later. The lifeboat service has a great tradition."

She took a step toward Dupin as if there was something important to follow.

"Do you know how many poor souls have been saved here over the centuries? Tens of thousands! Antoine has made a list of all the life-saving actions, you can find it on the Internet. Back in 1762 the Duc d'Aiguillon proposed to the islanders a wholesale transfer to the mainland, offering them all the finest pieces of land. And why? 'Who needs to care about the victims of shipwrecks when the island is going to waste?' That was in the official letter. As a gesture of thanks, the duke sent us tons of biscuits. Tens of thousands we saved the lives of. In 1804 we even saved two hundred and eight English. Up until the lighthouse was built a big ship was wrecked here every two to three years."

She took a step backward and smiled. "So, what can I show you? What are you most interested in?"

"Anthony here," Dupin was quick to reply, "wanted to show me something."

"The treasure chamber. The commissaire wants to see the treasure chamber. For police reasons."

The last sentence was supposed to signal authority.

"That room isn't open to the public, you know that. It doesn't belong to the museum! And it's pure chaos at present. We simply can't let anyone in."

A clear-cut decision.

"I'm sure it will be fine, Madame Coquil. I just want to take a brief look inside."

"And for what reason, if I may ask? Your inspector has already been here."

The boy ran on unheedingly straight to the door.

"At the moment we are on the track of different clues, investigative routine," Dupin said.

"It's off-limits."

Anthony was rattling the handle.

"Yes, it's now closed during the season. Order from Antoine Manet."

"I really just want a brief glimpse inside."

Dupin liked Madame Coquil, and he tried to show it in his tone of voice. It seemed to be working.

"All right then." She fumbled around in the pocket of her canary yellow cardigan, which today she was wearing over a crimson dress, and produced a key.

"We never used to close it in the season." Anthony was still looking unhappy. "Even I have to ask now when I want to go in."

"Who has a key to the room?" Dupin asked.

"Monsieur Manet and I. And there is one in the drawer in the kitchen where the brochures lie." She nodded her head.

While still wringing her hands, Madame Coquil had opened the door. She held it open.

"Afterward you must come by the historical museum. The history of the island should interest you at least as much as that here. Without our history we're nothing. Just ghostly phantoms! Never forget that!" She added with a smile, "For a competent tour of the treasure chamber I'll leave you in the hands of the future leader of the island."

And with that she turned away.

Dupin entered the room.

It was very basic and clearly hadn't been renovated in ages. The walls that had once been white had taken on a dirty yellow shade and smelled bad. The whole room smelled bad. An intensive mix of dust—which in places lay centimeter-thick on the floor—mold, Dupin guessed, some sort of glue and oil. There was something biting to it. One single window let murky light into the room.

Chaos was certainly the right word for the state it was in. Narrow painting tables were laid out in a long *L*. On top of them, next to them, between them, against the walls, everywhere there were cartons piled. With big yellow labels and abbreviations. All in the same format: *S.-28-20/ Georges Bradou/ 05/2002.*

The boy had noticed how Dupin stood there looking at the cartons.

"It's only the best pieces on the tables. All the rest are in the cartons. The stickers tell all the important stuff: the coordinates of where the piece was found, who found it, and so forth. *S* stands for

Sein. It's Antoine's system. It's the same everywhere in Finistère. He's in an organization, you know. They lay all that down."

It would be the organization in which Professor Lapointe had been a member.

"Look, Monsieur le Commissaire, these here are genuine Roman." Anthony was pointing to the middle of the tables. "This is Caesar Mazamian, that's my favorite coin. And this is Carausius. Caesar entrusted the protection of Brittany against the Germans to him. Real bronze. And here," he pointed to a handful of other coins, "these are silver." He was in his element.

Dupin walked the length of the *L*. It was a curious, magnificent ragbag of stuff. Every single piece had been given a little tag which gave the exact details as to where it was found, when it was found, and by whom.

He saw something.

An engine. Under the table between two boxes was an engine. A big rusty motor. Clearly more than a meter long. He stooped.

"That belonged to a fishing boat that sank on the west side of Sein, in a storm, found directly on the beach not far from the lighthouse."

"How long has it been here?"

"Oh, a few years. A long time."

"There's no plaque." Dupin had been looking in vain for the registration.

"Hm." The boy had no answer.

"Did anybody recognize the boat?"

"Yes. It belonged to a coastal fisher from Douarnenez. He had run it aground himself, he was okay."

"I understand. You saw this engine lying here, let's say, from the beginning of the year? And before that?"

The boy gave Dupin a quizzical look. "Yes."

"Are you quite sure?"

"I just told you."

In which case that couldn't be it.

Dupin got down on his haunches. He had never seen an un-mounted boat engine before. It had been built lengthwise but on one side there was a shaft that went downward, some thirty, forty centimeters, with a rusty rod in it, probably connecting it to the ship's propeller. And on the other side, clearly much farther up, a pipe, ripped away after a few centimeters, maybe the pipe to the fuel tank. If you turned the engine on end, and threw a tarpaulin over it, it would only take a little imagination to envisage the outline of a cross. Dupin took another look: a *lot* of imagination.

He got up.

"And the door to this room here didn't used to be closed?"

"No. Never before."

"When where you last here?"

The boy thought a minute.

"I don't know. Two weeks ago, maybe. Or three. There hasn't been anything new found recently."

"Nothing? Nothing at all?"

"No. Just the little iron horse." He pointed to the end of the table. A rusty horse made of iron and coarsely designed. "Jumeau found it."

"Where do you think the two women could have taken their big object?"

"That's the big question, isn't it?"

Dupin nodded.

"Not here. Home, surely. Or first to one of their two sheds. And then home. In the middle of the night when there's nobody around. Or very early in the morning." Once again he seemed to be think-ing conscientiously. "That's how I would have done it."

Dupin let his gaze run around the room once again. Along the tables. He ran his fingers down the back of his head.

"A fabulous exhibition. Thank you for the tour, and in particular for your excellent investigative work. You have done a great service to the police, Anthony."

The boy's eyes lit up. Then suddenly he looked gloomy. "Do I have to go to school now?"

"I'm afraid so. But by now you've already . . ." Dupin said with a glance at his watch, "been out for substantially longer than half an hour."

The light returned to Anthony's face.

Dupin headed for the door. "I think we'll be seeing one another again soon." He reached out his hand to the boy. The boy took it slowly, and then shook it hard.

"Feel free to take me out of class anytime you like. You know now where my classroom is."

With a broad grin he took off.

Dupin had to smile.

He closed the door of the treasure chamber.

Shortly before the exit he found Madame Coquil suddenly standing in front of him, as if she had just materialized out of nothing.

"And? Did you find what you're looking for?"

Dupin hesitated. "A gripping collection. But what I'm interested in are—more recent finds. Things from the past few weeks."

He gave Madame Coquil a penetrating gaze. It was pointless. Even if she had known anything there would have been nothing to see in the expression of the woman he had come to know. She showed not the slightest reaction to his sibylline question. Instead she just stared straight ahead.

"Now, I shall show you a little of the history of the island. We only have to go next door. We'll start with Sein in prehistoric days."

"I have to—"

Dupin's telephone rang. The commissaire gave a sigh of relief. Kadeg.

"I'm afraid I have to take this call, madame. I'm sorry."

He took a few hurried steps out into the courtyard.

"What's up?"

"There are no fingerprints on the knife. They tried it there and then with special fingerprint lifting papers," Kadeg said. "But the knife is now on its way to the laboratory, where they'll check it for DNA traces. And analyze the blood on the blade. A car is taking

Madame Gochat to the headquarters in Quimper. I'm off there too now. Naturally we'll wait for you if you also want to take part in the interview. Also the IT experts in Rennes have come back on the anonymous email. So far they can only give us the email client's service provider."

"We're going to have to let Madame Gochat walk free, Kadeg."

"We're . . . what?!" Kadeg was finding it hard to control himself. "You can't do that!"

"We're setting her free. Here and now. Did you hear me?"

"We found the murder weapon at her house. She has no reliable alibi. She had Céline Kerkrom tailed."

It was still not certain if it really was the murder weapon, almost nobody she had had anything to do with had an alibi, and Gochat was in no way the only person who had had Céline Kerkrom tailed. Of course naturally it had been enough to take the harbor chief temporarily into custody and have her interrogated—naturally it was possible to classify the facts to be as conclusive as Kadeg had done. The commissaire was concerned with other matters.

"If it was her it's more interesting to watch what she does when set free."

That was true, Dupin was convinced of it.

"I want to see what she gets up to. And you, Kadeg, will have her followed step by step, inconspicuously. Maybe she has something hidden away or knows where something might be hidden." Dupin was speaking less to Kadeg than he was to himself. "Or she might at least have an idea."

Kadeg had pulled himself together. "Have you something specific in mind?"

It wasn't yet time to divulge anything about vague and maybe completely crazy ideas, without it being a state of emergency.

"I mean in general."

"I think it's a mistake, but fine, you're the one who gives the orders here."

"Exactly so, Kadeg. I'm the one who gives the orders."

Something else had suddenly occurred to Dupin, an alternative, one that was an excellent extra idea.

"Kadeg, before we let Madame Gochat go, I want to talk to her one more time. Bring her here to the island. Straightaway." Dupin was liking the idea more and more. "Set off right now. With bells and flashing lights. Straight to Audierne. Directly on a speedboat." Kadeg was confused. "What if she refuses? I mean, if I tell her she can go and won't be interrogated, except that before-hand she has to go through an interrogation on the island . . . Her lawyer . . ."

"If she has anything to say about it, tell her she has a choice: she can go free, but has to talk to me once beforehand, or she goes straight into investigative custody. Which means numerous inter-rogations. It's up to her."

There was a brief silence. Then Kadeg said: "I think we'll see one another soon, on the island."

"I think so too. I'll wait for you."

Dupin hung up. While they had been talking he had carefully slipped out of the museum.

There was one thing that had remained on his mind the whole time. The phone call with his mother. One way or the other, he had to deal with it before long. And there was no way he wanted her to end up calling Nolwenn again. He took the telephone in his hand, bravely.

* * *

"Boss! Boss!"

Yet again Dupin had headed down to the quay and once again Riwal had emerged from one of the small alleyways just in front of him.

"You were busy, boss. Jumeau is there. He's sitting in the Chez Bruno."

"Let's go."

Dupin headed straight to the bar's little terrace. The call with his mother had been awful. But quickly over. It may have been the circumstance—lucky for him that the florist had just arrived and she was "occupied." He had poured out the truth to her, that the case had become more complicated since their last conversation, that there had been a third victim, that they had so far seen no sight of land in their investigations and that therefore it appeared more unlikely than ever that he could come tomorrow.

Despite him setting it out twice, she hadn't accepted his conclusion for a single minute, even at a rudimentary level, but had remained basically where she was. It was a technique—completely ignoring his information—which she had mastered perfectly. Anything she didn't want to hear she simply didn't hear. End of story. And that was the merciless but nonexistent punch line. She had mastered completely the ability to leave whomever it was with a bad conscience.

The lean young fisherman was sitting with a *petit café,* and seemed almost pensive.

"I would like to know," Dupin began to say before he had even reached the table, while Jumeau had just turned his head toward the commissaire, "what the large sum Laetitia Darot had transferred to you was all about."

Dupin sat on the facing stool, Riwal next to him. The question didn't seem to bother Jumeau in the least.

"I'm in financial difficulties. Have been for the past two or three years." He said it with no sign of self-pity or regret. It seemed nothing to him to admit it. "Fishing is a complicated business, for somebody like me anyhow."

"And she just sent you a bank transfer of ten thousand euros? Just like that, a large sum like that?"

"Yes."

"And I'm supposed to believe that?"

Jumeau gave Dupin an indifferent look.

"Was it meant as a loan?"

"No."

The problem was that Dupin himself hadn't the faintest idea

what the money transfer might have been about. Not even to what extent it might or might not be criminal. Even given the—extremely speculative, extremely airy-fairy—considerations that had come to light over the past few hours, no scenario occurred to him. Even so, ten thousand euros was a hell of a lot of money.

"Do you have debts?" Riwal took over.

"A loan from the bank for the boat. And I already had an over-draft on my account. I didn't ask her for it in any way. She had got hold of it by chance. And without another comment, asked me for my account number."

For Jumeau, that was a remarkably thorough answer.

Laetitia Darot had a regular income, and not too bad a one. But even for her it must have been a lot of money. Riwal would have mentioned if there had been irregularities on her account, such as large deposits, for example.

Riwal continued: "What if Laetitia Darot had paid you for, let's say, specific tasks? Perhaps for your help in recovering something? Or"—he wrinkled his brow—"for you to observe Morin and his boats taking part in something illegal?"

Obviously, that was easily plausible, although Dupin was getting more and more interested in the former idea.

"She just gave it to me like that. To help me."

"And," Riwal continued, "you did nothing for her in return?"

"Nothing at all." Jumeau fell silent. "She was like that. Money meant nothing to her."

"At the beginning of June, during the heat wave"—Dupin was keeping his eyes on Jumeau, alert for the slightest movement of his eyes, his mouth, his facial muscles—"the two women were out one day together in Céline Kerkrom's boat and came back relatively late in the evening, as the sun was already going down."

"I remember the hot days. So what?" He showed no reaction.

"You docked your boat shortly before the two did. At the front of the quay."

"That's where I always dock."

Jumeau didn't even appear impatient, something that would have been understandable enough given Dupin's awkward behavior. Riwal looked as if he was waiting for the punch line.

"Do you remember that day, Monsieur Jumeau?"

"I can only remember one of the evenings when Céline came in late. I had everything tied up when I spotted her boat at the back on the first jetty. I didn't notice whether or not Laetitia was with her."

"Was it already dusk?"

"I think so, yes."

"Did you come back down later to the moorings? To the sheds?"

"No."

Dupin thought for a moment. Then he spoke deliberately, sharply: "Where did the pair of them take it, Monsieur Jumeau? Where is it now? We know about their find."

The surprising question was initially met with nothing at all. This time too, Jumeau hadn't shown even the slightest reaction.

"I have no idea what you're talking about," Jumeau said.

Was Dupin deceiving himself or had the fisherman sounded unusually sad?

"And I don't believe a word you say."

"The decision's up to you."

"We know . . ." Dupin was about to try it again, then gave up.

The message that they knew about some discovery hadn't had any visible effect on Jumeau. Maybe it hadn't been a good idea to mention it at all. Dupin was annoyed. Without warning he got up and said: "Thank you."

It would have been a good opportunity to drink another *café*, but Dupin had lost enthusiasm. He was extremely annoyed. With everything. But most of all with himself. The whole case was going against the grain. Everything kept going head over heels. They weren't even managing a rudimentary investigation, to follow a thread properly. Figures were marginalized, then suddenly surfaced again, tasks left undiscussed. He felt everything was falling short.

He turned around and left the terrace silently.

Riwal stood up indecisively, looked at Jumeau, who didn't seem to be bothered by Dupin suddenly leaving, murmured, *"Au revoir, monsieur.* We'll be in touch," and followed the commissaire.

At the end of the quay Dupin turned onto the path that led directly to the sea, and inevitably, like all the others, to the lighthouse. Next to the path lay a gigantic rusty steel ship's screw, just like the other bits of shipwrecks that rose up around the island, like sculptures in a vast open-air museum. And under the great ship's screw there was a family of rabbits with little ones.

"Have we got anything yet on Morin's alleged sunken smuggler's boat?"

"I've asked for all the checks to be carried out at maximum priority, but it's going to take a while yet."

That was how it went. Follow-up checks took time. No matter how much Dupin resented it.

"Nolwenn is helping out. She has a good contact in the authorities."

"Perfect." That reassured Dupin.

"Do you really think"—Riwal made a serious face; something seemed to be worrying him—"that it's really all about the sunken boat, that it's Morin we're after?"

"I don't know!" That was the truth. "We have to keep looking in every direction."

Riwal cleared his throat, not particularly discreetly.

"Has anyone ever told you that Professor Lapointe was a particular specialist on Ys?" Riwal held back, then reformulated what he had just said: "I mean, he was an expert on local archaeology in general, but in particular on Ys. For the past two or three years, the legend-soaked city was his chief point of interest."

"Ys, really?" Dupin wasn't in the mood for the rich treasury of Breton legends.

"Kerkrom and Darot might have made some archaeological find on the seabed, that's what I mean. An important find. Something precious, of high value. And maybe that's why they sought out

Professor Lapointe and his expertise. Advice. The business with the analysis of the material would be plausible in that case. Darot and Kerkrom's purchase of technical stuff too. The new lifting arm, and the high-quality sonar which was capable of scanning the seabed beneath the mud and layers of sand. They could find anything with that."

Dupin was silent.

"It would also explain why Kerkrom and Darot were out to sea in a region where they had never been before. Maybe Darot had found it first. In the entrance to Douarnenez Bay, where the dolphins go in summer to hunt squid. And then she had taken Kerkrom there. Kerkrom's boat is vastly better equipped for salvaging something. And when they spent some time in the relevant region somebody noticed. The harbor chief and Vaillant for sure, as we know. But maybe someone else too. And they were watched. It could all have happened like that."

"You mean"—Dupin was trying to keep a neutral tone in his voice—"this is all about some sunken treasure in the end?"

This time it was Riwal who fell silent while the commissaire tested out the theory.

Dupin chose to follow the adventurous thread: "Say the two of them made a hugely important archaeological find? A cross, for example? Or something similar?"

He had spoken as absolutely casually as he could. But even so, at the word "cross" Riwal raised his eyebrows. "What leads you to the cross idea?"

Dupin made a dismissive gesture. "At the beginning of June the Anthony boy had been watching Kerkrom and Darot when they came back in aboard Kerkrom's boat at dusk with something on board. An object as big as he himself, he says, wrapped in a cloth. As far as he was concerned the object had the shape of a cross." Dupin interrupted himself and added—he clearly found it difficult to do—"He said it *was* a cross. The next day he asked Kerkrom and she told him it was a wooden beam she needed for her house."

Dupin had reckoned it was important to put it all in as matter-of-fact a tone as possible, but it wasn't exactly easy to treat the business with the cross as matter-of-fact.

Riwal had stopped in his tracks. For a moment he had looked pale. Then a light appeared in his eyes. Just the reaction Dupin had feared. The commissaire quickly added: "I think it might have been the engine or a part of the stern end of the sunken boat, a piece of a plank maybe. With the identification number on it."

"You know what they say about Ys, boss, don't you?" Riwal was trying hard to keep his excitement under control but not succeeding. "When they read mass in the big church in Ys on Good Friday, the city will arise again. And Dahut will come back. The legendary empire will rise again. And here comes the crucial bit, even if you aren't going to believe it: the mass, according to one of the reports"—*reports* rather than legends, Dupin noted—"that day has to be read under the *great gold cross,* standing on the church altar! The emblem of the legendary cathedral."

In fact Dupin wasn't unhappy: the more fantastic the stories got, the less he had to bother with them.

Another two rabbits appeared just in front of them; they only ever seemed to appear in pairs, again with daredevil speed.

"And are there some versions of the legend in which there actually is a great golden cross that plays a role?" Dupin had asked the follow-up question against his will.

"There are indeed."

"Tell me about it." He was sure he was going to regret asking. "Briefly. In as few words as possible, just the important bits of the myth, in a nutshell."

Riwal took a deep breath. "King Gradlon the Great was the king of Cornouaille, a famous king, repeatedly victorious and extremely rich, the son of Conan Mériadec, the first king of Armorica. The historic score could have been settled in the fourth or fifth centuries. Gradlon met the magnificent Malgven in the fjords of the north, and she bore him a daughter, Dahut, but herself died in childbirth. Dahut grew up to be an even more beautiful woman than her mother. Gradlon loved her more than life itself. Because she loved the sea more than anything else, he had a city built for her directly by the sea, the most splendid city the world had ever seen— with roofs of pure gold. And a spectacular cathedral. Great walls, the size of houses, surrounded the city, protecting this little empire from the sea. There was a single great gate, to which Gradlon alone had the key.

"Gradlon was a wise king loved by all and had an important adviser called Guénolé. Dahut was self-obsessed and greedy, but her father considered her a ray of sunlight and didn't see it. He named her queen and gave her the key to the gate. No man was good enough for her until one day she met a young prince at a ball, considered him the most handsome man on earth, and wanted to have him. She was a queen now and had power and vast riches, and now she also had love. The prince wanted a sign of her commitment. One night of the full moon she handed him the key. But the prince," Riwal caught his breath briefly, "was the devil himself. During the night he transformed back into his diabolical form and used the key to open the great gate. Within next to no time the whole city sank into the Atlantic. The king and his adviser saved themselves initially by climbing to the highest tower of the castle. Suddenly two horses emerged from the sea and took Gradlon and Guénolé to safety on the shore. The king called ceaselessly after his daughter—Dahut! Dahut!—but he caught no more than a glimpse of her in a wave. 'It's all my fault, I'm cursed,' she called to her father. Then she disappeared beneath the waves, of her own choice." Riwal was clearly moved.

"Poul Dahut, they called the pond into which she disappeared. It's still there today, to the east of Douarnenez. Her legs turned into a fishtail, and she herself became a siren, swimming through her submerged city at the bottom of the bay, where she has lived ever since. And she will only be freed when—"

"I've got the message, Riwal."

"Every day to the end of his life Gradlon stood on the coast of the bay looking out for his daughter, but he never saw her again. But on certain days he heard the bells of the cathedral, a strange distinctive sound, 'not of this world,' no ordinary bell ring. More like a sort of thunder, but changed and amplified by the water and the depths, suddenly lying over the entire region."

Dupin was reluctantly reminded of the extraordinary noise the previous night, that mad phenomenon; he did his best to banish all thoughts of it.

"Even today it can sometimes be heard at night. And that's it, boss, the story of Ys. Short and sweet."

Indeed, Riwal hadn't overdone it too much. He knew it wouldn't be wise to risk testing Dupin's extraordinary willingness, even briefly, to take account of such legendary stuff in an investigation.

"All in all, you could say it is at heart a story of the devil—*An Diaoul*!"

That was one of the favorite Breton genres, Dupin knew. Their "devil stories." In Brittany God and the devil were an inseparable pair, you couldn't have one without the other. Dupin's favorite story was the one about the slug, *ar velc'hwedenn ruz*. From the dawn of time, the devil had continuously tried to emulate God's creation, to hold his own in a war of opposing creation. Only he never quite got there—he always came close but there was always something missing. That was why there were so many incomplete, half-done, awful things in the world, an idea that had a strange power of conviction when you looked around you in reality. When God produced the delicious edible snail, the devil also had to have a go. That was what gave the world the slug.

"The devil led people into temptation, seduced them. But he was really only testing them. A test of character. Not everyone succumbed to him. Only those in whom greed, envy, vengefulness, and selfishness were stronger than all other traits." Riwal sounded deeply miserable now. "Just as in the case of our perp here, not because it was their tragic destiny, but because they permitted it. People have a choice."

"Good."

Dupin himself wasn't sure what he meant by "good" here.

"Don't think you're going crazy if you take something like this into consideration, boss!"

Dupin had in no way taken "something like this"—Ys—into consideration.

"Like I've said, the search for Ys is the subject of serious scientific interest. Think of the expedition I told you about, or of the many reputed historians intensively involved in it." It was as much to say, *you shouldn't find it irritating*.

By this time they had reached the cholera graveyard where Laetitia Darot had been so gruesomely laid to rest.

"The story about the beam, the wooden beam, that Céline Kerkrom needed, it all sounds a bit implausible, don't you think?" Riwal cautiously suggested.

Dupin didn't go into the matter. Instead he came back to another point.

"Was Professor Lapointe seriously concerned with the story about Ys?"

Dupin hadn't seen anything in Lapointe's study to suggest anything of the sort, nor was there anything on the list.

"It was a hobbyhorse of his. I know that from my cousin. He belongs to the same cultural organization Lapointe belonged to. Manet as well."

In which case there could have been many reasons for Darot and Kerkrom to have turned to the professor. He was also a doctor, and a biologist.

"Did I mention that my cousin is also an amateur historian? That he studied in Paris?"

"Was your cousin any more closely acquainted with Professor Lapointe?"

"Only superficially. In recent years he attended organization meetings so frequently because of his engagements for the *kouign amann*."

"What does your cousin do for a living?"

"He's the fire chief in Douarnenez, has been for many years, started out as a volunteer."

Dupin was massaging his temples. "Kerkrom and Darot must surely have known that Lapointe was advising the citizens' movement against the use of poisonous chemicals during the cleaning of Morin's boats. And they had been looking for an ally."

"But what for? An ally for what? Why would they have needed Lapointe in connection with the story about the sunken smugglers' boat? How could he have helped them with that?"

That was one of the unanswered questions. And in the end Riwal was happy enough to come back to it.

Dupin's gaze had drifted across the island, noticing nothing, but suddenly, he saw a single rabbit in front of them. It didn't seem to be the slightest bit afraid, showed no intention of fleeing. Dupin gave the animal a wide berth, briefly wondering if rabbits could carry rabies.

"What happens"—once again Dupin was trying to sound neutral—"if a private individual makes a major archaeological find. Is there a reward for the finder?"

"Five percent of the calculated value. At the moment the value of gold is around thirty-three euros a kilo. And we're undoubtedly looking at a serious weight in kilos here. A large cross could be worth several million. And that just goes for the sheer worth in weight. The real worth of such a find would be even more." Once again Riwal got carried away. "Just imagine! A relic from the legendary city. Immeasurable, the value would be immeasurable. And one thing is clear: the finder would become world-famous and rich."

He gave Dupin a guilty look. But only for a fraction of a second. Then he went on the offensive again.

"You heard the story about the arrival of the Vikings. Told precisely as it is today. And even these stories are today considered by non-natives as fantasies, legends! But these are just the exact historic events and venues passed down orally over a millennium, a little embellished in the process. No culture has preserved the oral tradition as that of the Celts. We've raised it to the level of an art form. All because of the legends." Riwal was talking in a fury of excitement. "Why should an event such as that which happened to Ys not be exactly the same sort of thing? An event even more important than the landing of the Vikings: the sinking of an entire glorious city beneath the sea, a massive rise in sea level, a fact we today know can occur." He was now supporting his fantasy with science, a clever tactic. "It could have been an ancient Celtic city, grown immeasurably rich through blossoming trade and fishing, which meant that Brittany in the early years of the Christian era belonged to the richest regions of Europe. Built directly on the coast, low down, below sea level, on a plain protected by high dunes and natural dykes, then continuously expanding. Until one day a devastating storm tide let nature break through."

Riwal looked Dupin directly in the eye. "A completely realistic scenario! Think of the greatest flood of the century following the solar eclipse this year! Or back to 1904, when the whole coast of Brittany disappeared underwater for two days. Including Douarnenez. And now imagine a once-in-a-millennium flood tide combined with an immense storm. And it's clear that within a hundred or five hundred years even some of the existing towns in Brittany will also literally sink!" Riwal was performing well. Presented like that, the story seemed a lot less fantastic, a much more prosaic picture.

"Do you know how many fishermen over the centuries have claimed at particularly low tides to have seen ruins in the bay? Above all the tower of a cathedral." He added quietly, "Reports come in to this day."

Dupin and Riwal were just going through another breathtakingly narrow passage of the island, on either side of which the sea had eaten its way threateningly into the land. At the same time the path forked to the right toward the lighthouse, to the left toward a stone chapel.

Riwal started up again: "You really must see—"

Dupin's phone rang. He pulled it out gratefully. It was Nolwenn.

"Your instinct didn't let you down, Monsieur le Commissaire. Morin did indeed deregister a *bolincheur*. One that was only ten years old! That's no age at all for a boat like that. He did it everywhere, with the fishing authorities, the harbor administration. And here's the crucial point. He did it almost exactly a year after the incident, and just two months before the technical inspection was due. In the light of your hypothesis, that's extremely suspicious behavior, I'd say."

"Splendid, Nolwenn, splendid! And this deregistered boat hasn't appeared since?"

"Obviously I can't tell you that."

"Or in the period between the incident and the deregistration?"

"I can't tell you that either."

"We need to talk to Morin. And to the head of his *bolincheurs*. This Carrière guy. We need to ask where the boat is and have them show it to us."

"I'm on it."

"Was any reason given for its deregistration?"

"No, it's not necessary. Obviously a boat owner can take it out of service any time they want to."

They had almost come to the lighthouse, soaring above them in the blue sky. Elegant, classical, bright white, a giant placard that said *Sein*. Above it a glass dome, an artificial metal construction with a black hood. The tower was on a building no less elegant, linked to the right and to the left in perfect symmetry by low connecting wings to two square blocks. An impressive piece of architecture.

"I'll keep searching, Monsieur le Commissaire. In the meantime, we're all getting ready for the major operation—it's about to start. Talk to you later."

Nolwenn had hung up.

Dupin would have loved to embrace her. Her discovery brought a touch of reality back to the investigation. At last they had a real lead.

Still in a good mood, he let Riwal take the lead again. Although there was a disappointed expression on the inspector's face, Riwal was professional enough to take account of the news, for the moment at least.

"If that's true, it means Morin was playing a bigger role in cigarette smuggling, because that can hardly have been a one-off job. We'll need to rethink."

Riwal was right.

"Whatever there was on Kerkrom's boat that June evening," Riwal blinked, "they must have taken it somewhere, and—"

"Hi there!"

A loud shout. Both of them flinched.

There was nobody to be seen anywhere.

"*Bonjour,* messieurs!"

There was still nobody to be seen, but Dupin was sure he knew the voice.

"Up here!"

It was quite a few meters above them, but they could clearly make out Antoine Manet, standing on the small platform at the top of the lighthouse.

"*Bonjour,*" Dupin called in return.

"Come on up!" It was easy to hear Manet, there was no wind to carry his voice away. "I was looking for you anyway."

"I—" Dupin caught himself for a moment. A chat with Antoine Manet was hardly a bad idea, since there were a few important new points to raise. Points that threw up new questions, new thoughts.

"You really shouldn't miss it, Monsieur le Commissaire. An overview can never do any harm. Fifty-two meters ninety, above the everyday reality."

"We're coming." Dupin sounded remarkably decisive.

"The door's open, come in, then turn right and come up. You can't miss me."

"But be very careful, boss, this big lighthouse, Goulenez, is very high and the steps dangerously steep. I think it might be better if we stay down here."

* * *

Dupin hadn't counted on climbing. Not this immeasurable number of steps. Not on a spiral staircase, which got sharply narrower as it rose, or to put it another way—not on an unventilated, extremely narrow space which got narrower with every meter it rose, and which collected very warm, very damp, stale air that stank of dust, oil, and machinery. The tiny windows were so greasy that it was almost impossible to see the—doubtlessly breathtaking—view. There wasn't a trace of any romance—this was a working lighthouse, not a tourist attraction.

And certainly no place for anyone claustrophobic.

Dupin had already broken into a sweat on the steep steps, pearls of moisture on his forehead. Even Riwal, who was younger and fitter—Dupin had wisely let him go in front—had to stop every now and then, and would then take a look back at Dupin.

The commissaire had no idea how long he'd been climbing by the time the steps finally stopped and they found themselves standing by a steel ladder which led recklessly straight up—the space was too small for a conventional staircase. At the top of the ladder there was a hatch like on a submarine. There was no air at all up here, at least no oxygen.

Riwal obviously had experience with lighthouses and their construction. Without hesitation he clambered nimbly up the ladder, turned the handle on the hatch, and threw it open. In a second he was through.

Dupin followed him.

"Close the hatch straightaway, boss. Otherwise all the doors in the building will slam."

Dupin knelt on one of the steel-riveted platforms inside the dome of the lighthouse, which housed the spectacular equipment:

a gigantic lens. It was still extremely clammy, but the air was a bit better.

"Ready?"

Dupin had no idea what for.

Riwal opened a tiny door in the dome, also made of steel, and vanished.

"Watch your head, boss!"

In the next second, Dupin was on a hazardous narrow construction that ran around the dome. He looked to the west.

An unbelievable immensity of light. Clarity. Freedom. An overwhelming view over the Atlantic into the far distance, which seemed to stretch forever, just as the view did.

The endlessness was blue. Everything was blue. Sapphire blue, turquoise blue, pale blue, azure blue, getting darker nearer the island: violet, then blue-black as far as the receding horizon. The sky was the opposite, the deeper tones of blue at first, the paler, lighter tones higher up. For a second Dupin felt as if he were drunk. He felt as if he were swaying, as if he were held aloft in the air by a magic trick between the sea and the sky. Majestic.

There was one other overwhelming effect. You could see—no, not just see, experience—the fact that the world was round. A ball. Here, fifty meters above the sea, and yet at the same time in the middle of it, it was clear to see: the horizon curved. It was an experience felt only by the sea. It had fascinated Dupin as a child. But he had never experienced it as forcefully as here and now on the lighthouse.

"The Chaussée de Sein," Riwal said. He was standing close by Dupin, not letting him out of his sight. Manet had also come over to them. "Yesterday on the boat, if you recall, you saw the first stretch of the rugged granite formation which leads from the Pointe du Raz out some twenty-five kilometers into the sea. Sein is about halfway. Right at the end is Ar-Men, the farthest out of the Brittany lighthouses, on an isolated barren cliff in the endless Atlantic. It is the lighthouse of Jean-Pierre Abraham. He lived there for several years."

Nolwenn's favorite writer. The one who had written the fine sentence about fishermen.

"And Henri Queffélec describes the building most exactly in his novel. *Un Feu S'allume Sur la Mer.* As well as the particular communal life of the people of Sein."

It was no moment for literary discussion, no matter how interesting the subject.

Dupin walked on a bit, along the narrow railing.

From here the view was to the east. The island had the appearance of a shapeless drawn-out strip of land: from above it looked like an inverted *S*. Madame Coquil's words came to him: "a fleeting little bit," her fear that it might soon sink beneath the waves. He understood her now more than beforehand. From up here the "little bit" looked even more fragile, more vulnerable. More open to the destructive whim of the ocean. Impossible to protect. Just grassy fields, rocks, and sand.

"Your first lighthouse? Not bad, is it?" Antoine Manet's voice was lively, fresh, and full of energy. He had a black camera in his hand. "Lighthouses play an enormously important role here in the most dangerous sea in Europe. They've all recently been classified as historical monuments. They save lives. They indicate directions. Absolutely reliable unchangeable safety symbols, more potent than any other. Real-life myths. I come up here, when possible, every day at the same time and take photos. A grand documentation plan."

He clearly had no intention of going into greater detail, and Dupin had no intention of asking for more.

"The original 1839 lighthouse," Riwal said, "was made of blocks of granite. It served for a hundred and five years, night after night. The Germans blew it up in 1944. This one here dates from 1951. It's very strong, very bright. You can see it from a distance of fifty-five kilometers. But, the islanders' hearts still belong to the old lighthouse. The two buildings—the one on the right and the one on the left—contain the machinery and equipment for desalinating seawater. They run on oil."

The deputy mayor leaned with both arms on the parapet and looked pensively at the village. "For people there, the history of the island is one of great storms, storm floods, and inundations," he said.

Something that applied to all of Brittany, Dupin had learned: storm floods shaped history as much as great battles, wars, or other decisive political events. There were hundreds of books on the topic, special editions annually of the Brittany magazine *Les plus grandes tempêtes: Les tempêtes du siècles, Les plus grandes tempêtes de tous les temps.*

"In 1756, Sein was hit by a tornado accompanied by a flood tide; for days on end waves crashed over the island and the Duc d'Aiguillon gave the order for it to be evacuated. The survivors refused, and holed up in their attics. The retreating sea took over a third of the population with it. The years 1761, 1821, 1836, 1868, 1879, 1896, and so on: those are the ones everything revolves around." Despite all the losses, Manet referred to them as if they were not defeats but great victories, acts of heroic self-confidence. They had defied the elements, again and again.

"The most recent serious floods struck the island at the end of 2013, beginning of 2014. It was absolute hell, the sea raged. The very ground of the island shook, the walls of the houses too. A five-ton chunk of the quay was twisted out of shape by a wave meters wide, a huge sandbag was thrown through the air like a feather and killed a man."

Manet's face grew dark. "There will be more and more hellish events in the future. And every time the island will lose a meter of land."

It was crazy. Despite the glorious high summer weather and the totally calm sea of the moment it was immediately possible to imagine the two extremes lying so close together on this unique island.

"And the rabbits"—Manet was staring at a brownish-white patch in a field—"contribute significantly to the damage. They tunnel through the ground and accelerate the erosion. Just like the day-trippers, who take stones from the beaches as souvenirs, stones we keep having to pile up again."

Manet had an impressive way of telling stories casually, yet making them enthralling at the same time, but even so Dupin managed to tear himself free.

"There's news, important news, Monsieur Manet. We now assume that Kerkrom and Darot . . ." He faltered, and failed to finish the sentence. While he was talking it had occurred to him that there was something else to do before they talked about it. Now. Riwal and the boy had been right: Kerkrom and Darot must have taken their object somewhere that evening. Somewhere here on the island, which wasn't exactly big, as was very clear from up here.

"What I wanted to say was: I would like to talk to you again, Monsieur Manet. Do you think we might," Dupin glanced at his watch, "meet later? In Le Tatoon? I'll call you when I have time."

The island doctor gave him an amused look. "Of course. But as far as I'm concerned, we could just talk now."

"Later in Le Tatoon. Excellent."

Dupin turned away and went back into the dome without further explanation. Riwal followed, shrugging his shoulders. Dupin clambered down the ladder hurriedly.

"You need to be careful, boss. Really careful."

Dupin was already on the steps. Riwal was falling ever farther behind.

Back down on the ground, Dupin waited for the inspector. "I want to go back into their houses, and the sheds again."

Riwal didn't waste a word on the matter, but his face showed exaggerated relief that Dupin hadn't had a fatal accident scurrying down the steep steps at that speed.

"You're thinking about where they might have taken the cross?"

"Let's forget Ys and all these stories, Riwal. Agreed?" It didn't sound unfriendly, but it did sound decisive. "We are going to concentrate totally on the idea that the objects might be a part of the sunken boat."

They walked rapidly to the exit. There was loud noise coming from the engineering area: a dull thumping sound.

"They have to have taken the thing somewhere during the night," Dupin said, "somewhere it has been for a long time, maybe up until the time of the murders. Until the killer got their hands on it. Or, on the contrary, didn't find it, and where it might still be."

Riwal wrinkled his forehead. "The stupid thing is we *have* to find it. Everything depends on it. Apart from that all we have is speculation."

They had emerged into the open air. Dupin headed silently toward the village. It didn't take them long to get to Darot's house. The commissaire and his inspector hadn't said a word all the way. Now Dupin's phone rang.

Kadeg.

"Yes?"

"Is that you, Commissaire?"

The last phone call had gone well. But now his aggravating habits were back.

"What's up, Kadeg?"

"We're down at the harbor, Quai Nord. Madame Gochat and I, on the main pier."

Dupin had almost forgotten.

"Okay, I'm on my way, but it will take a while."

"What exactly do you mean by 'a while'?"

Dupin hung up. And turned back to Riwal. "Okay, let's go. We'll take a look at the house."

It was small but in perfect order. It had to have been repainted not too long ago: the white was clean and bright. There was a little strip of rugged grass, and a waist-high white-painted concrete wall.

Riwal let his eyes rove over the house. "The neighbors didn't notice anything unusual, not even last night."

Dupin undid the police off-limits band outside the little gate, which had looked ridiculous in any case, and opened it. Instead of heading for the main house door, he went round the back of the house. The scrub grass here was twice as thick as in front and could pass as a garden.

Dupin was disappointed. There was no shed, no annex. Nothing. All that was remarkable was the view: a couple of strangely shaped granite rocks and the glistening Atlantic beyond them. There was a narrow terrace door, next to a big window. Dupin tried the door handle. It wasn't locked.

He walked in, Riwal just behind him. On his guard, a tense expression on his face. Almost immediately they were in the living room, which also served as a dining room. It was a cozy room with bright blue walls, a wide, ancient-looking sofa in the opposite corner, a little table covered in magazines, an armchair positioned so that it had a view of the picturesque panorama.

Dupin glanced at the magazines. Technical magazines, all to do with diving: *Dive Master, Plongée, Scuba People, Diver,* loads of glossy magazines. Dupin flicked through a few.

Then he went through a narrow door and into a galley kitchen, barely wider than the door itself. There were the remnants of a croissant on a plate. A mug next to it.

A steep staircase led upward from the little hallway. There was no storage room, no wardrobe; the house really was tiny. Upstairs there was a minute bedroom, another equally tiny room, that gave the impression of being completely unused. The bathroom had an unusually large window facing the sea. Next to the tub was a tiny table with a mug and several more newspapers.

Somebody had lived here. There were traces of everyday life. But at the same time it was deeply disconcerting. "Nothing was brought here. Nothing the size the boy referred to, anyway." It was Riwal, his face disappointed, who had made the brief summary, when Dupin was back downstairs.

Five minutes later the commissaire and his inspector were standing outside Kerkrom's house. It was quite substantially bigger. Made from light gray stone. The same layout as Darot's with an impressive panorama view to the rear. The land area was larger too, surrounded by a partially dilapidated stone wall and a blue gate. There was a low, level annex to the rear, in front of it a wooden terrace with a table, two folding wooden deck chairs, and three terra-cotta pots with camellias that were doing remarkably well for the climate of the island.

The terrace was unusually high with a steep set of steps up to it. Dupin nearly stumbled. It had a proper garden, looked after, quite unlike Darot's, but then Darot had only been on the island a few months.

"Maybe . . ." Riwal was looking back and forth slowly between the house and the annex. ". . . they brought the object here at night as a temporary hiding place, then took it elsewhere."

"That would only be increasing the chance of them being seen. And there aren't that many possibilities on the island: buildings, places, squares to which people have access, and were safe enough."

Dupin tried to open the door to the annex: just a temporary wooden lath door that looked like a bit of amateur carpentry. He only managed to open it with a strong shove.

Immediately to the right was another narrow door, open and with a few steps leading into the main house. A tiny window in the corner let some dull light into the annex. To the right was a switch for a bare bulb, which only just managed to do its duty. But it was just enough to make out all the stuff that Kerkrom had piled together in her annex. A large number of lobster cages next to the entrance, but piled up in an orderly manner here, unlike in her shed down by the harbor, just as everything else here seemed to be in a certain order. Next to the cages was a collection of buoys in different colors and sizes. Dupin checked out the gaps between the cages and behind them. He moved around some of the larger buoys. Farther behind them were three old cupboards with fishing rods lying against them. In the middle of the room was a stretch of free space. There was a smell of over-ripe rotten fruit, an aroma from Dupin's childhood. That was how it had smelled in the cellar of his old family house, in the tiny Jura village where his father had been born. At the end of the room he made out a big wicker basket of apples.

Riwal had begun opening the cupboards.

Dupin moved into the center of the annex. He had automatically glanced over everything. If the object was even nearly as large as the boy had described it, it would not have been easy to hide it here. Even the cupboards were too close to the walls to hide anything behind them.

"The cupboards contain inventories, clothing, some old files, all neatly sorted."

The floor was flat trodden soil.

"Look at this," Riwal called out from between the lobster cages. Dupin had already seen it: a frame with two large wheels, some fifty centimeters high.

"It's a trailer for boats, to be used for canoes and kayaks."

Riwal looked like he'd been struck by lightning. "It's brand new. She couldn't have had it long." There was a tremor in his voice. "She could have used that to transport a big, heavy cross easily, without a problem."

Dupin walked over to Riwal.

"Look, boss, you'd just have to bring a car close to the heavy object, tilt it against it, lift it up, and it would almost automatically slip on. You could drive around anywhere with it like that. Very practical. Made out of enameled aluminum, very light to use and very flexible."

Riwal's renowned sense of the practical. Dupin felt a tingling. Riwal's idea was brilliant.

The commissaire had hunched down to take a closer look at the trailer.

Suddenly he stood up. "We'll take a look at it outside in the light."

Riwal maneuvered it easily out of the annex. The wheelbase wasn't big so the door wasn't a problem. They immediately began a careful examination.

"It's new, all but unused. The enamel is pristine all over, I would say no more than a few weeks old, but," Riwal said, and pointed to a particular spot, "just here, exactly where the object would have been attached, between the rubber appliqués to the right and left, where the canoe or kayak would have lain, there are serious scratches, proper scrapes."

Dupin had seen them too.

It was incredible. The tingle had increased. He looked closely at the scratches in the dark green enamel. They went deep. He ran his fingers over them.

"Riwal, ask at the post office. Either Kerkrom bought the trailer on the mainland or had it delivered. In a large package. I'd like to know when. If anyone at the mail office remembers a big package, and then ask the ferry people. Or she brought it in her own boat."

The inspector already had his cell phone in his hand.

Dupin took another look at the scratch, trying to imagine in detail the scenario described by Riwal. They hadn't found either a canoe or a kayak at either Kerkrom's or Darot's.

"Madame, Inspector Riwal here . . . Yes, the one who asked yesterday about Céline Kerkrom's registered letter, yes . . . We've got another question . . . no, something different . . . Was there a large package delivered to Céline Kerkrom recently? At least one meter, eighty centimeters long. And sort of . . ." He didn't need to finish the sentence; the answer must have been quick.

"Oh, really? . . . And that was the only large packet? From a well-known chandler in Douarnenez . . . and you wondered why Kerkrom needed a boat trailer? . . . Yes, particularly as she didn't have either a canoe or a kayak . . . No, she certainly doesn't need it now . . . No, unfortunately I can't tell you why . . . But yes, indeed, like I said, you've been a great help. Thank you very much."

Riwal didn't seem quite to trust that the "thank you" would be taken as the intended close of a conversation that clearly wasn't easy to terminate. He hung up.

"She says—"

"I got it all, Riwal."

Dupin prowled up and down the terrace. Things were coming

together, the lifting arm, the high-tech sonar, the boat trailer—
even if they were all very tenuous, highly speculative clues. For a
very tenuous, highly speculative theory, which at present only covered part of this murderous story. But there were possibly more
people involved in the cigarette smuggling. And there was a craftily
organized system in place. An entire apparatus. One that was using another existing apparatus for its own ends—the harbor, for
example, the fishing industry.

They needed more solid clues. Something really substantial.
It was just as Riwal had said; whatever Kerkrom and Darot had
found, *they* now had to find it. Otherwise everything would remain
a ghost.

Riwal pulled aside the police tape on the door that led from the
terrace into the house.

"I can check out the house on my own, boss, I mean if you
don't . . . The harbormistress is waiting. I can look over everything
in detail and report back to you."

Riwal was right. He had to go.

Dupin's mood had darkened in the past few seconds. One of
those little investigative depressions often followed a moment of investigative euphoria which turned out not to clarify anything. And
his chat with a worked-up harbormistress was definitely going to be
extremely unpleasant.

Dupin turned to leave. "Not a word to anybody, Riwal. About
anything."

"Jumeau already knows . . . that we're looking for something.
And that we assume Kerkrom and Darot found something."

"I know," Dupin grumbled. Even as they were on their way to
the lighthouse he had got noticeably angry with himself. That had
been extremely rash. Stupid. It would have been better for loads
of reasons if nobody else had known about their hypothesis. But it
was probably out in the open now. Even if Jumeau wasn't the chatty
type.

"See you soon, Riwal."

Seconds later Dupin was on the street, reluctantly heading for the harbor. Unpleasant interviews were best faced head-on.

He had already gone a few steps when he came to a sudden halt. A thought had just occurred to him.

He turned around on the spot.

He went back into Kerkrom's house through the front door. Theoretically he only had to go straight ahead through the house, a hallway, living room, and dining room. He reached the annex through the narrow open door with the steep steps.

"Riwal?" He called loudly once inside the house. He hadn't seen the inspector.

It took a moment.

"Here, boss. On my way. I was in the kitchen. There's a little larder in there but nothing in it, except for crazy quantities of milk and oats. And Volvic mineral water." With those words he arrived in front of Dupin. "What about Madame Gochat?"

"I want to try something first." Dupin grabbed hold of the trailer that Riwal had set back next to the lobster cages. "Come along."

He took the frame out onto the terrace and wheeled it to the edge, glancing all the time back and forth between the house, the garden, the annex, and the terrace.

"The ground is only flat to the front." Dupin was focused as he was speaking. It had just occurred to him.

He pushed against the entrance door. It wasn't wide either.

Now they would see.

It worked. The trailer got through without any problem.

"The object," Riwal remarked, "can't have been much wider if it was to get through. But if we're assuming it was in the shape of a cross, some one hundred and forty centimeters long and no more than eighty wide, then it could work."

Dupin stood there in silence. From the little square lobby there were three doors. Straight ahead led to the living room, which led out into the extension—steep steps—apart from that was the door to the kitchen and left to the bathroom.

Dupin pulled the trailer into the living room. If it had happened, this is the way it would have come.

A little combined living and dining room with an old, rustic wooden table, creaking floorboards. A plush sofa with shabby velvet cover. Crude but artistic paintings on the walls: crabs, langoustines, sardines—all in rich Atlantic colors—giving the room a merry, happy air. An old glass-windowed cupboard. To the right a closed door.

Dupin took a look around.

Where could you keep anything large here?

He went over to the sofa. It stood too close to the wall. Dupin checked it out even so. The distance to the floor was too small too. But he checked that as well.

Nothing.

He opened the glass-doored cupboard.

Riwal had checked the table and the tabletop.

"Solid."

Dupin took another look around, thinking feverishly.

Then he took hold of the trailer again and pushed it over to the closed door.

A bright bedroom, with a view of the garden, the cliffs, and the sea. He walked in, pulling the boat trailer behind him. That wasn't a problem either.

A double bed, two wooden chairs used to hang clothes on, an old wardrobe, a little bedside table, and the same worn floorboards.

Riwal had immediately gone over to the wardrobe and opened it.

"Negative."

"Goddamn," Dupin swore. "They must have taken it somewhere."

For a while they stood next to one another in silence.

Then Dupin went over to the bed. He knelt down, looked under the bed. He had to turn his head sideways on the floor.

Nothing here either.

Nothing except dust. Lots of dust. In thick clumps. The whole room had a fine but visible layer of dust, but here, under the bed, the dust had nothing to stop it coming together.

"To hell with it, yet again," Dupin exclaimed in frustration.

"Boss, an idea's just come to me," Riwal said carefully. "If the material analysis *were* to have any connection with the events of this case"—he was speaking cautiously but insistently—"then they would have had to take the test sample somewhere, on shore or on the water; they would have needed tools." There was a certain defiance in his speech.

Dupin wrinkled his brow.

"I'll take a look in the annex."

It was up to Riwal to do what he felt was right.

Dupin was about to get up again when he suddenly hesitated. He bent his head down again to the floor with an extremely concentrated look.

He hadn't made a mistake.

There was no doubt.

On the other side of the bed the layer of dust ended abruptly. He had only seen it with one eye and only half paid attention to it. The dust ended in a straight line. It had been brushed away there. Quite clearly.

He shot to his feet and went around the other side of the bed. On this side stood the wooden bedside table, with two packets of tissues on it, as well as a book and hand cream, along with the lacy-shaded bedtime lamp.

From the bedside table to the corner of the room was about a meter and a half, the wall roughly plastered and whitewashed, as throughout the house. And—from here it was even clearer to see— the floor was completely clean.

It would have been no problem to bring the boat trailer here, a straightforward direct way through the house.

Dupin went carefully down on his haunches again. He tried to imagine it as exactly as he could, to make the fantasy work. He inspected closely the broad floorboards, the floor in the corner between the bed and the wall. Where the object might have lain, or, more plausibly, stood. They could just have tipped it upright from the trailer. That would have been the most likely.

Dupin got down on his knees. Slowly, carefully, he shuffled closer to the wall, his eyes on the floor.

A moment later he stopped. All of a sudden he saw it.

Clearly.

A scratch.

A good long scratch, a groove. Some fifteen centimeters long. Dupin shuffled closer to it, felt it, stroked his index finger the length of it. It was deep, at least half a centimeter, and sharp-edged. The object must have had a sharp edge. And been heavy.

Obviously the floorboards were covered with scratches and traces from decades of use. But it was quite clear that this scratch was recent: the places where the wood had been pushed in it were clearly lighter and more open-pored.

Dupin knelt there a while, looking at the groove.

Eventually his gaze rose higher up the wall.

He tried to measure the height with his eyes. The object would have been leaning a bit, no matter how stable it was.

And then he discovered it.

An impression in the white of the wall.

Horizontal. Just about as long as the scratch below, but fine here, just a line. Nonetheless—and this was the crucial point—it was easily identifiable. Dupin shuffled back a bit and fixed his gaze on the two places, concentrating. He felt ever so slightly faint. Even so. Something had stood here. Something heavy. It was quite clear.

It seemed he had found the place.

But *what* was it that had stood here?

Part of a heavy ship plank with an identification number on it?

An engine could also have parts with sharp edges, metal edges: iron, aluminum. But was a wooden plank that heavy? And would an engine have left its mark only on these two places? And precisely marks like these?

There was an uneasy feeling hanging over Dupin. One that merged with the faintness.

Hesitatingly he shuffled—still on his knees—a little to the left.

Here there was nothing to be seen. Nothing at all. Dupin was somehow relieved.

Just to be sure, he had to check out the right side, too.

He inspected the wall there closely.

There was something.

It was undeniable.

Not a long groove like above, but even so an indentation. Barely a centimeter, but here too, sharp-edged.

It was all too fantastic, too ridiculous; the stupid thing was it all fitted too well.

"Boss," Riwal said. He came back into the room with a depressed expression on his face. "I've found nothing."

"Good," Dupin said abstractly.

"Why are you kneeling on the ground in the corner?"

Dupin got quickly to his feet. Absently, he said, "They brought the object here, Riwal. Right here."

Riwal stared at him with an expression of disbelief.

"Come over here, I'll show you."

* * *

Kadeg had picked out a bar on the Quai Nord where they had by now already been waiting more than an hour for the commissaire.

The harbormistress had already fired off a first sharp tirade, even before Dupin sat down. She was up and ready for it, prepared to fly out of her skin. Dupin had acted as if he hadn't noticed. His first words were to order two *cafés* when the waitress turned up. Dupin was pleased they were alone; there were no other tables taken at the moment.

Riwal was seeing to it that the crime scene people examined the groove in the ground and the impressions in the wall. His reaction had been the same as Dupin's. The difference was that he was more excited than the commissaire, but had denied himself the slightest mention of Ys. And absolutely any celebration.

"This is going to cost you dear, Commissaire! That was police bullying. A purely arbitrary act, forcing me to make a decision either to come along without my lawyer or to be remanded into custody!" The harbormistress had lowered her voice, without losing any of its contempt or aggression. "Those are dictatorial methods."

"I am certain," Dupin said, nodding over to his inspector in solidarity, "that Inspector Kadeg did not put it like that, and certainly didn't mean it like that. It's not the sort of thing he would do, nor any of us." Dupin changed his tone from unashamedly smug to unapologetic. "You should think yourself lucky to be on the loose, Madame Gochat. I will find it hard to explain to my superior officer." That was actually true, it occurred to Dupin. It had been a while since he had thought of the prefect. "And the public prosecutor too. We found the murder weapon on your property and have the statement from the fisherman who was tracking the first victim on your orders. Also we have a series of pieces of withheld information. That's just the facts."

"My lawyer . . ."

"You won't be on the loose for much longer, Madame Gochat, if you don't talk. It's your choice."

Dupin was sure she knew something. And she could actually genuinely be the person they had been after all along.

Madame Gochat drilled the commissaire with a penetrating stare, but remained silent.

"Direct from the island into police custody. In that case I have no alternative but to yield to the forceful evidence of the facts"— Dupin clearly enjoyed saying it—"no matter what my own personal opinion might be."

There was pure hatred in her eyes, her face was pale, her expression strained. She thrust her chin forward as if ready for a fight.

"I am innocent. I haven't murdered anyone. That is all I have to say."

"Where is the find?"

For a fraction of a second, no longer, she flinched.

"Where is the find?" Dupin repeated.

"I don't know what you're talking about."

"Where is it?"

"I have nothing to say. Not a thing." She snorted, her lips pressed together, her eyes squinting together, staring straight ahead. She wasn't concerned about the consequences.

In the meantime the two *petits cafés* had been served and stood there in front of Dupin with their seductive aroma.

"In that case our conversation is over."

Without haste he drank down one *café*, then the other. Madame Gochat stared at him, aghast. With the last slurp, he got to his feet.

"This is monstrous." She was on the verge of losing her composure.

Dupin calmly gave instructions to his inspectors.

"We'll do things as we discussed," Dupin said, as if the harbormistress wasn't present. "We let her go for now. We can arrest her again whenever we like, when charges have been pressed."

He turned round and left.

"Oh, Kadeg," Dupin said when he was already down on the terrace. "Report straightaway to Riwal; he'll tell you about the new developments." Dupin had seen that Kadeg too had flinched at the word "find," but then quickly regained control of himself.

"What should I do here?" He heard Gochat cursing behind him. "Here, on this miserable island? The ferry doesn't leave until the afternoon. You can't just leave me sitting here."

Dupin didn't even slow his pace. It happened in every case that the commissaire would break off conversations or interviews, but here it had become the rule, which frankly fitted such an infuriating case. His mood had hit rock bottom. But at the same time he knew he had to think positively, even though it was an expression he hated.

In a recent irritatingly sleepless night—Claire had had yet another of her nocturnal emergency calls—he had watched a documentary about the first American who had reached the North Pole alone, without technical assistance, in forty-six crazy days. He had been literally half-dead when he got there. But he had done it.

He was asked how he had survived waking each morning despite serious frosts, fearsome pain, and ever new tortures—the changes in the weather, problems with the sledges he was dragging behind him—and setting off again. He had replied: "I had only permitted thoughts that reflected the positive about the situation, and cut out all the negative." In the middle of the night, around half past two, Dupin had been deeply impressed by how simple it sounded.

He tried now with all his strength to concentrate on the positive. So, the object had been here. But even more important: it existed. That was the decisive factor. And a huge advance. It was no longer a pure hypothesis. The two women had found something, and that was what it was all about—that was it, that was the story they were hunting down. Dupin was convinced of that. There were too many indications, too many secondary lines that matched too well, even if they had no proof. Something that despite "positive" attitudes, they naturally desperately needed. They needed to find the find!

Dupin knew the risky point in an investigation when one had to commit oneself, when you otherwise would fail to achieve anything at all and in the end would go down with all flags flying. Obviously it was possible that they were on the wrong track and were leaping over a blind cliff. But he wasn't afraid of that. Dupin had never been afraid of that.

He had reached the area of the harbor that lay between the two quays, where the sheds were. He stopped. Right at the spot Kerkrom always docked. As always he stood far too close to the water. And looked out at the harbor.

He had made his mind up: everything depended on this find. Only, was the find really part of a boat sunk by its crew? That was what he had decided. But what if Kerkrom and Darot really had made an archaeological discovery? In principle Dupin had so far never had problems with strange, wonderful, or bizarre ideas and theories in an investigation; certainly not since he had been in Brittany.

Reality outdid fantasy by a long way, especially when it came to things that were odd and strange in the world. He was no beginner: if things initially seemed mad or even totally crazy, that was no argument in favor of reality. But there were clear lines between the romantic and the fantastic! There was no need to speculate about Ys. If so, then it was a spectacular archaeological find, the kind there were dozens of in France every year—he was always reading about them. Even if it was a cross.

Dupin shook himself and set off again. He had worked himself up into a strange mood—was it the influence of the island? He had to keep a cool head.

There were two options. Question number one: Who had taken the find from Kerkrom's house? Answer number one: Kerkrom and Darot themselves. But where to? To somewhere else on the island? Where the killer had then found it? Or, equally plausible, where it still was, because the killer hadn't found it? Or the second scenario: the killer had taken the object with him immediately after the murder, from Kerkrom's house. And taken it off the island. Or—and that was another possibility—had left it there and come back to get it. Whatever the case, if they had their hands on the find, it would lead them sooner or later to the killer, Dupin was convinced of that.

He found his phone.

"Riwal, where are you?"

"Behind you, boss. Right behind you."

Dupin turned round. The inspector was barely fifteen meters behind him.

"I came to look for you on the Quai Nord."

Riwal didn't hang up. He left that to Dupin, who impatiently came a few steps toward the inspector.

"We need a systematic search of the entire island. Every remotely possible hiding place. Every unused building, every empty shed, storeroom," he said. "Plus the chapel and the church. Rooms that are rarely or never used in public buildings."

"Possibly it's no longer on the island."

It was on the tip of Dupin's tongue to object to Riwal's use of the word "it," but he let it go. There was no point.

"Possibly. How many staff do we have on the island right now?"

"Eight."

"Good. Why were you looking for me, Riwal?"

They had walked farther toward Quai Sud.

Riwal pulled himself together: "Ah, yes, the island seems to be particularly popular today."

Dupin looked at him uncomprehendingly.

"Our pirate captain, Vaillant, has docked at the first quay. Jumeau met up with Morin's *bolincheur* fisherman Frédéric Carrière when he came back to the island after his meeting with you, and the scientific chief of the *parc* was here in his boat too for half an hour to take readings at his station."

"What does Vaillant want here?"

"Nobody has talked to him yet."

"Do that. Talk to him. I want—" Dupin said, then changed his mind. "No, leave it, Riwal. Let him do whatever he wants to on the island, but follow him, step for step. Shadow him."

"Sure thing, boss. Jumeau, in any case, thinks Carrière is following him. And you know Jumeau doesn't say much. Carrière has spread his net near him. And normally he never hangs out around here. There isn't much for him to catch. All of this can't be a coincidence."

A chain of thought was running through his mind.

"One more thing, Riwal," Dupin said as calmly and soberly as possible. "I want you to speak in confidence with your cousin the historian. Extreme confidence. Ask him what would occur to him as a meaningful archaeological find here in the region. If there are any local stories or historical incidents." He stopped, seeing the thrilled expression on Riwal's face. "Yes, ask him on my behalf about a massive gold cross. Ask him about anything that could be relevant from an archaeological point of view." It was a risky, crazy thing, he knew; he had to limit it. "Just nothing about Ys, Riwal. Everything but Ys. I want something real, scientific."

There was a glimmer of protest in Riwal's eyes, but he managed to suppress it.

"That's it for the moment. I—"

The phone rang. Nolwenn.

"News, Monsieur le Commissaire!"

Just the tone of her voice revealed two things: that the call was important, and that she had no time to deal with it; that it was a bad moment but clearly there was no alternative.

"I've spoken to Carrière, and the harbormaster at Le Conquet, where the suspicious boat was registered, with the fishing authorities, and last of all with Morin himself."

Dupin could hear car doors at the other end, car doors slamming loudly.

"Most interesting of all is what the harbormaster says. He was very surprised when the boat was deregistered, because he knew it. It was in perfect condition. Officially it had been moved to another harbor, but according to the fishing authorities, that wasn't the case. None of Morin's boats are reported in any other harbor with that registration number."

"What do Carrière and Morin say?"

"I had an extensive conversation with Carrière. He was making an effort to appear relatively cooperative; the topic itself didn't seem to disconcert him in any way. He claims the boat has massive rot problems at the stern. That it needed to be laid up in dry dock in a private area of Morin's, along with a couple of other, smaller boats. That the work to be done was very complex and it still wasn't clear when it could return to water. I told him we'd like to see the boat— and he referred me to his boss."

Even if Carrière hadn't been bothered by the matter, it all sounded as soft as butter, exactly the sort of excuse to be expected.

"Monsieur Morin himself was extremely brusque, if not un-friendly. Basically he said nothing at all. Only that everything was completely in order and that it was up to him alone to decide which boat was seaworthy and which not. Unlike Carrière, he didn't ask why we were suddenly interested in this boat." Dupin was familiar with Morin's self-confident manner; that meant nothing. "Nonetheless he didn't give us permission to inspect the boat, nor tell us where it was."

Obviously not.

"What's the boat called anyhow?" He had been wanting to ask all along.

"*Troisette*."

"Find out where Morin keeps boats or boat parts."

"If there is something dodgy about the business, Morin probably won't have moved it there."

That was true.

"And if we search all those places and don't find it, that doesn't mean by a long way that it's lying at the bottom of the sea somewhere in the entrance to the bay." Nolwenn's razor-sharp mind was operating on full power, as ever. "It wouldn't even be approaching proof."

"What if we have the seafloor in the area searched?"

"Forget it, it would be easier to find a needle in a haystack. If everything we're speculating about here turns out to be true, there's only one solution: to find the parts of the boat that Kerkrom and Darot came across. That's if the perpetrator hasn't already gotten rid of it. *Or*, Monsieur le Commissaire, if it isn't something else altogether. Riwal has kept me up to speed. Don't forget: you're investigating in Brittany."

Her lower tone of voice implied the conversation was at an end.

"The convoy is setting off, Monsieur le Commissaire. And I'm in the lead. I'll be in touch."

She had already hung up.

Dupin and Riwal had taken exactly the same route that they had followed an hour and a half earlier, along the waterside to the cholera cemetery. From above—a bird's-eye view, like that of one of the many seagulls, for example—it would have looked amusing to see them walking up and down the little island, Dupin thought.

"What did Nolwenn say?"

Dupin passed on her news.

"I'll deal with the search now."

"Riwal?"

"Boss?"

Dupin didn't quite know how to put it. He didn't want to attribute too much weight to the matter.

"Nolwenn—and her aunt—are leading a convoy. They . . ." He was best to leave it.

"The 'great vehicle convoy' beginning in different places but primarily in Lannion, and they're all heading for Quimper: cars, trucks, tractors, down the four-lane roads." The "Brittany highway," and all the main traffic arteries. "It's going to hold up traffic for hours on end."

Dupin was trying his hardest to banish the images that sprang up in his mind. A state-employed police staffer was, in her normal working hours, leading an illegal operation to create massive traffic hindrance, which the police would have no option but to act against. A drive to Quimper—it would have to be Quimper! The head office of the prefecture.

The wisest thing to do was not to have anything to do with it. His inspector seemed to see things the same way.

"See you later, boss."

With that farewell, Riwal turned around.

Dupin kept going, glad to be on his own at last.

* * *

The commissaire found himself halfway between the cemetery and the lighthouse, on his right hand the pier, the only one outside the harbor area. A Zodiac with one of those colossal engines was moored at it. Riwal would have automatically recited the technical details: the cubic capacity, horsepower, length.

Probably Leblanc, here to take the readings.

Dupin wondered if it was time to start going on the offensive about the "find." Mention the various possibilities—they didn't have to use Morin's name if they mentioned parts of a boat. The islanders would get the message anyhow when the police began searching all the buildings. They would make wild guesses, which would get expanded on. There was no way of keeping secret any such large-scale search operation. Sometimes a revelation could exert interesting pressure at a specific stage of a case. Get things going. They hadn't even spoken about it, but Riwal would have to tell the officers what it was they were to search for.

It would, in any case, have an effect. The perpetrator would be scared, and ideally do something careless, overhasty. One could even specifically ask the populace for help and suggestions. Dupin had no scruples on things like that. It only mattered if it was wise or not. Whether it would help them reach their goal. There was always the possibility that something like that could make the killer extremely careful: to disappear. Or just lie low.

Dupin had left the asphalt path and climbed up the substantial hill of pebbles on the shore of the sickle-shaped bay directly to the pier. At the edge was a small, low building, not unlike the concrete shed in front of the harbor, on its roof a steel cage for technical equipment. The pier was longer than it looked from a distance, with an elaborate technical construction at the end. A sort of elongated cage which extended into the water. The apparatus for taking the readings, probably.

"Monsieur le Commissaire!" Leblanc had suddenly appeared from behind the shed and waved at Dupin. The commissaire moved toward him. "Has there been any progress with the investigation?" Leblanc asked.

"We know the story and the motive. We know what it's all about—we just don't have the murderer."

"That relieves me enormously." Leblanc lowered his gaze. "I still haven't come to terms with it. Here on the island I'm perpetually waiting for Laetitia to turn up any minute in her boat." Now he looked Dupin straight in the eyes. "I assume you want to keep the story to yourself? What happened here?"

"I'm not quite sure about that."

Dupin hadn't intended to answer like that. There was a pensive look on Leblanc's face. It prompted him to ask more questions, but he let it go.

"I've just taken the readings for the past week. Do you want to take a look at the equipment on the pier? It's quite small but brilliant. It gives everything the most advanced analysis requires." He was back to being the enthusiastic researcher again.

"What's in the low building?" Dupin asked.

"Technical stuff. It belongs to the measuring station. That's where the rest of the equipment is: for measuring wind, precipitation, air pressure."

"Nothing else?"

"A few bits and pieces to do with building works. And equipment. Things like that."

"Any objections if I take a look?"

"Not at all. But honestly, there's nothing very exciting to see."

Dupin walked over to the building.

A steel door. A solitary window overlooking the sea. An aluminum table in the corner near the entrance, a chair next to it. A laptop, connected to a piece of apparatus made of steel with lots of buttons and lamps, hanging on the wall. Cables that went upward and through a hole in the wall to outside, presumably to the devices on the roof.

"From here I can take all the readings from the measuring equipment out at the end of the pier: pH values, oxygen levels, things like that."

Dupin was only listening with one ear. The room was a lot more interesting to him.

"Laetitia Darot would obviously have access to this building, wouldn't she?"

"Theoretically yes, of course. But I doubt she was ever here. I can't think of any reason she would have had to come here. Once or twice she took the readings for me, in extended spells of bad weather. But only then."

Dupin had begun to move slowly around the room. Four meters by four, he reckoned. There didn't seem to be any electric light.

On two sides there were bits of aluminum that looked as if they belonged to the construction at the end of the pier. In one corner lay a formidable-looking anchor, several plastic canisters, probably for oil or gas, Dupin assumed, and in the middle of the room there was a ladder on the coarse concrete floor. Layers of dust everywhere. In the corner opposite the table lay an inflatable boat, small but professional-looking.

Leblanc had noted Dupin's glance. "Sometimes I have to fix something in the station from the sea. In that case I take the little boat."

Whatever the object they were looking for might be, it wasn't here. Which meant: it wasn't easy to hide.

"Is there . . . any other room, an annex or something?"

"No. Just this."

It was clear from Leblanc that Dupin's questions were increasingly puzzling him.

"I'd also like to take a look at the measuring station at the end of the pier."

The find had lain for ages in the sea; it wouldn't hurt it to be put back in the sea. A calm, secure place under the sea would generally be no bad place to hide something.

"Gladly. Once we would have needed whole laboratories to do what this can do. Come along!"

Leblanc left the shed. Dupin took a last long look around and followed him.

"Did Laetitia Darot have access to all the institute's rooms on Île Tristan?"

"Yes, in principle. But apart from in the technical area I never saw her anywhere. Like I said, she didn't even have her own office."

They walked down the pier. They could hear distant voices; snatches of voices, more like. Dupin turned around. He saw four policemen in uniform heading toward the end of the island. The operation had begun.

Then something occurred to him.

He took his phone out. "Just one minute, Monsieur Leblanc. I'll be with you in a moment."

Dupin walked a few meters out onto the beach.

"Boss?" Riwal was speaking so softly he was almost impossible to hear.

"You absolutely have to take a look around the lighthouse. And the adjoining buildings with the power supply and the desalination works."

"I'll see to it. Four colleagues are on their way to the chapel."

"I've just seen them, Riwal. They need to look into every room."

"Meanwhile, Vaillant"—Riwal spoke even softer—"has left his boat with three men. I'm tailing him."

"Where are you heading?"

"To the little supermarket."

"The little supermarket?"

"Exactly."

"What are they after there?"

"I don't know yet, but I'm watching the checkout. I can see them clearly. They haven't paid yet."

It was bizarre. Not least because Dupin was imagining Riwal cowering somewhere behind a wall.

"Call me again if something happens."

Dupin put his phone back in his pants pocket.

Leblanc had walked on to the end of the pier, and was waiting for him there.

"Are you looking for something in particular, Monsieur le Commissaire? Can I help you?"

Dupin had caught up with him. He walked to the farthest edge, where the frame met the sea.

It was incredible how clear the water was. In the sun it shone emerald green and turquoise blue. He could see every little stone, every mussel, every single little wave of sand. A swarm of green fish shot by, their bellies shining silver for a second, as if someone had exploded a splendid firework in the sea. Two jet-black crabs hurried past.

It didn't take long to see there was nothing here.

Dupin turned away. "That'll do, Monsieur Leblanc."

"Do you know any more now?" Leblanc couldn't hide his amazement.

"I need to go," Dupin said, frowning. "Thank you for your help."

"I hope you'll soon be able to draw a line under this case. It's a catastrophe. Totally." He looked sadly into the distance. He looked altogether even more upset than the day before.

"Yes."

"On the subject of the readings"—the topic caused Leblanc to brighten up—"the air pressure has fallen hugely over the past half hour. That suggests a storm. If you want to get back to the mainland in good time, you need to leave soon."

Involuntarily, Dupin looked up and stared around earnestly in all directions.

The sky was every bit as blue, glorious, and innocent as before. Not even the tiniest hint of a problem. Not the slightest indication of a change in the weather, let alone a storm. Naturally Dupin, compared with a genuine Breton, was no expert in predicting the weather, but he was also no longer a beginner, considering he had been training for years. He knew the signs. And the ones he was seeing didn't look like an upcoming storm. His gut feeling didn't indicate a storm either.

* * *

The searches of private buildings on the island were finished for the moment. The police had looked into every room. Madame Coquil had initially refused to hand over the keys to the non-public rooms in the museum, and in the end only agreed under protest. She was also in charge of the keys to the church and the little lighthouse on Quai Nord.

There were a few buildings—such as the old, empty Bureau du Port—which Dupin hadn't thought of, but Riwal had. Toward the end there were only a few left, and the police were acting one by one.

Without finding anything. No suspicious boat boards, no engine, no metal object in the right dimensions, and not a cross. Not one suspicious trace. Nothing unusual, strange, conspicuous. Nothing at all.

An operation without result.

It was discouraging; the negatives had piled up, it was extremely difficult to see beyond that and turn one's eye wholly toward the positive. As far as Dupin was concerned, there was nothing to see.

On the way back from Leblanc's measuring station, he had taken a look himself in a couple of buildings that had already been searched without anything being found. In the fire station, in the church. He had become nervous, more so than he had so far admitted to himself, and his nervousness had only got worse as the operation went on.

The nervousness had gradually become ill humor and petulance. Not a situation he hadn't been in before today, it had to be said, only now it was worse.

The word that the police were after "something" had, as expected, spread around the island in the blink of an eye. It was even said they were expecting to find another corpse. Then again there was talk of a "treasure"—a gold staff encrusted with precious stones. As if it had been created by a magician. Or druids. Found on the bottom of the sea. Antoine Manet had also got in touch and kept Dupin updated with all the latest. Before long, Dupin had no illusions, there would be online headlines and eccentric radio broadcasts.

He had told the uniformed police not to let slip a word about what it was they were after. Not even to deny anything, just to stick to the formula: "no comment." The rumors didn't worry him at all.

The perpetrator probably knew by now—or soon would. And he would assume that they knew.

Riwal had news. He was waiting for the commissaire in Ar Men, the only hotel on the island. Where Riwal had spent the night. The ferry today had brought a particularly large number of day-trippers, who had made themselves comfortable in the bars and cafés next to the harbor. Dupin had every understanding of that, but unfortunately it meant the cafés were no longer right for discreet police interrogations.

Riwal too looked depressed. The élan had gone; he looked jaded. He had been on his feet since five in the morning. And almost certainly—just like yesterday—without anything to eat. It was certainly not without ulterior motive that Riwal had chosen the Ar Men, which was also a restaurant. Dupin's stomach had begun to grumble noisily. Leblanc's report about the enormous drop in the air pressure had affected his stomach in the form of a small but persistent queasy feeling. Eating would certainly help; an empty stomach was never good. There were still no clouds to see anywhere, only that the blue sky had got just a little whiter, a little milkier if you preferred. But really only just a little.

"You're saying Vaillant and his men have come back to the boat from the little supermarket? With cola, chewing gum, chips, and beer?" Dupin shook his head unbelievingly.

Riwal had just reported in on his stalking.

"That's the way it is. As if they were having a laugh at our expense."

"And have they since set off from the dock?"

"Straightaway. They docked, went to the little supermarket, back to the boat, and set off again. Carrière meanwhile is no longer to be seen out at sea. Nor is Jumeau. He'll probably have headed off toward the Chaussée des Pierres Noires."

Dupin thought to himself. He ought to have Vaillant shadowed at sea also. But that wasn't going to be easy. If they wanted to be inconspicuous they'd need to get hold of a fishing boat. But at the same time they ought to shadow all the others, all their "special candidates." That would need a lot of fishing boats.

The sea was a difficult place for investigations. It made things more complicated than they already were.

Riwal interrupted Dupin's fruitless reflections. "As you asked, I've spoken to my cousin again. According to his scientific opinion, a find of that nature—let's just say a cross made of solid gold at the bottom of Douarnenez Bay—I'm quoting here, boss, even though you won't like it," he hesitated again a moment, "would *unquestionably* have to be seen in connection with Ys. There are no churches in Douarnenez, and none of the towns or villages around the bay have churches, monasteries, or any sort of place that could even rudimentarily be home to such a cross or similar archaeological find." He was speaking faster all the time for fear Dupin might interrupt him.

"In any case there are not many gold crosses of this size in the whole of historically Christian France, he said. And none of them are missing. 'It would have to be an improbable importance to an improbable place.' Those are his words. There's nothing else imaginable."

Dupin hadn't interrupted. He was too tired. Apart from anything it was he who had told Riwal to talk to his cousin. He should have known.

Dupin had hoped for something else. A realistic historical context, possibly including a cross. Something like: in the great cathedral of Quimper or Rennes there was a great golden cross up until some century or other, when it was stolen at some stage by the Normans, the Angles, or Saxons, and brought to Douarnenez on a ship that sank in a stormy night . . . something like that.

He said nothing.

"What do we do now, boss?"

"I want us to concentrate on Morin."

He had spoken forcefully, but it sounded pathetic. He hadn't got a clear attitude. It was enough to make him fly off the handle.

"No," he corrected himself. "From now on we'll focus on all the others as well." It didn't sound quite so hangdog. "The killer isn't going to make things easy for us," Dupin grumbled. "It's going to be a clever hiding place. Nonetheless, we'll extend the search systematically. To the mainland. We need to keep the teams at it."

It would be a lot of effort. A lot of frustrating effort. Dupin let out a deep sigh. But obviously it did no good.

Riwal just offered a battle-weary, "Let's get on with it."

"But beforehand, Riwal, we're going to eat."

The inspector's face immediately brightened. "The restaurant's specialty is known throughout France. *Ragoût de homard!*" He had announced it like a fanfare. "You will be delighted, boss. The ragout is served in large crockery pots. Lobster finely cut up, partly removed from its shell, pink onions from Roscoff, celery, fennel seeds, smoked mussels all seared in groundnut oil, rinsed with cider *eau de vie*, with two or three glasses of very good white wine added." It certainly sounded like poetry. "Then the incomparable potatoes *amandine*, a dash of cream, Espelette peppers, sea salt and lots of salted butter, then let it sit and braise, braise, braise."

"Yes, please?" A slim, dark-haired woman was standing in front of them, friendly but clearly not with unlimited patience, a little notepad and pen in her hands.

"Two, please," Dupin announced.

"Gladly, sir. Two—that would be two what, precisely?"

"The lobster ragout!" Riwal blurted out. "And two glasses of Quincy."

"Make it a bottle," Dupin corrected him.

The woman nodded appreciatively and disappeared.

This was a great place to sit too. From Ar Men's daringly pink painted tables and benches you looked out onto the rear of the island, the lighthouse and the chapel, down the road to the cholera cemetery, fields of the tiny pink flowers here and there. And on either side: the sea.

The milky white of the sky that had replaced the magnificent blue—there was no doubt about that—had gradually but inexorably turned to a hazy gray. Riwal looked as if he were still in another world. And he was once again in story-telling mode.

"Merlin, the most famous magician in the world, was a good friend of the nine witches of Sein. He came to the island regularly, to talk with them about the art of magic." With every word his story gained vitality. "They told Merlin of their visions, including the future of a great king, that of the Arthur we all know, whom Merlin met a little later. One day Arthur was wounded in a fierce battle at Camlann. So badly that not even Merlin could save him. To cut to the quick, he brought Arthur here to the Île de Sein. To the nine witches. Who made him a shrine of pure gold. Veleda, the healer amongst them, 'the woman from another world,' took charge of him. He was as good as dead. But she restored him to life. Not even Merlin knew how. She had the power to open the doors to the underworld. You see, the island plays an important role even in the legend of Arthur." Riwal's eyes were gleaming.

Dupin said nothing.

He felt helpless.

"Monsieur le Commissaire!"

Dupin flinched in shock. Kadeg. He had almost forgotten him. The next moment the second inspector was standing, breathing hard, next to the table. For him, he was making something of an impression.

And there was a reason:

"She got away from me," he said, his tone a mixture of embarrassment and anger. "She's crafty! After the conversation with you she had to phone her husband straightaway. She walked around the harbor, not looking at all suspicious. Between the piers—"

"What are you talking about, Kadeg?"

"Gochat! She's gone. She's left the island. Her husband came to collect her with a boat. At some time she wandered down to the big pier, and all of a sudden a boat pulled up to the big rocks by the entrance to the harbor, pulled up next to them very briefly, and then she was gone."

It didn't really surprise Dupin. Even so, it was irritating.

"How do you know it was her husband?"

"I recognized the name of the boat, *Ariane DZ*. It's registered to François Gochat, and I saw a man."

"You can get anywhere with that boat," Riwal, the expert, chipped in, "and fast. It has an excellent engine, I saw it yesterday in Douarnenez."

Kadeg looked grief-stricken, a rare sight.

"Make sure that Gochat is watched as soon as she reaches Douarnenez harbor. And then take over yourself. Now." Dupin spoke extraordinarily perkily. "Would you like to eat something first, Inspector Kadeg?"

Kadeg had been on his feet longer than either of them. And you could see it. At the moment, however, he looked astonished; he had expected a totally different reaction.

But he didn't protest. "The lobster ragout?" he asked, anticipation in his voice.

"Yes." Not long later he was sitting peacefully alongside Riwal on the bench, Dupin opposite them, each of them lost in their thoughts. Happily it wasn't long before the waitress arrived with the bottle of Quincy and three enormous plates, then the vast cooking pot, full to the brim, lobster claws sticking out left and right. As if the cook had known the state of their stomachs and wanted to cheer them up. They could have invited a couple of ordinary uniformed police to join them and all of them would have been full.

"Phenomenal, isn't it, boss?"

Dupin nodded, a nod of serious agreement. It really was magnificent, hearty and full of flavor. You could taste the sea itself, the character of the island, compared with which the lobster meat was sweet and tender; a confusing but wonderful mixture. And the cold white wine with it. Pure happiness.

The ring of Dupin's phone tore them out of their mix of exhaustion and enchantment.

It was Nolwenn.

"Yes?" Dupin swallowed the last bite.

He could hear the satisfaction in Nolwenn's voice: "I've found the eighty-six-year-old brother of Lucas Darot, Laetitia Darot's alleged father. He lives a solitary life in a tiny hick town near Pointe du Raz and sounds pretty sprightly to me."

It sounded confusing, but promising.

"A nephew of my husband has a butcher's shop nearby, and the brother sometimes shops there."

Dupin still couldn't quite follow.

"I've spoken to him. It's all true. It was an affair, Laetitia's mother and Morin. A very short one. Lucas forgave her. And brought up Laetitia as his own child with all his love. He never told anybody. Except for his brother, who had kept it in his heart until today. But now with Laetitia's death everything is different."

So it was true. And that was what his gut feeling had been telling him all along.

"A moving story, Monsieur le Commissaire. This case gets right down to the nitty-gritty. It demands everything from us. But lobster ragout gives you strength—you'll see."

How could she have already found that out?

"We're sitting here, Riwal, Kadeg, and me," Dupin said. "All together in the Ar Men. We can talk it over peacefully here."

He could hear engine noise over the phone; somebody had just shifted down into lower gear. Nolwenn seemed still to be in the car. Dupin could imagine the chaos. Cars, trucks, tractors, crawling along at a snail's pace. The "four-lane roads" would be crippled.

"I'm afraid your mother's party is going to be wrecked. But that's the way it goes," Nolwenn said, her tone of voice totally lacking in irony. "There's nothing to be done. Work is work. See you later, Monsieur le Commissaire."

Dupin put his phone away and raised his eyes to the sky. The light gray had now become a threatening gray. And it was getting thicker, looking like it was growing into a cloud bank. It covered the whole sky, like a shapeless, diffuse gray wall. There was still not the slightest wind, the air was still. Dupin had never seen anything like it, despite having experienced so many tricks, sensations, phenomena of the weather in the last five years—exposed to the most basic elements of Brittany—that he thought he had seen it all.

They needed to get going again. To pick themselves up.

"We're going to extend the search to the mainland." There was an urgency in Dupin's voice. "There's nothing more for us to do on the island for now."

"Where exactly are we going to spread the search to?" Kadeg said with his mouth full. He had to rub it in, of course.

"We will locate all the properties, plots of land, houses, second homes, third homes, sheds, storerooms, and cellars that belong to our protagonists. Starting with Morin."

"They'll never tell us," Kadeg said while appreciatively cracking the last lobster claw, "where they've hidden the thing." The supremely tender, endlessly delicious final tip of the claw disappeared into his mouth. "*If* there even is such a find! Nobody has seen it yet. The whole thing might just be a fantasy. A small boy who gets bored and dreams up fantastic stories! A new boat trailer, and a few scratches on the floor and in the wall! It's all very thin."

It had been a stupid idea to let Kadeg gain new strength. Dupin should have known. The bad bit was Kadeg hadn't intentionally set out to make a malicious impression. It hadn't been his intention to insult Dupin; he meant what he said. And up to a point he was only raising the doubt that kept haunting the commissaire.

"We're finished here." Dupin stood up unexpectedly. "We can discuss the details on the boat." His gaze had again turned to the sky; he was getting ever more queasily worried. He added a postscript intended to be as determined as possible: "First I'll meet up with Morin again."

* * *

They were ready to set off. The commissaire and his two inspectors had gathered in the bow of Goulch's sleek boat.

"The slip lines are loose," shouted one of the lanky young men to Goulch, who was already at the bridge. One moment there was just a gentle puttering, the next the mighty diesel engine roared away.

Dupin had left four uniformed police officers on the island and given them precise instructions. One each of them should mark Kerkrom's and Darot's houses, one at their storage sheds, and one down by the harbor to coordinate the little team. You never knew.

To be on the safe side, Dupin hadn't asked Goulch about the weather. Could a storm really develop out of this nebulous gray mass? Goulch would let them know in good time if he saw changes worth mentioning in the weather coming toward them.

"First I want us to . . ."

All of a sudden the diesel engine fell silent. Dupin paused in irritation.

Within seconds Goulch had clambered out of the bridge house, looking extremely worked up, by his standards.

"A radio message, just came in. Charles Morin! They just fished him out of the water. Wounded, bleeding, totally exhausted. He almost drowned, was seemingly saved at the last minute."

It couldn't be.

"Morin?"

"Exactly."

"What happened?"

"They don't know yet."

"Who's 'they'?"

"A coast guard boat. Morin was saved by an algae fisherman. A *goémonier*. He took him on board and called the coast guard, who had come out from Molène. They must have got to him in a few minutes."

"I need to know what happened."

"Like I said, we have no more information for now."

"Didn't Morin say anything to the algae fisherman?"

"At least the algae fisher didn't say anything to the coast guard. It only just happened, I mean the report just came in."

"Where was he fished out?"

"Four sea miles from Molène, toward the south, toward the Île de Sein, that is. An area with extremely strong currents. And think about the reduced visibility."

It seemed to have been a lucky chance that they had found him at all and he was still alive.

"Is it possible to talk to Morin? I mean is he fit enough to answer questions?"

"I can't tell you that either."

"Where are they taking him?"

"Douarnenez. To the hospital."

It was obvious what they had to do.

"We head for Douarnenez, as quickly as possible." Dupin knew what that meant: maximum speed. But there was no alternative.

"Okay, take charge of my radio. The coast guard will come through again." Goulch handed Dupin the bright yellow device.

A few seconds later the engine was screaming, twice as loud and fierce as before. The boat took a real leap forward.

A quarter of an hour later they were well out into the open sea. Theoretically they ought to have been able to see the Pointe du Raz to the east, but the diffuse gray wall had turned into a horrible, deep dark brew that had nothing in common with normal fog or mist. The sea itself had taken on a pale concrete gray; it was hard to see more than two or three hundred meters. The horizon had long since been swallowed by the ominous mass. Even Goulch wouldn't be able to see anything, neither the steep cliffs, or worse, the hidden flat rocks, of which there were swarms around here. That meant he would have to rely totally on his high-tech navigation equipment. And he clearly trusted it, because they hadn't slowed down from maximum speed for even a second. Dupin had passed the quarter hour in silence.

"*Stelenn Bir,* come in, please."

The broken voice emanating from the radio in Dupin's hand gave him a shock.

"Yes, here *Bir*, Dupin." He had to pull himself together. "It's me, Dupin. Captain Goulch is at the helm."

"We have Charles Morin on board. He's refusing to be taken to the hospital in Douarnenez. He wants to go to Île Molène. He says he has a house there and the island has a good doctor. Morin is extremely weak and hypothermic. He really needs to go to the hospital," the coast guard man said professionally and calmly. "But he insists he's fine. Even if we can hardly understand a word he says."

It was unbelievable.

"Did he say what happened?"

"He says it was a spot of bad luck."

"A spot of bad luck?"

The man from the coast guard was unperturbed. "He says he was out line fishing and fell overboard when he leaned too far over the railing to pull the line in. He was caught in a current. His boat was taken two kilometers away. He was spotted by another algae fisherman. The trouble is that these positions simply don't agree," the man continued as dryly as ever. "The position where Morin was fished out of the water, and the position where his boat turned up."

"What do you mean?"

"The currents go the other way."

"So how can it be that he turned up where he did?"

"No idea." The coast guard man wasn't the type to speculate.

"When did this happen?"

"Monsieur Morin says he swam for about half an hour. That makes it around one forty-five that he must have fallen into the water."

Dupin was silent for a few seconds, different thoughts rushing through his head. Or more accurately, whirling around in his head, like in a snow globe shaken fast and hard.

"Are you still there, Commissaire?"

"Yes."

"He is conscious and has made clear his wishes." Dupin knew what that meant, he knew the formula. "We will have to take him to Molène."

The commissaire didn't hesitate for a moment. "I'll come there too." He had to see Morin.

"As you wish."

"Where is he injured?"

"His upper arm. It's bleeding substantially. He says it happened when he fell out of the boat. But when I ask myself how . . . what the hell. He's bleeding."

The whole thing sounded completely absurd.

"You don't believe him?"

"When he says something like that . . ."

"You have doubts about his story, am I right?" Dupin also had doubts, great doubts. "It wasn't an accident, was it?"

"I don't think so," the man came back as calmly as ever. "We're already on our way, monsieur. Over."

Riwal and Kadeg had come over to Dupin, and despite the wind noise had overheard every word. Dupin just had to tell Goulch on the bridge. He was back in no time.

"Obviously it wasn't an accident." Riwal sounded decisive. "The coast guard man is undoubtedly an expert on the currents here. It will be exactly as he says."

That was exactly what Dupin felt too. An accident would be far too much of a chance.

Riwal's features were dark. "It was an attack."

"Attempted murder," Kadeg said more precisely, "an attempt to murder Charles Morin."

Dupin said nothing.

The consequences were enormous. And turned Dupin's current scenario to dust. Either that or somebody wanted revenge? Because he had been particularly close to one of the victims and knew Morin was the murderer? That could explain why Morin lied. Why he gave no explanations. Why he'd dished them up the fairy tale about the accident.

Dupin leaned far out over the railing, dangerously far. The wind could blow your head off. He breathed the ferocious airstream in and out a couple of times. Then he went and stood in front of his two inspectors. When things were going bad and you didn't know how to proceed there was only one thing to do: charge headlong.

Dupin's voice was clear and steady, strong in presence: "I want to find out from all our suspects where they are now and where they've been for the past hour. I want to know precisely, and I want witnesses. Proof. Nothing vague. From now on that's all we're interested in. Nothing else anymore."

"Precisely which individuals?" Riwal asked, just to be sure.

Dupin narrowed his eyes: "Our young fisherman Jumeau; Vaillant, the pirate; our charming harbormistress; Pierre Leblanc; and of course, Frédéric Carrière, Morin's *bolincheur.*"

* * *

Morin was half sitting, half lying down, in a brown leather chair in the living room of his house, which was very different to the one in Douarnenez where Dupin had visited him. Simple, plain, not even very big. The one thing that at first glance made it different from the other was the magnificent location: right behind the old harbor with the laguna-like sandy beach, not that there was much to see in the dark gray soup that engulfed the island.

Morin was wearing a jogging outfit and was wrapped in several brightly patterned woolen blankets. He looked to be in a worrying condition. Totally exhausted. It was easy to see that the strain of what had happened had taken its toll on him. He was overwhelmed by shivering fits at irregular intervals, during which he appeared so weak that he looked like he might collapse. At the same time, however, Dupin thought he looked upset, deeply upset, his face muscles contracting and his features distorting.

The doctor had bandaged up Morin's upper arm so that Dupin unfortunately couldn't see the wound—"an ordinary wound." The doctor had also given Morin a painkiller and something for his circulation. And he had made it clear to Dupin that—for medical reasons—he would not leave Morin's side.

Dupin was on his own; Riwal and Kadeg hadn't come in with him. "I was fishing, yeah, at one of my secret places, I was standing in a stupid position and fell overboard, wounding myself in doing so—that's it. That simple."

"You nearly died. The fact that you're still alive is pure luck." Dupin was annoyed. He had no sympathy.

Morin had not made any fuss even over his minimal greeting, made clear he regarded the interview as unnecessary, and—unlike previously—was not remotely interested in the commissaire or their conversation.

"The positions at which you and your boat were found don't co-ordinate at all given the currents here. Explain that to me, Monsieur Morin."

Dupin was standing in the middle of the room. He had refused the chair opposite Morin, who had offered it to him with a weak wave of his hand.

"Think whatever you want," Morin said with complete indifference, his glance turning demonstratively toward the big window.

"What sort of boat were you out in? How big was it?"

"Eight meters ninety. An Antares, an old model."

An easy boat to run on your own, Dupin knew from Riwal's numerous explanations, ideal for fishing. Not a speedboat, but not slow either.

"How did you injure yourself?"

"I don't know." He didn't even bother to think about it. He was making a mockery of the whole thing.

"I don't believe a word you say, Monsieur Morin."

"I don't care."

"You were set upon. It was an attack. Somebody wanted to be rid of you."

Morin just repeated: "Think whatever you want."

Obviously Dupin had intended to confront him with the smuggling boat saga, with what they already knew. To threaten him with incontrovertible evidence. But Morin would just have dismissed it with a sardonic smirk.

"You know who the murderer is. Somehow or other you found out." Dupin had begun walking up and down while he talked.

"It was only a matter of time." Despite the shivering that had again afflicted Morin, there was a satisfied smile on his face.

"So you admit it."

Dupin had tried a shot in the dark. Successfully. But right now another thought had occurred to him. It was easily possible that Morin had already been successful. That there had been a hand-to-hand fight in which Morin had killed the other man, even if he had fallen overboard somehow. Or both of them had fallen overboard. But only Morin was rescued. But what argued against that was Morin's vast internal tension, which suggested that for him, whatever had happened was not yet over.

"I admit nothing. I had an accident, and I think," he said slowly, "that I need to rest now."

"That is clearly the case, from a medical point of view," the pale, stubby doctor butted in. "I suggest that as a matter of urgency, Monsieur Morin."

"Indeed. I need my strength," Morin mumbled. Dupin hadn't missed the fact that for fractions of a second he had balled his fists. Morin had noticed Dupin's glance, but it had seemed irrelevant to him.

There was a distant rumble, not particularly loud, but clearly audible. A roll of thunder that came with a storm. A long way away, that was clear too. But even so.

An aggressive silence filled the room.

Morin wasn't going to breathe another word. And they couldn't force him. If it came to a legal matter, Morin would stick to the accident story. There would be nothing Dupin could do, nothing at all. He was condemned to impotence. And for him there was nothing worse. It made him furious.

"I'm going to sleep for a bit now, if you'll excuse me," Morin said, and fussed demonstratively with the blankets.

"We've spoken with Lucas Darot's brother. We know the story now. Laetitia was your daughter."

It was as if Dupin hadn't said a word, the statement vanished into the air.

"I promise you, Monsieur Morin. We'll find out everything." Dupin paused briefly. "The whole truth." But the words from his mouth were as nothing. They had long since become useless. Laughable.

Dupin turned around. Went to the door. A few seconds later he had left the house.

He turned sharply to the left, onto a steep clay track that quickly led to a narrow path directly down to the water. After a few meters he came to a halt.

"What a load of shit."

The curse had come from his heart. His top and bottom molars pressed so hard together it hurt. Things were going completely out of control, and there was nothing he could do about it.

"What a load of shit!"

The swear word resonated across the island.

* * *

The air was heavy, warm, damp, oppressive. The nebulous mass swallowed all sound. It was as silent as a graveyard. Not even the slosh of a wave in the viscous sea to be heard. No seagulls. No people. No engine noise. It was an eerie dusk.

To the left, spiky, strangely shaped cliffs alternated with large flat granite slabs. All of which sank within a few meters into the dark Atlantic, which had already worked its way close to the innermost coastline. A flood tide was coming. Somewhat farther out were hazy patterns, silhouettes of small, rugged, rocky islands, some of them with dark green canopies. A surreal realm. Images recognized from science fiction films, imaginary landscapes from alien planets.

The air didn't smell, it stank: a cocktail of moldy, rotten seaweed and decomposing fish innards, brought up by the rising tide around the island. On the other hand, the commissaire could no longer hear any more rumbling, not even in the distance. The storm had calmed.

The distance between Sein and Molène was hardly great, but the difference between the islands was. Molène was completely different, even in shape. If the Île de Sein was long and misshapen, extended, torn, then Molène was a harmoniously rounded, almost circular picture-book island. Even at the water level it was two or three meters higher than Sein, and from there it rose steadily toward the center of the island. People believed it could resist a tempestuous storm. Everything seemed more gentle than on Sein, more balanced, even if the vegetation on "Moal-Enez"—the "bald island," as the Brittany expression had it—didn't have anything more to offer: here too there were no trees, large bushes of hedgerows. The village with its two hundred residents lay around the harbor to the east.

Dupin had followed the sole footpath along the water, which seemed once to have gone all around the island. He had tried to regain sharpness and clarity of thought. To calm himself down. He was thinking far too strenuously, feverishly, flushed. He was trying to wring the answers out. By force. Hastily. That only led to distraction.

He had begun to calmly review everything. Everything that had happened since yesterday morning, when he had first stood, overtired and freezing in the small tiled room of the fish market hall. Maybe he had missed something. Somewhere, at some time maybe someone had said something, maybe he had noticed something and maybe even scribbled it in his notebook; something that contained a clue that he simply hadn't so far recognized as such. He had pulled out his Clairefontaine and flicked through it without standing still. He had almost tripped up a couple of times in so doing.

Suddenly a noise shattered the strange silence. Dupin was sure his phone had never rung that loudly. It was an unknown number.

"Yes?" he said sullenly.

"I've been thinking it over, Georges." His mother. It was hardly possible! She had an unfailing feel for the most unsuitable moment. "I don't know if I made myself clear this morning when the florist was here. It is simply unthinkable for you not to be there tomorrow. There is simply no circumstance we would excuse. I know you are on an investigation and that it's an extremely unpleasant story—I really am sympathetic—but you are simply going to have to have it sorted out by tomorrow morning."

"I—"

"You have things to do, Georges, I know. I'll let you get on with the job. See you tomorrow, my darling."

That was the end of the conversation.

A totally insane conversation.

But before a stunned Dupin could put his phone back in his pants pocket, it rang for a second time.

Yet again an unknown number.

"Ah, Monsieur le Commissaire!"

Unfortunately he recognized the voice straightaway. And at the same time he wished downright it had been his mother again. This was worse: the prefect. Once again—and in one respect this was the happiest of his Breton cases to date—he had completely forgotten him.

"There's trouble," the prefect fired out, "a lot of trouble." The words made clear they were about to be followed by one of his notorious tirades. The only puzzling thing was that his voice wasn't more hot-tempered. "Madame Gochat, the harbormistress, has made a formal complaint. Against you and the police action. She knows a few powerful people in Rennes. The fishing industry lobby." His voice got harder and harder with the latter words; maybe the attack was imminent. "Coercion, unlawful detention, and so on." A rhetorical pause followed. Dupin feared the worst. "We are not going to let ourselves be bullied by this arrogant snob! Even if she swears like a trooper and carries on like Rumpelstiltskin. Do you understand? No velvet glove! Be merciless. Do everything that has to be done."

Dupin thought he was hallucinating.

"I, er . . . I'll do just that, Monsieur le Préfet. Everything necessary. Everything needed from a police point of view."

"Police point of view, my ass! Don't be so fainthearted! You know my wife is from Douarnenez. We still own her parents' house." Dupin had naturally no idea what this meant and didn't understand why he needed to know. "We got ourselves a new boat a few years ago, and obviously we wanted to moor it in the Vieux Port. Where else? By one of the nice places directly at the front. Gochat refused flat out to do anything for me in that respect. Pure nastiness!"

So that was the way the wind blew. Dupin should have known.

"And one more thing, *mon Commissaire*." It was a formula that suggested the greatest caution was required, and Dupin braced himself. "You are aware that this extremely important exercise being carried out for safety on the streets of our nation, in which I am taking part, will last until Sunday evening, six o'clock. Right?"

"Absolutely," Dupin said. At least he would be able to investigate in peace until then. But he still didn't know what the prefect was aiming for.

"Like I said, urgent national interest! I'm also not going to be able to give a press conference declaring the successful conclusion of the investigations before Monday morning."

He stopped and gave no sign of carrying on. He must already have made his point.

Dupin needed a moment for the penny to drop.

"I—" he said, but the words he wanted failed him.

"There's no need for you to rush into things, no need for an exaggerated, hectic pace. It's perfectly satisfactory for you to arrest the perpetrator at the beginning of the week." A complicitous tone, worse for Dupin to bear than any ferocious tirade. "That would then be a wonderful start to the week. The announcement of our common triumphant investigations."

It was absolutely monstrous. With every case Dupin thought that this beat everything the prefect had tried so far, and there could be no way to top it. And every time he'd been taught a lesson.

"Oh, Commissaire, and while we're speaking, I've heard something about a protest action on account of this sand dune, that there's going to be a big closing demonstration right outside the prefecture office in Quimper. Do you know anything about that?"

"I—"

"Boss!"

Dupin started.

"Is everything okay, boss?" Riwal said. He was coming along the narrow coastal path, Kadeg in tow.

Dupin reacted immediately: "I'm terribly sorry, Monsieur le Préfet. Urgent news. I'll be in touch."

He hung up quickly; he didn't want to take any risk.

"You need to be careful. There's slippery granite hidden amidst the clumps of grass on the path here. You could easily fall over."

Dupin didn't reply.

Riwal immediately changed the topic. "You were on the phone. We bumped into the doctor. He had seen you take the island circular path. Did you know that there are seven hundred and twenty blue benches along this path, placed at all the best viewing points?" Dupin had been too deep in his thoughts to notice even one of them. "It's the official island circular route."

Riwal's sentence was like a call to action. With those words the three of them set off again.

"If you could see anything," Riwal continued, "you would have a breathtaking view from here on the northwest side. Above all, if it still were low tide you would have a perfect impression of the whole archipelago. To the south"—Riwal gave a meaningless wave at the gray soup—"there are a few larger islands. On one of them there's a ruin of a house, inhabited from time to time by one mad fisherman or another, and on one of the other the *parc* has a measuring station. On yet another still there's a blind for birdwatchers. The whole archipelago is a paradise for birds. From a geological point of view the archipelago is a gigantic granite plateau that during the last ice age formed part of the Brittany mainland and only slowly became part of the seabed, out as far as the island even. Do you know what they say?" It was a rhetorical question. Dupin was still too busy with phone calls to get involved. "At high tide this is a land in the sea, at low tide a sea on the land."

Riwal stopped and gave Dupin a searching look, apparently an attempt to fathom the commissaire's state of mind. Then he quickly followed his digression with a question about the case.

"How did the conversation with Morin go?"

Dupin had to sort something out; he had no choice, even if it was against his own maxim: "Riwal, do you know anything about the protest march holding a 'major demonstration' in front of the prefecture offices?"

"Of course. The march began on the Quai de l'Odet, and the demonstration is obviously to be outside the prefecture. It should be beginning any time now: several hundred people. The mood must be pretty worked up, people are stinking mad. And rightly so. There'll be a lot of newspaper photos, even if the prefect himself isn't there."

That was precisely the problem. Dupin could imagine the pictures. A close-up of Nolwenn holding a banner in the front row directly outside Locmariaquer's office. He could see the eggs and tomatoes flying. Windowpanes being smashed.

But then all of a sudden Dupin had to grin. What was he worried about? It was Nolwenn. She wouldn't need his help. And if she should, obviously he would be there, at her side.

"So, what did Morin have to say?" Riwal asked again. He was completely correct, there were more important things to talk about.

Dupin went over the conversation as well as he could.

"This is completely unacceptable. We need to force Morin to talk," Kadeg said.

"How do you plan to do that? Torture him? From now on, Kadeg, keep a permanent eye on Morin. Permanent! And no problem with letting him know it. Stay here on Molène. Somebody else can take over Gochat. And get help. Whatever he does, stick with Morin."

"He's not going to make any mistakes now."

"Even so," Dupin insisted. He felt his hawkishness return. "And now for the main thing. Who was where between one P.M. and two fifteen P.M. today. Friday."

There was a muffled growl in the air, and this time it no longer seemed far away.

"That came from the south," Riwal said, and once again made a ridiculous gesture into the invisible. "The business with Morin must have happened out there somewhere."

Kadeg had even more ridiculously followed Riwal's gesture with his eyes. "Also, we've checked out the algae fisherman who pulled Morin out of the sea. He seems innocent enough. There's no reason of any sort to think he could have had anything to do with the business."

"Good." Dupin nodded in acknowledgment.

"He's from Lanildut," Riwal added. "The most important harbor for algae in Europe. There are about a hundred algae fishermen there. They call algae 'the reed of the sea,' and the *laminaires*, which can grow up to four meters long, they call the spaghetti of the sea."

Algae was one of the big topics in Brittany, Dupin knew, and for good reason.

By now they were walking slowly; the coastal path was so narrow that they virtually had to walk one behind the other, as closely as possible so they could hear each other. Dupin, then Riwal, and then Kadeg.

"The legends talk about a 'magic seaweed of multiple colors' fed on by the magical sea cow Mor Yvoc'h." Riwal began rambling on again. "But it's only nowadays that the fantastic potential of the different sorts of seaweed has been discovered. They have medical potential as well as for biotechnology, pharmacology, natural fertilizer, insulation material. But the greatest potential of all is for nourishment. How are we going to feed what will soon be nine billion people on our planet? With algae. We'll only manage it if we use algae!"

"Let's get back to the case," Dupin said.

"Algae are extremely healthy. Rich in iodine, magnesium, fiber, and antioxidants. And Brittany's haute cuisine creates the most wonderful delicacies with it. There's soon going to be a seaweed channel too: Breizh Algae TV, which is—"

"The alibis," Dupin interrupted. "What about the alibis?"

"Gaétane Gochat is still not back in her office and so far can't be reached." Kadeg had jumped ahead of Riwal and snappily started his own report. "Nobody down at the old port where her boat's mooring place is has seen either her or her husband . . ."

"Shouldn't she have been back ages ago?" Dupin was wide awake.

"There's no way they came straight from Sein to Douarnenez. That much is certain."

"And you don't find that extremely alarming?"

"Should we arrest her again if and when she surfaces?"

"As soon as she surfaces again, she'll be questioned. And obviously, if details of Madame Gochat's report as to where she was after she left Sein are even slightly incorrect, then we arrest her again."

Kadeg rolled his eyes.

"Riwal, how many helicopters does the coast guard have?"

"I can't say exactly, boss, maybe five in Finistère Sud."

"I want you to search for Gochat."

"I don't think that makes much sense in this weather."

"True," Dupin moaned.

"Do you think it was her?"

"It's possible. One way or another she's looking for something. Just as we are. I'm convinced of that. But go on, what about the others' alibis?"

"You saw Leblanc still on Sein at midday." Riwal had obviously checked out the scientist. "After that he went on to Ouessant, also to take readings. I got through to him there. At two thirty-three, from the boat still. The institute has a tiny research station on Ouessant. Two staff. I spoke to one of the two, who confirmed that Leblanc had been there for a while but couldn't say exactly for how long. Leblanc insisted it was about one forty-five. If that's true then there wasn't enough time for a clash with Morin. If not, and if he got to Ouessant half an hour later, then it would look very different. It also depends to a great extent how fast his boat can go."

"Hmm." A rough grunt from Dupin. That was one of these dubious alibis of which they had heard far too many since yesterday. Taken literally, it meant nothing.

"I think . . ."

All of a sudden Dupin flinched. And stood motionless. Riwal nearly walked into him.

In front of them they could see four strangely shaped granite rocks, right next to the path. And one of them had just moved. Slowly, calmly. But quite clearly.

Dupin fixed his eyes on the spot.

"A fat gray seal, tired from eating too much. They go out hunting and then come back here to eat comfortably." Riwal sounded delighted.

The seal had turned its head toward them. It seemed for a moment to be studying the little group of humans to decide if there was anything to indicate they weren't dangerous. It carefully put its head back to the rocks. A perfect, chameleon-like blending in with the granite it was lying on. And it wasn't just one seal, Dupin saw now, but more of them. Eight altogether. The others hadn't found it necessary to raise their heads even slightly and look to their right. It looked rather cozy; they were all lying there stretched out beside one another, classic examples, about two meters long. Nobody seemed amazed, except for Dupin.

"Regarding Vaillant," Kadeg said, while Dupin remained somewhat impressed by the seals. "He was west of Ouessant when I heard him over the radio. They were out fishing for mackerel."

"Could he have been at the spot where it happened around one forty-five?"

"Under the right circumstances, definitely. Just like Leblanc. It's not out of the question."

Unbelievable. It went on and on.

"He came to the Île de Sein to buy cola, chewing gum, chips, and beer, and then went out fishing? What did he do before visiting the supermarket?"

They had left the seals behind them, though not before Dupin had turned around for a last look.

"He said he'd been asleep a long while."

It was absurd.

Kadeg's phone went off. He took a few conspicuous steps on one side and picked up.

"Inspector Kadeg?"

He listened for some while.

"Three of his big boats? Three of the deep-sea trawlers?"

There came an answer, and then a follow-up question from Kadeg: "What about the coastal boats?"

Once again Kadeg stood there listening for a while. Then he terminated the call.

He came back to Dupin and Riwal with a meaningful expression on his face.

"Three of Morin's deep-sea trawlers, which were in the Douarnenez harbor, had left at the same time. They weren't supposed to go out to sea until tomorrow."

Dupin ran his fingers through his hair. That was no coincidence either.

"Where are his other big boats?" Dupin asked. He recalled six of them, if he remembered correctly.

"Between Scotland and Ireland. Far away. Too far."

"He'll have sent all his coastal fishermen out," Riwal said grimly.

"Without doubt," Kadeg said.

Dupin wasn't in the least surprised. That was why Morin had needed to get his strength back. To launch a major operation.

"The search for her still won't be easy," Riwal mumbled. "The sea is big. And the woman in question could have been on land long ago."

"Could we have Morin's fleet followed?" Dupin asked.

"Even if we wanted to, we don't have enough boats."

"Keep going. What about Jumeau? Where has he holed up?"

They had set off again. Now in a line the other way around: Kadeg, Riwal, Dupin, one on the heels of the other. They would soon have completed the entire circuit of the island.

"I got to him first. To the north of Sein, where he was yesterday. He claimed to have spent the whole time in that region, which would have been about ten sea miles away."

"Of course." That too had been vague. As was more or less in the nature of things, Jumeau too had been out at sea. To measure distances and times and make estimates on the sea they had to combine engine power, plus the strength of both waves and currents. All of which necessarily complicated the calculations and left them extremely elastic.

"Frédéric Carrière, Morin's *bolincheur*," Kadeg began again. "He was just two sea miles from Ouessant at two fifteen. That's not far from the area we're talking about. He was seen from the other boat, a *bolincheur* that had nothing to do with Morin. Carrière himself said he had been a lot farther north. Almost outside national waters. That means he was lying, that he lied to me directly."

Maybe Morin's fishermen really had played a central role in this drama.

"Call him, Kadeg and—" Dupin cut himself short. He had stopped dead. As if he had been struck by lightning.

"What was that you just said, Riwal?"

The inspector turned round in confusion. "What did I say? In connection with Jumeau or Vaillant? The sea is big and—"

"No, no. The thing about the *parc* measuring station. That the Parc Iroise has a measuring station out there"—Dupin waved out into the murky gray, just like Riwal had done—"on an island, in the south of Molène, you said, more or less close to where the business with Morin took place."

"Yes, the Île de Trielen. But . . ."

"Wait a minute," Dupin said. He had speedily produced his cell phone. He had already called that number today.

Riwal and Kadeg stood clueless in front of him. It took a while.

"Hello?"

A cheery female voice. Full of spark.

"Am I speaking with Monsieur Leblanc's assistant?"

"That's me."

"Commissaire Dupin. I came by yesterday . . ."

"I remember."

"Just one question. When Monsieur Leblanc does his Friday tour around the measuring stations, what route does he take?"

"Always the same: Sein, Trielen, Ouessant, Béniguet, then Rostudel and the Crozon peninsula."

Dupin fell silent briefly.

"Trielen, the island to the south of Molène?"

"Exactly."

"Always the same route, in the same order?"

"Only in extremely bad weather does he make a change. Trielen is the most difficult, what with the swell and the currents. In difficult conditions he skips the island and collects the data the following week."

"What about today?"

"I think," she began, then hesitated. "To be honest I don't know. We've been waiting for a heavy storm since midday. But on the other hand the sea so far has remained calm. Should I ask him?"

"No. Leave it for now. I'll call him myself. Thank you."

Riwal and Kadeg had come closer and closer to the commissaire as he spoke on the phone. Kadeg was first to speak.

"Leblanc told me he was going directly to Ouessant. He didn't mention Trielen. He must have canceled that stop today."

"You think," Riwal said sharply, "Leblanc was on Trielen, don't you, boss? In which case he could well be our man."

Dupin was silent.

"But even if he had been on Trielen and Morin had been waiting for him there, and that would fit perfectly . . ." Riwal paused. "How could we prove it? Somebody would have to have seen Leblanc. And that's extremely unlikely, particularly in this weather. Out of the question, effectively."

Dupin remained silent.

Unfortunately Riwal was right. It had felt like an unexpected inspiration—the sort of thing they desperately needed.

"There has to be a way." Dupin's sentence sounded like a prayer.

"I want to speak to Vaillant. He knows . . ."

Dupin froze again. And a moment later he had his phone to his ear again. He called the same number once more.

"Hello?"

"There's something else I need to know. The readings Monsieur Leblanc takes, and uploads onto his computer." All of a sudden he was feverish; something else had just occurred to him. "You only see the values when they're in the system, correct? When Leblanc gets back to the office. I mean that's when he feeds them into the system, and not by wire beforehand?"

"No, only then."

"And if he erased them beforehand, you would never see them."

"That's correct." He could hear justified confusion in the assistant's voice. "I've already spoken on the phone with Monsieur Leblanc. There's a couple more things I have to clear up with him before the weekend. And as you asked, he did leave Trielen out for now today, because he thought the storm would be well under way by now. But he's going to pass by there now, on his way to the Île de Béniguet."

"I . . ."

For seconds Dupin was incapable of saying any more because of the force with which the thought had shot through him. And this time it was a crystal-clear thought. One that illuminated everything. Dupin was sure of it. "Did you tell Monsieur Leblanc that I had asked about his route?"

"Only in passing."

She could hardly have done otherwise.

That was it. That was the solution.

"I need Goulch. He has to pick us up immediately."

Riwal and Kadeg stared at the commissaire.

"No time for explanations, Riwal, tell Goulch he needs to come here right now."

Dupin had left the path and walked over to the water. They needed to be quick. Quicker than him. Or else the game was lost.

"Where should he pull in here?" Riwal already had his phone at his ear. He could hear the urgency in Dupin's tone of voice.

"He needs to get here immediately."

It was serious for Dupin. He kept on walking toward the sea.

It was going to be tight. He needed not to destroy the evidence. It had to be there. Dupin had reached the water. He looked around. There was no sign of sand or gravel, just huge black rocks. Luckily it was high tide. Maybe Goulch would be able to make it some way or other after all. That water was dark gray, somber. There were thick mats of seaweed.

A moment later Riwal and Kadeg were next to him.

"Goulch is coming."

"Good." Dupin was deep in thought.

"Where are we going to?" Kadeg's question was cautious, not pushy; even he seemed to feel that this wasn't the moment to be outspoken. Dupin didn't hear a word. He had begun to pace up and down, his head bowed.

"The *Bir* will be here in a second," Riwal said. He seemed to want to calm the commissaire.

All of a sudden, Dupin came to a stop, deep determination on his face. The next minute he stormed off, straight into the sea. Kadeg and Riwal stood there, open-mouthed, without moving from the spot.

Dupin rushed into the water up to his knees, then to his waist. Then he stopped, not feeling anything of the chill of the sea. He waited.

"Boss, this wasn't a good idea." Riwal had finally got moving and rushed down to the water's edge. Suddenly there was a loud noise—the twin engines of Goulch's boat, coming from the right, even if it still couldn't be seen in the pea-soup fog.

"Here, we're over here," Dupin called as loudly as he could.

"Got you, Commissaire."

Goulch, calm itself, as always. He was speaking through a megaphone, clear and easy to make out. It only took a moment for Dupin to see the shape of the *Bir*.

"I'll send out the tender, Commissaire, but I'm not coming much closer."

"That'll take too long."

Dupin walked forward, briskly if a little more carefully than minutes before. It wasn't easy to keep his balance, with the ground stony and covered in seaweed. The water was up to his chest. And now he could feel it. Sixteen degrees, Dupin guessed. Or fifteen. Or fourteen.

"Watch out, boss! You'll lose your footing!" Riwal's voice betrayed the fact he could see catastrophe staring them in the face.

Dupin stopped one last time. There were still ten meters to the boat. Then without taking a single step farther, he slid completely into the water.

And swam.

He swam up to the high stern. Goulch had been watching everything and run to the rear of the boat with two crew members.

Riwal and Kadeg were now also wading into the water. Deeper and deeper until they began swimming. Faster toward the end; it was clear the commissaire wasn't going to wait for them.

Dupin had reached the boat, the steps of the flat stern. With Goulch's help he was immediately on board. One of the others handed him a blanket, but Dupin turned it down.

"To Trielen. As fast as possible," Dupin said. His heart was hammering madly.

"Got it," Goulch said and vanished into the bridge.

Riwal and Kadeg did the crawl the last few meters. They heaved themselves on board just as the engines roared into life.

* * *

"We're here!"

Dupin had joined Goulch on the bridge during the high-speed trip. His polo shirt, pants, shoes, and socks were saturated with seawater but he didn't notice. He had strained to keep a lookout the whole way, despite how crazy it was. The murky air seemed to have become even more impenetrable.

"There are two passages." Goulch had a detailed map chart on his impressive monitor. "The measuring station is here at the narrow end. It looks as if you could get to the station in the same time from both north and south. We're coming from the north."

Kadeg and Riwal had in the meantime pushed in to join Goulch and Dupin, which made it very crowded on the bridge.

There was still nothing of the island to be seen: no rocks, no silhouettes.

"How close can we get?"

"Just a few meters, and that's it. Even at high tide."

"Isn't there a pier?"

"No. You need a tender."

"Turn the engines off, Goulch."

As they couldn't see anything, they had to work with their ears. But above all they had to hope they wouldn't be too late. From one moment to the next everything fell silent.

Totally silent. All that could be heard was the gentle slapping of the water as the boat slid through it.

"Three possibilities," Dupin said in a subdued voice. "He may already have gone again, so far that we can't hear his boat anymore; he could be here now on the island but with his engines off, in which case he knows someone else has arrived; or he might still be on his way here and we'll soon hear his boat."

Nobody said anything for a while.

Dupin ran up to the stern. "We'll go onshore. I want to get to the station."

"This time I'd advise taking the tender," Goulch said.

Suddenly they could make out shapes, dark low rocks in silhouette. Maybe twenty meters away. They really were next to the island.

"It'll be quick," Goulch said. He pressed a big yellow button, and the two massive arms released the tender to the water.

"Good." With that modest comment, Dupin was already standing on the hard rubber of the tender. Kadeg and Riwal followed.

"Take this with you." Goulch handed the commissaire a walkie-talkie radio. "I'll stay right here with the boat. When you reach land, the station will be about a hundred meters to the right. Directly on the water."

Dupin nodded.

Goulch released the tender.

Kadeg and Riwal had each grabbed a paddle, and pushed the boat off.

It glided toward the rocks almost silently. Instinctively Dupin reached for his gun.

In just a few meters they reached the island.

Riwal kept an eye on the spot where they were to get out. Still not a single other sound to be heard. No seagulls here, no people. Nothing.

Riwal was first to get out of the boat. "It's fine here."

Dupin did the same, then Kadeg. The water was up to their hips.

There was no doubt about one thing: if Leblanc was already on the island, he knew they were too, but not where exactly. He wouldn't be able to see them either. Dupin waded to the shore.

He climbed onto the dark rocks until he reached the stubby grass. He headed right, as Goulch had said, the inspectors two or three meters behind him.

It was eerie. The thick pea soup, the absolute silence, as if nature, the island itself, and the sea were all holding their breath.

Dupin moved slowly, his hand on his Sig Sauer.

After a while the land went uphill.

To the right, on the rocks by the sea, they could see concrete constructions, probably a form of defense for the measuring equipment. All of a sudden there was a mighty noise.

Dupin had immediately identified it: the howling of a boat engine.

He was there now.

"It's coming from the other side of the island." Riwal had immediately shot off, Kadeg too. Even Dupin didn't hesitate. The sound had died down a little but was still constant.

They ran over grass and stone without seeing where they were going. Heading for the source of the noise. The island was larger than Dupin had thought.

They reached the shore. And could see nothing here either at first.

The boat had to be farther to the left. The rocks looked higher and steeper than on the other side. They needed to take care not to slip and fall. They could break their arms or legs.

Just a few meters on, they spotted the boat. Dupin recognized it straightaway: a Zodiac. They could see a line that was provisionally tied to a prominent rock.

There was nobody to be seen.

"He's left it ticking over on idle."

Of course, Riwal was right. Even on their way here, Dupin had noticed the monotony of the engine noise.

It all happened in a fraction of a second. Dupin turned with a sudden jerk and ran back in the direction they had just come.

"Back! All back! To the measuring post. As fast as possible."

He'd been leading them by the nose. It was a decoy. And they'd fallen for it.

He had wanted to pull them away from the measuring station. And he'd succeeded. That was how Dupin knew that it was actually all about the station.

The commissaire ran as fast as he could. It was unbelievable. Would it all fail as stupidly as this? At the very last minute? All because of a stupid trick?

Without slowing down he pulled out his gun.

"Police! Stay away from the station," he called as loudly as he could, into the murky soup.

He ran on without waiting for a response.

"I'm about to shoot. Get away from the station, and put your hands up."

No reaction.

Still running, he raised his gun to the sky.

And pulled the trigger.

Once, twice, three times.

There was no reaction.

Before long he could see water again. They were back on the side of the island where they had moored. He heard Riwal and Kadeg behind him and veered left.

His sense of direction had let him down. A few meters more and he came across the concrete construction again, the protection for the measuring post.

If the whole station was laid out like the one on Sein, the shed should also be nearby. Dupin stumbled, nearly falling over, then he ran on.

Suddenly he stopped still.

To the left was an outline of a shape. That had to be it. A bit farther and he could see it: a low shed made of concrete, with a door on the right. It would be a matter of seconds, split seconds. With one leap he was in. Ready, his pistol leveled.

Nobody. Kadeg and Riwal stormed into the room after him.

"He's not here," Kadeg gasped.

"Never mind." Dupin had already caught his breath again. He seemed fully concentrated.

His eyes searched the room. The inside too was like that on Sein. An aluminum table, a chair in front of it. Technical equipment on the wall above the table, a box, small diodes, blinking red.

He had to remember. Where was the cable connected?

On the side somewhere.

Right.

There were two connectors here. Two USB connectors. Normal USB connectors, if Dupin was right.

"I want to know what's going on here, once and for all," Kadeg barked, no longer trying to play it calm. "What is this all about, Commissaire?"

Before Dupin could answer, a howl of engines erupted.

"He's escaping," Riwal said, and leapt toward the door. "He's had one over on us again!"

"Let him go. If he's already been in the station, then we've lost everything anyhow. And if he hasn't, then we've everything we need."

Dupin's walkie-talkie sounded. "Goulch here. It sounds as if a boat is leaving the island. What should I do?"

"That's Leblanc. Follow him."

"Should we arrest him if we catch him?"

"I'll tell you that then."

"Good. Over."

Dupin turned to the measuring apparatus. "We need a laptop here." He hadn't thought that far.

High-powered engines fired up again. Once again the noise was deafening.

"You want . . ." Riwal began, then paused, and beamed—he had understood: it burst out of him: "You want to link up to the apparatus here. There is the time the last data was registered. He *had* been here after all, he lied to us. Leblanc had been here and taken the readings.

Just before the business with Morin. That here—that's proof," he said delightedly. "Incontrovertible proof. The measuring station will tell us. That's why. That's why he had to come back. He needed to erase all trace of the transmission. The time on it betrays him." You could literally see the jigsaw puzzle coming together behind Riwal's eyes.

"He was especially worried after his assistant told him you had asked about his route. The time the data was taken down was recorded in two places: his own computer and here. He can easily erase it from his own computer, but to erase it here, he had to come back," he concluded. "There was no way Leblanc went direct from Sein to Ouessant; he was here. And this was where Morin tried to tackle him. Here on the island! He laid in wait for him here. Presumably as Leblanc was trying to leave the island again. He had to have transmitted the data again."

That was more or less the conclusion Dupin had come to also.

"We'll have a laptop sent from Molène. They must have two police boats on the island." Kadeg was already on the job. He left the shed to make the call.

"In any case, we now know it was him," Riwal said.

"But if he managed to erase the data from the midday reading, then our hands are empty."

"Just the fact that he found us on the island and made fools of us is hardly definitive evidence." Kadeg came back. "They're bringing us a laptop. It won't be long." His tone made clear he'd roused somebody important.

"Good."

Dupin walked slowly around the room. He was extremely calm but with an internal tension that could go off at any time.

It was a terrible few minutes. They had nothing to do but wait. Have patience.

Dupin tried as hard as he could to divert his thoughts. Another question came to the fore. Where was the object at the center of all this? The thing Kerkrom and Darot had unearthed? Dupin was convinced that in that respect nothing had changed. It was all about the find. It was at the heart of everything. But what was it about the object? Now that he knew they were after Leblanc, not Morin—at least as far as the murders were concerned—then everything had changed. It wouldn't have to do with a plank or the engine from a smuggler's boat.

Dupin had intuitively left the two inspectors in peace. He continued walking around the room.

"Give the order to have Leblanc's house searched. All the buildings and pieces of land that belong to him, or with which he has any connection. Sheds, storerooms, outbuildings, whatever. The same goes for the institute, all the buildings belonging to the Parc Iroise. On the Île Tristan in particular. But not only there. They also need to check out the other *parc* measuring stations. That announcement to the public should say we are searching for an item of value. Approximately one meter forty tall, possibly of gold." Only then did he turn round to his inspectors. "I want a major operation."

"Got it, boss," Riwal said, relieved. Kadeg nodded brusquely. Both left the room, leaving Dupin on his own. He had come to a halt before the apparatus.

He stared at it without moving.

* * *

Kadeg brought the laptop over as if it were a holy object. He put it down on the narrow aluminum table with exaggerated care. Dupin was impatient.

"And here's the USB cable," Kadeg said as he pulled it out of his pants pocket.

Dupin took it and put it rapidly into the connector slot.

The laptop booted up. Riwal took over, standing in front of the keyboard. Kadeg yielded to him.

"Naturally we don't have the program the institute uses to transmit and store the measurements. I'm trying to do it at OS level. All we need through the USB port of the apparatus is when it was last contacted."

Dupin had only the faintest idea what the technical stuff Riwal was talking about meant. He couldn't care less.

Riwal was typing enthusiastically.

"That's not it." A buzz, clicking keyboard, another buzz. "Not that either."

A pause.

Riwal typed with all ten fingers.

"Shit!" Riwal took a deep breath. "But . . ." A sustained pause, then: "Yes!"

All of a sudden he was in top form.

There wasn't much to see on the screen. Just at the bottom left edge, a row of commands. Letters, signs, numbers. In a tiny type size.

Dupin's gaze hung on the final line:

Synchronizing run 22.06–13.25.

"That's it, that's our proof. Somebody here transmitted data at one twenty-five. That is reliable proof."

Dupin stood there motionless. He didn't say a word. For a few moments they stood in silent celebration.

Until a different noise struck them suddenly: furious, rattling rain. It had begun to hammer down as if from nowhere with apocalyptic strength.

Then an ear-splitting clap of thunder seemed to cause heaven and earth to tremble.

The storm. At last it had arrived.

"Tell Goulch, he's to arrest Leblanc as soon as he's caught his boat." There was a small smile on Dupin's face.

"Goulch got in touch as soon as we were outside. They have Leblanc's boat on their radar, they're on it. But he's doing the best he can to shake off the *Bir*. He's making zigzag maneuvers at breakneck speed. Despite the raging sea he's heading for the little islands near Quéménès where the water is very shallow."

A gigantic blinding flash illuminated the sky and the island, a stroke of lightning that seemed to have come through everything,

even the massive walls. The thunder that came with it was instanta-
neous. The crash was even louder than the first.

"We need to get away from the island and onto solid dry land
as fast as we can. It's really going to take off now." Riwal sounded
seriously worried, which was no good sign, given that of the three
of them he was toughest in extreme weather conditions.

On top of the rain, thunder, and lightning, now came ferocious
gusts of wind.

The boat that had brought the laptop was now moored just about
where Goulch had been. Two police officers had come to the island
with it and were now waiting by the tender. Kadeg's forehead too
was now creased with worry lines.

"Let's go."

The commissaire had extremely unwelcome memories of a storm
on the Glénan islands, which had ended up with him being forced
to spend an unexpected night on a miserable folding cot in a damp,
narrow room along with Riwal and another policeman. And there
wasn't even a folding cot to be seen here.

"I'm going to leave the readout from the laptop as it is. But I'm
taking a screenshot for safety's sake."

A few clicks and Riwal closed the computer.

"How are we going to get it onto the boat dry?"

A good question. They couldn't just tuck it under their clothing.
That was already soaked from them coming through the sea.

Dupin looked around. In one corner, next to all the other junk,
there were some pieces of polystyrene. "That'll have to do." Dupin grabbed it. "We can squeeze the laptop in between." They were
dirty and smeared, but dry.

"Okay," Riwal said. Dupin laid the laptop between the two
sheets of polystyrene foam.

Another mighty crash of lightning, another mighty thunderbolt.

"To the boat!"

They stopped briefly in the doorway.

"Kadeg, as soon as we get to land, you make certain that the laptop gets to Quimper safely and as fast as possible."

"And where are we headed now?"

"To the Île Tristan."

"To the institute?"

"Yes."

They ran off. Into the monstrous rain. Into the storm that was now right above their heads.

* * *

The sixty-seven minutes on the police boat from Trielen to the Île Tristan on that twenty-second of June were—Dupin had absolutely no doubt—the most horrid, terrifying, unspeakable of his life.

It hadn't been long from them setting off until the symptoms of massive seasickness manifested themselves. Not just the basic symptoms of seasickness, such as nausea, dizziness, and vomiting, but at the same time every other possible reaction that seasickness could provoke.

Dupin hadn't just gone pallid, but a pale white, and a thick film of sweat had covered his forehead. His heartbeat hadn't just increased, his heart was pounding like mad. Just as his headache pounded. And his head was not just dizzy but swirling.

This was no matter of pitching *or* yawing—in most people seasickness was caused by one or the other—this was both at once. The most terrifying sensation was not just that the boat and he himself along with it and the whole crew were inescapably being tossed *forward and backward* but that at the same time the whole of the sea, the Atlantic itself, was doing the same. It was as if the Earth was being tilted, the whole planet, a sudden shift in the Earth's axis, some cosmic catastrophe. It was remarkable how long panic attacks could last.

It was a nightmare.

The previous day's trip, which had severely stressed Dupin, mentally and physically, had in hindsight been child's play.

Comical as it sounded, he had been taken by surprise. He had been so taken up on Trielen by the new developments, so fervently obsessed with new thoughts, that when it came to the journey he had assumed things would be as they usually were at such moments of an investigation when it came to dealing with the rest of reality: for the period of his feverish obsession with the solution of the case, the remainder of reality would sink into the background without any involvement from him. It would temporarily cease to exist. But not today. The seasickness had won out.

The mountainous waves had become monsters, totally erratic and at irregular intervals, as if a titan in a fuming rage had slammed a mighty fist down here and there across the surface of the water, each time creating new, unpredictable, dramatic spurts of water. There was no more wind anymore, just foam and spray with every breath. Even the sound of the water was deafening, the sound of the water, not the storm. When the monstrous crest of the waves broke, the water was blown away horizontally, something Dupin had never seen before.

The Atlantic had literally roared. Dupin had always thought the term, which he knew from lots of stories of great storms, was a metaphor, a spectacular poetic picture. This was no metaphor. The sea really could do all of that. It roared. It raged. Riwal had on countless occasions explained the signs that indicated the classification of storms. Now Dupin had experienced all of them. Wind strength nine: severe storm, meters-high waves with spray blowing, sea begins to roll; wind strength ten: severe storm, crushing waves, higher still, in excess of hundred kilometers per hour; wind strength eleven: hurricane-style storm, sea roars; wind strength twelve, hurricane, a pure hell of white foam.

On top of that Dupin was certain that sooner or later a lightning bolt would strike the boat. Given the monstrous number of lightning bolts that continually seemed to strike nearby it was a statistical miracle that they hadn't been hit.

He wasn't helped by the expression on Riwal's face, which had gone stony as soon as he'd lain down. The inspector didn't say a word throughout the whole journey, and nor had Kadeg, whose face had gone chalky white. Only once, and it could have been his imagination, Riwal had suddenly turned to Dupin and with a horrorstruck face said something that was hard to understand in the noise of the storm. He thought he had heard "There's no escape," but that was obviously nonsense. Like the whole scene the previous morning, with the seven graves. It was ridiculous, but involuntarily the thought of the curse had come back to him during the crossing. In confused, flashing pictures Dupin had seen himself in the cholera graveyard, standing by the seventh grave.

The stupid thing was that even back on solid ground the heaving and lurching—though not the spinning—didn't go away. And still hadn't: even when Dupin was on the soil of the Île Tristan, he was still reeling.

Even while leaving the boat Dupin had had to hold on for every step he took, last of all onto the railing. Now, with nothing to hold on to, he had to be careful not to stumble.

Determinedly, he tried to sway in the direction of the institute, which Kadeg and Riwal were already hurrying toward with fast strides. The nausea was still bad too.

The rain hadn't even relented any, it had just got seriously colder, dropped a few degrees.

Dupin was soaked through. The only good thing, if it could be put like that, was that he wasn't aware of just how miserable a state he was in. Mainly that he was freezing. He headed for the wall of the house between two windows. He wasn't yet in a state to carry on a sensible conversation, not even half sensible.

He would lean here for a bit.

As soon as he felt the wall at his back he forced himself to breathe in and out in a regular rhythm: to hold his breath for five seconds after breathing in, and another five seconds after breathing out. A method that Docteur Garreg had recommended for extremely stressful situations.

The most important thing, and hopefully that would help, was that he had to get his concentration back on the case, pull his thoughts together. Bring them into order, which above all meant consistently concentrating on the matter in hand, the searching of all the rooms with any relation to Pierre Leblanc and his arrest.

It took some minutes before he trusted himself to carefully move away from the wall. Coffee would be fatal to his stomach still, even if he needed it more right now than he ever had done in his life.

Even in the entranceway the institute was abuzz. A troop of six uniformed police came toward him, led by Inspector Kadeg, who was already telling them: "Then we'll take a second look at the technical building. And properly this time!"

Precisely the building Dupin was most interested in.

One of the officers, a chubby young kid, stopped in front of Dupin.

"We just searched the building systematically, Monsieur le Commissaire," he said self-confidently, clearly. "And found nothing."

Dupin just nodded. It still wouldn't be a mistake to take another look. The first time couldn't have been all that thorough, the team couldn't have had all that much time.

Dupin wondered if he should join up with Kadeg. But he ought to take an overview first. He stumbled on, through the small hall, then another door to a sort of reception, where he spotted Riwal. He still wasn't well, not nearly.

Riwal came toward him, clearly excited.

"Leblanc has now turned toward Le Conquet, maybe to take shelter from the storm. Goulch is still on his heels. Even though, if it comes down to it, Leblanc's Zodiac is faster and more maneuverable. The crazy maneuvers won't help him, though. Goulch will soon get him. I suspect you'll see Leblanc shortly."

"Shortly?" Every word was an effort. "Here, on the island?"

Dupin couldn't wait.

"Here in the institute?"

"Here."

There was no way the commissaire was getting on a boat again in this storm, even for the two hundred meters to Douarnenez. Even the thought of it brought on a new wave of dizziness.

"Okay, boss. An initial search of Leblanc's house has been completed." Riwal sounded frustrated. "As well as that of the little weekend house he owns. Not far from the Pointe du Raz, in Kermeur. Both without result. The same goes for the rooms here. So far nothing found. And the object isn't small. We're seeking out people in Leblanc's circle who might know whether he owns other buildings. Professionally and privately."

Dupin winced.

He needed to lean on the wall for support. He had that terrifying feeling again; to be more precise he once again actually experienced the earth falling steeply away in front of him.

He waited, took deep breaths; his five-second ritual.

"All okay, boss?" There was deep concern in Riwal's voice.

"I need to go out for a moment, Riwal."

It was only after Dupin had been walking for quite a while that he felt better.

The fresh air did him good. The wind and rain had died down a bit.

Only slowly the horrible sensation diminished and he could consciously get his thoughts back into order. He had to go back, continue the conversation with Riwal. There were still a lot of important points.

He turned round. After a while he made out the brightly lit windows of the institute.

And a figure, hurrying toward him.

"Boss, is that you?"

Riwal.

"I've been looking for you."

"Everything's fine, I . . ."

Yet again Dupin winced.

But this time it wasn't dizziness, but a thought. A thought that came as if from nowhere. He shoved a hand in his pants pocket. His Clairefontaine.

Being given a bath so many times—in the Atlantic, in the Breton rain—wouldn't have done it any good.

"What are you intending, boss? Shouldn't we go back in? It's not raining quite so hard, but . . ."

"You go on," Dupin said absently.

His notebook did indeed look in a miserable state. The cardboard cover was soaked through, and the thin protective film had come away on all sides. Despite the fact that the notebook pages had been pressed tightly together in his pants pocket, the water had naturally soaked all the way through from the cover to the inside.

It was only a thought. But it could just be right. Even if it sounded fantastic. But what did that mean?

"I want to take a look at something, Riwal."

Dupin's eyes glanced along the island path: without intending to he had walked quite a long way.

"Should I . . ." Riwal hesitated, "come with you to look?"

"No, no. It's just . . . just a thing."

"Are you sure you're okay?"

"Absolutely." Dupin did his best to sound steady. "I'll be back in a minute."

He turned around and marched off again. Riwal shrugged despairingly when he knew the commissaire couldn't see him.

Dupin's footsteps were fast and determined.

He didn't need the Clairefontaine. At least not to be sure of what it was the wonderful owner of the Ty Mad hotel had mentioned yesterday. The semi-derelict pier at the western end of the island—and the grottoes. Grottoes that served as entranceways to underground caves and passageways, believed to be legendary, where the fantastic treasures of the fearsome pirates lay hidden.

Leblanc could only have taken the object off Sein in the boat. A pier, therefore, would almost certainly have played a part in his choice of hiding place. It was like in Kerkrom's house: they had to think absolutely concretely and practically, from Leblanc's point of view. Where and how was it going to be easiest to move such a heavy object? So that it would be best hidden? The island rose substantially toward the center. The sky was still letting only a little light through; here and there you could see little more than the outlines of low-hanging cloud clusters.

High trees stood on both sides of the path, making it into a wild avenue. If Dupin's sense of direction was still more or less functioning, the path ran virtually straight.

The commissaire panted for breath. He had set a high pace. But internally he was far from stable. His moment of inspiration, which was extremely interesting, had now been followed by huge doubt. Very basic doubts that had reversed his conviction at one go. What if the whole story of the "find" really was just a fantasy? If the thing under the tarpaulin really was just a wooden beam for the house? What if it had just been something banal standing in Kerkrom's bedroom that had left the notches? What if his own fantasy had simply run away with him, as so often happened with Riwal? And the business with Leblanc and the island, maybe even that was nothing out of the ordinary? What if it really was all about Morin's boat? In some complicated way that he simply didn't understand, didn't remotely imagine? Or was it all something different altogether? And that out here on the island he was just chasing a figment of his imagination?

The sudden doubts—which hopefully were just the results of his distraught condition—had caused him to slow his steps.

Nonetheless he carried on. His eyes focused straight ahead.

In the meantime the heavy banks of cloud had been ripped open everywhere, and in a curious way Dupin was glad of it, genuinely relieved. Above anything else it seemed to have restored a touch of reality. The dominance of the obscure dark matter that had unleashed the capricious storm was at an end.

The path now turned steeply downward, toward the sea. Dupin

had to be careful. Before long he saw the outline of a building. An old stone house, without a roof for the most part, the wall on one side totally collapsed. The path led right past it.

Then Dupin made out the semi-dilapidated pier. There were only a few meters left. One of the huge storms must have long ago taken the rest with it.

Even if the weather seemed to have calmed down, the Atlantic was still working at it. Dupin went down to the start of the pier—paying attention to keeping a safe distance of a few meters from the tossing sea. It was easily possible to dock a Zodiac. A good place to go ashore. Dupin turned around. Concentrated. Leblanc would definitely have had something to help him, like Kerkrom's boat trailer. It was unimaginable otherwise.

The old stone house was some twenty meters away. The path was in reasonably good condition, stony, but sound. Another path, also reasonably smooth, led off to the right. Behind it were huge rocks and a warning sign: *Keep Clear—Danger of Death*. And another with a symbol Dupin knew well from the Brittany coast: cliffs from which the rocks had broken off and crashed to the ground. With a large red exclamation mark next to it.

Dupin headed on along the shore path. A few gentle turns, the cliff wall to the left, the sea to the right. Twenty, thirty meters.

Then the path ended abruptly in a sort of stone platform. Two jagged, tall, dark holes were visible in the rocks. One directly behind the platform, one that required clambering over a few meters of rough gravel. In this weather, and this light, they looked like wide-open jaws. Next to the pair of them was another "Keep Clear—Danger of Death" sign.

Dupin pulled out his phone, one of the modern "outdoor" models that Nolwenn had equipped the whole commissariat with, which had withstood the past few hours better than he had expected.

He turned on the flashlight function. It would be a laughably weak light, but it was all he had. Without hesitation he entered the first grotto.

Inside it was pitch black. And astoundingly cold.

Dupin stopped and shone the light around the stone chamber. The phone's light reached a lot farther than he would have thought possible, revealing imposing dimensions. Not so much in the width or length—the grotto was no more than ten meters long, and maybe six wide. But in height it was another matter altogether. The light disappeared above, with no ceiling to be seen. In some places the rocks glistened brightly when Dupin shone the light on them, patches of mineral: quartz.

There were thick layers of dried seaweed on the floor, with only a narrow stone corridor left free in the middle. The seaweed would be brought in during high tides and heavy storms. It seemed it had piled up here over the years. There was no sign anywhere of any activity suggesting that anybody had been here recently. Dupin walked around a bit, shining his light on the ground. The grotto had to be astonishingly dry; the seaweed crackled under his shoes.

He stood there a few moments, ankle-deep in seaweed, and involuntarily shook his head. He turned around and headed quickly toward the exit.

The second grotto was surely twice as large as the first. Here too there was no ceiling to be seen. But in contrast to the first, the rocky floor here was clear, no sign of a single piece of seaweed. On the other hand, directly behind the entrance on the left, there was a crack, about one meter fifty high and a meter broad. Dupin shone the light inside. It didn't reach very far, but far enough to see that from the crack there ran a sort of natural passage in the rocks.

Should he explore the passage? Or would he do better to come back and do it with reinforcements and suitable equipment? Such as a proper light. Riwal would know what to think about such a spelunking expedition.

Dupin hesitated. Then he ducked down, ready to go in.

The minute he set foot in the crack, leading with his head in an extremely cramped position, something suddenly occurred to him. He nearly rocketed up.

A mental image of the cave with the seaweed, when he had pointed his phone at the ground.

Something had flashed, he had just seen it from the corner of his eye, which was probably why he hadn't immediately noticed it, because the quartz had shone in various places. But when he thought back to it now, it was clear to him that it wasn't just the walls that had glittered, but something else. And that something had been on the ground.

He turned around quickly, left the cave, and just a few seconds later was back in the first grotto, out of breath.

The seaweed looked the same everywhere. He would just have to try. He squatted down in the middle, holding the phone flashlight toward the ground, and turned slowly in a circle.

Nothing.

He went two steps farther, did the same again.

Still nothing.

And again.

Had he just imagined it?

"What a load of shit."

Dupin stood up. The softly spoken words echoed notably, his voice sounding strangely distorted.

"Then that's the way it is," he muttered defiantly.

He went straight over to the right-hand corner by the entrance to the grotto, then turned round and began systematically pushing the seaweed aside with his right foot.

The rocky ground was uneven, as one might expect, with dips and cracks that were covered over by the seaweed at the surface. He made slow progress. It hadn't been possible to see that the layer of seaweed reached up to half a meter in thickness in places. Then the next minute it would be no more than a few centimeters. It reminded him of autumns in his childhood when he would run through thick layers of fallen leaves, or when he whirled around in the heap of them that his father had carefully stacked up in the garden.

Suddenly he lost his footing. For some reason or other he slipped. He swayed, tried in vain to keep his balance, then fell over. Straight forward, instinctively putting out both hands in front of him. And hit something hard. A piercing pain in his hands, arms, and shoulders overwhelmed all other sensations for a few seconds.

He tried to get his bearings.

He was lying on his right shoulder. Thousands of tiny shreds of seaweed swirled through the air. He coughed.

His phone with the flashlight app must have fallen into the carpet of seaweed. It took a while for his eyes to accustom to the darkness. The only light was a dim glow coming from the entrance to the grotto. Dupin tried to prop himself up, only to be rewarded by a strong, sharp pain in both wrists. He carefully felt around with his left hand.

He felt the edge of a rock, about forty centimeters high. Now he understood. He had fallen into a depression in the rock floor. A real dip. It had to be a few square meters in size. He now noticed that his shin too was aching badly. He must have landed with it on the sharp edge. Dupin moved his leg carefully. Even though he was a bit stunned from the impact, the pain wasn't as bad as in his wrists. But this was not a rock ledge, it felt quite different.

In the semidarkness he could make out a sharp, straight line in the seaweed. Dark. There was something lying there.

He quickly brushed some seaweed out of the way, and felt the object. The upper surface felt soft, organic, but below it was hard. He rashly got to his knees, ignoring the pain in his hands.

A sort of brace, four-sided. Maybe fifteen centimeters long, five wide.

He tried to move the thing a bit. Impossible. He hastily felt his way upward.

Then he stopped as if struck by thunder.

He lost his breath.

A crossbar. A right angle.

He exposed the horizontal bar completely. It was shorter than the other.

He still couldn't breathe.

A cross.

It was a cross.

A large cross, made of a heavy material.

Dupin felt goose bumps creep all over him.

It was completely mad. Too mad. It couldn't be true. Had he fallen on his head or something? Was he hallucinating? But the pain in his hands—for example—felt absolutely real. It lasted until he got free of the spell he had fallen into.

He shook himself and looked back at it. He couldn't make out much. It looked as if a sort of moss had formed over the brace.

All of a sudden he found something lying right next to the cross. On the bare rocks.

His phone. It was only when he had it in his hand that he realized that the display had shattered. The lower part of the glass was missing altogether, while there were holes in the housing. But the worst was that the light no longer worked. Dupin pressed the On button but nothing happened.

He needed to get up. No matter how painful it would be. And it was. Not just his hands, arms, and shoulders hurt like hell, but all his other bones too.

He squatted down, which hurt no less.

A shining material appeared. That must have been what he had previously seen glittering in the seaweed when he shone the light on the ground.

In the light it was hard to tell if it was golden; but it certainly couldn't be ruled out. Dupin used his fingers to touch the place. And felt a notch. With a sharp edge. The material was damaged, or to be more precise there was a bit missing. Not much: a long, thin piece.

Once again Dupin was frozen.

What was it Riwal had said about the thing Kerkrom had sent in?

The material test which the Paris laboratory had identified as pure gold?

Dupin sat up.

This had to be it.

Kerkrom and Darot really had found a cross. A golden cross. On the bottom of the sea. In Douarnenez Bay. They had brought it up in Kerkrom's boat and taken it to her house. Leblanc had brought it here after murdering them.

Maybe they had involved both him and Professor Lapointe to examine their find. To work out what it really was. To decide what to do. Perhaps they then would have given the cross to a museum, a regional or national museum—and Leblanc wanted to do nothing of the kind. Or perhaps he had just somehow found out about it by chance and they didn't know someone else was on to it.

In theory the cross could have been from any year at all; from the nineteenth, eighteenth, seventeenth centuries or even from the Middle Ages, no matter what Riwal's cousin had said. There were the craziest stories, and history was full of them. Brittany had created so many saints after the end of the western Roman Empire, faith was so acute, who knew what people would have done to be as sure as they could of getting to heaven. Or what Napoleon's troops had secretly brought back from their Russian campaign. From some immensely rich Orthodox church. There was without doubt an endless number of wholly realistic possibilities.

"I have to . . ." Dupin was speaking aloud. ". . . I have to fetch the others." The loudly echoing sentence had the effect of building up his self-confidence.

He struggled to climb out of the dip in the ground and stared once again for a moment at the dark cross lying there. He saw it, and yet it seemed completely unreal. It was monstrous.

He turned around and headed as fast as he could toward the exit from the grotto.

Once outside he was blinded by the bright light. He had to hold his hand in front of his face.

The sky was torn open theatrically in places, with rays of sunshine breaking dramatically through chaotically jagged holes.

* * *

"A cross, Riwal. An . . . archeological find."

The inspector's eyes were open wide. Dupin thought he noticed a gentle shiver run through his inspector's whole body. The fact was, it was just that which Riwal had expected, hoped, but now that it was reality it seemed to be too much for him. Something Dupin could easily understand.

Kadeg, standing next to him, was no less shocked.

"You think they . . ."

"Back to Leblanc. What's happened, Riwal? Tell me."

The two inspectors had stormed toward Dupin the minute he stepped into the institute. Riwal had excitedly reported something about Goulch, Leblanc, and "still on the run." Dupin interrupted him: it just burst out of him. His discovery. He tried to tell them about it simply, remaining as prosaic as possible in his choice of words and manner. Out of the grotto, in broad daylight, the discovery seemed even more fantastic.

Riwal was still palpably under the influence of Dupin's news, but was trying to pull himself together to present his report. "Just by the entry to the harbor, before turning past the rocks in the channel leading into the port, he suddenly spun the rudder round, turned the motor up to full, and shot off northward. You know how fast those Zodiacs are. But Goulch will get him whatever tricks he plays."

"He doesn't have a ghost of a chance," Kadeg said. "There are by now also two speedboats of water police involved in the operation."

"Good. We need four men for the grotto, I think." Dupin was in a hurry.

"Do we have a car?"

"An old Land Rover Defender. We were about to take it out on a search. I was trying your phone the whole time, but—"

"Where is the car?"

"Just to the left behind the building when you come out."

Dupin set off. The pain in various parts of his body had slowly eased, although that in his wrists had gotten worse.

Half a minute later they were standing, along with reinforcements, next to the Land Rover.

Dupin took a seat up front. He had difficulties climbing into the car. It was one of the many peculiarities of the vehicle that despite a built-in step it was necessary to pull yourself up by a handle.

Riwal let the engine rev up and then put his foot on the gas.

The vehicle's violent jolting on the unsurfaced path made Dupin's stomach churn again, but before long they had reached the half-collapsed house and jumped out into the open air.

Dupin headed in front, the rest of the troop behind him. The high rock walls, the short winding way along the shore, the little stony platform. The Keep Out signs.

At the entrance to the grotto, Dupin stood still for a moment. The others nearly walked into him. Then he went in.

Riwal, following directly behind him, turned on one of the powerful flashlights. On its own it illuminated the whole grotto. Others blazed on.

"There, in front."

Dupin moved forward carefully. He had already reached the carpet of seaweed.

"Here! You have to be careful, it's half a meter down, it's easy to fall over. It's underneath . . ."

He didn't finish the sentence.

He had uncovered the cross. And pulled a serious amount of seaweed out of the dip. But now the dip was almost no longer visible, just a rocky edge at one point. The seaweed was spread evenly all round, creating an even surface. A gust of wind must have blown into the grotto and swept it all around, even though Dupin hadn't felt a single breath of air.

He felt around with his right foot until he found the edge of the dip and then—extremely carefully—stepped into it.

"Here below the seaweed?"

Kadeg had also stepped down. Dupin didn't react. He moved his right foot backward and forward in the mass of seaweed. Took one step forward and repeated the exercise. Kadeg copied him.

Riwal and the others had stayed by the edge, and were watching the commissaire and the inspector, shining their flashlights on the seaweed.

Nothing.

It was impossible.

"There has to be another dip."

Riwal had gone a step farther into the cave.

That had to be it. Of course. Even if Dupin would have bet this was it. In fact, he was dead certain. Nevertheless.

The other policemen followed Riwal's example and swarmed out.

"Here. There's something here."

Kadeg had squatted down.

Dupin walked around.

The inspector was holding up his hand in a comically triumphal manner, with Dupin's broken phone in it. The commissaire had simply left it there.

Nobody said a word.

Dupin's disbelief was soaring by the second.

It was one of the four other policemen who, after a period of depressed silence—and further futile combing through the seaweed—finally gave voice to the obvious.

"There's nothing here. No cross. Nothing at all."

"That's completely impossible. It *must* be here. It was just there. In this cave. In this dip in the rock."

"But no longer," Kadeg said.

"I was only away for twenty minutes," Dupin said. "From leaving the cave to the moment we entered, no more than twenty minutes passed."

"It seems that was enough," Kadeg said. "Enough for somebody to get the cross out of the cave. Or," he added quietly, "there was no cross. If you didn't have a light and your phone was broken, it must have been very dark here."

What was that supposed to mean? That he had mistaken the edge of the rock for a large golden cross? That he had been hallucinating?

"After the journey on the boat," Kadeg said without the slightest ill-meant nuance, which only added to the effect of his words, "completely blown away by the wind, Monsieur le Commissaire. I would describe it as seasick in the highest order. Something like that confuses everything, including sensory perceptions. And the mind. With after-effects that can last hours. Or, and this would be perfectly understandable, you hit your head somewhere on falling."

Dupin was too busy with the situation to go into Kadeg's impertinences.

"Maybe it was the other grotto, boss?" Riwal tried to keep on Dupin's side. "Shouldn't we search it too?"

It was well meant, but only made things worse. He wasn't wrong. He had, even in the wake of the admittedly serious attack of seasickness, long since got his five senses back. He hadn't had some pipe dream.

"It was here!"

The only possible, logical explanation was Kadeg's first suggestion:

"Somebody has taken the cross. Somebody was watching me and then took it themselves."

That meant, however, they had to have been working at lightning speed.

Without waiting for any of the others, Dupin headed for the exit.

"Whoever it was can't be far away. Riwal, Kadeg, give the order to seal off the island and search it systematically." Dupin knew he had already given the same order today on another island. "And they should deploy more boats and check all the ships in the vicinity of the island." He hesitated, but only slightly, before adding: "Best of all, every boat in Douarnenez Bay. Every single one needs to be searched, big or small, no matter what its purpose is. And find out where Gochat, Jumeau, Vaillant, and Carrière are right now." It was another order he had already given. "And what Morin is doing on Molène. I want you to speak to every one of them personally."

He had had it. He had had the cross! Just twenty minutes ago. And then he had made a fatal mistake. He should never have left it here alone.

Leblanc could have worked out that they had begun searching on the Île Tristan. Did he have an accomplice? Had they been getting it wrong the whole time? If so, would he have warned him immediately after the incident with Morin? So that the accomplice had been on the ball all along, and either arrived when Dupin had already left the grotto, or while he was still there, but without Dupin noticing him? In that case he would have to have waited a bit in order to get the cross off the island.

That was how it would have been. Someone had stolen it from them.

Dupin ran to the pier, with Riwal, Kadeg, and the four uniformed police at their own distance after him. Puffing, he came to a stop at the pier, looked around, turned on his own axis, and scanned the sea and the island.

"We need to go up the hill. To a spot where we can see the surrounding area and the sea."

Dupin sprinted off again, up the steep path.

"Up to the left." Riwal was now hard on his heels. "I'll show you."

Dupin heard Kadeg, who had stayed behind on the pier, bellowing orders into his phone.

Dupin's heart was pounding.

By now Riwal had reached the same point.

"Here, along here." Riwal left the path. They ran cross-country between huge trees. Not long, but long enough to make Dupin's wrists ache again from the constant impacts.

Then, suddenly, a breathtaking panorama opened up in front of them.

The whole bay of Douarnenez lay before them. The fifty meters above sea level was enough for an impressive outlook. And overview. Riwal had been right. At first Dupin stood dangerously close to the abyss.

Over the past few meters he had begun systematically to seek out the water. The sea was still wild. Huge waves were crashing against the cliffs. Dupin felt the fine spray in his face.

There wasn't a boat to be seen. Not a single one.

"With a sea whipped up like that," Riwal gasped, trying to calm his breath, "the smartest thing would be to take the left hand from the pier and straight along the coast, preferably into the Port de Plaisance in Douarnenez. There are dozens of boats there. Moor there to start with. And move the cross on by land, or wait and then head out at the same time as the other boats, when the sea has more or less calmed down."

Dupin got the message immediately.

"Have the leisure boat harbors searched, every single boat."

"Straightaway, boss." Riwal got out his phone.

Dupin walked along the rocks for a bit, running his fingers through his hair. Again and again.

"To hell with it."

* * *

The commissaire and his inspector had walked from the cliff to the vehicle next to the semi-dilapidated house, and from there driven back to the institute.

Kadeg and the four uniformed police officers had begun their search operation directly from the pier. Several other officers had joined them.

But with no luck so far, either on the island or the water. They had four boats out on the sea, and six police combing the leisure harbors.

Dupin had become grimly angry. Leblanc had pulled one over on them properly, and was still doing it with a vengeance, with his latest attempt to escape, above all with his chess games here on the island.

They shouldn't underestimate him again. Leblanc was cold-blooded, cunning. He was one of those criminal types you shouldn't trust with anything. Dupin knew the type. He was literally burning to get his hands on him.

He was furious at Leblanc, but it was primarily anger at himself that was driving him on. Not just because of the stupid mistake he had just made, but because he had several times let himself be led up the path.

Dupin pushed the institute door open, Riwal right behind him.

"We need to concentrate on this question: Who could be his accomplice?"

Riwal's phone rang. "It's Goulch."

Dupin snatched it from his hand.

"Have you—?"

"A deep-sea trawler, the *Gradlon,* came out of Lanildut bay. Out of the harbor there, he . . ." Goulch stammered. Dupin had never come across the self-confident policeman like this. "There's absolutely no visibility in the area. It just plowed right over the Zodiac. We had to watch it happen. The boat burst."

"What?"

Dupin stood there as if paralyzed.

He could hear shouts, calls, hectic orders, Goulch's crew members.

"It only just happened, a few seconds ago. We're looking for Leblanc now. The Zodiac went right under the trawler's keel, at high speed."

"Morin."

Goulch got it immediately. "Yes. The trawler belonged to his fleet. We signaled to him to turn back into harbor immediately. He's just turning now."

Dupin was dumbstruck.

"He'll have heard the police radio." Goulch sounded resigned. Of course. That's what had happened. Morin was definitely perfectly equipped. "There were several boats out there."

It was insufferable. Too much.

"There, there he is." A loud shout. One of Goulch's men. A moment passed before Goulch commented:

"We can see Leblanc's body, he's . . . certainly no longer alive, Commissaire, we . . . I'll call you right back." Goulch hung up.

Dupin still hadn't moved from the spot.

Suddenly he sprang to life. He rushed out, Riwal's phone to his ear.

It took a while before the call was answered.

"Yes?" An indifferent grunt.

"They *executed* him." Dupin stressed the word hard. "They set their boat on him. That's murder."

"Ah, Commissaire Georges Dupin," Morin said calmly, at peace with himself, no trace now of exhaustion. "Obviously I fear I have no idea what you're talking about."

"One of your deep-sea trawlers ran over Leblanc and his Zodiac."

"You mean there's been an unfortunate accident?"

Morin didn't even try to sound surprised or shocked. At the same time there was no hint of provocation. He had no intention of humiliating Dupin, or laughing at him. He was interested in something else.

"You lay in wait for him on Trielen, and now your work's over."

It was enough to drive you mad. How could they get their hands on Morin?

"There's no point in denying it. We know."

"Apparently," Morin said calmly, "you also know who the murderer was. Which means you've solved the case. That must be a tremendous relief. A tremendous relief for us all. Congratulations." It was unreal how satisfied Morin sounded. "The killer was a man of extreme brutality and pure greed. He has three people on his conscience. Two wonderful young women. If I understand correctly, he would seem more or less to have suffered the punishment he deserved."

"You admit it?"

"I admit nothing."

Dupin stalked up and down feverishly outside the institute.

"We'll prove it was you, monsieur, you can count on that."

The reality was different. Dupin wasn't promising himself anything; it would be extremely difficult to prove anything against him.

"In weather like that, with such a turbulent sea, there are unfortunately tragic accidents all the time. Particularly in such a rugged landscape with all the rocks. And I imagine Leblanc was going at a dangerously high speed."

"Had your trawler any business in Lanildut harbor?"

"I can't tell you. You can imagine that I am not continuously in contact with all my captains. I suspect, however, they were looking for shelter from the storm. He probably set out for Douarnenez, heading for the channel. It's wise to make for land there."

It was shameless, but that's the way it would go. Exactly like that.

The captain was the only one who could cause trouble for Morin, and Dupin was certain the man wouldn't say a word. He'd be true to his patriarch.

"I don't think it's going to be a major issue for the people and the press if a triple murderer fleeing from the police died as a result of an accident he himself was guilty of."

The worst was: Morin was right.

That's how it would go.

"Apart from everything else," Morin said slowly, a sharp tone in his voice now, "remember how complicated it would have been really to have placed the crime at his door. Obviously he would have denied everything. And you had no more than a chain of more-or-less plausible hypotheses and circumstantial evidence. None of which would have ever made the thing certain. And you know that.

"Is that what you wanted? You would have been left to depend totally on my statement. Everything would have depended on me making a statement. And maybe even presenting some proof . . ." He spoke ever more softly. "Maybe, and this is obviously just hypothetical, one of my fishermen really had seen something incriminating. Or I had said how Leblanc tried to kill me."

He didn't expect any reaction.

"You're a clever man, Monsieur Dupin. You know I had no interest in seeing Leblanc in jail. Even if my statement could have landed him there forever."

It kept getting worse, ever more ironic. And at the same time ever clearer. Dupin understood—and that was the awful thing—exactly what Morin meant. The last thing he would have wanted was to see Leblanc protected in jail. He wanted to see him set free. So he could carry out his revenge. And if Leblanc had tried to disappear from the scene, Morin would have hunted him down mercilessly, until he was found.

It was appalling.

There was something defensive in Dupin, they couldn't just take it, just let it happen.

"The cross, Monsieur Morin, the cross is gone." Maybe that was the way to get to him. "Somebody took it from the hiding place where Leblanc had kept it."

Morin didn't reply.

There was a long silence. A very expressive silence. It seemed as if Morin had also known about the cross, but not that it had now disappeared. Maybe that was the only thing he hadn't known.

"Leblanc had to have had an accomplice," Dupin said. "It might have been the accomplice who killed your daughter, and not Leblanc himself."

Morin still didn't react.

"Or you might have had the cross fetched yourself," Dupin said.

Morin could have used force to make Leblanc reveal the hiding place during their confrontation on Trielen. Before he had been overcome himself. He would only have had to wait for the right moment and had the cross fetched. Maybe by one of his coastal fishers. Their boats were only a few hundred meters away.

"I couldn't care less about the cross, Monsieur le Commissaire," Morin replied with the deepest scorn.

The line went silent again. Dupin could hear Morin breathe.

"Let it go, Monsieur le Commissaire." Morin's voice was for once almost upbeat. "If you really must, go look for the cross. Do what you have to do. Come and look around my place if you will, my doors are always open to you. And just so you know: there is no accomplice. But in any case, it's over."

"Nothing is over, Monsieur Morin. Nothing."

Dupin hung up.

Without noticing it, he had walked to the end of the quay, then walked on, along the stony beach. Quite a way.

"Boss? Boss?"

Riwal, somewhere in the distance.

"Here."

He could see the inspector now. Riwal had been standing on the grass outside the institute and now came running toward him. Dupin walked in his direction.

"They've taken Leblanc's body on board. The body was horribly mutilated. The ship's screw must have caught him. It must have been a terrible death, his left arm and the whole shoulder are—"

"That'll do, Riwal."

"I've spoken with the captain of the trawler. He's in shock, or so he says."

But of course. Dupin had expected as much.

"He had seen the Zodiac coming. They had been happy finally to get out of the storm. There are three police cars on their way to Lanildut. We'll bring the captain and the whole crew to Quimper and interview them."

"Do that."

It was a waste of time. But they had to give it a go.

Riwal had already come to terms with Leblanc's death. Just as everybody else would. Morin had predicted it. Nobody was going to be much bothered by the death of a brutal murderer.

Dupin put his hands behind his neck.

"I want—" Then he stopped. "I need to think."

He turned abruptly away.

He needed to be alone.

* * *

Only a native of Brittany would believe it. There wasn't a cloud to see in the whole sky, not one. The fuss over the heavy storm was over. As if the world hadn't nearly drowned two hours ago. The only reminder of the storm was the fact that everything was wet—including Dupin, his inspectors, and all the uniformed police who had been on duty.

Dupin had walked on farther. A long way farther. As far as the little bay.

The whole world was steaming, Douarnenez, the town—on his right hand—the island, the trees, the rocks, the ground. Everything had now warmed up, as the cool rain had sunk into the land. It was an entrancing sight, one Dupin normally loved: these dainty, ethereal plumes. But now he barely noticed them. Nor the warmth and strength of the sun, even in the evening.

He turned his eyes to the water, hazy, empty. His wrists ached endlessly.

"Boss?" Riwal was approaching him cautiously from the side. Kadeg next to him. "We've—" Riwal began.

Kadeg interrupted him. "We've searched all over the island. It isn't big. Without finding anybody or anything. Unless there are more hidden caves, then I don't know where anyone could hide a one-and-a-half-meter-high cross. Especially if you didn't have much time. We've also, by the way, checked the fissure in the other cave. After a few meters it gets ever narrower and more inaccessible. Nobody could get through there."

Dupin didn't reply.

"Two boats in the bay have been searched." Riwal made no secret of his disappointment. "They were the only ones to come out after the storm had ended. Nothing suspicious about either. We haven't found anything yet in the leisure harbor either. The harbormaster couldn't think of any boat that came in during the time in question. His office is right at the front by the entrance and he has a very good view."

"Somebody took it." Dupin spoke in a low monotone. "Somebody has to have taken it." The second sentence sounded as if he was pleading. "There's no other way."

"Or," Kadeg said calmly, "it was the seasickness, like I said. These things happen." This time too he didn't want it to seem he was making fun of Dupin.

"Where were Vaillant, Jumeau, Gochat, and the others in the last hour?"

"Gochat and her husband turned up back in Douarnenez, we actually caught them at home on their landline. Gochat had something to do in Morgat, she went from the Île de Sein directly there, we checked it out. Out of the question that she could have made a trip to the Île de Trielen during the time in question."

"What about Frédéric Carrière, Morin's *bolincheur*?"

"We haven't managed to raise him yet. I have the number. I'll try it again now." Riwal reached for his phone.

"Same goes for Vaillant. Not to be reached."

"If you don't reach him soon, send out a search warrant for him."

Kadeg raised his eyebrows. "Don't you think that's a bit over the top?"

The commissaire ignored Kadeg's comment.

The inspector tried to adopt a friendly tone of voice, which was bad news: "I don't want to offend you, Commissaire, nor do I think that you've really lost your mind, but like I said: lots of people have had seasickness and—"

"That's enough, Kadeg. Do you understand? That's the last time!"

Dupin had made the sentence as forceful as he still could. "Try Vaillant again. Now!"

The inspector moved away, looking insulted.

Dupin saw that Riwal, already a few meters away, was on the phone. He seemed to have gotten through to somebody.

Before long the inspector was back.

"Carrière headed for Ouessant before the storm. He was there the whole time, in a bar by the harbor. There's a whole crowd of witnesses. If you want . . ."

"That's fine, Riwal."

Yet again the wrong tack.

"And Jumeau?"

"Sitting in Chez Bruno. He went back to Sein when the storm broke. He's out of the question too."

It was cursed. Somebody had to have taken the cross.

Riwal seemed embarrassed. "You shouldn't despair now, boss. You solved the case."

Riwal meant well, but it didn't help.

It was unbearable. They had found the killer. A solution to one of the hardest and most challenging cases in his whole career. Then, however, the killer was caught and killed before their very eyes. By the father of one of the victims. Who was himself a criminal—and now a murderer, too. A last brutal twist in an otherwise brutal case. A case filled with dark, devastating moral chasms. A murderer they wouldn't catch.

Everything else was laudable enough. But at the same time it wasn't sufficient. The "spoils"—the thing it had all revolved around—a massive golden cross of inestimable value, had escaped them. Dupin had had it, and had it stolen away from him. When it came down to it, that was a sorry defeat.

The day had been long, terribly long. Just like the day before. He'd had hardly any sleep either night. And he hadn't had any caffeine since midday. On top of that his wrists were still aching. To make everything worse, Dupin had to deal with the prefect. Who didn't want the case cleared up before Monday and would now learn that the case had been "solved." Anything but a stroke of luck.

"Boss." Dupin had almost forgotten that he wasn't alone. "I've been thinking." Riwal was trying to speak as softly as possible. "To be honest, there was very little time to take the cross. I mean"—he seemed uncertain if he should continue—"twenty minutes isn't much. Somebody must have been watching you from a boat as you were going to the grotto. The island was full of police. Then, when you came out again, he must have waited until you were some distance away, then moored at the pier, gone into the cave, loaded the cross into a car or something of the sort, maneuvered his way out, and taken it back to the path to the pier. Then loaded it onto the boat, and"—Riwal was using long, awkward phrases—"got away so quickly that we never saw him again. It has to have been a semi-military operation."

Dupin had had similar thoughts, a few times, even if he had put them to one side. There was really nothing plausible about such assumptions. Nothing.

"We're not getting anywhere with a natural explanation. There's no doubt about the following: the cross exists. You saw it. Then it was gone," Riwal whispered, meaningfully. "Something mysterious happened here."

Those weren't the thoughts that had struck Dupin.

"This isn't the time for things like that, Riwal." Something else had just occurred to him. "Where is Leblanc's assistant, by the way?"

"She was down in the reception with us the whole time. She behaved extremely cooperatively, even if she's a bit agitated."

Then it couldn't have been her.

"I think . . ." Riwal started again in a whispering voice, "it was the cross . . ." He didn't finish the sentence.

Dupin wasn't pleased. He could tell from Riwal's tone what it would have been about: Ys. Or something else fantastic. And that was the last thing that Dupin would have been able to bear now: a serious mention of the supernatural.

"Vaillant is in Ouessant," Dupin continued.

Kadeg had come closer unnoticed and said, "They went there for safety's sake. Obviously reception was patchy during the storm. There are witnesses, he says, we can . . ."

"—speak to him any time," Dupin said. "Damn."

"Another thing: the units who searched Leblanc's house and weekend retreat want to know if they are still needed."

"They can go home," Dupin said wearily.

"I think so too." Kadeg marched off.

Dupin took a few weak paces along the shore. And then stopped. Riwal followed him discreetly.

The commissaire and inspector stood there silently together in the bright evening sun for a while.

"Kadeg and I will deal with the interview with the captain in Quimper. Maybe, maybe we'll come up with something." Riwal was trying to be somewhat circumspect.

"Do that."

"And," speaking decisively now, "I think you should also go home, boss. That's it for today."

Nothing happened. It wasn't even clear if Dupin had heard what he said. Then he gave a deep sigh.

"You can rely on the fact that our colleagues will carry out the searches at the harbor conscientiously. If they find anything we'll hear about it straightaway. And obviously we'll leave a few uniformed police officers on the island to keep watch on everything. Through the night as well."

There really wasn't any more they could do.

"You should also have your wrists looked at."

Dupin glanced at his hands. There were notable large swellings on both wrists. As far as the base of his fingers. They hadn't been there until now. There was a blue sheen to his skin.

"I . . . right, Riwal." Embarrassed, he tried to stick his hands in his pants pockets. Which was a stupid idea.

"Let's go."

Riwal's face showed deep relief, which clearly meant more than just Dupin's readiness to let things be for the evening.

"You're through now, boss. You actually were lucky. Good luck amidst bad. Things can go like that. You should be glad."

Dupin had no idea what the inspector was on about.

"You have the aura of the island to thank, its *bright* aura. They say the grave of Tristan and Isolde, their last and eternal reunion on the island, wards off harm. It's supposed to be somewhere near the cliffs above the grottos."

Dupin still hadn't understood, but had got enough to be sure he didn't want to.

"Do you understand? The evil spell is diminished by the other, the good spell. The curse of the seven graves was too strong to be completely neutralized." Riwal shot a stolen glance at Dupin's hands. "It so often ends in death. But . . ."

"Enough, Riwal. I don't want to hear any more about it."

His harsh reaction didn't seem to have any effect at all on Riwal. The relief on his face had even turned into a smile.

"Fine, boss. I'll let Kadeg and the captain know. We'll meet up on the boat."

Dupin winced at the mention of the word "boat," but then got a grip on himself again. It really was only a stone's throw to the mainland.

More important, he had had another thought. A wonderful thought, such a seductive promise, that it gave him new strength. In an hour's time he would be sitting in the Amiral in front of a wonderful *entrecôte frites* and a rich, velvety Languedoc wine.

"Can I just borrow your phone for a moment, Riwal?"

The inspector handed it to Dupin. "You can give it back to me on the boat."

Riwal turned away.

It was one of the few numbers Dupin knew by heart, one that his head had no problem retaining.

"Hello?"

"Claire, it's me."

"Georges? This isn't your number."

"I'll explain later. Could we eat together tonight?"

"I . . . I can't, Georges, I thought . . . Are you finished already?"

"More or less."

"I didn't think you'd have the time. That's why I agreed to stay on to midnight. I could do it after that. But that's ridiculous. The earliest I could get to the Amiral would be a quarter to one. But I'll come to your place, naturally. As soon as I can. I'm sorry."

"It doesn't matter, Claire." Dupin did his best to sound convincing, but didn't succeed. "We'll see each other later then, at my place. I'll look forward to it." There was only real enthusiasm in the last sentence.

"See you later, Georges."

That was a shame, a real shame.

He had to rely on the vision of the delicious entrecôte to help him. Which it did. Even if it couldn't rescue everything.

* * *

The sun hadn't gone down yet, but it wouldn't be long now. It had already spectacularly colored the western sky in all imaginable, softly merging shades of red, orange, lilac, and pink. The sea too. The sun itself had chosen a classic yellow for its performance.

Shadows had grown endlessly long, of everything, including the row of plane trees on the big Quai Square where Dupin had for ages parked his old Citroën. The soft light covered the trees and the rest of the world with a warm golden sheen. Made them light up magically.

The shadow of the restaurant—a fine old building from the end of the nineteenth century—stretched almost as far as his car.

Only the sight of the Amiral changed Dupin's mood.

The anticipation of the entrecôte had made him put his foot on the gas. But even more urgent was the desire to get home. Back home to Concarneau. And, above all, unquestioned reality. To leave behind the island of fantasy, the whole region of fantasy with its legends, myths, and wild stories. The sinister case and the grim fatalities.

Dupin opened the heavy door, and went in.

And saw his regular seat. In the corner on the left near the bar. It was free. Dupin relaxed. He hadn't warned the owner, Paul Girard.

He had made a few calls from his car phone. First and foremost he had tried to get hold of the prefect, feeling unwell about the idea of somebody else summarizing the events. He himself didn't know exactly what he would tell him, and how. But the prefect had only his voicemail turned on. Dupin saw him in his mind's eye, hidden in a ditch next to a hugely busy highway, enthusiastically bent over the latest high-tech radar equipment which they were currently testing.

The fact that his regular seat wasn't taken also meant, however, that Claire definitely hadn't arrived; he had secretly hoped she might have managed it.

Paul Girard was standing at the other end of the bar, opening a bottle of wine. He gave Dupin a long look, warm and friendly. A surprisingly emotional greeting by his standards. The long look was also asking if there was any difference to the usual order, the meal for particularly stressful, difficult days.

Obviously not.

Dupin sat down at the already laid table for two.

More accurately, he collapsed onto the dark blue, pleasantly up-holstered bench. With the last of his strength. He pulled off his jacket. It was still damp and smelled of salt and seaweed. Like everything he was wearing. It occurred to him he must look com-pletely disheveled, all the worse for wear. He didn't care.

The first tables were already empty, the big ones, for families. The others, the tables for two, were already being served dessert.

It was Friday night, the mood was relaxed, easygoing.

Dupin liked the noise in the room, a cozy background noise that created a jovial, animated atmosphere.

The captain of the deep-sea trawler would be in Quimper by now. Kadeg and Riwal were probably beginning the interview in the next few minutes. But Dupin wasn't going to think any more about that. It only made him angry. And would change nothing.

He knew less and less what he should be thinking about the vanished cross, and everything had seemed more unreal with every kilometer he distanced himself from the mythical island. There again he had seen it. With his own eyes. Which might have played a devilish prank on him; there were more than enough devils in the many wild legends. This cross existed—of that the commissaire was certain—a remarkable archeological find that had been the cause of three brutal murders.

And he would have to talk about the cross. The cross of gold. The whole truth, the whole story. Even though it would cause a huge fuss, a riot in the media. But whatever it caused, he was putting it aside for this evening.

What he did have to do was give a quick call to his mother. To relieve her. And above all to relieve himself. No more hardnosed putting her off. Yes, he would be there tomorrow. The party had been saved. And so had his soul.

He would ring Nolwenn too. The "big operation" had to be over by now. A chat with Nolwenn at the end of a case belonged anyhow to his fixed rituals.

Paul Girard headed toward him with a decanter carafe in his right hand, which he put down on the table with an unusually ceremonial gesture.

"I've found a last bottle of Le Vieux Télégraphe, your favorite Châteauneuf-du-Pape, 2004. The secret last bottle for extraordinary occasions, and emergencies. There was a lot of talk this evening." A conspiratorial smile.

"Wonderful."

Dupin adored this wine; he was moved.

Paul poured the wine, rather more than one normally poured into this round-bellied glass. He meant well toward the commissaire.

He set the carafe on the table and was gone in a flash.

Dupin lifted the glass, ignoring the pain in his wrist the movement caused.

He sat there rather reverently.

The first sip.

"You're not going to drink it without me?"

Dupin looked up. Wine spilled over the rim of the glass and splashed on his polo shirt.

It didn't matter, nothing mattered.

"I had to freshen myself up, I've just got here."

Claire sat down without ceremony, took the bottle, and poured herself a glass. No less than Dupin had in his glass.

"My assistant doctor managed to come earlier."

Dupin hadn't said a word. He was too perplexed, and too pleased.

Claire.

No matter what he said, it wouldn't have been able to express how happy he was.

Now everything was good.

Claire had that effect. She didn't need to say a word. She just had to be there.

In this first year of being together in Brittany, they hadn't seen as much of each other as he had hoped. But that wasn't what it was about.

She was there. She would always be there.

"I . . ."

"Georges." Paul Girard came over to them. "Telephone, for you . . ."

Dupin didn't want to answer, whoever it was. He took the phone reluctantly.

"Yes?"

"*Bon appétit*, Monsieur le Commissaire. I won't disturb you long," Nolwenn said in a quiet voice. "You have to see things positively. You solved the case. You made everything clear. You did your job. But"— she spoke now immensely seriously—"you still don't have everything in your hand. No one has. Not even you. I know, it's hard for you to accept that. It is hard. But unalterable. And we'll get Morin eventually. You'll see." She changed to an aggressive tone. "Nobody in Brittany gets away with lynch justice just like that. Where would we get to like that? No matter how unscrupulous a character Leblanc might have been. You absolutely mustn't have your conversation with the prefect before tomorrow. Not until all the searches have been carried out. That way the case is still live. Right, now"—her voice became more lighthearted—"enjoy your evening with Claire. Tomorrow you have to start early. Call from Paris when you get there. Then we can talk over everything else. Until then, forget it all. We're going into the *brasserie* here now to get something to eat. So, *bonne nuit*, Monsieur le Commissaire." Clear instructions.

Nolwenn waited a few moments before hanging up—just long enough for Dupin to pick up all the threads. He would actually have talked to Nolwenn about the cross, at least a few sentences. But he'd let the moment pass.

And as soon as he had set the phone down on the corner of the table so that Paul could pick it up again, he had forgotten everything again.

Claire glanced at him curiously.

"Everything's in order. Just a few—things—that need sorting." Dupin hesitated briefly, then the words flowed with surprising certainty. "But they'll sort themselves out."

"Does that mean we're going to Paris tomorrow?" Claire was genuinely pleased.

"Tomorrow morning. Paris!"

"Then we can spend Sunday morning in the park? And not come back until the evening?"

On Sunday mornings on fine summer days they used to go into the Jardin du Luxembourg, not far from Dupin's apartment, and sit there in the sunshine in the brightly colored chairs, buried for hours in the Sunday newspapers with all their amazing supplements, the chairs close to each other so that their arms touched. Meanwhile Dupin had fetched both of them a *café*, a croissant, a brioche.

"Yes, we'll do that."

All of a sudden, Paul Girard was standing next to them again. This time with a really big plate. One of his waiters was standing behind him with a round metal rack.

"I just really fancied them." Claire's eyes sparkled. "And we've got the time. The entrecôte comes afterward."

The waiter had put the metal rack in the center of the table, and Paul placed the large plate on top: oysters, langoustines, *praires, palourdes*—the little sea creatures, and the big ones: an immense crab.

It was perfect.

"Lots of time."

Dupin looked at Claire.

And took a large sip of the wine.

Epilogue

Four weeks had passed.

Dupin had told the world the dramatic story, exactly as he had known it.

The prefect had for the very first time allowed him to speak on his own at a press conference, the matter having become too awkward for him in many ways, he had admitted frankly, although he welcomed the media fuss.

For Dupin things hadn't become awkward.

He had spoken completely seriously. Leblanc's crime had to be spelled out: his cold-blooded murder of three human beings. He related the story of the murders in minute detail. Part of that was the possibility that he had had an accomplice, something that was for Dupin a particularly important hypothesis because of the question of the location of the cross.

Riwal, Kadeg, and he had continued the investigation in every direction, had gone through everything again in the smallest detail, had talked once again to everybody, as well as with those they hadn't spoken to. Leblanc's telephone calls, his computer, email account, bank accounts, all of them had been thoroughly examined. But they had found no hint of an accomplice, and no mention of a cross or an "archeological find."

Leblanc had acted very cleverly, very cautiously. The result was that the accomplice hypothesis was officially dropped. Eventually even by Dupin himself. Something—like so much else in this case—that he found incredibly difficult.

Dupin also felt obliged to report with the same exactitude on the crime committed against Leblanc, his unscrupulous murder. Dupin had calmly set out that he was totally convinced it was a revenge murder. Surprisingly the prefect didn't object, even though he hadn't a trace of evidence.

Obviously, as Dupin had expected, the press, media, and public saw the brutality of the killer as such that Leblanc's death was nothing more than the punishment he deserved. Once again Dupin saw the influence of Morin in that he himself didn't turn up, but a whole row of influential people did, and gave lengthy interviews in which they repeatedly referred to a "chain of unlucky circumstances." That was the way it went. But Dupin didn't let himself be influenced. He was continuing the investigation into the "police pursuit of a *bolincheur* suspected of smuggling." A few actually applauded, while others shook their heads heavily. He wouldn't rest until they knew if the boat still existed. If not, then they would really get started.

Charges were laid against the captain of the *Gradlon*, although the chances were slim of it coming to a trial, never mind a conviction. This "incident" had also been thoroughly reconstructed. Reports were submitted, thorough reports. The captain and seven seamen stated that it had been an accident. It was not them but a Zodiac traveling far too fast and too near the coast on a turbulent sea that was itself to blame. The reports had all referred to the adverse conditions. Nonetheless there remained a series of puzzling questions—for example why the trawler was coming out of Douarnenez harbor at all, when the sea fifty kilometers farther had suddenly been too rough for them?

The police investigation into the harbormistress on account of the discovery in her garden house of the murder weapon—which did indeed bear traces of the blood of all three victims—was dropped. In return Madame Gochat had dropped her charges against Dupin and the police and admitted she had guessed there was something to do with a "treasure," which was why she had Kerkrom followed.

But what people had most been absorbed by over the past four weeks was the cross. The big golden cross Dupin had told them about. Despite the fact it hadn't been found yet.

There was no hint of it, not a trace. No more witnesses. Just Dupin. A team of forensic experts who had specially come down from Paris had searched the cave, and in particular the dip in the ground. Without bringing the slightest thing to light.

The crazy thing was: the fact that the cross was missing was no bad thing; quite the opposite. Its absence gave free range to the boldest speculation, free fantasy and fable. A riot of imagination had broken out. Whether it was at the baker's in the morning, at the Maison de la Presse, in the Amiral, it was the subject of discussion everywhere. The newspapers, the radio and television—local, regional, national—and of course the Internet, the most ripe medium for gossip, were filled with the most exotic tales told for days and weeks. Naturally most were about Ys. Some—and it was more than just a handful—saying a mythical realm was about to return, to the extent that even Riwal, reading the morning papers, furiously cried "Ridiculous!" and "What a load of humbug!"

The leader of the scientific expedition that was due to look for the ruins of Ys in Douarnenez Bay next year had announced he was bringing the whole thing forward, as they'd had three large donations. The regional council had turned head over heels to give permission to the plans. Only a few scientists and art historians had meticulously passed around Dupin's description of the thing, which had in any case remained very vague. But none of them had dared to offer a guess, or place it in the context of a history of art.

What wasn't reported was that the police search for the cross had meanwhile been called off. Dupin found that hard to live with.

It took a while, but gradually the press reports tailed off, primarily because there was no follow-up. It had been three days now without a single item on the subject.

Even at the commissariat the cross no longer seemed a topic of conversation.

Only Dupin couldn't rest, found no inner peace.

In conversations with Claire or Nolwenn he heard himself saying that one day the cross would turn up again. But he realized it only made it seem more mysterious.